CLEAVER

Born in Manchester in 1954, Tim Parks moved
permanently to Italy in 1980 and presently works
in Milan. Author of novels, non-fiction and
essays, he has won the Somerset Maugham, Betty
Trask and Llewellyn Rhys awards, and been
shortlisted for the Booker. His works include
*Destiny, Europa, Adultery and other Diversions,
Italian Neighbours,* and *A Season With Verona.*

ALSO BY TIM PARKS

Fiction

Tongues of Flame
Loving Roger
Home Thoughts
Family Planning
Goodness
Cara Massimina
Mimi's Ghost
Shear
Europa
Destiny
Judge Savage
Rapids

Non-fiction

Italian Neighbours
An Italian Education
Adultery & Other Diversions
Translating Style
Hell and Back
A Season with Verona

TIM PARKS

Cleaver

VINTAGE BOOKS
London

Published by Vintage 2007

2 4 6 8 10 9 7 5 3

Copyright © Tim Parks, 2006

First published in Great Britain in 2006 by
Harvill Secker

Vintage
Random House, 20 Vauxhall Bridge Road,
London SW1V 2SA

www.randomhouse.co.uk

Addresses for companies within The Random House Group
Limited can be found at: www.randomhouse.co.uk/offices.htm

The Random House Group Limited Reg. No. 954009

A CIP catalogue record for this book
is available from the British Library

ISBN 9780099507253

The Random House Group Limited makes every effort to
ensure that the papers used in its books are made from
trees that have been legally sourced from well-managed
and credibly certified forests. Our paper procurement policy
can be found at: www.randomhouse.co.uk/paper.htm

Printed in the UK by CPI Bookmarque, Croydon, CR0 4TD

PART ONE

I

IN THE AUTUMN of 2004, shortly after his memorable interview with the President of the United States and following the publication of his elder son's novelised auto-biography, cruelly entitled *Under His Shadow*, celebrity journalist, broadcaster and documentary film-maker Harold Cleaver boarded a British Airways flight from London Gatwick to Milan Malpensa, proceeded by Italian railways as far as Bruneck in the South Tyrol and thence by taxi, northwards, to the village of Luttach only a few kilometres from the Austrian border, from whence he hoped to find some remote mountain habitation in which to spend the next, if not necessarily the last, years of his life. Ratting on your responsibilities, had been Amanda's interpretation. She is the mother of his children. The responsibilities of a man at my time of life, the eminent and overweight Cleaver told his partner of thirty years, can be no more than finan-cial, and, acting on a decision taken only hours before, he signed over to her a very considerable sum of money of which neither she nor their three surviving children could possibly have any immediate need, with the exception perhaps of the younger son Phillip who was always in need, but never accepted anything.

The following morning, climbing on the train to Gatwick, still rather dazed to find himself taking such a momentous step, Cleaver switched off his two mobile phones. This is not just another of your many projects, he repeated to himself. He was sitting opposite a young man cradling a CD player, his lips silently singing. You are not, as has been the case on other extended trips, planning to write a book, or to make a documentary. The young man, he noticed, had a glazed look in his eyes. He hasn't recognised me, thank God. The CD player was whirring. The culture, such as it may turn out to be, Cleaver told himself firmly, of the South Tyrol need not be analysed, ironised, criticised or eulogised. A recorded voice warned that the doors were about to close. The business of living in a remote mountain cabin need not be dramatised or serialised. Nor written up à la Thoreau into a sort of *Walden*. The train began to move. The Thames was suddenly beneath, then behind. The familiar sprawl of South London accelerated away.

Nor can there be any question of *recommending* anything to anybody, Cleaver was still reflecting an hour later as the airport shuttle took him to the North Terminal, or of reporting home on any wisdom supposedly acquired. He was lucky to be able to purchase a ticket for almost immediate departure. I have no baggage, he declared. Nothing. Nothing, Cleaver finally muttered, as he adjusted a safety belt to his girth, will be brought back from this trip for insertion in the national debate. For so many years a master of the public voice, he would now leave it behind. Such is the extraordinary idea that has somehow thrust itself upon Harold Cleaver during these last few days of remarkable public notoriety and intense private turmoil: I must shut my big mouth.

On the train that took him from Milan to Verona, Cleaver shared a compartment with a young woman absorbed in the study of what appeared to be some kind of marketing report. There were bar charts and he noticed the subheading *Bacino di afflusso*. Moving back and forth across the print, her eyes would occasionally hesitate before she stopped to underline a word or phrase with a rapid, predatory jerk of the wrist. Every five minutes or so, distractedly, she resettled a white shawl that continued to slip down over slender arms, and sometimes, in her pensiveness, she smiled, or frowned, and her free hand slowly twisted a strand of dark hair between knowing fingers. Cleaver was pleased, at Verona, that he had not tried to talk to her. Only as he stood up to leave the compartment did their eyes meet in the mutual awareness that they would never see each other again. This is an excellent start, he thought. It was Mother's constant complaint, his elder son had written in the opening lines of *Under His Shadow*, that my father was as *utterly incapable* of leaving any woman alone as he was utterly, absolutely and *irremediably* incapable of turning down any offer of food or drink or cigarettes, or, even more chronically, any opportunity to appear in public at any moment of the day or night. He was *ambition, avarice and appetite* incarnate – the three As as he called them – at once and always *carnal and carnivorous*. I have not eaten, Cleaver suddenly realised as he studied the departures board at Verona Porta Nuova, since my early morning tea and toast.

From Verona a second train followed the river Adige north up the Valpolicella into the gloomy mountains of Trentino. There were few houses on the slopes here. The barren formlessness closing in on either side of the train promised a solid barrier. It was fascinating how people had reacted to his son's book, Cleaver thought, or rather to his son's book in combination with the famous interview of the President of the United States. He was weary of thinking of such things. When a group of teenagers with knapsacks climbed on at Rovereto, Cleaver felt in his pockets for his earplugs. It was not that he had brought any reading material. There will be no more reading, he had decided. He just did not want to hear, even in a language he did not know, their shared life, their noisy collective identity. If I must shut my mouth, he thought, I can stop my ears too. There would be no more voices of any kind.

Almost alone on the platform at Franzensfest, just below the Brenner Pass, Cleaver was struck by the sweetness of the air. What smell is this? Of cut grass, cow shit, sawn wood, of snowmelt running on stone. He stood there, unsettled, listening to the insistent clang of the station bell announcing the arrival of his train. He looked up to see a waterfall tumbling down from slopes high above. I will write no letters, he thought, aware now that he was approaching the end of his journey. He had not brought a laptop. Or even a notepad. Or even pen and paper. Whatever is about to happen to me, or around me, need never be told or expressed.

From Franzensfest to Bruneck, the railway is reduced to a single line. Cleaver gazed out of the window as the train crossed and recrossed a grey river flowing in the opposite direction. Only one other man shared the carriage. At Ehrenburg they stopped for almost twenty minutes to wait for the westbound train. The twilight deepened in the deep valley. A slamming of doors left the air quieter and colder. Well before Bruneck, the other passenger was standing impatiently, switching his briefcase from hand to hand.

Luttach, Cleaver told the taxi driver. It was the first word he had spoken since the purchase of his ticket at Gatwick, since calling Amanda from Victoria to say goodbye. It was his destination. At least tell me where it is you're going, she had demanded. The whole world's trying to contact you. Luttach? The driver asked for confirmation. He filled the name with catarrh. Cleaver had refused to tell her. Luttach, he repeated in the cab, altering his pronunciation to satisfy the driver. The man was wearing a green felt hat above a ruddy face, a heavy moustache. He can't believe his luck, Cleaver thought, as the meter began to measure the distance. That's a London thought, he corrected himself at once, an old thought. If my father, his elder son had written, could take a taxi to go to the end of the street, he would, he *did*. After all, he was always on expenses. The only *account* I ever give of myself, he used to joke at dinner tables, is *an expense account*. This taxi ride is the last, Cleaver decided. He was paying with his own money.

The car proceeded sensibly northwards up the Ahrn valley. Again they were crossing and recrossing a river flowing against them. The water was faster now, flecked with white. They were climbing steadily. By the time they passed the village of Gais the autumn darkness was complete. Lights pricked out here and there on the slopes far above. This is what Cleaver has always remembered from his one previous visit to the South Tyrol: isolated lights high up in the alpine night. This is what has brought him here.

When the valley narrowed to a gorge above Sand in Taufers, the driver asked: Wohin wollen Sie? I'm sorry? Cleaver has forgotten what little German he once knew and has no intention of recalling it. In part, he has come here *because* he doesn't know German. Address, the man said. Hotel, Cleaver told him. He couldn't remember the name of the place he had stayed in with Giada. It didn't matter. Any hotel. The driver shook his head, risked a quick glance over his shoulder. Alles geschlossen. He pronounced the

7

words slowly and emphatically. Sommer ist zu Ende. Der Winter ist noch nicht da. Alles geschlossen, he repeated.

Cleaver waited. The man will have seen I have no luggage, he thought. On the flat again above the gorge they passed the modern development around the base of the ski lift. The whole complex was in darkness. Hotels, alle geschlossen, the driver insisted. But he keeps driving, Cleaver observed. Five minutes later the car pulled up in the tidy main street of Luttach. The shop windows were dark. Everything is shuttered. Cleaver didn't move to get out. Hotel? he asked. A taxi driver always knows where to find a bed for the night. The meter is still counting, time now rather than space. Zimmer? the man suggests. Ja, Cleaver told him. Perhaps he knows more German than he thought. An O level is an O level in the end. Or was. The car proceeded along the main street, and turned left up the hill.

Kommen Sie doch. The driver took Cleaver by the elbow and leaned on a heavy door. It's a bar, a bare room with wooden floor, wooden benches and tables, a dozen red-faced men in two groups talking loudly over cards. But there's a woman serving. The driver went to speak to her. They're old friends. Standing at the door, Cleaver savoured the foreignness of it, the hubbub of words one could treat as mere noise, the difference of the decor, the men's clothing, the smell. A wood smell, Cleaver thought, and there's smoke and leather and beer. It was exciting. The wall too, he saw, was clad in wood and there were old wooden skis arranged crosswise above the counter and dusty porcelain dolls on a mantlepiece over a fire of smouldering logs.

The woman came to speak to him. She is the kind of woman one calls handsome, past her best that is. Wie viele Tage? She was wiping her hands on a blue apron. Her skirt was grey wool. Cleaver shook his head. Then he was irritated when he realised that he was imagining himself on camera. He was acting the eminent man in the back of beyond for an imaginary audience. Just look where Cleaver's doing his show this week! Observe, he would tell the audience, the unusually large, carved wooden crucifix hanging over the bench in the corner, the Christ's twisted limbs, the sombre resignation of the upturned eyes. Armin! The woman went to a door and called down a dark passageway. Armin! You must stop doing this, Cleaver decided. Armin, kimm iatz! You must just *be* here, he told himself, and nothing else. No running commentary. The men at their tables showed no curiosity. Someone slapped down a card and started to laugh quite raucously. It's not even German they're speaking, Cleaver realised, but some rough mountain dialect. So much the better.

A boy in his mid teens appeared, reluctant. His hair is long and seems to have been dyed coal black. He wears an earring with a silver skull. How many days you want the room? he asked. I'm not really quite sure as yet, Cleaver said. He corrected himself: I don't know. The woman has seen, he saw, that I have no bag. At least three or four. Drei, the boy tells his mother and immediately turns to go. The taxi driver is tapping Cleaver's elbow. Fifty euros, he says, in English. It seems excessive, but how can I ask to consult the meter? One of the card players darts the new arrival a know-ing glance. Out of habit, Cleaver starts to ask for a receipt, then says, Nein, das macht nichts, and hands the man fifty-five euros. Until he spoke, he had no idea he knew the expression.

On a series of ledges and tables up three flights of wooden stairs and creaking landings, there are more porcelain dolls, dressed in the traditional peasant costumes of at least a century ago, their hard bright faces beaming, their glassy blue eyes wide open, as Cleaver labours upward, breathing heavily, led by the handsome woman, past her best. Only a foot or two from his face are her long brown socks, green slippers. He can smell them. He finds the stairs hard going, steeper than home. On the third-floor landing there is a huge old dolls' house, perhaps five feet by four by four. White and pink, porcelain faces beam out of all the windows. The light in the stairwell is dim and yellow and the dolls' frilly clothes seem musty. The wall is clad with vertical strips of dark wood and a splintery old scythe has been hung between drawn curtains. Cleaver smiled. In many ways it really is a shame there is no camera.

But to the eminent man's surprise there is a smart TV in his room with an impressive remote. How impressive it would be, he thinks, to say, No, take it away! A bait I must not rise to. As he is trying to get his breath back, the woman has already started speaking. She is talking very rapidly. She gestures here and there. Why is she doing this when she knows he can't understand? She is pointing to a door further along the corridor, showing him towels, repeating things she has said a hundred times before. She is doing her duty regardless of his ability to understand. But now the word Frühstück does ring a bell. Heißes Wasser, the woman waggles a finger. Noch nicht. Then she was gone.

Here I am then. Cleaver lay down on the bed. He is wearing a leather coat, a jacket, pink shirt and lemon tie, dark trousers. When he left the house that morning, he could perfectly well have gone to the studios and withdrawn his resignation. Was there anyone who was anyone who had not begged him to change his mind? And that was only yesterday. Think it over, Michaels insisted. For Christ's sake! The room was damp. It hasn't been heated. No one was expecting guests. You're a fat pig, Cleaver announced, hands folded on his stomach. A man of your girth, he spoke the words out loud, ought to create his own warmth. The room is quite large, but largely empty and dusty. How my father loved to rhyme the words girth and mirth, his elder son had written. Cleaver has no reason to open the wardrobe and drawers. What's the view from the window? He gets off the bed. Nothing but a narrow alley, a facade without a window. Turning round, he notices yet another doll sitting on the chest of drawers in a puddle of dusty frills; its face is set in that same changeless expression of blank complacency. The eyes are blue and wide and unblinking.

Cleaver shivers. Here we are then, he repeats and lies down on the bed again. The one blanket is definitely damp. Turning on his side, he becomes aware of his mobile phones. I can finally lose weight, he thought. Lose touch and tension, unwind. He took the phones out of his pocket and laid them on the bedside table. A pine surface. All the furniture in the room is untreated pine. Or ash, or birch perhaps. Cleaver knows nothing about wood. To be quite consistent, I shouldn't even have brought a phone, he reflects. On the other hand, one could hardly become a saint over night. Is there any signal up here in the mountains? he wondered. He smiled and shook his head, but then deliberately succumbed to a different temptation. He stood up, walked over to the TV set, clicked on the power and picked up the remote.

Settling back on the bed, he was aware his feet were cold. How can one be so fat and have cold feet? A man was taking a microphone into a studio audience. At once Cleaver felt anxious. He checked his watch. At this very moment one of his two stand-ins would be in make-up. Have I really left? After making mincemeat of the President of the United States? At the acme of my career? He watched the presenter push the microphone towards a pretty, pouting mouth in a convenient aisle seat. Cleaver has no doubt that the girl has been placed there on purpose. She begins to speak, urgently, confidently, in German. They must have a camera tracking down the aisle from the back of the studio to pick up the presenter's nods. Standard fare. The egregious man is agreeing. Cleaver has no idea what they are talking about. Something serious, he guesses. Suddenly everybody is laughing. An overhead camera pans. People always laugh together. The lighting is a little harsh, Cleaver decides. An isolated laugh is an embarrassing thing. The studio has olive-green seats, orange screens, matt black fittings. Very German colours. Don't all German subway stations, Cleaver remembers, have green and orange wall tiling? He changes channel. An earnest and voluptuous woman is reading the news in Italian. Cleaver listens. She is deploying the same rigid patterns of cadence, he observes, the same sudden extravagant emphases, at once routine and dramatic, of which he himself is such a master. But this is an old observation. He has noticed the same things in French, a language he understands, and in Spanish, a language he doesn't. Everything must be urgent, yet the routine confidence of its delivery reassuring.

He gets to the tenth channel, the twelfth. Suddenly it's English. BBC World. They have a satellite. This is unexpected. Perhaps at the top of the hour there will be a word about his, Harold Cleaver's, surprise resignation from Britain's most serious, most successful talk show: *Crossfire*. But for the moment an old acquaintance, Martin Clabburn, is interviewing a man in a turban. Surely you're not going to pretend that you were unaware of collaborating with one of the most ruthless governments of modern times? Martin appears to be outraged, but poised too. The man in the turban gives a poised and combative reply. They are allies.

The show proceeds. Cleaver sucks his teeth. Nothing, a voice has started to repeat in his head, could more emphatically confirm the rightness of your decision to bail out than this rehearsal of a completely fake confrontation. Clabburn again makes some piously offensive remark to which the turbaned man once more replies with offensive piety. How wearying. Yet so long as you lie here watching the show, you haven't really left. The viewer is always complicit. A close-up suggests that the only real emotion Clabburn is experiencing is his pleasure in the discomfort he imagines he is causing the man. Cleaver Carves Up President, was how the *Guardian* had described his famous interview. The fellow in the turban seemed to be relishing the fight.

Then Cleaver must have missed a few minutes – perhaps he actually dozed off – because now quite unexpectedly the theme music explodes; the screen is a kaleidoscope of dramatic scenes and hi-tech items that appear to be whirling through space between riots and bloodshed and exulting athletes. Television has been taken over by these clips, Cleaver's elder son had written in his discussion of his father's many controversial TV debates and topical documentaries. How the boy could have claimed the book was a novel is beyond Cleaver. A mixture of the air-raid siren and the sexiest, state-of-the-art gadget, his son had written: the intention being, as my father once told me in one of his interminable attempts to *coach* me as a journalist, as a writer, because it must be understood that my father couldn't speak to someone, to anyone, without trying to *seduce* them if they were a woman or to *coach* them if they were a man – the intention being, my father explained, to instil in the viewer both intense anxiety and extreme complacency, *simultaneously*. Did I really say something as intelligent as that, Cleaver wondered? He smiled. Certainly his son had become a past master. I coached him well. My elder son. Then in the shifting red lights of this grotesquely long, end-of-show clip, Cleaver glanced at the doll on the chest of drawers. She is watching; her porcelain eyes are rapt, her smile enviably vacant. Cleaver lifted the remote and killed the screen.

At once he became aware of singing. The men downstairs are singing something. There's the strain of an accordion. I'm hungry, Cleaver realises. I mustn't expect to be compos mentis today of all days. Just stick to plan. Compost mentis. That was an old joke. He put on his shoes and went out on the landing but couldn't find the light switch. Perhaps the handsome landlady had explained something. From the dark stairwell the singing swelled up louder. Cleaver ran his finger blindly over the walls. They were male voices singing boisterously, in German. This was risking a splinter. He went back into his own room, turned the light on again and, leaving the door open, found his way to the top of the stairs. From every shadowy ledge, as he descended, the dolls stared and smiled in facile approbation. There is something noisy about these dolls, Cleaver decided. Something choral. From beneath, the male chorus grew louder as he trod carefully down past the mute, female dolls. There was something military to the rhythm now. Almost all the politicians I interviewed, Cleaver reflected, pausing to let his eyes grow accustomed to the darkness, were men; while almost all the viewers and readers who wrote to me were women.

Then, on the very last stair, imagining he was already at ground level, he stumbled and fell forward against a table where two shiny eyes stared blindly. A door banged open and there was bright light to his right; the card-players were cheering and thumping the table in self-congratulation at the end of their song. A tall bearded man paid Cleaver no attention as he stamped off down the corridor. Cleaver replaced the doll in a standing position and walked into the bar.

He had been sitting five minutes at a corner table before the woman detached herself from the far wall and came to him. She stood still in her apron, hair gathered beneath a white headscarf. Most of the dolls had headscarves too. Cleaver did not want to be reduced to pointing fingers at his mouth. He smiled apologetically: Do you, um, have anything to eat? She passed her tongue over her lower lip, watching him steadily. She is unaware of course that Harold Cleaver is used to talking to audiences of upwards of ten million people. Bread? He asked. The woman raised her eyebrows and looked around in evident impatience. Two men were singing softly, clinking their glasses on the table. Bier? she enquired brusquely. Cleaver surrendered and made the timeless gesture. He lifted his right hand and pushed three fingers toward his ample mouth, widening his eyes in what he knows any audience would register as a charming smile of self-irony and supplication. Zu spät, the woman said. Her face is attractive – there are friendly wrinkles round bright eyes – but the cheeks betray the slight jowliness of early middle age. Trinkn, trinkn, trinkn! the men have begun to chant. The knocking of their glasses has become a clatter. The woman pushed her cardigan off her wrist and tapped her watch. Zu spät. Brot, Cleaver remembered and then, Speck? She pursed her lips and turned away.

Cleaver ate with his head forward over a wooden platter. The beer is icy. He wonders if the men have stopped singing because of his presence. More than fifty million had watched his interview with the President when CBS picked it up stateside. I put it to you, Mr President – Cleaver realised he would have to cut the speck into smaller pieces – that you have simply allowed your agenda to be driven by a series of ongoing debates and conflicts, the Middle East, terrorism, the white-collar tax burden – while the real challenges for the future – global warming, excessive consumption, alternative energy sources, you have largely ignored. When the President had hesitated, Cleaver added: Or do you think that in a democracy it's inevitable that the successful politician will be no more than a choirmaster for the loudest chorus? The stringy ham keeps catching in his teeth. Let me get this straight, the handsome President said aggressively, I am my own man. Then Cleaver smiled his famously dangerous smile. He smiles it again now, chewing his food: Mr President, you have just used two clichés, one right after the other. He needed a toothpick. A robot could be programmed to give better answers than that.

Suddenly the card players were arguing. Someone was being accused of cheating. Or so it seemed to Cleaver. The only man wearing a jacket and tie threw his hand down on the table and pushed his chair back in disgust. As he stood up, another jumped to his feet and pushed him back. Incongruously, he wore a leather cowboy hat. The well-dressed man stumbled and almost fell. Everyone was shouting or laughing. The landlady ran to the table. A younger man, a boy almost, in green corduroy trousers and chequered shirt lifted a red accordion from the floor and began to play, softly and squeezily, some peasant dance. Perfect background, Cleaver decided. All at once the quarrel was over and another tray of beers was crossing the floor.

My room is cold, he told the woman. Do you have an extra blanket? He made the gesture of snuggling into wool, of pulling something up over his head. She concentrated on counting coins from a pouch at her waist. Blanket! Or I'll freeze. Brrr! It had been a mistake to order cold beer. But now the man in the cowboy hat came over. A big blanket

16

for a big man! he boomed. He said something to the woman. She nodded. Welcome to the Südtirol! he went on expansively. He has a thin, almost cylindrical head, a hooked eagle nose, twinkling eyes. You want to ride a horse while you are in Luttach, you come to Hermann! Onkel Hermann's Stable! Already he was putting a business card in Cleaver's chill fingers. A big horse for a big arse! He clapped and laughed. You want a woman, you ask Frau Schleiermacher. She knows everybody. Ha, ha, ha! A bigger whore for the man who has more, Cleaver quipped. My father's quips were interminable and interminably crude, his son had written. But Hermann couldn't follow this. The Südtirol welcomes you, he repeated nodding and laughing and offering his hand. His grip was iron.

Cleaver had been back in his room five minutes when the boy with the dyed black hair brought the extra blanket. His satanic earring made Cleaver smile. But he couldn't remember the kid's name. Had it really been Amen? Foreign names find no pigeonholes in our minds. Cleaver's elder daughter, Angela, had been through a phase when she wore all kinds of rather grotesque emblems of death. It was gross misrepresentation, surely, to describe this as an attempt to reveal the depth of her unhappiness to her distracted parents. There are droves of adolescents, Cleaver announced out loud, wearing satanic bric-a-brac. Mainly earrings and bracelets of dark silver, or grey steel, or black T-shirts with orange, hellfire motifs. It is part of the modern world's parody of everything that once meant something and made us tremble. But Cleaver had never considered confronting his son over the account he had given in his book. Almost as soon as he lay down, he realised that the extra blanket would not be enough.

The problem is his feet. The extra blanket would certainly be enough, Cleaver thought, if only his feet were already warm. He turned off the bedside lamp. As it was, he couldn't feel them at all. He reached for the wire and turned the lamp on again. The Tyrolese doll is still staring at the blank TV screen. Oh to be as thoughtless as a doll! As careless of heat and cold!

Cleaver got up. He had stripped to his pants and vest. Leaving the door open, he padded out onto the landing – what a fat figure he would cut now – and tried the door that the landlady had indicated as the bathroom. What he did at home when his feet were cold was to take a hot bath. The times when Amanda would warm them between her thighs were over almost before they began. To say my parents had a stormy relationship, his elder son had written, would be like saying that Arafat and Sharon enjoyed the occasional tiff. The water in the shower was cold. Cleaver waited, advancing a finger from time to time. Sometimes my son's analogies leave a tad to be desired, he thought. He even laughed. The water gushed from the shower head but stayed cold, cold as the streams tumbling from alpine rocks in the night. Heißes Wasser. She had definitely said that, though now Cleaver began to wonder if the idea hadn't been associated with Frühstück in some way. Noch nicht. Returning to his room, he had the first inkling that this was a serious problem.

Cleaver put all his clothes back on, including his leather coat and climbed back into bed. Then he got out again and arranged the two blankets so that he could roll himself into them. Roly-poly pudding, he muttered. His face and his bald spot are covered now. He breathed his own warm breath in the dark. This room smells, he realised. He hadn't noticed before. My feet aren't warming up at all. They seemed to be separate from the rest of his body, as if what he perceived as cold was in fact the famous ghost pain after amputation.

Damn! Suddenly he wants a cigarette. Cleaver turned on the light. There was no doubt that the sections of *Under His Shadow* that dealt with the narrator's father's chronic hypochondria were among the cruellest and the funniest in the book. Cleaver unrolled the blankets, sat up, hauled in his feet and began to massage them. Fuck the book. The skin is a queer, greyish colour. The wonder, his eldest son had written, is that my father's *constant* conviction that he was only a few moments away from a heart attack never prevented him from eating and whoring and drinking and smoking. However hard he rubbed them, Cleaver's feet remained exactly as they were, grey, cold and slightly damp. He hadn't had a cigarette for at least three months, nor a woman for six, so it was depressing to feel he wanted one now. How can I pass the time till my feet get warm? He looked around for the remote. And this is the man who is planning to go and live in a mountain cabin! Tomorrow he must sort himself out. I'll get all the kit.

He put his shoes back on and began to walk up and down the room. He was moving on blocks of ice. After fifteen minutes, no change. The doll is staring. Just go and bloody-well ask for another bloody blanket, a voice announced, or four, or a quilt, or a hot-water bottle. Didn't the Germans all use quilts these days? But Cleaver isn't going to go and ask. He knows that. It is something to do with the language problem. And a challenge too: he knows he would feel ashamed. The landlady has judged that two thick blankets should be enough. It isn't really a cold night. It's autumn, but not winter. Cleaver doesn't want to draw attention to his weakness. My father, his son had written, would have competed with Carl Lewis at the hundred metres, with Muhammad Ali in the ring, with Pete Sampras on the tennis court. He was quite simply the most *competitive* man who ever lived. Sometimes I felt that he had chosen Mother and she him because, since they both worked in the media, they would be able to compete with each other day in day out their lives long. It's a lie that I competed with the children, though, Cleaver thought. Damn these feet. He grabbed the TV remote and pointed it.

As if he had turned on on purpose to hear the news, BBC World launched directly into its top-of-the hour bulletin. Eleven p.m. European time. BBC World! an authoritative voice declared, Demand a broader view! Cleaver sat on the bed and took his shoes off again. Anyone who truly took an intelligent view, he thought, would deny himself the use of the slogan. What my son lacks, Cleaver realised then, watching the camera pick over the ruins of some Palestinian village, which is what makes him so successful perhaps, is any sense of pathos. The pathos of journalism's interminable superficiality, the pathos of marriage and parenthood, the pathos of cold feet, damn it. Though of course he and Amanda had never married. Every time Mother asked, my father said no, and every time my father asked, Mother said no. We're the perfect mismatch, my father quipped. A match yes, but always a Miss, Mother would answer. Match, as in incendiary device, my father would come back. Cleaver massaged his miserable feet. My son is a genius of caricature, he decided. Everything and everyone was described in such a way that he, she or it could be slotted into some available cultural pigeonhole. Hence character and action were always memorable. That's the key to success. A name the public can recognise. A situation where everything is clear. The boy missed all the pathos of it, Cleaver thought, and the fun too. I myself forgot the half and more long ago.

Without thinking, Cleaver reached for the bedside table

and turned on the red mobile. I must get away from this sterile engagement with my son, he decided. It was exhausting. The small screen glowed. You did not come to the South Tyrol to conduct conversations with the world you left behind. The name HAROLD CLEAVER appeared together with his home phone number. I'll have to change that. Then there was a few seconds' wait. Cleaver had often tried to visualise this business of the little gadget sending its feelers out into the busy air for some welcoming network to lock into. At such moments, even the mobile has a pathos, he thought, an imagined pathos, the desire to lock in to the collective mind. The BBC began its ritual analysis of the world's stock markets. By now everyone has a pigeonhole for the NASDAQ, the dollar against the yen.

OST-NET, the screen suddenly decides. Almost at once the phone began to vibrate. One message. Two messages. Three, four, five, six. The number stopped at fifteen and a small image of an envelope began to flash in the top left corner. Memory full. Cleaver felt in the inside pocket of his coat. He felt in his jacket. Don't say! He can't find his reading glasses. Rapidly he went through all his pockets, his jacket, his trousers. Could I have been so stupid? But perhaps it would be better not to read them. He had meant to give up reading in general. Straining his eyes to focus, he wondered what order the messages had been written in. Is there any way of knowing? All from Amanda. No, he couldn't make out the letters.

Turning away from the television, Cleaver had to put the mobile under the lampshade right in the naked glare of the bulb. There, just.

What am i supposed 2 do with yr stuff mr renegade because if u've really gone no way i want it cluttering the place here

As soon as Cleaver pressed the erase button, the phone vibrated with the arrival of another message.

BTW u shld see the phonebill yr daughter has run up.

Again Cleaver erased and again the phone vibrated. Amanda could text, he reflected, while cooking, while driving, while on the john. Amanda loves texting. He squinted:

Michaels has called 5 times in 15 mins I reminded him deserters shld b shot as they ran

Cleaver smiled, clicked again.

I knew u wldn't have the balls not 2 take yr phone

Now he had to close his eyes a moment. The letters had begun to blur. The BBC had started a feature about a language on the edge of extinction, in Siberia. It is extraordinary how much enthusiasm and drama a TV troupe can put into such reports that in no way affect the lives of 99.99 per cent of their audience. Apparently the marvel was that these Mongol-looking people needed only one word to say, I'm going out bear hunting.

I really will throw yr stuff out u no – he went back to the phone – 1st editions included

Though there were hardly any bears left, the journalist was lamenting now, and even fewer language speakers to hunt them.

Dear mr fugitive i imagine us meeting by chance some day at angie's graveside. Don't worry i'll pretend not 2 recognise u

Cleaver shook his head. She hit below the belt to elicit a response. Angela's accident, he muttered, could in no way be described as the chronicle of a death foretold.

Michaels has just phoned AGAIN 2 ask if i wanted 2 do yr job. Little old me! Can u believe it?

Cleaver didn't believe it for one moment.

If u don't tell me where you are i'll go 2 the police and tell them u've disappeared.

Every time Cleaver erased, the phone vibrated. There was no end to it.

I love u. U're the only man i ever wanted 2 live with, the only possible father 2 my children

Cleaver wondered if she was drinking.

Don't hope i'll kill myself, she wrote.

I know u're only pretending not 2 read these

I hate u

Bill white phoned about selling the balkans doc 2 french TV. He wouldn't tell me about money

Sleep tight harry wherever you are. Did u remember yr tranquillizers?

I always said u were a coward

Still the messages kept arriving. Cleaver's eyes hurt. Without reading them, he repeatedly pressed the button that opened and then erased the messages, until, after three or four minutes, the phone was still. He turned it off. I won't reply.

The BBC was now marvelling over the special effects used in a new film about the paranormal. Apparently the computer graphics were more interesting than the subject. Cleaver turned that off too. There is nothing for it but to lie here, he thought. He took off his leather coat, wrapped himself in the blankets again and placed the heavy coat, folded in four, on his feet. They were aching with cold. What on earth am I doing so far from home and simple comforts? He had brought no drugs. This is stupid. The doll was watching as he turned out the light.

He couldn't sleep. Think of nothing, Cleaver told himself, determinedly, of nothing, of nothing, of nothing. Like a doll. The minutes passed. Count all the women you've had. That was a reliable pastime. He wearied. Oh, but I should have thought of the trick with the coat before. His feet finally began to warm and before he knew it he was waking in the early hours to find himself too hot. This is fantastic. He went to the bathroom, stripped to his underwear, rearranged the blankets. His feet were glowing now. Welcome to the Südtirol, he told them. He was chuckling. His whole body was wonderfully present, wonderfully comfortable. He couldn't remember such physical pleasure, such relaxation. What a disproportionate reaction! Lying in the dark now Harold Cleaver enjoyed an enormous sense of well-being. Done it. Escaped.

II

THE NAME OF the house is Rosenkranzhof, some two thousand feet above the village of Steinhaus, a ski centre to the north-east of Luttach. But Cleaver didn't find it at once. The first day he bought boots, warm clothes, toiletries, walking poles, a good waterproof and a backpack. His whereabouts would be evident from his credit card bill, he thought, so he phoned the bank and asked for payments to be made by direct debit. He would inform of his new mailing address anon. Then he did the same with his private mobile contract. Turning off the phone after making the calls, ignoring the new messages that were still arriving, Cleaver decided he would turn the thing on only once every forty-eight hours. Briefly. In the evenings. His work mobile, on the other hand, which was also his flirt mobile, he wouldn't turn on at all.

At the Tourist Information Office the girl couldn't get it into her head what he wanted. Perhaps she hadn't really understood the word remote. She is pretending to understand, Cleaver thought. Here is our list of farms with rooms to let, she said. Her pretty young hands opened a printed brochure with pages and pages of photos and prices. There were the usual coded descriptions of what was on offer. Five minutes from the ski lifts at Sand in Taufers. Self-catering. It was an English edition. Easy walking distance from the cable car at Steinhaus. Sleeps eight. Parking for two vehicles. I want something remote, Cleaver repeated, high, high up. He made a gesture with his hand. For months, not weeks. Years perhaps, he thought. The girl stared. She wasn't unattractive: honey blonde, pink cheeks, generous, uncomprehending eyes. Not unlike his younger daughter, Caroline. She went behind a door to call for help. A man in his early forties appeared. Such a place, sir, he pointed out, so far from anything, would probably not have electricity, it would not be easy to live in. That's what I'm looking for, Cleaver insisted.

Clean-shaven, solemn, chinless, the man spoke with a bureaucratic we. We only advise accommodations that meet our high standards. We inspect them all. That is our boast. As Cleaver turned to leave, the man advised: If you rent a place on your own, you can be as isolated as you wish, even here in the village. The people of the South Tyrol are very discreet. Cleaver hadn't expected this wisdom, this level of English. After all, the Tourist Information employee went on, and he smiled knowingly, it might be unwise to find yourself too far from essential services. The girl also smiled. They were telling him they had taken note of his age, his weight. I want a remote place, Cleaver repeated. Absurd as it was, his success in warming his feet last night had given him the determination to press on. I want to be one of those isolated lights, he thought, high up on the mountainside at night. When the heart attack strikes, so be it.

On returning to Unterfurnerhof, as he now saw his guest house was called, Cleaver found there was a quilt on his bed, but when he went down to talk to Frau Schleiermacher she made no mention of this change. Armin, she called, Armin! My mother, Armin translated without enthusiasm, does not understand why you want to find a place so high high up. The boy has blond eyebrows beneath his coal-black hair, pale blue eyes. Today his earring was a triple six. Distorted guitar music drifted from his room along the passageway. I have decided to be alone, Cleaver said. It was hard to eliminate the pride from his voice. Far from being angry, he felt pleased that there had been no quilt last night: I survived my first test. Allein, the boy referred. His mother's eyes narrowed. She has shrewd, lively eyes. She spoke for perhaps a whole minute. She knows no place, Armin abbreviated. There was a frank sullenness about him. Dying your hair coal black and wearing satanic jewellery was not as radical as deciding to be alone, Cleaver thought, even in the South Tyrol. It's exactly this supposed rebellion, he had once told Angela when she got heavily into piercing, that confirms your constant engagement with society. Don't you see that? Frau Schleiermacher was still talking. You're involved in a battle, which is about as involved as anyone can be. There are many, many abandoned Häuser up on the mountains, Armin interpreted, but if nobody is living in them, it is because they are . . . He got stuck. His mother had said a word too long and complex to translate. She repeated whatever it was. His puzzled eyes moved from her to their guest and back. Then his face lit up in a smile: Because they are shit.

Cleaver bought a map and began to walk. Above Luttach the Ahrn valley curves from north to north-east. To get the best of the morning sunshine, he tackled the south-facing slopes. It was strange not to start the day bombarded with information, with e-mails, fact sheets about the next show's guests, summaries of everything each of them had ever said on every possible issue. What questions are tabled in Parliament today? The name *Crossfire* had begun to irritate him recently.

He walked up a narrow road signposted Weissbach, Rio Bianco. Without his glasses he was unable to find these places on the map. Only after seeing the same sign three or four times along the winding road did it occur to Cleaver that these places were in fact the same place – Weissbach, Rio Bianco – one name was the translation of the other. He stopped and stared. One translates a name to appropriate it, he thought. As Amanda always insisted on calling me Harry, rather than Harold. She wanted me to be *her* Harry. Cleaver knew very little of the history of this part of the world, only that it had changed hands from Austria to Italy at the end of the First War. To everyone else he had been Harold. Imagine them changing all the names, he suddenly thought, and the language in London! Arc de Marbre! St Johann's Holz. At a stroke all the popular pundits and celebrities would be impotent, deprived of the power of their masterful voices. Ponte della Torre! Though that might prove a relief in the end, a release. Bäckerstrasse! Cleaver remembered laughing with Giada about the relief that forthcoming impotence would be. Coming at the fourth attempt, you mean, she giggled. She was a bubbly girl. They had been in the Tyrol to ski, not to walk. People like Giada didn't walk. Find me a ski resort, he had told his travel agent in the King's Road, where there is no chance whatsoever of anyone recognising me. Just once, though, on the last day of the trip, they had joined a group on a guided hike with snowshoes. The deep silence of the snow-filled gullies had made the chatter of the other hikers all but unbearable. My father's position on noise, his elder son had written, and on conversation in general for that matter, was that it was only tolerable when *he* was making it. Perhaps I brought the mobiles in case Giada tries to get in touch, Cleaver wondered. Or various other women for that matter. But no, he hadn't. Nor would they. There will be no more romancing. The Lord giveth, Cleaver muttered, and the Lord taketh away.

He soldiered on to Weissbach. The name sounded more believable than Rio Bianco. He smiled. But after twenty minutes steady climbing he was exhausted, overheated. I'm carrying two stone too many, at least. He took off his jacket and stuffed it in the backpack. Three perhaps. He grabbed a fold of flesh on his belly and squeezed. It's got to go.

Breathing hard, he sat on a log and surveyed the scene. Named, he now saw, after the stream that tumbled by beneath a low, wooden bridge, Weissbach amounted to four shuttered guest houses, converted farms by the looks, their owners holidaying off season, in the Seychelles perhaps, or perhaps London, Maifoire even. To spend a whole day, Cleaver suddenly and surprisingly found himself thinking, really grasping a fact like that, a scene like this: these old houses, half wood half stone, built at an altitude of some four thousand feet, used for centuries to store hay and shelter cattle; then their recent transformation, under altered economic circumstances, into hotels, mainly for skiers, the old names repainted in fancy Gothic script on timber facades. Yes, to master the obvious, he thought, shifting his fat hams on the rough log beside the path, there was an ambition: without making a documentary, or even planning an article; to stare and stare at something real, solid, uncompromising, not a photograph, not a clip, not something you could edit and reorganise, to get a sense of its smell, its gritty presence – the wood smoke in the air and the rush and gurgle of the water – until you felt quite sure you had really got the thing fixed in your stupid head, hammered home hard, once and for all, like a long nail in an old beam. That is what I must do. That is what I have come here for.

Disturbingly, it took two attempts to get back on his feet. For Christ's sake! He was only fifty-five. Cleaver crossed the road, pushed open a door under the painted sign, Unterholzerhof, and found himself in a large shabby bar. But already the word Stube seems more appropriate. These places mustn't be confused with pubs. No one was about. The light is gloomy. Every day, Cleaver reflected, lowering himself down again on a bench that resembled a pew, every hour even, news bulletin after news bulletin, for years, decades, one revised one's opinion on Thatcher and Reagan, on Blair and Bush, on genetically modified foods, corporal punishment, Afghanistan, the never-ending pathos of the Lib Dems, idea after idea after idea coming at you through words and pictures, but without anything ever being nailed home. Once again there was a crucifix in a corner. Everything could always be edited, reorganised for a different public. This seat is very hard, he thought. Nothing was ever settled and resolved. He looked around. There was a brooding quality to the grey light. When am I going to get served? he wondered. He was thirsty.

Aside from the crucifix, the dark, timber-clad walls were hung with what Cleaver was already beginning to recognise as the standard South Tyrolese bric-a-brac: antique farm implements, shotguns, a stuffed hawk, flowers dried decades before, a troll with an axe. These are other things one might easily spend days contemplating. The curtains were a dusty red. Not to mention, Cleaver returned to his thoughts of a moment before, constantly rearranging your position on privatisation, homosexual marriage, cloning, rap. It was a stream of ever varying phenomena, a frenzy in a sorting office. Still, it was curious, he noticed now – his calf muscles were aching – that despite the fact that he was in no hurry at all, absolutely none – he nevertheless felt rather impatient to be served. Where is everybody? It had to do with the dynamic, he supposed, of entering a place whose function is to serve you things. I could be dying of hunger, he thought. You walk into a place that serves food and at once you're locked into the logic of exchange: you want things to get moving, food one way, money the other, despite the fact that actually you're in no hurry at all. On the contrary, you could do with a rest. Cleaver frowned, bending down to massage the backs of his legs. I should remember to carry a flask of water in future, he thought. If there was one thing, his elder son had written, that my father wouldn't be seen dead drinking, it was water: My contribution to the conservation of vital resources, he would say, uncorking the customary bottle of Bordeaux.

Bitte? a quiet voice enquired. Looking up, Cleaver found an old man had materialised. Tall, bent, with incongruously long ears, he wore a leather apron. Trinken, Cleaver told him. Bier? The man asked. His gnarled hands held a dish-cloth. Nein. There was a pause of some seconds. The waiter's watery old eyes made no attempt to focus. Apfelschorle? he proposed. Cleaver hesitated. He hadn't understood. Das ist Apfelsaft, the old man said. Okay, ja. Cleaver lifted a hand above the table to indicate the size of the glass he wanted. Big. The man gave no sign of acknowledgement. He walked stiffly to the bar and busied himself, quietly and very slowly, behind the counter, washing glasses, wiping surfaces. He has no concept that I might be in a hurry, Cleaver reflected. Eventually, in a slow shuffle, wrists tense, face concentrated, the waiter returned with a tall glass of some cloudy yellow liquid, wobbling on a tin tray. Danke, Cleaver took a sip. It was fresh, sour. Bitte schön, the old man said quietly.

While Cleaver drank, the waiter drifted over to the window, mottled hands folded over his apron, pale eyes staring between the curtains at the wooded slopes. Although his bench was facing the other way, towards the counter and the crucifix, Cleaver could not help but be intensely aware of this silent presence. While he is hardly aware of me at all, he realised. Certainly he is not thinking of me.

Twisting his head, Cleaver sneaked a glance. There was a fantastic painted stillness to the man, standing with one hand in a pocket beneath his apron, his wrinkled face blank, waiting for his customer to go. He doesn't care, Cleaver realised, whether I take five minutes or fifty. It makes no difference. For some reason this made him feel anxious to be on his way. Again he twisted his neck to look at the bulbous nose, long ears, pale closed lips. There was something doll-like about his steadiness. He wants and expects nothing of me, Cleaver thought. At the same time he felt irritated. Why? He drained his glass. Why should I want him to want something of me? But when he stood up to leave it turned out that what the old man wanted was an exorbitant five euros. Five euros for a glass of apple juice! The waiter pocketed the coins with the smallest of bows. Aufwiedersehen, he muttered.

A hundred yards beyond the settlement the road came to an end and Cleaver had to start using his walking poles in earnest. That was what I bought them for. He felt pleased with himself. Norwegian walking poles, apparently. He shook his head, smiling. A steep path zigzagged up into thick pine woods. It was nice to thrust the poles into the ground, nice to look through the shadowy light beneath the trees, not unlike the quiet, timeless gloom in all these Stuben. The larches have begun to turn, Cleaver told himself. How else would he have guessed they were larches? Do I want to start filling the vacant mental space by naming everything here, he wondered, now that there are no more briefs, no more e-mails, no more newspapers: the twigs, the brambles, the mosses, all the little plants with their different leaves? The insects. Cleaver has never known the names of plants or flowers. Never mind toadstools. He never had much time for the countryside. When my father bought flowers to placate my mother, his elder son had written, he would just go into the florists and say: ten o' them red uns – he liked to fake a lower-class accent – five o' the yeller, three o' the pink, oh and some green stuff for background, you choose. Not quite, mate, Cleaver objected. I used to say roses, actually. Amanda only liked roses. Green stuff, perhaps. But what were you supposed to say? Foliage? He distinctly remembered waiting to be served, impatiently, in the muffled damp half-light of the florist's near Edgware Road Tube, holding the twins by the hand. Daddy only buys flowers when Mummy's angry, Angela told the girl as she rang up the price at the till. Certainly I never scrimped, Cleaver thought. Oh really! the shop-girl laughed, Well I think I'd make a point of being permanently furious if it meant getting lovely presents like this. Sometimes there were pleasant flashes of complicity, Cleaver remembered now, at the florist's. Why did I never take advantage? He remembered eyes glancing up brightly while practised fingers tied knots of twine round stiff green stems.

Cleaver rested and pushed on. No danger of not losing weight if you keep this up every day. Again, it was strange, he thought, how sweet and resinous the mountain air was, and at the same time how loudly, even after walking so far, the noise of the traffic still rose from the main road in the valley far below. No, it isn't really loud, he decided, but insistent, ensnaring. I want a house above the noise line, Cleaver told himself. He has no idea how he is going to find such a place. At a certain point, seeing four abandoned walls in a hollow below the path, he decided to explore. Almost at once his foot slipped into a hole full of leaves and slime. He banged his knee painfully on stone flagging. So much for the Norwegian walking poles. When he pulled his boot out of the mulch, it stank. The purpose of this retreat, he reminded himself – he had to sit and nurse his knee for some minutes – though I really don't like the word retreat – the purpose of this whatever it is, is to extricate my mind from all that has bound it, for too long. I will learn to be free.

But there was no hurry. He toiled very slowly up the steep slopes for about an hour and a half. How the old flesh weighs on you, the sheer bulk of one's body! If there had been an original sin . . . no, that was the wrong word, if there had been a defining impulse that had made him who he was, he thought, it was this always being in a hurry to achieve. Cleaver stopped for breath. He was panting. You were always hungry for praise. He looked upwards through the tall trunks. I'm not going back down, he decided, without having climbed above the trees. His eyes searched. There was no sign of an end. The air seems strangely still, as if trapped in the tangle of dark ivies and twigs. And that included your own praise, oddly enough. The branches of the larch drooped like loose sleeves. You were hungry for your own praise, he thought. You were in a hurry to admire yourself. He shook his head. I'll make it to the treeline, he thought, or just above, take a quick look around, then turn back.

Cleaver walked. Using the poles was jarring his shoulders. His left boot was rubbing at the heel now. He has blisters. All this was to be expected. With each hairpin twist he

paused a moment; he had begun to notice the play of difference and sameness each time a new section of the path
appeared: roots embedded in mossy rock; white fungus on
brown bark; the ground thick with pine needles and cones
and huge anthills; sparse wet grass and scrubby vegetation
where the sun broke through in little streaks. Occasionally
something moved, or rustled, or wings beat in the branches
above. If I knew how to read all this better, Cleaver muttered,
if I had lived here for many years, each turn of the path
would be as different to me as people are different. And as
similar. You're going to let everything die, are you, just like
that? Amanda demanded. She had woken him in the middle
of the night. Less than forty-eight hours ago, come to think
of it. Her mouth was tight with anger. She had been drinking. After all we've been through? Just because of that stupid
book you're going to abandon everything we've built
together? You're going to chicken out? I was right not to
answer, Cleaver told himself. Who cares about a stupid book?
she demanded. Who cares? You've just interviewed the
President of the United States, for God's sake! You're the
most important journalist in the United bloody Kingdom.
She turned on the bedside lamp. He remembered her tight
lips, the extraordinary energy of her contempt. When
Amanda drank, she drank seriously. Answer me! she
demanded. However painful it might be, he thought, not
answering Amanda must be the first step, not accepting any
back and forth. Nothing would appease her but capitula-
tion. Phillip had been pleasant on the phone. Dad, you do
whatever you want. Phillip is always pleasant, impenetrable.
It's your life in the end. Text me from time to time, Dads,
Caroline whispered. She was in a library. She couldn't talk.
Caroline hasn't understood yet, Cleaver thought. His younger
daughter understood books not people.

He sat down on a stone, completely exhausted. Why am I not relaxing? The wood was truly hushed now. Pine needles and moss. He strained to hear the traffic. Gone. No sound. He waited. Suddenly he felt disorientated. Hey! Cleaver shouted. Oy! There was no echo. Anyone around! No one. It was strange. He picked up a pine cone and threw it. I feel like an overripe fruit that has fallen from its branch, he announced. Perhaps that was what he should text Amanda. That would explain. But it was trite. My feet are in shreds. Last night they ached with cold and now they are burning with blisters. One has to get used to new boots. I knew that. Cleaver turned back. By the time he entered Luttach the afternoon was growing chill and he could barely walk. I must learn to take things slowly.

The President of the United States will be re-elected President of the United States regardless of his disastrous interview with me, Harold Cleaver thought. He was watching television again. He had eaten alone in the big Stube. The sooner I'm living in a place without a television, he told himself, the better. That was obvious. The card players hadn't arrived yet. My father always argued out loud with the television, his elder son had written in *Under His Shadow*. In fact, he talked more to the television than he ever did to us. It is also clear that I'm never going to lose weight eating dumplings and stew. But how could you refuse the only thing on the menu? Especially when you couldn't understand what was written there anyway. Knödel. Cleaver flicked through the channels. He must remember that word. They were all talking about the presidential elections in languages he couldn't understand: a scandal that wasn't really a scandal, or so it seemed, in the Democratic camp. He had gathered that much. And regardless of our interminable war of attrition, our betrayals on either side, he reflected, my partnership with Amanda always continued. The first lady, if not the first wife, as she always said. He was tempted to turn on the phone. Do I hope there will be messages, or not? Actually, they weren't really betrayals, Cleaver decided. When will this old territory come to an end? This echoing on and on. With the exception of Priya, perhaps. A lifetime has been spent, Cleaver thought, and untold megawatts of mental energy, revising my position on the word betrayal. It is a concept he has never got his mind around, not to his absolute and final satisfaction, the way one is never sure if one wants to believe that the universe has a boundary, or that it goes on beyond and beyond forever. Either way is inconceivable. Life with betrayal, life without it.

Priya was definitely a betrayal, he told himself.

Cleaver stood up, crossed the room, picked up the big Tyrolese doll from the cupboard and sat it beside him on the bed. The body was enamel hard under brittle grey frills. The baby face retained its vacant smile. Olga, he decided. Meanwhile, a German TV channel was putting little orange circles around the head of a handsome woman who, it appeared, was never more than a couple of yards from the Democratic candidate at his various would-be charismatic appearances. Scandal too, Cleaver thought, is a word that one increasingly struggles to get to grips with: is it a stumbling block, a form of promotion, or an initiation ceremony? For me to be found in this hotel room with you, for example, he told Olga, is that a scandal? Two tiny TV screens flickered in her eyes. Cleaver changed channel.

An interesting game he had learned to play over many years in foreign hotel rooms was to see how much he could guess about the leading news stories in languages he didn't know and then compare what he'd deduced with the BBC and CNN. Tonight it turned out that he'd missed the twist that the supposed mistress was married to a Republican senator. The Democratic candidate wasn't despairing of his chances. He is getting more airtime. Every time, Cleaver remembered, that a betrayal or a scandal seemed to have blasted them apart forever – Harold Cleaver and Amanda Cunningham – it later turned out, on the contrary, that the crisis had fused them together in new combinations of cohabitation and conflict. I always thought this was a good thing, he remembered, though a little frightening.

Suddenly, the Democrat evaporated and the frightening President was smiling at the camera, waving, congratulating himself. Cleaver stared. He put a hand in the doll's hair. Perhaps the most curious thing about this sudden turn his life had taken was how, precisely in the euphoria of self-congratulation that had followed that interview – Mr President, I can remember no other administration that has presided over such a loss of moral capital – he had become aware, even before he was out of the studio, that something was about to change. But in Cleaver's life, not the President's. What made it almost impossible to escape from my father's shadow, his elder son had concluded one of the central chapters of his fictionalised autobiography, was his completely castrating take on all the things you have to be able to treat seriously for life to make any sense. He rubbished *everything*, then went on subscribing to it all *anyway*, exactly as he had before, exactly as everybody else did. Television debates were *meaningless*, but my father was the undisputed master of them. Documentaries were always *falsifications*, but he went on making excellent documentaries and accepting praise for their authenticity. Marriage in particular was *utterly pointless*, yet in a way my father was more married than all his divorcing friends. Paper gatherers, he called them.

Cleaver had read these comments in his elder son's auto-biographical first novel the day before the great interview, less than twenty-four hours, that is, before the culminating moment in his long career as one of the country's most authoritative commentators on public life. An English interviewer would be a neutral figure, that was the bait they had hooked the President with. I always felt, his elder son had written, that I wanted to emulate my successful father, to write the way he did, to make conversation the way he could, since no one was wittier and sharper than my father when he put his mind to it, no one enchanted a dinner party, a studio audience, more *completely* than he did. But then when the guests had gone and you were alone with him, moving the dishes back to the kitchen perhaps, putting the corks in the bottles, he would tell you that it was a *farce*, an *illusion*. You were stupid for having been taken in. He told you that his documentaries were successful only because they played to the public's desire to be shocked, to feel guilty, that his conversation was only attractive because it followed well-worked riffs. The artist is always a puppet, my father said. Never the puppeteer. The public is the puppeteer, he insisted. Shakespeare's Prospero, he used to say, *begs* the audience to set *him* free at the end. He puts all the other characters under a spell but then has to beg to be set free *himself*. By the public. I must have heard my father say this at least a dozen times. So that, thinking back on it now, Cleaver's elder son had written, to live with my father meant to be told that *nothing you admired and aspired to* was actually worth doing and, in any event, even if it was, *he* was already doing it far better than you ever could. He was a better talker, a better film-maker, a better writer, a better viveur, than you could ever be. Viv*eur*, as it *were*, he would rhyme. Nothing could have been more paralysing. Our whole family – Harold

Cleaver must have been reading these words only hours before the interview with the President of the United States, when he should have been scanning through pages of statistics and election promises – our whole family was as if *frozen* in the high noon of my father's celebrity. The words frozen and celebrity were still reverberating in Cleaver's head in the taxi on the way to the studio. My twin sister Angela got locked into drugs, his elder son had written; what is there to do in life when your father has done everything and informed you that it's pointless, when he is famous and has told you that fame is ridiculous? She was paralysed and reckless. My younger sister, Caroline, did *nothing* but study. Study, study, study. She hardly spoke to anyone. My little brother, Phillip, lived, and *still* lives, in a complete fantasy world; reality, after all, had already been entirely cornered, occupied and written off by my father. For my part I always felt, almost from the moment that I became conscious of myself, as if I were under a strange spell. I so much wanted to get started in life, to make things change and move, but I couldn't, because my father had explained to me – and my father was nothing if not convincing – that life, or at least the kind of life I wanted, was *meaningless*. So why start? Until the night the Berlin Wall came down. That was the turning point. Two days after my twentieth birthday and maybe two months after Angela got herself killed. Perhaps that shake-up was important. Anyway, the night the Wall came down I finally decided he was wrong. The people of Berlin, I realised as I watched the drama unfold on the television – do you remember, the crowds, the masonry torn down, the dancing? – the people of Berlin are *proving my father wrong*. The world *can* be changed. Only then, on that fateful evening, awestruck by the pictures, the jubilation, the unexpected triumph, did I push a first tentative foot into the light beyond my father's shadow. Only then did I realise how *completely* he had been suffocating me.

This account, Harold Cleaver had reflected, as he climbed out of the cab that evening, marvelling at the levels of security in force around the TV centre – and in particular this sentimental stuff about the night of the Berlin Wall – was pure fantasy, pure effect, pure fiction, in a book that called itself fiction, a novel indeed, while at the same time making it perfectly clear to anyone halfway in the know – to wit the entire British public – that it was fact, when actually it wasn't, not quite. Angela died *after* the Wall came down. It was disgraceful, brilliant.

And yet, Cleaver told himself now, in his room in the Unterfurnerhof, watching, on a generous TV screen, as the President of the United States repeated the very line he had gone on repeating throughout that extraordinary interview – Let's get this straight, I am my own man – and yet it was thanks to my son's mendacious book, that I was so devastating that evening with the President. I was furious, fearless, I who usually avoided head-on confrontation. And it was thanks to the completeness of that success, that tidal wave of media attention, my coronation, no less, as the most effective, authoritative and above all intrepid figure in British political journalism, with an interestingly troubled private life to boot and a son who was making a remarkable literary debut, that I had to give up and get out.

For Cleaver had understood at once that even this devastating interview would change nothing, for the President. I was right that such things are meaningless. The President of the United States, Cleaver sensed immediately upon leaving the studios, would be re-elected anyway, regardless of how foolish he had made himself. We have gone beyond the days when interviews change things. And indeed here the man was, less than a week later, seen from a dusty guest room in the South Tyrol, entirely at his Texas ease and quite confident that he was on his way to re-election; no more perturbed or changed, Cleaver said out loud, than you are, dear Olga. In the glow of the screen, the doll's expression appeared to be one of rapt attention as the President assured her that he would defend the American way of life from every threat. Even that of English interviewers. Perhaps my evident contempt for his simplistic evangelicalism, actually helped him, Cleaver thought. Viveur as it were, he told Olga. Incredible, he thought, how his elder son had missed the point there. No, I am the one who was changed, he decided. Verily, if any of ye were paralysed by my celebrity, he announced out loud in the cold room, take up your beds and walk. Killing the TV shortly after eleven, Cleaver slept easily that night, quietly pleased with himself for not having turned on his phone.

III

WHAT AT ONCE gave Rosenkranzhof a sense of fatality for
Cleaver, of a choice already made for him, was this business
of finding, in the thickest of these foreign woods, but so
near too to the most awesome of views, where the land fell
dizzily away over Steinhaus and St Johan and the white water
of the Ahrn – this business of his finding a name he could
recognise, a place that already had its pigeonhole in his mind:
Rosenkranz and Guildenstern are dead. For the most guile-
ful aspect of my son's book, Cleaver realised, on spying this
name in flaking paint on rotting wood, was the way it created
a caricature image of me, precisely in order to rub me out:
My father thus died, his elder son had written – and quite
probably, for the so-called reader-in-the-know, it was the
only patently fictional episode of the whole novel – hoist
with the petard of his own determination to be in the limelight.

Waking up on his second morning in the South Tyrol,
Cleaver appreciated that a change of plan was necessary. To
spend the day, as he had intended, resting in his room and
nursing his sore feet, would mean to pass the time watching

television and, sooner or later, he had no doubt, reading Amanda's text messages, which in turn would feed his general anxiety that nothing was being accomplished, this despite the fact that one of the major goals of this retreat, this exit rather, was to stop thinking in terms of accomplishments and live life in the simplest possible relationship with himself and the world. It was complicated. Overcome by a sudden fear of lost direction, an insecurity that had frequently haunted him whenever he was away from work and home for more than a day or two, Cleaver got out of bed, ate breakfast rapidly in the shadowy Stube, and set out into Luttach to find plasters and perhaps even a bandage for his blisters.

This is one of the things my elder son knew nothing about, he reflected, waiting in a surprisingly slow queue in the village pharmacy, this anxiety I have always experienced away from home, this extraordinary insecurity. There seemed to be an awful lot of consultation going on between customers and pharmacist. Sometimes it was as if a void were opening up – Cleaver began to grow impatient – not so much beneath his feet as all around his head. Away from home but, above all, from work, he became a consciousness anxiously adrift in empty space. My son knew nothing about this. A swarthy young man with a ponytail and black leather jacket seemed to be purchasing a remarkable quantity of medicines. It wouldn't fit in with his caricature picture of me. A man half my age, Cleaver thought, considering the young fellow's coarse, unwashed hair, but with twice my problems. Suddenly, away from home, or rather work, he would be swept by a feeling of vertigo, of having nothing to touch or hold, an inexplicable but absolutely urgent fear that would at once be dispelled, Cleaver knew, if someone put a microphone in his hand, or stood him in front of a camera, or told him to write a one-thousand-word editorial on some controversial issue for publication tomorrow morning. I always needed a yoke, he told himself, and a load to pull, if I wasn't to feel I was merely floating in nothingness, underachieving. Perhaps home had been a kind of job, in the end.

An elderly woman had removed her cardigan and was rolling up the sleeve of her blouse to show the pharmacist an ugly skin disorder all around the elbow. I always saw life as a task and a competition, Cleaver reflected. It was disturbing. The man adjusted his glasses to examine it. Psoriasis, perhaps. When will Harry write his masterpiece, Amanda would laugh and shake her head, and what she meant was: when would he, Cleaver, write that book they had always imagined him writing, or, more probably, make that film he was one day bound to make, that work of genius that hadn't been ordered or commissioned with a contract and a deadline and a publicity budget, but that would come unbidden, unplanned-for from his brilliant head, without the need for any yoke at all. Take a break, she would whisper to him in their rare moments of intimacy. Amanda was ambitious for the father of her children. It was important for her to believe she lived with a man of genius. Take a break and do something all your own, Harry. You can do it, she told him. My father's promised masterpiece, his elder son had written in *Under His Shadow*, was at once the longest standing joke in our family and the most sacred cow. The boy didn't seem to have appreciated – Cleaver shook his head, spying the plasters on a rotating display beside the counter – that all that drinking and eating and smoking he satirised could only occur at the end of a day when his father felt he had achieved something. He had performed. Even if somebody else had called the tune. I pulled my weight. Even

45

if there was nothing to be achieved and every performance a sham. You are a pig, Cleaver, Cleaver told himself, a great fat pig.

Sitting on a low stone wall right outside the shop, unlacing and removing his boots, Cleaver decided that he must make a list of all those aspects of his personality that his son had known nothing about, all the things that made this slick presentation of himself as some sort of caricature tyrant absolutely implausible. Have I really left? he suddenly found himself asking. He spoke out loud. The good people of the South Tyrol walked by pretending not to notice this balding tourist, peeling off his socks to inspect two damp and delicate feet. You could be home in a matter of hours, Cleaver thought. Two or three phone calls and your diary would be full. You would be busy for the rest of the year, the rest of your life. The soft layers of skin above the heel presented four or five concentric holes, each slightly redder and moister than the one above. Harden up, he muttered.

This morning Cleaver walked a mile or so northwards before striking up one of the many ramblers' paths. They were signed with a rectangular red-and-white flash on a rock or tree trunk beside the road, and inside the flash a combination of numbers and letters – 8A, or 13B & C, or 3, 5, 9B. No doubt these corresponded, Cleaver imagined, to the tiny numbers beside the twisting dotted red lines on his map, if only he could have read them. I should have asked in the pharmacy, he thought, if they had any of those off-the-shelf reading spectacles. He hadn't seen any. A magnifying glass would do. Not that he had the slightest intention of opening a book or newspaper. The sky was dull today and a light breeze had begun to blow. The highest peaks were lost in cloud. Climb to the cloud, Cleaver ordered himself. Far too much of his life had been spent reading newspapers, thinking of things that didn't directly concern him. Except there was also the question of whether or not he should buy a charger for his mobile. What is the point, Cleaver demanded rather sternly, striking up a broad path at random, of buying a charger for my mobile while searching for a remote property at high altitude that will quite probably have no electricity, be wrapped in cloud half the time and never receive even the ghost of a signal? More than a path, it was a broad track he had taken, an access road for logging vehicles perhaps. Though no doubt when he came down into the village for supplies he could always ask someone to charge the phone for him for a few hours and hence pick up any messages there might be while he was down in civilisation. Frau Schleiermacher perhaps. He sensed the beginnings of a mutual respect between himself and Frau Schleiermacher. She had served him swiftly and generously at breakfast. Curious, too, he reflected, the absence of a Herr Schleiermacher. Oh please! Cleaver muttered. What possible need do I have of a phone?

Striding up the timber track, swinging his walking poles vigorously, Cleaver tried to increase his pace. Piles of pine logs were stacked at regular intervals. He breathed deeply. Too fat, he muttered. Pull your weight is a strange expression. Then a chainsaw started up. A low moan rose and fell, biting into wood somewhere. At once Cleaver realised that until the noise stopped he couldn't be happy. There was a roar as a branch fell and the motor revved. He couldn't think even. He felt angry. How far do you have to walk to get out of range of a chainsaw, to find a remote place to live in? Was he walking towards it, or away? It seemed to be above him. Try to keep a brisk pace, he thought.

The path climbed steadily, monotonously, through tall trees, random undergrowth, small clearings with boulders and scrub. Ten minutes, half an hour. The noise seemed no nearer and no further, groaning, roaring, stopping and starting. The forest stretched away, austerely shapeless. There was no peace. How can I possibly find a place to live, Cleaver demanded, if I don't know where I'm going? I'm so unfit. Only the slope gave direction. Up or down. Life isn't a fairy tale, he muttered – he was panting now – where you stumble on your tailor-made Gothic castle, or suddenly find yourself the wilderness-wise master of a log cabin. I don't even own a penknife, for heaven's sake!

Suddenly tired, Cleaver sat down on a tree trunk and with unexpected perversity pulled out his phone and turned it on. Apparently, part of his mind had known he was going to do this, while another part was scandalised, disappointed. Only to check how much battery is left, he murmured. Three notches. Not bad. Now it was vibrating with arriving messages. So there is a signal! Impressive. I'm in touch. If necessary, he told himself, I could call California. Already the little envelope was winking. Memory full. He opened the message file. They were all from Amanda. Or rather, BOOTS. That was how he had her in his address list. Cleaver frowned, scrolling down the list.

BOOTS
BOOTS
BOOTS
BOOTS
BOOTS
BOOTS
BOOTS
BOOTS
BOOTS
BOOTS

He shook his head. One of the things that had made him

suspect a certain amount of collaboration between his elder son and Amanda in the writing of the famous fictional auto-biography, was the detail the first-time author had been able to give of how his father and mother had so fatefully met when, three years older than himself, Amanda was Cleaver's boss on *The Times Saturday Review*. So he called her Boots, for short, his elder son had written. The Pretender, was how Mother referred to him. My father always claimed he should have sued for sexual assault in the work place. Talk about being bossed about, he would quip. In any event the two had just broken up and my father had left the paper (was this the first attempt to write the masterpiece?) when Mother realised she was pregnant. With twins.

Cleaver turned off the phone without opening the messages. The chainsaw had stopped and he thought he heard other noises now through the trees from the slope above. The cloud was sinking lower. A horse neighing perhaps. Is that possible? Perhaps voices. Amanda had put the book in his hands exactly thirty-six hours before the most important moment in his career, his interview with the President of the United States. That in itself was an act of terrorism. Hot off the press, she told him, and already on the shortlist for the Booker. Our boy.

It was breakfast time and, opening the stiff new pages beside his cereal bowl, Cleaver was at once concerned to find his elder son holding forth about the origin of his parents' relationship. Why did I know nothing about this? he asked. On the Booker list? Despite all their vaunted *modernity*, his elder son had written, their habit, that is, of presenting themselves to the world as bright, rebellious young things, my father and mother caved in at once to received moral-ity and, even before Angela and I were born, *stayed together for the children*, something they would then make us pay for throughout our childhood, which means, of course, for the rest of our lives, since each of them, having bowed to the parental yoke, then had to do absolutely everything to establish that they had *independent lives* apart from the family, apart from each other, apart from us. How many times would a guest at lunch or dinner – because we *always* had guests both at lunch and dinner; in fact, if there were no guests, more often than not there was no lunch or dinner – how many times, Cleaver's elder son had written, would a guest say Your wife, or Your husband, and *immediately* my father and mother would chime in, Actually, we're not married you know. Actually, we never tied the knot. Probably it was the only time they spoke *in unison*. How irritating, Cleaver thought, was his son's silly habit of using italics. Not *knotted*, you know, he had written, quoting his witty father. I should get royalties for all the jokes in that book. And how utterly reductive this was, Cleaver felt sure, as an account of the tension there had been between himself and Amanda in those feverish and beautiful days, the decision they had taken: that twins were a gift, a sign. You can't abort twins. Though of course Cleaver never did believe in signs. Certainly we loved each other. Or something. It was so long ago. And Amanda was the most atheist woman in the world. Still, it did seem, Cleaver was now convinced, that the all-too-accurate details in his son's book of how he, Cleaver, had given up what would have been, at that point, a rather precocious masterpiece, to make his breakthrough move to the Beeb, was a story his elder son could only have had directly from his mother. Hot off the press the book might be, but Amanda seemed all too familiar with the contents.

A horse snorted quite near by. At once the chainsaw started up again. But quite definitely there had been a jingle of harness, the snort of an animal. If there is one sound that more than any other sums up the horror of invasive noise, Cleaver decided, as the motor started up again, it is the moan of the chainsaw, its insistent, straining aggression, the way, even when it abruptly stops and the world shrinks into wounded silence, nevertheless the mind remains tense, on guard, waiting for it to start again, to start demolishing things again, above all, demolishing your thoughts, your peace of mind. With this pregnancy, his elder son had written, and the consequent decision to get back together and have not one baby but two, my father was obliged to acknowledge that this literary ambition of his was impractical and so . . .

Look, doesn't the Booker, Cleaver had shouted to his wife at breakfast that morning – he seemed to remember she was grinding coffee beans – have to be a novel, fiction? I mean, should I turn to the last page and find out what happens, or what? The coffee grinder fell silent and Amanda was laughing. Better not, she said. They hardly ever looked each other in the eye. The bloke casting the long shadow gets killed, hoist with his own petard.

Breathing deeply, fighting the insistence of the chainsaw, Cleaver decided he was unwell. There are times when he feels he has stepped into an oneiric space of pure, motive-less anxiety. His palms sweat. His head feels hollow, his flesh is impossibly heavy. He can trace these experiences right back to university days: this difficulty breathing, a fear of emptiness that is actually a physical tension in the mind. On your feet, Cleaver ordered himself. You old ox. He thrust his poles into the dirt. Neck in the yoke now. And as he stood up, the horse appeared. It was a small stout Haflinger, brown and gold, round as a barrel, pulling a cart. Cleaver knew the names of horses from the times he had taken Angela riding. Then he wanted to burst out laughing. Directly behind the animal's fat butt, flapping the reins, sat the flamboyant

Hermann, he of the big horse for a big arse. There was the same comedian's grin about his thin lips, though he had substituted his leather cowboy hat of two evenings before for something old-fashioned and black, a black trilby with a green band. Somehow this allowed Cleaver to notice his moustache properly, a generous blond brush in the shrewd red intensity of his narrow face. An exhibitionist's moustache. Cleaver was about to wave when he noticed the passengers sitting in the cart behind. Everyone was strangely well dressed: a man of fortyish sitting slightly bowed, a green sash across his short jacket, his black hat forced onto thick tawny hair; beside him, a creature who seemed no more than a dark bundle crumpled against the cart's backboard. The face was hidden in a loose hood. Two women sat opposite, swaying together with the uneven progress of the cart, both wearing black headscarves, one elderly, one young.

As the cart approached, Hermann met Cleaver's eyes and quickly touched the brim of his hat, but as if to indicate that he couldn't speak. Cleaver smiled, standing back against a tree. The horse stumbled, pushed hard by the weight of the cart trundling down the steep track. Up above, the chainsaw must be biting deep into some old tough wood. It whined and groaned. Hermann was staring straight ahead now. As the cart passed, Cleaver saw that the younger woman was still an adolescent, seriously overweight, her hair cut boyishly short, the sunken eyes blank, mouth wide open. The man had a hunched alertness about him, his hands gripped tight on his knees. Only the elderly lady picked up Cleaver's gaze and held it a moment, despite a sudden lurch of the cart. Her cheekbones were high and flat. Her hard eyes locked into his and glittered. Cleaver was arrested. Turning to watch as they rattled away, he saw that between the passengers' feet a black cloth had been draped over a low platform or box. They were sitting with their knees tucked under their benches so as not to touch it. Even so, it was only when the chainsaw roared out and fell silent, leaving the valley bare to the distant clanging of a bell, that Cleaver realised this must be a funeral.

Without thinking, he turned. He could still hear the Haflinger's hoofs and the faint clatter of the wheels. But the cart had disappeared now. The air seemed limp, drained of tension. It had come on to drizzle. This isn't a day for getting above the treeline, Cleaver decided. Strangely relieved, as if released from some difficult assignment, he pulled his waterproof cape from his backpack and started striding back to the village as swiftly as possible. Why the hurry? Because the clouds were coming down. Yet he couldn't explain a vague sense of excitement as his legs led him briskly after the cart. Just before the track met the main road, a jeep drove past. No doubt the chainsaw man.

The church stood in a large cemetery surrounded by a low wall. A small crowd was milling under umbrellas outside the gate, but as Cleaver approached, a band struck up and they began to move in. He tagged behind. A procession was forming along the wall of the church. At its head was the priest, and beside him a man in black carrying a huge, almost life-size wooden crucifix. Death-size. Then came the coffin, borne by six men, including Hermann and the other fellow on the cart. All wore sprigs of flowers in their lapels. The chief mourners it seemed were the three women who had been sitting with him, the oldest supported by the other two. Beneath the black hood, Cleaver glimpsed a face whose skull seemed to have risen right through the sunken skin.

All in dark uniform, the band began to play some slow dirge. It was soft and solemn. The drummer had muffled his drumsticks. The rain muted the brass. Who are they burying?

Cleaver wondered. It seemed a very public occasion. And he recognised Armin. The boy was blowing a trumpet. He wore a black cap like the others, but he hadn't removed the earring with the sign of the Beast. It can't be a child, he told himself. There wasn't that anguish you saw when there was a child to bury. To this day, his elder son had written, I shall remember my father's face as . . . No. Cleaver shook his head.

The music surged forward. Leading the procession, the swaying crucifix turned the corner behind the church. Cleaver watched from among the graves. Frau Schleiermacher was there, almost at the back, stepping slowly, face handsomely intent. She has a fine chin, steady eyes. Not even forty-eight hours here, Cleaver thought, and already you recognise people. They were singing a hymn. The voices swelled, but softly, tunelessly. The sound was strangely solid. He didn't understand the words. The rain came harder. How concentrated everyone is, Cleaver noticed, how intent and sure of what they are doing. His eye moved across the graves. They formed a grid of small ironwork crosses, arranged in rigid symmetry, a low black rail around each grey tombstone. There must be firm rules here, he thought, or no desire to be different.

Then just as he was going to tag on at the back of the crowd as it wound round behind the church, he heard a voice intoning a prayer and, turning his head, saw the priest now reappearing from the other end of the building, the tall crucifix swaying beside him. The priest half sang, half spoke in a flat, guttural voice and the crowd were murmuring a collective response. They had done no more than march right round the building.

Cleaver stopped on the path beside the church wall to watch, to listen. The man beneath the crucifix was finding

54

it hard going. Indifferent to the rain, the bleeding Christ gazed away amongst the graves. Hermann shuffled slowly beneath the coffin, his thin lips and bright moustache moving to the responses. No doubt I look ridiculous, Cleaver thought, in my red waterproof with my tourist's backpack. But Hermann gave no sign of having seen him. Tourists should not come to funerals. A car door slammed and a woman came hurrying into the cemetery. She wobbled on heels along the wet gravel path, belting a raincoat as she ran. Seffa! Seffa! The elderly lady half raised her head, but turned away.

The procession was heading straight towards Cleaver now. To get out of its way, he stepped aside and stood with his back pressed to the church wall between two buttresses. The coffin passed very close in little lurches, resting on the bearers' shoulders. I can reach out and touch it, Cleaver thought. There was a small wreath of flowers on top. Very small. Carnations. The man who had been riding on the cart was hunched under his burden, coarse features tense. The rain drummed on the dark wood. No one seems to notice me, Cleaver thought. The new arrival, a petite, blonde town-dressed woman, fortyish perhaps, had grasped the big girl's arm. Both were staring at the coffin. How fixed everybody's face is! How promptly they muttered their responses to the priest. A collective voice speaks through them, Cleaver thought. He couldn't have said even to himself why he was so taken by this. Armin must have seen I am here, but he pays no attention. The rain doesn't touch them, he noticed. They let it run down their cheeks and onto their black jackets without concern.

Once again Cleaver was on the point of joining the back of the procession when once again the priest and the crucifix bearer reappeared behind. They had circled the church a second time. A second time he stood pressed to the wall to let them pass. The murmured responses dissolved in the damp air. Water ran swiftly in a gutter. The tall, straight woman with the glittering eyes is the chief mourner, Cleaver realised. She was austere, expressionless. There is something quite remote about her. The flat cheeks and pale pressed lips passed only a couple of feet away. Even if I jumped out in front of her, Cleaver thought, she wouldn't notice, her eyes would pass right through me. Then he understood that the woman was burying her husband.

I wldn't mind, the fourth or fifth message said, if u'd gone away to DO something. Cleaver lay on his bed. E.g. to write the famous masterpiece, said the fifth or sixth. Remember? And the eleventh or twelfth added: Or even if u were with another woman . . . How does she know I'm not? he wondered. He smiled at the Tyrolese doll. The porcelain face seemed softer now he was getting used to it, the glittering eyes more credible. The sharp glitter, Cleaver remembered, in the mourning woman's eyes was quite riveting. Olga, he said out loud.

Having succumbed to the messages, he was resisting the temptation to turn on the TV. Outside, the rain fell heavily, as it had fallen heavy and hard on the crowd gathered round the graveside. Three turns around the church – why? – and then the short procession to a fresh grave beside the outer wall. The woman was not grieving for her husband's death, Cleaver reflected now. The set lips and fixed gaze, the chin held high, even as she sprinkled water over the coffin with a sprig of pine, were a declaration of self-assertion, of survival. What grieves Amanda, he decided, is the idea that I have got away, clean away, while someone in his grave can always be kept tabs on. You can sprinkle holy water over them. Of course, my father was away that fateful night, his elder son had written. Did he really have to write fateful? Do they really give literary prizes to people who use words just because they ask to be there? Fateful night. Tragic accident. Hopeless attempt. Breathed her last. Holding the phone inside the lampshade, right beside the bulb, Cleaver opened another message. These things happened years ago. His eyes strained. After all, he read, when u were with another woman, i knew u'd soon be coming back to me. My father would regularly stay out for the night, his elder son had written in his purportedly fictional autobiography, with this or that excuse, this or that story, the comedy of it being the way he tried to make his stories credible and the way Mother pretended to believe them, so that we twins were actually on the point of leaving home before we finally twigged. It is not so much, Cleaver decided, replacing the phone on the bedside table, his being wide of the mark that irritates me, nor even the thought of more or less everyone I know reading these hurtful half-truths, as that he couldn't have written this without her collusion. Only Amanda could have told him that the Indian woman at the funeral was his father's girlfriend. To this day, his elder son had written, etc. etc.

Cleaver stood up, found the remote, turned the television on. There was a noisy slither of violins. The flat grey screen was transformed into a deep field of colour where ballet girls spun in dizzying white. Furious, he turned it off at once. I must have the television removed from my room. He felt shaken. Seeing the quiet despair in his eyes, his elder son had written – could the boy really remember the expression on my face fifteen years ago? – I imagined I was discovering the vulnerable, human side to my father for the first time. My heart went out to him. Instinctively, I forgave him for not being at home the night it had happened. In the end they did not have the perfect relationship, and Mother, it has to be said, was no saint. What utter crap, Cleaver had fumed, reading this sanctimonious account of what, after all, was a thirty-year partnership, only hours before he was to interview the President of the United States. For two whole days he had been riveted by the book, entirely ignoring the piles of documents his research assistants had sent him. Instead, his elder son had written, when I realised that he had brought his girlfriend of the moment along, to his daughter's funeral, when I saw him talking to the TV cameras outside the porch of the church, my blood ran cold. It seemed to me it had all been a show: my father had no real grief. Perhaps he had no real personality at all.

Cleaver found himself looking out of the window at the blank stone facade across the narrow street. You keep telling me you love me, Priya had said, but you won't let me anywhere near your real life. There is no limit, it seems, to the years some words will reverberate. But how could he write, My blood ran cold? Watching the heavy rain come down, Cleaver wondered vaguely who that woman had been, jumping out of a taxi, dashing through puddles in the grave-yard to catch the mourners. Was it a name, the word she had called? He couldn't remember it. No real grief, he muttered.

Then all at once he knew he was in peril. I must react. He was trapped in this shabby room with a TV and a mobile and a doll. Cleaver glimpsed his jowly reflection dissolving in the wet glass. Perhaps I am about to have some sort of fit. I must not not not watch ballet, he announced out loud, not unless I go to watch it in the flesh, not unless I sit there for the dura-tion in the flesh-and-blood presence of the real-life dancers. No, he actually wanted to have a fit, he realised now, to feel his mind seized and confounded. And I must not not not go to funerals unless they are my funerals. What business did I have scrutinising the faces of the mourners, a fat fifty-five-year-old in a red hiker's waterproof, with no real personality?

Cleaver snatched open a drawer and pulled out a dry pair of trousers. What had become of his composure on the journey out here, he asked himself, of the decision so swiftly and confidently taken to live in silent dignity in some remote mountain habitation? Why can I never win this battle of being alone? It was his being alone that so shocked Amanda. He dragged the trousers up his thick legs. She doesn't believe I can do it. Where was the sweater he had bought? I must get out of this horrible room, rain or no rain. He pulled the new wool over his eyes. My father was a quick-change artist, his elder son had written. He put on emotions like hats, yet at the same time, and however quickly he changed from one thing to another, he was always convincing. That evening, after Angela's funeral, for example, I turned on the TV and saw the interview he had given to *Newsnight*, and he really was awesomely convincing: Disbelief, my father told the viewers. He was standing in the porch outside the church and he spoke softly and very slowly, you might even say seductively. His eyes were bright with pain. Nobody knew how to look into a camera like my father, to look right into a viewer's heart. Nausea, he said. You know? Loss. His face really did seem as if only the most extraordinary act of will was keeping it from breaking into sobs. And then that terrible anger, he said, that comes from thinking, if only, you know, if only this, if only that . . . When all the while his mistress was standing not five yards away, the woman he had been sleeping with when my sister was bleeding to death on the pavement.

Who told you that? Cleaver demanded, buckling his trousers viciously into his paunch. He was aware that his mental state had taken a dramatic turn for the worse. Your mother of course. Why does it have to rain now? Why can't I go out and walk? The idea of living in a remote mountain habitation had been to walk and walk and walk. To walk himself into tranquillity. The South Tyrolese peasants were so composed at the funeral, Cleaver found himself remembering, so compact in their mourning, and that business of everyone sprinkling holy water over the grave, with pine sprigs. He turned his daughter's funeral into an advertisement, his elder son had written, while cruelly showing off his mistress to friends, his Indian actress intellectual. Perhaps even at the graveside he was already planning his documentary on bereavement, screened not six months later, a truly excellent piece of work, all the critics and specialists agreed. Perhaps . . .

Rebut him, if that's the problem, Amanda insisted when Cleaver had warned her of his imminent departure. Write a denial. Sue for libel. For Christ's sake, take the envious little bastard to court! Show who you really are, Harry. You don't have to throw our lives away after all these years just because your son's written a spiteful book. You told him! Cleaver shouted in the gloomy room of the Unterfurnerhof. Why hadn't he said it to her face? The doll's eyes glittered unblinking. You play the lover when we're making love, Priya complained – fifteen years ago if it was a day – but you never let me anywhere near your real life. I have to go, Cleaver had told her, hurrying into the night after receiving that call. That terrible call. Your daughter has had an accident. My father could act any part, his elder son had written, mimic any voice, only to tell you an hour later that all parts and voices were meaningless. No wonder Angela got lost in drugs and drink. I don't let you into my real life, Cleaver told Priya, because there is no such thing. Which brings us, his elder son had concluded one of his chapters, to a curious contradiction in my father's career: that while half the country was convinced that he had invented a masterful voice and TV manner that everybody else imitated – *the* news voice of the eighties no less – the other half was equally sure that he merely copied whatever flavour of the day was successful.

Who gives a fuck! Cleaver demanded. I am really shouting now, he realised. Who could ever begin to distinguish between imitations and originals in this crazy world! Who cares? Suddenly he kicked out at the cabinet holding the television. He has forgotten he only has socks on. Not wishing to walk dirt around, he had left his wet shoes downstairs in the porch. His toe crunched against the stout wood of the cabinet. Idiot! The pain shot up past his knee. Oh Christ. The doll stared. Then, as Harold Cleaver sat on the floor to grab and nurse his toe, swaying violently back and forth, the bedside table suddenly and strangely buzzed. Twice. Two sustained vibrations. Meanwhile, his elder son had written, Angela was really dead, there was nothing fake about that. The mobile, Cleaver realised. I should throw the thing out of the window. My sister had lost her way looking for something intense enough to be a counterweight to the constant drama of my parents' unknottedness. BOOTS the message list said. Squinting, holding the phone at arm's length, Cleaver could just make out the letters: Lovely afternoon in the park. Having tea with Larry. Wish it was u.

Cleaver crashed out of the room and down the stairs. Running on wooden boards in just his socks, he stumbled twice. Perhaps he had picked up a splinter. The foot was already painful. The dolls kept watch, floor after floor, window ledge after window ledge, in noisy silence. Why would anyone want so many, and all alike? Like quiz shows.

The Stube was empty, echoey, stale. Pulling on his walking boots in the porch, Cleaver isn't sure whether he is planning to hobble up the mountain in the heavy rain, on and on upwards till he drops from exhaustion, or whether he will find a taxi somehow in the main street in Luttach and be back in Chelsea belligerent and bloody-minded before the clock strikes midnight. Even in the porch, there are two dolls, both with red ribbons in golden hair, and on the wall a large bunch of plastic flowers in a brass vase. There was no point, Cleaver knew, in rebutting this or that claim his son had made. Why would people living in the country keep plastic flowers? That wasn't the problem. It isn't. He hasn't left the UK because of his son's book. The mystery, for example, of Amanda's having invited Priya to come to the funeral without even telling him remained one of the great unexplained mysteries of his life. Why didn't I have it out with her? But fifteen years ago. And the beginning of the end of his relationship with Priya, of course. Who cares now? I don't care. I've forgotten these things. The problem is living, Cleaver decided. Or rather, having lived, having a version of some kind that you can tell yourself. I couldn't offer a more convincing one, he knew. My son's book is nothing if not convincing. But I would never try. The more convincing a documentary is, my father used to say – and this, his elder son had written, was typical of his defeatist strategy – the more you can be sure it is omitting, or just plain lying. *Under His Shadow*, Cleaver remembered, made no mention at all of the fact that Larry Shiner was also at the funeral, that Amanda told me to say a quick word to *Newsnight* to get them to go away. A convincing story is always a lie; that was one of my father's favourite lines. But this was still not the problem. I don't need to be convinced of what happened, let alone convince anyone else. The porch smelt of wet dog, damp doormat. It was curious Amanda didn't understand this. It's curious he hasn't seen the dog, since evidently there is one. Somehow the situation wouldn't have arisen had it not been for the extraordinary farce of the interview with the President of the United States. I must shut my big mouth, Cleaver repeated. This is your only hope. Say nothing.

Wet shoes on his feet, wet waterproof on his back, wet hood pulled over his big bald head, Cleaver pushed open the door on a soaking street. The gale flung the rain at him. His cheeks were stinging. At least I never wrote my masterpiece, he thought. The temperature must have fallen ten degrees in a couple of hours. Already his trouser bottoms are damp. It doesn't matter. With no idea where he was going, Cleaver forced his way against the wind to the corner of the street where he collided with Armin in full flight for home, his trumpet in his hand. Hurrying behind the boy were Frau Schleiermacher and Hermann. 'tschuldigung! Armin was shouting. He raced for the porch. Mister Englishman! Hermann cried. He was fighting to keep an umbrella over their heads. Mr Harold, where do you go bei diesem Wetter? He grabbed Cleaver's shoulder. Rain was clattering on an awning. A van raised a slap of water from the cobbles.

Suddenly they were all back in the porch. Cleaver was aware that Frau Schleiermacher was telling him something quite animatedly. Her face seemed younger. The fine wrinkles round her eyes were alive with energy. What was she saying? She seems excited, happy. I have to look for somewhere to live, he protested. I want a place, high up. In this rain! Hermann had a naturally loud voice. His laughter was explosive. Everyone was cramped in the porch, unlacing shoes, struggling out of coats. We have a drink, Englishman, a drink! The man's face was chill and bright, his blond moustache glistened. Hanging up his jacket, Armin turned and smirked. They've been drinking, Cleaver realised. Wonderful, Südtirol funeral, don't you think, Mr Harold? Why do you not come after for the lunch? Lots to eat. Somehow, Cleaver had allowed himself to be pushed back into the Stube and was sitting damply at the big wooden table that the card players had sat at the first evening. Old Tyrol tradition, Hermann insisted. The crucifix was directly above him. Everybody welcome at a funeral! Now he had an arm round Cleaver's shoulders. Katrin, Bier! Hoi, halt a mo!

Armin had been slipping off into the passageway by the stairs. Hermann called him back. Blos di Trompete! he boomed. The boy didn't want to. His mother was fussing and humming behind the bar. She had turned on the lights. There were four heavy plastic shades pretending to be parchment. For some reason the bulbs seemed exceedingly yellow. The room was actually darker in their glow. Blos, blos, blos! Hermann clapped. He had a manic energy. He turned to Cleaver. Do you want that he plays? Cleaver nodded. Always merrier with music, he said. He was collecting his wits. Armin's pale eyes flickered under the lank, dyed hair. He had stripped to his vest and his feet were bare. Why isn't he freezing? Spiel là!

Unexpectedly, the boy lifted the trumpet to his lips and blew out his cheeks. The mournful notes of the funeral dirge rang out with a piercing sadness. Nein, nein, nein! Hermann was remonstrating. He said something rapid and persuasive, then turned to Cleaver: We are not in the Friedhof now! Cleaver didn't understand. Armin had stopped. Friedhof, Hermann insisted. He was gesticulating. Grab. Tomba. Cimitero! Not now. Not yet! The man exploded with laughter. Pouting, Armin said something that ended in whisky. Shush! Hermann brought a dramatic finger to his lips and glanced over his shoulder in pantomime caution. He banged a fist on the pine table. Whisky! he shouted. Katrin! Do Engländer will an Whisky trinkn!

The trumpet began to play something jazzy, muddled and fast. Armin! Frau Schleiermacher protested. She was carrying a tray with beers. She had put on a blue apron. Haben Sie schon gegessen? she asked Cleaver. Nein, he said. Möchten Sie noch? Ja. He speaks German, Hermann shouted. Recht gutes Deutsch! Sitting with legs planted wide apart, the cowboy had begun to clap a rhythm. Is he really drunk, Cleaver wondered, or at that critical stage when people like to act drunker than they are?

Armin sat down to play his trumpet. Sitting near him, Cleaver was struck by the boy's youthful presence, the smooth freckled pallor of his oval face. Clap! Hermann insisted. He had pulled his sleeves up on thick forearms. Cleaver laughed. It's scandalous, he thought, how rapidly I can rediscover my party personality. Then he asked who had died. Whose funeral was it?

Hermann kept clapping. The trumpet squeaked and wheezed and slid over the notes. The boy was trying not to laugh as he blew. Oh when the saints, he began. He threw back his head, hamming it. Frau Schleiermacher returned with a platter of bread and speck and cheeses. She has a lovely, businesslike walk. There was a glass of whisky too. Whoever it was, you don't seem very unhappy, Cleaver was saying.

Unhappy! Hermann roared with laughter. His eyes were brimming with tears. He pulled a face of mock misery. Katrin, Katrin! He caught Frau Schleiermacher's long skirt as she turned to go, said something loud – et traurig! – clapped his hands in exaggerated mirth. She pulled a wry face, but with a shrewd, girlish grin. How erect and solemn she had been in the procession. That was a terrible man! Hermann shouted, a terrible man. No one is sad!

Armin gave a great blast on his trumpet, stopped, turned it upside down to shake out the spit and picked up the whisky that Hermann had supposedly ordered for Cleaver. Turning away for a moment, he downed it in one. Hermann spluttered applause. A terrible man! Better dead. But a lot of people came to the funeral, Cleaver objected. I thought he must be well loved. To celebrate! Hermann cried. A lot of people want to see sure he is dead! For a moment it seemed he would choke. Traurig!

Noch einmal Whisky, Cleaver called. Hermann was delighted. Der Engländer spricht Deutsch! Frau Schleiermacher turned with a look at once suspicious and indulgent. While I was plunged into crisis, Cleaver realised, the funeral has cheered everybody else up. The woman had fine ankles. It's a cause for celebration.

Hermann was saying something to Armin. Cleaver turned and found himself looking straight into the young man's pale blue eyes. He was an old Nazi, Armin said brutally. Everyone hate him. Hate hate hate. Lifting the trumpet again, he began to play Deutschland Über Alles. Armin! His mother yelled. Hermann was banging the flat of his hand on the table. Brüderlich mit Herz und Hand! he sang. Einigkeit . . . but as the music reached its crescendo he burst out laughing again. He was out of tune. Don't you have to take the others back? Cleaver asked. The family. In the cart? Hermann shook his head. Tomorrow. Weather too bad. Bier, he shouted.

In an instant, then, Cleaver made a conscious decision to enjoy himself. Really a Nazi? he enquired. The evening I am about to spend, he thought, will exactly confirm the portrait of me in my son's fictional autobiography. Ja, ja! Hermann insisted. I'm going to drink everything I can, Cleaver told himself. Nazi Polizei, very old man, Hermann said. Deutschland über alles.

Hate, hate, hate. Armin repeated. We hate him and he hate everybody. He tossed down the second whisky. Hate die Engländer, die Franzosen, überhaupt die Walschen. Walschen? Cleaver interrupted. Italian, Hermann laughed. Bad name for Italian. Walsche, Scheiße! So he went to live, high on the mountain. Never see anybody.

But all the village came to the funeral, Cleaver protested again. Hermann referred the comment to Frau Schleiermacher who was bringing more drinks. She sat down herself now with a glass of wine: Er war ein Mann, she said simply. At the same moment she must have caught a whiff of Armin's breath. Na, du bisch a bledo Bui! She began to scold. My fault, Cleaver interrupted, I gave it to him.

The woman stared. Armin translated. But suddenly, Hermann was saying: You want to live high high on the mountain. Right? His eyes were gleaming and his lips pressed tight with suppressed mirth. That's right, Cleaver said. Rosenkranzhof, Hermann cried. Do Engländer konn afm Rousnkronzhöf bleibn!

There was a moment's silence. Cleaver hadn't understood a word. Armin lifted his trumpet to his lips and blew out one loud note that shrieked upwards and died. Na. Frau Schleiermacher pushed her chair back and stood up. Na, bisch du a bledo! All at once the two adults were arguing back and forth with vehemence. They are lovers, Cleaver thought. He felt no nostalgia. Or they have been. Old lovers. Draining his beer, he turned to Armin: What's all this about? Hermann, Armin said, thinks of a house where you can live, but my mother says, if you will go there, you are . . . kaputt.

Some five hours later, gripping the banister tight, Cleaver pulled himself up the stairs to bed. No amount of drink could sink my father, his elder son had written. Whores,

Cleaver told the watching dolls. Above all, no amount of drink could stop my father from holding forth. What is your job? Hermann had asked. They had been playing cards. Seven or eight at the table, all strong loud men. I must have lost quite a lot of money, Cleaver thought. Why do you want to live in the Südtirol? Hermann insisted. Why do you want to go high up? To keep my mouth shut, of course. That was the proper answer. And instead Cleaver had held forth. Just as his son described. He had begun to tell this and that, to explain himself. So you will write a book about us! Hermann shouted, thrusting an arm round the Englishman's neck. You are famous. You will make a film. Cleaver opened his wallet. He was betting money without having really got his mind round the rules of the game. Gerhard! – Hermann pointed to a fat solid man tugging a red ear – you must write about Gerhard! He has had more women than, than . . . than me! Hermann translated himself for his friends. Gerhard raised a wry eyebrow. Two or three others were silent, stony. They all wore plaid shirts. They kept their damp hats on.

Why in God's name did I try to explain? Cleaver pulled off his shoes and collapsed on the bed. Drink. Quite probably we children were all conceived, his son had written, in a drunken stupor after my father had spent all evening holding forth. About 250 euros, Cleaver thought. I must be careful. And he thought, the only good thing – he took aim with the remote – about holding forth to foreigners, is that they don't understand you. You could only do so much damage. Journalism, he had explained to Hermann (it was my father's pet phrase, his elder son had written), substitutes the mysterious disturbance of reality with the digestible fast food of the sound bite. You know? God, I had a lot to drink. Hermann was nodding eagerly, studying his cards. He hadn't understood a word. So that we can all go on eating and shitting as if we knew what was what. Eating and shitting, Hermann yelled. He downed his beer. And oo, oo, oo! Half standing, he pushed his pelvis out in an unequivocal gesture. C'est la vie! The other men barely glanced. Hermann did not impress them. The man understood nothing, Cleaver reassured himself. He changed channels. Thank God.

All over the world the satellite networks were piling up the corpses. German and Italian TV showed the same clips of various victims. Somewhere in Asia an excavator was digging a neat rectangular trench. The bell never tolls for the viewer, Cleaver told Olga. He remembered how re-assuringly neat the graves had been in the cemetery. Quite the contrary. I came to the Tyrol so as not to write, he had explained to Hermann. So as not to hold forth. Yet I was looking for recognition, he told himself now, for admir-ation. From a man who understood nothing. He had drunk a great deal. It's ridiculous. Cleaver felt sick. I was looking for admiration for having given up looking for admiration. At least, he thought, I didn't accept the offer of cigarettes. I didn't say I needed a woman.

Resigned to his perversity, Cleaver turned on the phone. Sure enough, it vibrated, but only once. Perhaps she is weary-ing. Competing visions of world order, CNN's anchorman was announcing. He seems very young, Cleaver thought. He squinted. My father would have explained his pet theories to a stone, his elder son had written. They were all defeatist. Remember the good times, Harry, Amanda's message said. Cleaver turned off the light and shut his eyes. Outside, it occurred to him, an old Nazi is spending his first night in a neat grave. You have achieved nothing.

IV

LATER CLEAVER WOULD tell himself he had settled too swiftly on Rosenkranzhof. He had not reflected. But this was true of so many of the major turns his life had taken. Still, if I hadn't accepted what was so surprisingly offered, Cleaver thought, staring into the flames of his evening fire in the empty house, what would have become of me? What would have become of the young Cleaver, sitting alone in a furnished bedsit, wondering how on earth one conceived a masterpiece, if Amanda had not called: You're so potent, Harry, she had whispered. Engländer! a voice had shouted. The knocking brought his headache to consciousness. Engländer, you come with me. There is a house for you! Ganz allein.

It was Hermann's voice. Without reflecting, he had gone. At fifty-five I am still rash. He had pulled on his clothes and a few minutes later he was sitting on the back of the cart, rattling along the road, then up the steep track. The woods were sodden with yesterday's rain, the air heavy and damp. Shreds of cloud clung to the branches. Jürgen and Frau Stolberg had gone back on foot yesterday, Hermann mentioned. To milk the cows. Cleaver found himself beside the fat girl, opposite the ancient creature wrapped in her cape and the younger woman who had arrived late at the funeral. Not a word was spoken, though Cleaver had the impression that the town-dressed woman was eager to catch and hold the girl's dull eyes. There was a pressure there. It is no business of mine, he told himself. He tried to respect their bereavement. The ancient lady kept muttering, rubbing her old hands together. The cart climbed steadily, far beyond the point where Cleaver had stopped and turned back the previous morning. The track became narrow and rutted. The fat Haflinger strained. Hermann talked quietly to the beast, imprecating, encouraging. Its big hams shifted jerkily. The man had a repertoire of intimate little whistles, cheerful clicks of the tongue. He shook the reins. Strange they don't have a jeep, Cleaver thought. The constant sameness of the pines, the undergrowth, the still air, was oppressive. Or perhaps they did have a vehicle, but had left it at the farm as unsuitable for carrying a coffin. The girl beside him seemed childishly dressed, he realised: her jacket didn't fit, the trousers were too tight. She stared at her feet, fleshy knuckles clutching an ear, fingertips squeezing the lobe. A case, Cleaver thought.

At last the track broke out of the woods at the top of what, looking back now, seemed a deep gorge they had climbed from. At once the sun grew warm, the air was alive, moving freshly across a panorama of forests and ridges and peaks and broad shadowy valleys. Directly ahead of them, a few hundred yards of gently sloping pasture merged into scree and rock where the mountain started to rise almost vertically toward its summit. Cleaver saw half a dozen cows switching their tails beside a pool of water and, perched right on the edge, above the gorge, a farmhouse, with battered outbuildings roofed with corrugated iron sheets held down by heavy stones. Trennerhof. There were chickens pecking by the walls. Beneath the black Gothic lettering painted between two windows a round green sign announced: Forst. Did the place serve beer?

Hermann stopped the horse and set the women down. A dog chased toward them, barking furiously. The fat girl lifted the ancient lady down. Cleaver glimpsed scaly eyes beneath the hood, the jaw working and muttering. The girl seemed mechanical in her movements, abrupt and resigned. Sniffing at everybody's heels, the dog began to bark again. An old, ugly dog, Cleaver thought, with a greying snout. The town lady carried a small, pale blue suitcase and looked about her with intense interest. Hermann was saying good-byes, then all at once he set the cart in motion again. Fünfzehn minuten now, he announced.

As soon as they were alone he began to chatter. Very traditional family, he said. He was shaking his head. You know? You could write about them, Mr Journalist. You could make a film. Here, it is a hundred years ago. One of the last houses without electricity, without a car. Frau Stolberg was his aunt, he explained. He brought up supplies from time to time. It was good exercise for his horses. He used the cart to take tourists for rides in summer, but now they had all gone of course. Right, Cleaver said.

The track skirted the neck of the gorge for some four hundred yards beyond Trennerhof, then plunged back into the woods on the further side, deteriorating rapidly. After a few minutes, a small rockfall forced Hermann to pull the Haflinger to a halt. We cannot move this now, he decided. Above the path, a high cliff was severely weathered with water trickling from a web of brownish cracks. They walked for a while in steep descent, slim pines and mossy boulders to each side, until, at a turn, there it was: a tiny house built against the sheer rock face and right on the edge of the gorge. Cleaver stood and stared. Hermann laughed. You say you want to be alone! he said.

Only at the front of the house was there any clearing at all; a few yards of rotting wood chips, sawdust and sparse grass. The building was made up of two low storeys: stone below, timber above. Hanging from two rusty nails on the door was a string of red beads. Cleaver touched them. Curious, he said. The place oozed damp. The door needed a shove to get it open; the planks squealed against the lintel. What are these for? he asked. The beads were shiny. Peering into the dark interior, Hermann hesitated: Ein Rosenkranz, he said.

Cleaver shook his head. There was a faint gurgle of running water. His guide stepped back and pointed to the faded lettering on the black timber of the upper floor: Rosenkranzhof. This – he touched the beads – ist ein Rosenkranz. The name startled Cleaver. Hoist with the petard of his own determination to be in the limelight, his elder son had written. You know, Englishman, Hermann insisted, Rosenkranz, Heilige Maria, Mutter Gottes. Cleaver wasn't paying attention. Already he knew he was going to take the place. I am going to live here. Gebet, prayer, Hermann was saying. He seemed glad of the excuse to linger outside. Santa Maria, Madre di Dio. Rosario auf Italienisch. They went in.

Five-hundred euros if you want meals also, Hermann told him later as they climbed back to the cart. Two hundred if you just want the house. He had discussed the matter with his aunt. Nobody seemed to have any qualms, Cleaver noticed, about renting the place only days after the old man's death. His belongings were scattered across the floor. The bed was unmade. It seemed he had lived alone there for fifteen years and more. Why? Cleaver asked. He felt shaken, excited. Those dark rooms are to be my home, my remote home. Hermann breathed deeply, holding the reigns. He whistled to his horse. Julia! She was called Julia, the j pronounced as a y. God knows, he said. Perhaps he wanted to be alone. He laughed, like Mr Cleaver!

Cleaver moved in three days later. For a modest fee, Hermann would take his things up in the cart. When the tourists departed, he said, no one wanted his horses. He ran trekking expeditions through the summer. He winked theatrically, the blond moustache waggled: Lots of divorced German women, city ladies. He made a happy noise in the back of his throat. They want to be girls again. They want nature, youth. He thumped a big fist on his chest beneath a blue work shirt. You should come! That's getting more and more difficult, Cleaver quipped. Hermann looked blank. Your stomach is no problem, he insisted. I have the horse that can carry an elephant! He roared with laughter. Why, Cleaver wondered, would Amanda have passed on all the intimate information she had to his elder son, if she was then going to encourage him, Cleaver, to take the author to court? The only reason my father gave up philandering, his eldest son had written, was because of a growing impotence, brought on no doubt by his various excesses, not to mention the sheer physical bulk he had accumulated by the time he turned fifty. What had Amanda been thinking of telling the boy crap like that? Cleaver shook his head in wonder as Hermann left him at the door of Unterfurnerhof. I should have asked her to her face. And how could they think of giving a literary prize to someone who wrote growing impotence? What did she mean now by alternating messages with threats and messages with happy memories and messages with her familiar, neurotic concerns about the children, all of whom, Cleaver was convinced, had long been beyond the reach of parental concern? When will I be free, he wondered, from asking myself what Amanda means? It was so tiring.

All the same, the need to make practical arrangements settled his mind for the moment, much as the business of buying plane tickets and consulting train timetables had given him a healthy sense of purpose during the journey out. I shall cook for myself, he had told Hermann, and he filled box after box with groceries. This is a rare achievement, he reflected, for someone who hasn't bought food for twenty years and more. DESPAR the supermarket was called. Far from abandoning hope, Cleaver felt cheerful. I will brighten the place up, he thought, I will cut down the vegetation that has darkened the windows. I will make Rosenkranzhof my home.

Frau Schleiermacher observed his comings and goings with scepticism. She went out of the Stube to call for her son. My mother says that you . . . Armin hesitated, looking for words. Today he wore a thick leather wristband with studs and spikes. These satanic accessories do nothing but set off your innocence, Cleaver wanted to tell him . . . that you can not live the winter at Rosenkranzhof. You can not. Cleaver had asked Frau Schleiermacher for another couple of cardboard boxes. He was stacking packets of pasta and rice. Anyone can cook pasta. Why not? he asked. On Angela's slim wrists those studs had looked even more ridiculous.

Frau Schleiermacher sat at one of the tables in the Stube, chopping vegetables. She was watching him with concern. Cleaver recognised the motherliness, the female shrewdness. But now Armin had to answer his mobile. There was a futuristic trill. Brushing hair from his mouth, the boy walked quickly to the window and began to speak in soft low tones. Cleaver smiled. His girlfriend? he asked the mother. Freundin? Frau Schleiermacher pouted in mock disdain. Then she stood quickly and came across the room. She crouched by the boxes. He could smell her washed hair, sense the movement of her thighs in her skirt. She was picking rapidly through the products he had bought, lifting and replacing. Women's hands, Cleaver told himself. Her lips were tight. Zucker? she asked. She looked into his eyes. Gibt's nicht. It was a second. Her face is no longer new to me, he realised. It was changing. Salz? She stood up, touching his arm a moment as she did so. Her calves are still slim, Cleaver noticed. She pressed a fist into her back, shook her head. Herr Cleaver, Der Winter ist sehr schwer da oben. Verstehen Sie? Es ist kalt, sehr kalt. Es gibt viel Schnee. Das können Sie sich nicht vorstellen.

Armin was returning with a smirk. You can not imagine the cold, he translated. Cleaver laughed. With all his stores laid out, he was in a good mood. Tell her I have salt and sugar in another box. And a torch. And a Swiss army knife. And a state-of-the-art sleeping bag. Armin was puzzled. Frau Schleiermacher interrupted. Warum? she demanded. Her concern is making Cleaver feel happier. She thinks you must have some big problem, Armin translated, perhaps rather freely. She thinks there is maybe some better way to . . . to . . . The old man lived there, Cleaver said mildly. I need to lose weight. He patted his paunch. Frau Schleiermacher replied with four or five sharp words. Krimineller, she repeated. Er hatte keine Wahl. He was a cri— I understood, Cleaver told the boy. He didn't know how to reply. Tell her I really have to try this.

The day before moving out he took a bus down the valley to Bruneck to buy bed linen, blankets, perhaps some thermal underwear, woollen long johns, good gloves, a serious hat. The sleeping bag would be for emergencies. When was the last time Cleaver had travelled on a bus? With Giada perhaps. Giada would have been fun to live with. Among the stone-and-glass facades of the town centre, the Tyrol chic of windows dressed with antlers and embracing marmots, he came across an Internet café. Don't go in. He bought two heavy blankets and a down quilt jacket and then, overloaded with plastic bags, returned to the Internet café and went in.

It was an amusement parlour with old men on stools beside slot machines and teenagers intent on war scenarios in fantasy cityscapes. My hands are trembling. He had promised himself he wouldn't do this. My father, his elder son had written, was one of those people who can no more stay away from his e-mail than he can from drink and cigarettes. And expensive food. After all, someone might have written him a fan letter. And the first thing he typed into any search engine was always his own name. cleaver@cleaver.com, Cleaver typed. The German keyboard was irritating. How do you do the @? The password was PRıYASAR. Just when you are achieving a little peace of mind, he told himself, you go looking for trouble again. He pressed ENTER and waited, one elbow resting on the desktop and a knuckle between his teeth. This is the position Cleaver always assumes, waiting for the mail to come through. Do I want peace of mind or not? he wondered.

232 new messages, the screen told him. Cleaver scrolled down through the names. Allison was there. And Anna, and Lisa and Sandra and Melanie. My fragmented life. Really, his son had no idea. Scandalously indiscreet, the book was also poorly researched. Cleaver didn't open them. His agent had written three or four times, despite having been warned not to. This is typical. And Michaels. Even Larry has written.

Object: Where are you? Be in touch! Miscellaneous invitations, reminders, offers. The Sarajevo Film Festival. Names he's never seen. Junk mail. Viruses various. Discount medicines. Editorial meetings. It's late in the day to enlarge my penis, Cleaver smiled. His accountant. Personnel. He breathed deeply, hand on the mouse. Am I going to click on something? My elder son hasn't written, he told himself. None of the children. If Caroline or Phillip had written, I would certainly read what they said. But they wouldn't. The bank yes, though. And an Australian media company.

Cleaver closed the mail window and typed in www.guardian.co.uk. The headlines were all war and elections. The President of the United States had the main photo. He is wearing combat gear, more square-jawed than ever. Cleaver's eye was caught by an orange square at the top left of the page: EXPERTS GIVE BOOKER ODDS. He hesitated, My son is on the Booker list because of my celebrity, it occurred to him. Was that a consolation? Or maybe not. Perhaps it really is an excellent book. He looked out across the street with its neat Teutonic facades. To be away from home, truly away, in the twenty-first century requires a constant effort. He remembered a story of a man who, in order to stop smoking, had had himself locked up somewhere and ordered his paid gaolers not to bring him any cigarettes, even if he begged for them, though when he begged, of course, someone promptly brought him some. He then paid this man not to tell the others. Cleaver did not check the paper Amanda worked for and did not type his name into any search engine. How sombre I feel, he realised, getting up to pay: a ghost shackled to old haunts, but unable to take pleasure in them, eager to be exorcised. Was it a triumph, having opened nothing, or a failure to have gone into the place at all? Why must I think of my life in terms of success and failure? Waiting at the bus stop, he saw a taxi and hailed it.

Barely had Cleaver settled in his room that evening for his last night at Unterfurnerhof than there was a tap at the door. He was sitting on his bed, surveying his purchases. The broad felt hat is particularly pleasing. The television was on. There was no point in fighting the small screen this last night it was available, just as there had been no reason to resist the lure of a cab only one day before he moved to where no taxi would ever go. Olga had her back to the wall beside the pillow. It can be a sort of stag night, he thought, flicking through all thirty-six channels. Pancake day before the fast. He put the hat on his big bald head. It is charcoal grey. The tap was repeated. Come in, Cleaver shouted.

Frau Schleiermacher stood in the doorway. She seemed embarrassed and determined. Herr Cleaver, she said. Her son is not with her, he noticed. The language barrier forced them to look into each other's eyes. He didn't register any colour, only the intensity of her unexpected presence. Ja? he asked. He took the hat off. She had noticed the doll sitting on the bed against the wall. A faint smile lifted one eyebrow. She said something he didn't understand, something ironic, he suspected. You came to this neck of the woods because you speak no German, Cleaver thought. You can't hold forth. Yet he was distinctly conscious now of wishing to speak to Frau Schleiermacher.

She had taken a step into the room. In her hands she had the notepad and pen she used for orders in the Stube. Hier, she said. She went to the window, put the pad on the ledge and started to write. She could have said whatever she wants to say when I was eating, Cleaver thought. Hermann had been there. He would have translated. She could have called

79

her son. The BBC was rounding up the financial markets. Every day we must know what the Hang Seng has done. Herr Cleaver, Frau Schleiermacher called him over to her. Möchten Sie . . . If I spoke German, Cleaver was thinking, I could explain to her my theory about the liturgical aspect of financial news, how it subtly disguises the ritual of ceremonial repetition by sending stocks up and down by a percentage point or two, as if it were these tiny differences that made us listen. The landlady has come to fix my bill, he thought. He got up off the bed. My father, his elder son had written, had become so obsessed by the meta-functions of the information culture that he no longer granted any importance at all to its content. All that matters is punctuality and packaging, he used to say, the repetition of well-worn formulas, reassuring signature tunes. The woman's hair had fallen forward over her face, her rather sharp nose. Writing, she moved her tongue across her lips. She just didn't want to be embarrassed, he decided, by letting the others hear how much she was going to charge him for his six days' room and board. He liked her old-fashioned, green wool dress. It was as if the syntax a person used, his elder son had protested, were actually more important than what they said.

Cleaver stood beside her. Next to his bulk Frau Schleiermacher seems slim, smaller. If anyone should be on the Booker list, he smiled to himself, it's me. She gave him the pad and watched while he read:

WENN SIE HIER DEN WINTER DURCH BLEIBEN WOLLEN – each letter had been printed quite separately – PREIS = 450 EURO/MONAT, MIT ESSEN.

She smiled. Verstehen Sie? Cleaver nodded. She is asking me to stay, offering a bargain. She took the pad and, writing as if taking an order in the Stube, added: NO PROBLEM.

When she had gone, he lay on the bed for perhaps two or even three hours as the television hurried him back and forth across the world. You are very generous, he had told her. She had not understood. He was determined he wouldn't hold forth. The language barrier helped. Do you like my hat? he had asked. He had squashed it on his head again. In the window he saw he cut quite a figure: a big bulky man with a cavalier hat. She shook her head too. Der ist schön, aber unpraktisch. It is a kind offer, he said. She didn't understand. You are simpatica. He felt a strong urge to touch her face. Katrin Schleiermacher has a small mole above the corner of a full upper lip. Aber ich kann nicht, he said. Nicht . . . bleiben. She tossed her head: Wollen Sie mir nicht sagen, warum?

She wants me to become part of the family, it occurred to Cleaver now, watching a French programme about child prostitution in the Philippines. He had been here six days, largely speechless, and already she saw the Englishman as occupying a possible role in her South Tyrolese household. Italian TV had a talent show for would-be tango dancers; some seemed barely pubescent. Even the audience were scantily dressed. She had liked the way he joked with Armin perhaps. He had said something light-hearted yesterday about the skull and crossbones on the boy's T-shirt. He had complimented the lad on his trumpet playing. Angela had had a go at the saxophone, but her real instrument was the piano. Keyboards rather. She sees me as a possible stepfather, Cleaver thought. She sees a Cleaver-shaped space in her family. He still hadn't figured whether the woman was divorced or widowed. Which was actually a pretty large space. Or rather, she sees a man with no history, no context of his own, and she thinks, He will do. Er war ein Mann, she had said of the dead Nazi. To the casual visitor, Cleaver's elder son had written, my father always seemed a very fatherly person. In the end that was all Amanda wanted of me, Cleaver thought. They had not had sex together since Phillip was conceived. She liked to retail the story of his impotence.

Does television help or hinder reflection? Cleaver wondered. Constantly changing channels, he recognised a familiar feeling of resignation. I could go to Manila and have sex with a twelve-year-old. Fat as I am, I could fit in anywhere. Don't you think, Olga? Now the BBC was marvelling that the US President's popularity ratings remained solid despite everything that had gone wrong during his administration. Better the devil you know, a young journalist was observing. They are all so young, so knowing. Nobody commented on Cleaver's devastating exposure of the President's neurotic concern for popularity polls. Deny it if you will, Mr President, but I put it to you that your policies are determined by an almost pathological craving for instant approval. It is as if my interview had never been, Cleaver thought. But you knew that would happen. Amanda . . . he tapped out the name on the phone's small keypad. The battery was down to its last bar . . . tomorrow I move to a place with no signal. Cleaver never used abbreviations when he wrote text messages. He always put in all the caps and all the punctuation. I want to be alone for a while. Please don't worry about me. Look after yourself. LOVE, HARRY.

Holding the phone at arm's length, Cleaver considered this message, then cut the last two words. How to sign off? he wondered. It was an old problem. LOVE seemed inappropriate. WITH AFFECTION would be ridiculous. After thirty years together you can't write, With affection. Harry was her name for him. I never called myself Harry. Not that there wasn't affection. He stared at a German programme speaking authoritatively, it seemed, about financial fraud. What word could there be now for all that had passed between himself and Amanda? There is no word for how I feel, Cleaver thought. Or how I don't feel. He didn't know. In comprehensive rebuttal of his elder son, he might have said: By convincing me to be a parent and partner, but only rarely and in recent years never a lover, your mother lured me into pursuing a dispersed and fragmented emotional life, since there are few women who wish to be clandestine lovers on a permanent basis. Yes, I could make that defence. Cleaver watched the television. Words mean less as experience accumulates, he thought. The more you have of both – of words and experience – the less they seem to have to do with each other. Back on the BBC, a survey on religious belief worldwide showed the British lagging behind. That was the expression the presenter used! Cleaver burst out laughing. I'm lagging behind! He shook his head. You backward freethinker, you! But in the end, damn it, you chose your life, he objected. You enjoyed your string of mistresses, you always changed channels obsessively. What point was there in whining? Let the boy make money out of me. I need no defence.

Then it occurred to Cleaver that he might close his message, FORGIVE ME. Tomorrow I move to a place with no signal. I want to be alone for a while. Please don't worry about me. Look after yourself. FORGIVE ME. But he knew he didn't mean it. I got so used to saying what women wanted to hear, he thought. Asking forgiveness became routine. He never imagined he had really done anything wrong. I was good at that. Though as a result he had never been quite sure what he felt. Or he could just sign off, YOUR OLD PRETENDER. The great crisis, his elder son had written, in my parents' relationship came some two or three years after my younger brother Phillip was born. No doubt my father was having one of his countless relationships with publicity girls, receptionists, sound-production secretaries, whatever, though we children knew nothing at the time. In any event, he walked out. Angela and I must have been thirteen. Mother went completely crazy. She had been abandoned with four children to bring up. She didn't even have a marriage certificate to protect her. In a fit of rage she went up to his study on the second floor. It was a big house in Kilburn. My father had all his books and old vinyls carefully catalogued. It is curious how meticulous he was in this regard, considering what a messy life he led in general. But as far as his work was concerned, he was always extremely professional. I remember in particular a filing cabinet with thousands of newspaper articles on the widest range of subjects, all very carefully classified and sorted. Anyhow, Mother began to throw everything out of the window and into the street. The study was at the side of the house and there was only a narrow passage, then a creosoted fence, then the street. After the books had been flying for half an hour and all my father's precious old LPs and all these files and files of newspaper cuttings, fluttering down in the passage or out onto the street, someone called the police. And someone must have called my father too, because he arrived to find a young constable trying to restrain Mother from kicking his belongings up and down the road. Afterwards, Angela and I helped him to bring everything back inside and carry it upstairs again. I remember there was dog shit on some of the books. But my father seemed to be in a very cheerful mood. This has helped him to decide to leave forever, I thought. I remember feeling upset, with a lump in my throat, though deep down, I already realised that it would be much better if they split up. I loved my father and very much wanted to be like him. Instead, a couple of hours later, when he had got everything more or less back in place, if not in order, he fixed himself a drink – I even remember it was a gin – sat down on the sofa, turned on the TV and generally made it clear that he had decided to stay. Angela and I were so happy. We chopped up lemons and filled the ice bucket. Now I understand he just didn't have the courage.

KISSES, Cleaver reflected, was how he signed off to most of his girlfriends. There was a safe mix of sexual promise and friendly affection in KISSES. If it became too perfunctory, you could up the stakes with some playful remark about nipple nibbling. Up the stakes! He shook his head. There really was no way to sign off this message to Amanda. It wasn't true I lacked the courage, he told Olga. He spoke out loud. The doll had her eyes on the TV. Words are so categorical, Cleaver thought. Courage. Love. The Nigerians were also ahead, BBC World claimed, when it came to the number of people willing to die for their God. Seventy-eight per cent (a little bar chart appeared) as opposed to only seventeen in the UK. No doubt that was courage. GOODBYE would be far too dramatic, and in the end hardly credible. I am not going to die, after all, Cleaver told himself, in Rosenkranzhof. He was bound to see her again.

For a few moments Cleaver was painfully aware of having no plans, no clear vision of what life would be like, next year, next week even. In part, it was this uncertainty that made signing off to Amanda so difficult. He had no idea what impression he wanted to create, what state of mind he wanted to leave her in. Regards to Larry? He chuckled. We exhausted ourselves with these affairs. The problem I had, Cleaver told Olga – I like a traditionally dressed lady, he decided – whenever I sat down to write my masterpiece, was exactly – he smiled – exactly this problem of credibility, of being able to say anything that remotely got it right. You know? All at once, he distinctly recalled the anxiety, the various quiet rooms, the desks, the windows opening on suburban streets, himself sitting there shoving a knuckle in his mouth, jerking his knee up and down, fretting – the anxiety that you would never be able to get it right. And the same now signing off to Amanda. Not that you were obliged to put down the whole truth – Cleaver had never been so ambitious – but at least to be pertinent, candid. Otherwise there was no point. Otherwise you might as well go back to broadcasting, or publisher's commissions, a short introduction to the Balkans, perhaps. Recycle the material from his documentaries.

He shook his head. I can't do it. Whereas nothing, he suddenly realised, could be easier than correcting someone who was claiming to tell the truth but had manifestly got it wrong. Nothing would be easier than a back and forth of claim and counterclaim over his son's ridiculous book. I did not go back home to stay the day Amanda threw my stuff into the street. Quite the contrary. His elder son's vaunted memory had let him down rather badly there. I stayed away at least a further couple of weeks. Unless of course the boy was lying for effect; it was supposed to be a novel after all. He had ordered a taxi and taken his certain precious belongings with him. Amanda was hanging out of the bathroom window shouting abuse. Be sure, he might write to her now, I'll be thinking of you. That would be true, guaranteed even, yet somehow even more inappropriate, more cruel, than the other solutions.

Then Cleaver remembered that he had already said goodbye to his partner twice. First the night before he left, in her bedroom – I'm really going, Amanda, he had told her;

he had spoken her name out loud – then the following morning, on the phone from Victoria station: Just to say I'm on my way to the airport. Had Siddharta Gautama gone on sending his wife text messages after his sudden and scandalous departure? Just as Cleaver was erasing what he had written, the phone vibrated in his hand: BOOTS. Cleaver clicked, squinted, held the little screen under the bedside lamp. U-no-hoo, he read, has given an interview to the *Torygraph*. You should see it!

V

CLEAVER ATE AN early and hearty breakfast and was already
sitting on Hermann's cart among a dozen boxes when Frau
Schleiermacher came out to say goodbye. She had a hand
behind her back. These people are never going to read the
Telegraph, Cleaver was telling himself. So why should I? A
man who is going to live on a mountain top has no use for
a reputation. Frau Schleiermacher offered her hand, smiling.
Her eyes are very alive. Gallantly, Cleaver bent down from
the cart to kiss her cheek. Then the handsome woman said:
Wollen Sie die Puppe mitnehmen? He didn't understand.
From behind her back she produced the doll. Olga! Cleaver
cried. Hermann said something rapidly and Armin burst out
laughing. Frau Schleiermacher appeared to be protesting, but
her voice too was full of mirth. What did it matter if Cleaver
didn't understand? Aufwiedersehen, he told them.

Yet no sooner was Hermann guiding the Haflinger up
the now familiar track than it seemed to Cleaver that he
missed Frau Schleiermacher immensely. The doll is no substi-
tute. He missed Armin with his black leather jacket, his neck-
lace and inverted crucifix. He missed them more than all

the people he had left behind in London. More than his daughter Caroline, his son Phillip. This is perverse, Cleaver thought. He even missed his place by the window in the Stube where Frau Schleiermacher had served him his breakfast in the morning, his Knödel in the evening. Only six days and already he had felt that that place was his and no one else's. I should have stayed perhaps. I felt secure. Economically speaking, Cleaver told himself, you could probably afford to live in the Unterfurnerhof for the rest of your days, regardless of what your son says about you in the London newspapers. My father, his elder son had written in *Under His Shadow*, never took less than half a dozen newspapers. As a child, it seemed to me that nothing could be more important, more urgent, more real, than a newspaper. The chapter, Cleaver remembered now, as the trees closed around the cart and the track grew steeper, describing Harold and Amanda's Sunday mornings, with the carpet, the sofas and the furniture all smothered in newsprint (there was barely a square inch of upholstery, his elder son had written, that wasn't stained with printer's ink) was clearly supposed to be one of the book's main comic set pieces. I don't miss the papers at all, Cleaver reflected, as the Haflinger pulled the cart higher and higher up the narrowing gorge. The air was still and strangely heavy. Cleaver put on his hat. He shivered. It was as if, his elder son had written, my parents could only feel confident about themselves once they had checked every section of every Sunday paper, once they had a grip on the whole world. And since that is an impossible proposition they shared the papers out between them and exchanged notes. So Sunday morning was also the moment when they were most a team. Or rather, they were a conspiracy against the world. They knew the name of every journalist, every pundit. They knew who would be offended by

89

this piece, who would hit back at that, who had persuaded so and so to write such and such. They were terrorists planning an assassination, or generals plotting reprisals. And for us children too, this was the happiest time of the week. Mum and Dad were swimming together in a jacuzzi of newsprint. They were happy. It was a sort of enchantment, a different world. I miss Armin, Cleaver decided. A jacuzzi of newsprint was a stupid analogy. He had the doll on his knees. I feel closer to Armin, at this moment, he realised, than to any of my own children. If anyone else, Amanda had told him, had betrayed you like this, you would have fought like a lion. She is jealous, Cleaver realised. She can't believe my restraint. If I had written this stuff, she protested, you would kill me. It occurred to Cleaver then that his partner had given his elder son those intimate and damning details in order to be sure that her Harry would hit back. She wanted a fight.

Es wird regnen, Hermann announced. Rain. He clicked his tongue gaily. Regen macht Spaß, nicht wahr? Is there a Herr Schleiermacher? Cleaver suddenly asked. Hermann turned. He looked puzzled. They were straining upwards round a tight bend between pines and boulders. The harness creaked. I never saw Herr Schleiermacher, Cleaver reformulated. Armin's father. A slow smile spread across Hermann's narrow pink face. My brother, he said slowly. He is weg. Wie sagt man? Away this week. He is ein Jäger, you know. Caccia. He is weg. The man gestured vaguely toward the mountains to the north. Mit seinem Hund. The dog. Er schießt. He shoots. Pam, pam! Die Rehe. Die Hasen. Rabbits. Cleaver picked up the doll and threw it into a corner of the cart. You are ridiculous, he told himself.

Even before they emerged from the gorge, the horse was climbing into thick cloud. You have Streichhölzer, Hermann asked. Feuer? Cleaver patted his jacket. The cardboard boxes will be getting soggy, he thought. The air is so wet. Then the dog was barking, the Trennerhof dog; they were out on the plateau. You could feel the space open out, though the cloud was dense. At intervals Cleaver noticed tall poles that must mark the track when the snow came. The farmhouse appeared as a grey silhouette in damp white air, strangely insubstantial, dirty smoke spilling from the chimney. Hermann raised a hand. A spectral figure was standing by one of the outbuildings, but Cleaver couldn't have said who it was. The house was already fading. We must hurry, Hermann laughed. Schnell, wir müssen uns beeilen. They rattled into a luminous mist. Crossing the high pasture, Cleaver experienced a sense of dislocation. It was a different world. The cart gathered speed, travelling downwards now. Heavy, cold drops were clattering on the boxes.

Along the track, the fallen rocks had been removed. Slithering and bumping, closely hemmed in on either side, the cart reached the small clearing in front of the house. The rain was falling steadily. How quiet the air is, Cleaver thought, but for the patter of the rain. Hermann had donned a cape. He began to work with great speed. The back flap of the cart slammed down. A box was in his arms. Cleaver forced open the door. He has Olga in one hand. The rosary swung and dripped on its two nails. A smell of old churches, Cleaver thought, looking into the dark room. Ten in the morning and it's dark. He set down the doll and turned for a box. Schnell! Hermann shouted. He began to laugh. We take down a . . . einen Sarg, he shouted, and bring up the shopping . . . The water was running off his waterproof as he lifted the boxes off the back of the cart and passed them to Cleaver. The Haflinger shivered and neighed. Sarg? Cleaver wondered. Like an idiot he had packed his cape in a bag somewhere. A box of tinned fruit fell apart in his arms. A can bounced on his foot.

The dark room was getting cluttered now. Cleaver tried to shift things to make space. Another box came apart on the stone floor. Packets of biscuits. Toilet rolls. His clothes were in a new suitcase. You imagined some sort of contemplative life, in a remote habitation, but not the practical details of arrival, the man you were paying singing loudly, as if the rain were a pleasure. The table was creaking with packages now. They were done. Hermann rocked it fiercely with one hand and shook his head: Gefährlich. He began moving the heavier things to the floor. A thunderclap rumbled among the stone peaks. The rain came heavier.

Fröhlichkeit! Hermann yelled. Satisfied the table was safe, he sat hard on a chair and pulled a flask from his pocket, stretched out his long legs. There is no sofa, no armchair. Cleaver looked about him and found some grey glasses on a shelf. Hermann shook his head. He gulped and offered. The two men's eyes met in the half-light. What is it he has understood about me? Cleaver wondered, taking the flask. I understood nothing about the Schleiermacher ménage. Whatever it was, the drink was fierce. My father, his elder son had written, always imagined that women were in love with him. The heat burned down into his stomach.

What am I drinking? he asked. Gebirgsgeist! Herman announced. He seemed unaccountably pleased with himself. Ge-what? Cleaver enquired. The horseman repeated slowly Ge-birgs-geist. Then in his clownish English: Ghost of mountain. Spirit, Cleaver corrected. You'd say Spirit of the Mountains. He took another swig. To the mountains, he toasted, to home. Hermann reached for his flask. Ja, Ja! Die Heimat! It seemed he couldn't speak without shouting. He drank deeply, then burst out laughing. Unsere Heimat ist in

Gefahr! Danger! Cleaver raised an eyebrow. What was this about? Die Walschen! Hermann shouted. Italiener, Scheiße! He is playing the ghost of the old occupant, Cleaver realised. The ghost of the mountains. Was that what Sarg meant? They had taken down the dead Nazi. Now we play his ghost. Heil Hitler, he said coolly. Hermann became almost hysterical. He had to put his wrist in his mouth.

Then it seemed Hermann wanted him to go straight back to Trennerhof for some reason. Vertrag, the cart driver said. Unterschrift. He made a gesture with his hand. Cleaver didn't understand. His clothes were damp and uncomfortable. The place smelt musty. Picking his way through the boxes, he lifted an old storm lamp from its nail by the door. On the timber panelling of the wall a framed black-and-white photo showed a line of young men in uniform. Polizeiregiment, Bozen, 1945. How do you light these things? Öl, Hermann told him. There were dusty bottles on a long rough shelf with rags or corks in the necks. Outside the rain was easing. The Haflinger neighed. Hermann unstopped the bottles and sniffed them, making clownish wrinkles with his nose. Öl, he repeated. He showed Cleaver how to fill the lamp, adjust the wick, light it. Cleaver watched his rough, practical fingers, his steady eye. What am I doing here? he wondered. As the yellow light came up, the space grew darker. Films never really got that effect. Cleaver carried the lamp between kitchen table and old stove, through a low doorway with a step down into the main room. It's been tidied, he noticed. There was a fresh pile of logs by the fireplace. Easy, he thought.

They took the cart back to Trennerhof. Cleaver had understood now that he must sign a contract. Despite the lack of all public utilities and the extreme remoteness of the place, these people wanted to be in order with the taxman. They wanted things to be clear. There was a decoration, he noticed now as the wheels began to turn, of gnarled white branches under the eaves of the house. They had been nailed there, intertwining along the wall like old antlers or bones. Everybody in Luttach knows you are here, Hermann explained. This is not Italy. Though it was to the Italian government that taxes must be paid. You can get milk, Hermann added. Cleaver gauged that the two houses must be a little less than a mile apart.

Surprisingly, at Trennerhof, the room he was led into was full of radios. Old radios, on shelves round the wall. Some of them looked like museum pieces. Cleaver took off his hat. There was even an army field transmitter, from the last war presumably. Coming in from the wet, he couldn't work out whether he was in a bar or a kitchen. There was a counter with a beer-pull to the left and against the far wall a huge stove, perhaps six-feet high, with a bench around the bottom, a fixed ladder and a wooden platform on top, a bed perhaps. In the middle of the room the long stone-topped table seemed to be where the family ate. The place smelt of smoke and soup. Frau Stolberg leaned forward to shake his hand, stiffly. The glittering eyes are a firewall, he decided. She doesn't want to be contaminated. Freut mich, Frau Stolberg said. She was wearing black.

Cleaver found himself sitting down at the long table with a piece of paper in front of him. He heard a muttering. The ancient creature was in an armchair by the fire, fingers fidgeting on her lap. I don't understand, he said. The paper was a photocopy with various gaps filled in, in a neat hand. Hermann came to sit beside him. He pointed a dirty finger at the key conditions. He has blond hair on his knuckles. Frau Stolberg stood on the opposite side of the table, her arms folded. The high cheekbones are expressionless. It was strange that they hadn't offered him anything to drink. He felt uncomfortable in his damp trousers. I must slim. You pay one month now. And two months' Kaution. Deposit, Cleaver guessed. Then you pay first day of the month.

Just as Cleaver was counting out the bills, a door opened and the town woman appeared. She wore a pale blue coat. Frau Stolberg spoke sharply to her. The woman said something to Hermann. Cleaver lifted his head. Hermann was embarrassed. She is pretty, Cleaver noticed. Late thirties, but well kept, in a relaxed kind of way. Yellow blonde. My father, his elder son had written, claimed he could size up a woman and his chances of scoring in something less than a millisecond. That must be another anecdote Amanda had fed him, though Cleaver would never have said such a thing in her presence. Suddenly, the three of them were arguing. The town woman raised her voice. These are recriminations, Cleaver realised. There was a large crucifix, he saw now, in the corner above the old lady's head, exactly like the one in Unterfurnerhof. Two dry corncobs hung from either side, as if dangling from Christ's nailed hands. Hermann was shaking his head. When they spoke in their dialect, Cleaver couldn't recognise a single word. Everything fused into an obstinate mass of sound. Frau Stolberg's voice was extremely sharp. She must be in her seventies. Pushing her hair from her face, the town woman suddenly looked like a girl. She is defying authority, Cleaver thought. She is the daughter. Hermann was mediating, retreating.

You will remain in Rosenkranzhof? the young woman turned on Cleaver. Her English wasn't perfect, but perfectly clear. Why? she asked. Why are you wanting to remain there? It is horrible.

Taken aback, Cleaver sighed the deep sigh he had made famous in so many interviews. She is more alluring when she is angry, he thought. Just when a woman's behaviour should have warned him off, his elder son had written, or perhaps especially then, since his real aim wasn't pleasure but conquest, my father would lay on the charm.

You cannot remain the winter in Rosenkranzhof, the town-dressed woman insisted. She was aggressive. It is horrible!

Perhaps, Cleaver told her quietly, if we meet from time to time, I will try to explain why I want to live there and you can tell me why it upsets you so much.

The effect of this exchange on Frau Stolberg was immediate. She addressed acid words to Hermann. She was angry. Does she understand English? Cleaver wondered. It seemed unlikely. Frau Stolberg thrust the money into her apron pocket. Or was she afraid of things being said that she didn't understand? She didn't like his tone of voice. Unterschrift, Hermann reminded him. His fingernail scratched the spot. Hier, Unterschrift. Your name.

We will not be meeting again, the younger woman said. Fortunately. She walked across the room toward the fireplace, speaking in German now: Großmutter, she whispered, Oma. Frau Stolberg is seething, Cleaver noticed. The crucifix seemed to have been carved from a gnarled root. It was curious the business with the corncobs, hanging there like the two thieves. By the fire, the ancient woman raised her glazed eyes. Can she see or not? The old lips quivered in a web of wrinkles. Hesitantly, she opened her arms for an embrace. Cleaver saw a string of red beads twisted round mottled fingers. Rosenkranz. He looked down at the contract. Frau Stolberg was glaring. Harry Cleaver, he signed.

Milch, Hermann said the moment they were outside. He set off towards one of the outbuildings. The cloud was lifting, but everything is wet. Cleaver saw the woman's blue suitcase on the back of the cart. Then the dog was at their

feet. Why all the radios? he asked. I mean, there's no electricity to run them, is there? The animal tried to thrust its
snout into his crotch. Down! The radios? That is Jürgen,
Hermann said. But he was preoccupied. The argument with
the town-dressed woman has upset him. He pushed open a
splintered wooden door that had strips of thick black plastic nailed all around. Inside the smell was fierce. Cleaver had
to pause on the threshold. Käse! Hermann announced.
Cheese, please! He had found his smile again.

The man Cleaver had seen at the funeral detached himself
from basins and taps on the far wall and came bustling to
meet them. He was taller than Cleaver remembered, but
awkwardly hunched, wiping wet hands on a black rubber
apron, a small round leather cap on his thick, dirty hair. Jo,
jo! The handshake was vigorous. He smiled idiotically. The
eyebrows were fat dark caterpillars only a millimetre apart,
the cheeks pitted, coarse and unshaven. Freut mich, Cleaver
remembered. There was a constant gurgling noise in the room.
There must be running water. Recht gutes Deutsch! Hermann
began his routine again. He clapped the new tenant on the
back. Jürgen was still smiling blankly. Through the pungent
tang of the cheese, Cleaver definitely caught a whiff of alcohol. The man's eyes are red. Ich will die Milch nehmen, he
said. Deutsch, Deutsch, Deutsch! Hermann applauded. Any
good director would have cut a while back, Cleaver thought.

Against the wall, two metal urns stood in a tank of dark
water; it must be filling from beneath and draining through
an overflow. Stream water presumably. Jürgen took down a
battered can hanging from a makeshift wire handle and
plunged it into an urn. His movements seemed unnecessar-
ily vigorous. Hermann was making some kind of appeal
now, speaking earnestly. His voice is less jovial in his own
language. Both men were wearing exactly the same kind of

rough, dark blue shirt, as if it were some sort of uniform. Why on earth did I sign as Harry? Cleaver wondered. He was tired of it all. But milk is important. He has packed five boxes of cereal. Having filled the can, Jürgen bustled over to the opposite wall where bowls were resting on stone shelves. In all my father's chaotic life, Cleaver's elder son had written, the one absolutely indispensable ritual, aside from the newspapers – and probably in Pavlovian connection with those newspapers – was his morning bowl of cereal. Serious cereal for serial and ceremonial evacuation, he would say when we had guests. The nice thing about our frequent guests was that my parents argued less, though you had to put up with all my father's ancient witticisms. Käse, Hermann said again. Cleaver found himself holding a plain white plate on which a gritty, grey-green mass had been squashed under a plastic wrap. Danke schön, he said. Jürgen was still smiling. It was a face from which reflection seemed entirely absent. The radios could remain a mystery, Cleaver decided.

Outside, the young woman had already climbed up on the cart ready to go. Goodbye, she shouted in English. She seemed friendly now. She has cheered up. Good luck! Hermann offered Cleaver his hand. Cleaver gave him an envelope with the money they had agreed. Danke schön! The horseman was his jolly self. When you have need of help, come to Onkel Hermann's Stable, in Luttach! He climbed on the cart. He is driving the woman straight back down, Cleaver realised. A cousin presumably. She came for her father's funeral, now she is going back home to Bruneck or Brixen. Carrying the open tin can with its creamy milk, the plate with the cheese, he set off in his damp clothes to walk down to Rosenkranzhof.

It isn't easy for a fat fifty-five-year-old to walk almost a mile along a steep track holding a can brimming with milk in one hand, a great lump of grey cheese glued to a dinner plate in the other. Am I elated or terrified? Cleaver wondered. He was really alone now. He was above the noise line at last. Or would the important step be not even to investigate one's own feelings, not to notice them, just live the moment? To his left, the rugged crags of the Speikboden towered into a white mist. Ahead the Ahrn valley dropped and wound far away through a northern panorama of cloud and stone and dark pine woods. It's not true that you have no sense of spirituality, Cleaver objected. He spoke out loud. It's not true you can't see beyond the lens of a camera. Damn! There was a sudden barking at his heels. Just as the track dived into the gorge, the Trennerhof dog caught up with him. Startled, Cleaver lost a splash of milk. Damn and damn! At once the animal was licking the dirt. Shoo! Go home. Haus. Heimat! The creature barked excitedly. Fuck off! A fat old dog, Cleaver thought, with a grizzly snout and rheumy eyes. When he made as if to kick, the creature yelped and cowered, but did not turn back.

Cleaver walked down into the woods to take possession of his new home. Rosenkranzhof, he muttered. Hoist with his own petard, etc. Needless to say, *Under His Shadow* had made hay of the great man's resistance to his children's desire for pets. My father was obsessed and oppressed, his elder son had written – first it had been hamsters – by the thought that a human being's relationship with an animal is always and exclusively one of domination. Then rabbits, budgies, goldfish. It pained him to think of us having dumb creatures – finally dogs – under our absolute power. I don't even care if that's true or not, Cleaver decided, resigning himself to the wet creature trotting beside him. He thought it was bad for us and bad for them, his elder son had written, because he himself could think of relationships in no other terms than those of power, competition, domination, and an animal, he said, was not a worthy opponent. It was a massacre.

How bloody right I was! Cleaver stopped and rested the milk can on a boulder. The woods around him dripped and whispered. He spied a mushroom. What was the publication of *Under His Shadow* after all, if not a devastating assertion of the young author's newly discovered power, an attempt to deliver his father a lethal blow? I even die at the end of the damn thing, for Christ's sake! More of a massacre than that! My father simply didn't see, his elder son had claimed, that it might be enriching to be intimate with other forms of life. Blah blah blah. The Trennerhof dog sat and waggled his rump in the earth and whined. Hit back, Amanda insisted. Take him to court, if you're so angry. First she confided all kinds of intimate details to the boy, then told Cleaver to hit back when he published them. Opening the newspapers, his elder son had recounted, my parents were always eager to see how so and so would hit back in response to such and such an accusation. That was the fun of the media for them. The news was an ongoing war, which kept all the antagonists, winners and losers alike, constantly in the public eye. Only conflict is newsworthy. Every relationship is a power struggle. When my parents weren't fighting each other, it was because they had found a common enemy.

You, Cleaver thought, you little runt. He picked up the can and decided to drink off some milk, before it got spilled anyway. There was a stone in his boot. I am now entirely, completely and utterly on my own, he reminded himself once again. How creamy it was! I am not obliged to think about my son's autobiographical novel. I do not have to choose my weapon. I won't even know, he told himself, if they give him the Booker or not. As soon as he started walking again, the dog padded along behind. Cleaver rounded on it: What's your name?

It was definitely chillier down here in the gloom among the trees. On the ground the dead pine needles squelched and the frequent rocky outcrops were slimy with lichens, rust-coloured and green. Wie heisst du? he tried. The stone could wait till he was back at the house. The dog let his tongue hang out. His eyes are pleading. Then for the first time it occurred to Cleaver that it was the interview with the President of the United States that had stopped him from hitting back at his son. Sitting stiff with fury in the taxi on the way to the studios, he had seen the painful conflict that lay ahead. An abyss opened before him. He would go to a lawyer. Amanda knew lots of lawyers. He would file a suit against his son. My eldest son. He would have the book withdrawn. Then the knives would be out in earnest. Then blood would flow and more blood. Mr President, Cleaver had asked – he had done none of the homework one normally does for such an interview – in your reactions to terrorism, your celebrated determination to meet violence with violence, is it possible, do you think, that you allowed yourself, and with you the American people, indeed the whole Western world, to be trapped into a cycle of escalating antagonism, strike and counterstrike, that can never produce a winner? If we hadn't hit back, the President retorted smoothly, we would certainly have been the losers. Cleaver stumbled on a loose stone. A little more milk splashed. Again the dog was there with his pink tongue. Recovering, Cleaver listened to the silence of the gorge. Is that a stream in the distance? The house, he had noticed, had water channelled from somewhere along yards of primitive wooden conduits. Utterly alone, he whispered. He felt vaguely anxious, as if at any moment he might be caught trespassing, somebody might be watching. With time these thoughts will lose their urgency, he decided. The dog barked and made as though to tug at his feet. He knows where we're going.

On reaching Rosenkranzhof, and it was towards two in the afternoon now, Cleaver noticed that the Haflinger had crapped barely a yard from his front door. Wasn't that supposed to bring good luck? The heavy rain had made the shit soggy. He looked over his property, the grey stone of the ground floor, the splintery black timber above, the grim trophy-like decoration of bleached and twisted branches. Why had they built it here, smothered in trees, on this cramped ledge, not quite at the top of the gorge? Looking closely, he saw there was a layer of moss between each strip of planking. No wonder it smelt bad. Does the track go on from here? he wondered. I must explore. He must change his damp clothes. His crotch is sore. This is your remote habitation, he told himself. You've got this far. The roof tiles were also wooden, warped. It was quite an achievement, he decided. The dog was pawing at the door. Perhaps he had been the old Nazi's dog. Now all you have to do is metamorphose.

VI

CLEAVER WAS PLEASED with his progress over the first hour or so. He changed his clothes, sorted out the groceries, the little miscellany of tools and equipment, put everything away in drawers and cupboards and shelves. The dog curled up on a mat that he clearly knew of old. There were four rooms in all. The front door opened directly into a kitchen, with stove, table and sink. Cutlery and crockery were old and muddled, but someone had rinsed them. They were grey, but not dirty. The walls were all roughly timber-clad. And someone had removed all the clutter and cobwebs he had seen on his first visit. Frau Stolberg, he imagined. Or the younger woman. Or the fat girl. Jürgen, on the other hand, would have removed the rockfall from the track.

Then you went down a step into the main room which had two shapeless black armchairs, a stone floor and a fire-place with threadbare hearthrug that the dog had claimed. It's only dark in here, Cleaver assured himself, because the windows are filthy and outside there are branches pressing against the panes. The owners had done nothing to rectify this, but then they had hardly had much time. There was a large stuffed bird above the mantlepiece. Could it be an eagle? It wasn't the town-dressed woman did the cleaning, Cleaver told himself, or she wouldn't have spoken as she had about his coming to live here. Frau Stolberg, perhaps, had tried to keep the business of my renting the house to herself. Open everything up, he proposed, on a bright clear day and that smell of damp upholstery will go. For lunch, he cut a piece of sausage and pressed it between two thin slices of Vollkornbrot. When the dog begged, he ignored it. Unfed, it would go back to Trennerhof. The irony, Cleaver smiled, was that when we did finally get a dog, because I always caved in in the end, who was it wound up taking the damn thing for walks? His son hadn't mentioned this. The great Harold Cleaver, more often than not. Taking the dog out, he had discovered, offered an opportunity to make the kind of phone call you couldn't feel easy about making at home. I don't think Amanda took the creature walkies even once.

Against the far wall of the main room, a rough wooden stairway led to the upper floor, but under the stairs was another door with a bolt. A deep cubbyhole had been hewn from the rock face against which the back of the house was resting. It was cold. Waiting for his eyes to adjust, Cleaver began to make out lines of unlabelled bottles under thick dust, then a keg, a sickle, an axe, a spade, a saw. They hadn't cleaned in here. There were other tools. It was the fat girl who cleaned, Cleaver thought, under the supervision of Frau Stolberg, while the town-dressed woman sat in the parlour in Trennerhof with her decomposing grandmother. Oma, she had called her. But I completely misunderstood the Schleiermacher ménage, he remembered. The big hooks emerging from cobwebs on the ceiling must be for hams and sausages. Or even game perhaps. The spade would be useful for removing the shit. He imagined a hare hung by its hind legs. With a dog I might learn to hunt. But he hadn't come here to ape the locals. It was not a question of going native, of adopting new habits to replace the old. Quite the contrary. I want no habits at all.

Then Cleaver tackled the stairs. The wood creaked. There was a faint chuckle of running water. It's little more than a ladder, he thought. He had done no more than poke his head up here on his first visit. One of the characteristics everybody noticed about my father, his elder son had written, and that invariably irritated or amused, depending on how vulnerable you felt, was the way he loved to give the impression of having understood from a conversation more, far more, than you had intended to tell him. Cleaver pushed his head into a small, dusty loft bedroom. You would say that you were having trouble preparing such and such an exam, you couldn't sleep, and he would say, Ah, re-eally? as if he had seen through and behind this fact, this symptom rather, to some tormented psychological scenario that could only get worse, the sort of thing he might make a documentary about, if only he could tear himself away from a thousand other projects. There was a single wood-framed bed against the wall to the left of the stairs, a small, smeared window opposite, almost entirely obscured by pine fronds. You would tell him a girlfriend had cancelled a holiday because she'd been taken ill, and at once you could see, from his knowing grey eyes, from a sudden narrowing of the pupils, that he had deduced that she was phobic, she had made herself ill to avoid taking this step toward a greater intimacy with you.

Carefully, Cleaver undid the catch of the window and tugged. After a little resistance, the frame swung toward him, letting in a world of damp air and pine resin. He put his nose over the sill. The offending trees rose from the steep plunge of the gorge beyond the handkerchief of flat ground on which the house stood. In short, his elder son had written, my father knew more and more profoundly about you and your friends than you ever would yourself. Leaning further out of the window to assess the feasibility of cutting the things down, Cleaver remembered the incident of his son's girlfriend. I was right in the end. The boy was wasting his energy. Every time the two of them were about to move in together, the girl – she was certainly pretty – would contrive to have some kind of strange ailment that obliged her to return to her mother. You don't go to bed with scores of the creatures, Cleaver said out loud, without acquiring a certain familiarity with the terrain. Then, trying the door to the small room above the kitchen, he discovered it was locked.

Cleaver looked around for a key. The door had been open when he poked his head up the stairs on the first visit. It was an old, rusty keyhole. This bedroom is remarkably bare, he realised. Not a thing had been left. He remembered a clutter of photographs, ornaments, clothes, boots. There had been a military cap on a nail. Now, on the same nail, there was a crucifix. So in a way every room becomes the same room, he thought. Or even a church. Then he guessed they must have stored all the old man's stuff in the small upstairs room and locked it up. Rather than cleaning the place, they had been removing the evidence, and preserving it too. Was it written in the contract he'd signed that he did not have the use of this room? The end result, his elder son had written, was that whenever you spoke to my father about anything personal, you came away feeling that there were dark forces at work in your life, forces you hadn't even dreamt of. But having those secrets unlocked, or perhaps only invented for you, didn't make things any easier. On the contrary, you felt more vulnerable than before. His documentary on anorexia, based no doubt on the experiences of some mistress or other, won an award for its "perception" and "uncompromising realism"; but the truth was that my father just enjoyed the melodrama of presenting other people's predicaments as fascinating and hopeless.

Maeve.

Cleaver hurried down the stairs rather faster than was wise. One plank in particular protested loudly. He collapsed in an armchair and stared at Olga in the other. She stood on the black cushion in her Tyrolese red and white. You plan to be here for months, he reminded himself. Maybe years. It was as though the doll were intent on something just behind his right ear. There will be hundreds of these days. She was watching a television perhaps. Or the stuffed bird. Its wings were outspread in dust. So what do you think of the place, so far, Olga? he asked warmly. For a moment, he couldn't help thinking of some fatuous reality show: *Cleaver Outcast*. You behave as though you're alone, he imagined, but really there is a camera crew all around. The director suggests the doll to provide a little dialogue. Otherwise I'd have to talk to myself. Armchairs could be comfier, couldn't they? Cleaver remarked. A little psychodrama. Reality Show is a contradiction in terms, of course. Though not as mendacious as Documentary.

The doll stared glassily, but on hearing Cleaver's voice, the old dog opened one eye. The tail wagged slowly, once, thumping on the rug, and the eye closed again. We bought the bloody dog, in the end, Cleaver remembered – actually rather a beautiful dog – because, after years of successful resistance, Angela made a huge effort to convince me. She had begged, pleaded, promised: It will sit at my feet and help me study, she told him. He can hear his daughter's voice, see her wry smile. She must have been sixteen at the time. Her hitherto brilliant schoolwork had taken a sudden turn for the worse. She was blooming. Cleaver was in love with her. You would do anything for Angela, Amanda told him when the announcement was made: We are getting a dog, folks. Why didn't his son's stupid book mention that it was Angela's dog? Why do I feel so incredibly tense? Cleaver demanded of himself. You're alone now. You can relax. Instead, it was as if something extremely unpleasant were about to happen, something that couldn't be put off. Angela's belongings, Cleaver remembered, had been preserved in her old room for years, though no one had ever locked the door. Is there something they don't want me to see? he said out loud. Damn!

Cleaver jumped up, went back to the filthy stone cubby-hole below the stairs, picked up the axe, hurried out of the house and round to the gorge side. There was barely a foot of slippery ground here between the damp wall of the house and the precipitous slope. The first thing I should have done was light a fire, he told himself, to dry the place, to make it mine, to get rid of that musty smell. But now, sitting down on a rock, he looked for a foothold among the soaking ferns and slim trunks and boulders atop the gorge. Another pair of trousers would get wet.

Stumbling, grabbing at a branch, he found a good foothold, and at once swung the axe to attack the offending pines. There were at least three that would have to go. This place needs some fucking light, he shouted. He hadn't bothered to assess the problem from a technical point of view. He was balancing awkwardly a couple of yards below the level of the house. When did I ever use an axe before? The blade sank so deeply into the slim trunk that he had to fight to pull it out. This job could easily have been left till tomorrow, or next week for that matter. You haven't even taken your bedding upstairs. But he wanted to do it now. He wanted to destroy those trees. Being alone hasn't calmed me down at all, he realised. Panting, he glanced back over his shoulder. The ground dropped away into the gorge beneath him. Fortunately there are trees and boulders to break a fall. His feet were well planted. Okay, one, he said. I'll cut down one tree. Cleaver swung the axe again. At least one. That way I'll have achieved something. I'll have made my mark.

Bastard! Cleaver was surprised both by his own vigour and the stout resistance of this apparently meagre pine. The weapon was heavy, it swung wildly. Shit. He is sweating now. I've had bigger Christmas trees than this, he protested. He knew he had lost his cool. He didn't want to know why. Something is threatening. Damn you, damn you, damn you! He slipped. He hit furiously. At last there was a loud crack. The slim tree spun and fell sideways onto the wall just beside the kitchen window. At once, the dog was barking. That woke the fucker up. The animal came bounding to the corner of the house and howled, his front paws just over the edge of the drop. Cleaver stood breathing heavily and wiped the sweat from his forehead with his shirt. The dog they had got – what was he called? – always howled when Angela played the piano. He was Angela's dog in the end. Ivan. A handsome Labrador. His son had mentioned none of this. He didn't mention Angela's remarkable piano playing. Only the piercing and tattoos, the joints and pills; all much exaggerated, as if she were some kind of terminal dropout. He hadn't mentioned that his twin sister was a musical genius. If anyone in this house produces a masterpiece, Cleaver had started to say when they teased him, it will be Angela.

Inevitably, a girl who played keyboards in a band experimented with a pill or two. Quite probably Armin does too. Haven't I, in my time? Not because of her parents' problems, for Christ's sake. Frau Schleiermacher seemed to be an excellent mother. My son was jealous, Cleaver realised. Why hadn't this occurred to him before? Jealous of my relationship with his sister. Trying to get at the next tree, he banged his ankle. Or hers with me. He slipped, had to grab at a trunk below, scraped his knuckles. Everybody was clamouring for my attention. The dog barked. Shut up! And for Angela's. Cleaver tensed his jaw and took a mighty swing. Why didn't he mention any of this? He created an image, Cleaver announced out loud, of Angela that would show me in the worst possible light, a version that would make me responsible almost for her death. Angela was a genius! Cleaver screamed. He struck the tree again. It was thicker than the other. The piano still has pride of place in the sitting room where the Sunday papers are read. It's there now, at this very moment. Why didn't he mention Angela playing the piano while we read the papers? You betrayed the memory of your twin to get at me, you creep! To his surprise, the tree came crashing down. It must have been rotten. Cleaver had to scramble to one side as the heavy thing fell toward him. There was a terrific cracking sound. The dog was going wild. Alex! Cleaver yelled. I shall call you Alex. Immediately, the fat man was pulling himself up the slope on his hands and knees. The phone! Where did I leave the phone?

Cleaver dragged his suitcase up the stairs – there should be a little more light here now – and emptied the contents on the bed. It was still gloomy. The phones were in a side pocket. He can't see properly. The problem is the panes are filthy. Opening the window, he risked smashing the damn thing. It jammed at a corner. But he needs light. My eyes are such crap. He wouldn't even be able to read the names on the phone's address list. There was still the biggest of the trees to cut. I'll do that tomorrow.

Leaning out of the window over the tangle of broken branches and the dark deep wound of the gorge, he turned on the red phone. On the opposite slopes were dense woods broken only by cliffs of grey stone, the white thread of a waterfall. In the palm of his hand, the small screen glowed and then died. The battery is dead. You knew that! He shook the thing. You knew it would be dead! Now the dog came scrambling and scratching up the stairs after him. Fuck off! Can't I be left alone a single instant? Amanda had been furious about the business of Ivan sleeping by Angela's bed. I didn't mind at all. Cleaver had never shared his partner's obsession with hygiene, the business of running to the bathroom after sex. He hated that. Your honour, I claim as just grounds for this divorce the fact that my wife always runs to the bathroom after sex. But you were never married.

Only now, though still dimly, and still pressing the button that should have turned on his phone, did Cleaver realise that what had disturbed him most about his son's book, was not, or not just, what it said about the past, but the past itself, quite independently of that book, the past his son hadn't spoken of. How could the boy talk about Angela without mentioning all that was healthy and even brilliant about the girl? Only now did Cleaver realise that the scratched and splintered varnish of the stairs must be the result of this smelly dog with his long claws dragging its fat carcass up here day in day out after its ageing Nazi master. Go down, damn you! I will never be anyone's master again, Cleaver decided. I want relationships with no one. He tried to push the animal with his foot. He didn't have the heart to kick. My father, his elder son had written, for all his cynicism and careless cruelty, was actually a big softy when push came to shove. Even that is to be held against me. And they were rewarding a writer who used expressions like when push came to shove! I'll shove the bastard downstairs.

But already Cleaver was rummaging in the suitcase for the grey phone, the office phone. Already the dog was lying on the bare boards beside the bed. The old Nazi slept with his dog, Cleaver realised. He was a softy. The creature could well be fifteen years old. He had that flea-bitten look to him. So the man hadn't really lived alone. He'd had his dog by his bed. How many years was it since Angela died? Fifteen? Seventeen? All kinds of things happened then that you didn't understand. Life changed. Yet my documentary on bereavement was widely praised. He particularly remembered the sequence about the pet that searches everywhere for its dead mistress. It was funny you used the word mistress with dogs.

Cleaver turned on the phone. It's what my son didn't want to mention that disturbs me. Good. Two bars of battery had appeared. So why am I planning to call him? Come on, come on, he muttered. There was no sign of a signal. To talk about what really happened. Let's talk. To get it out in the open, to have him admit a few things. Let's really have it out. How could he write a book like that without saying what really happened? There is battery now, but no signal. Cleaver hung out of the window, holding the phone at arm's length. The bastard. The sill sawed into his paunch. He had definitely scraped the skin off an ankle. I took a knock. The utter bastard. Nothing. You came here, a voice reminded him, precisely in order to be beyond the reach of a mobile phone signal, and here you are hanging out of the window over a thousand-foot drop in the hope of catching one.

Cleaver hurried down the stairs. It's the fourth from the

top that groans so ominously. He is now extremely aware of behaving irrationally. Why? What is it that has driven me so crazy? Just when I was finally alone. The dog came clattering down the stairs after him. Cleaver turned on him. Fuck off, dog! Go write a book!

He ran out of the house and began to walk briskly back up the track. It's the gorge that's cutting out the signal, he decided. I'll make one last phone call. Above Trennerhof there would be something. To sort things out with my son. I'm not a coward. I'll confront him. I should have confronted him the moment I saw the thing. I should at least have spoken to him before I left. What's the point of taking on the President of the United States of America if you can't speak to your son?

But now he had to stop. He was winded. His chest is hurting. There's a taste of blood in his mouth. Jesus! As soon as he sat down, on a wet slab of rock, the dog was there. Cleaver gasped for breath. The stupid creature has decided that I must replace his master. Unless he was a she. To him I'm no different from an ancient Nazi. Ghost of the mountains. In his documentary, Cleaver had shown a dog that howled whenever it heard the sound of a violin. Its dead master had played in an orchestra. In our house nobody played the piano after Angela died. He and Amanda had not insisted, Cleaver remembered, that Phillip and Caroline go on with their lessons. Angela was the musician. Angela was dead. The kids were all too happy to stop. His son had mentioned none of this. Alex! Cleaver fondled the dog's ears. The pain was passing now. The music died with her, he thought. In a stupid road accident. Despite being convinced that he would die at any minute, his elder son had written, my father always refused to get a proper medical check-up. He was afraid that theatre might become reality, or alternatively that he might find he had no cause for panic. What I am going to ask him – Cleaver got to his feet – is why he blew up that year or so of Angela's rebellion into something so portentous, yet entirely omitted to mention his twin sister's musical genius, the encouragement I gave her, the expensive Moog, the permission to travel with a band when she was barely seventeen. She died because I gave her permission, because I believed in her.

Cleaver began walking up the track again, a little more sedately now. He held the phone in front of his eyes. No signal. He really didn't feel well. The dog waddled along beside him. This dog is as unfit as I am, Cleaver thought. He's ancient. He shamelessly seeks company, while I just want to be alone. Why are you trying to make this phone call then? He stopped. I could vomit, he thought. Bereavement, the voice-over in his documentary had said, is a form of enchantment in which the most constant presence in your mind is the person in reality absent.

Cleaver climbed on. The same could also be said of lost love, he reflected. In fact he had stolen that line, he remembered now, give or take a word or two, from some tearful novel about mid-life crisis. What a bore. Coming out of the wood onto the high plateau, he suddenly realised that there was a breeze. I'm sweating and it's chill. The dog barked. Then the screen lit up. There's a signal. Cleaver stood still. It was gone.

He took a step back, moving the phone around as if it were a Geiger counter. Nothing. In the distance, Trennerhof released a wreath of smoke into the gathering dusk. The breeze snatched it eastward over the gorge through failing light. One bar of signal appeared, disappeared. What am I doing here? Cleaver wondered. The battery had shrunk, he saw, from two bars to one. His son would answer, of course, if I do actually speak to him, that he hadn't talked about these things because the book was a novel. It's *fiction*, Dad. Italics in his voice to make me foolish. My son is waiting for this call, Cleaver suddenly realised. When you write a book attacking, no, destroying, a member of your family, the most powerful member, you naturally expect a tough phone call, at the very least. You are ready for it. It's just a novel, Dad. He can hear his elder son's rather high-pitched, defensive voice. There's a disclaimer, remember. It's *not* a memoir, Dad. The younger children, Cleaver thought – Caroline, Phillip – were left very much to their own devices after Angela's death. He watched the screen attentively, waiting for the signal to reappear. Your relationship with them never had the same intensity. The moment the signal appears, he decided, I call. Neither he nor Amanda had had the energy to impose piano lessons. The sound would be a terrible reminder. On the other hand they hadn't actually got rid of the piano. And it was surreal, Cleaver suddenly decided, obscene, that Amanda had invited Priya to the funeral without saying anything at all to me. You can't – he would tell his son the moment this signal deigned to connect with his mobile – just rearrange the past, my past, to have your father appear in the worst possible light, and then get away with it by claiming it's fiction. Precisely through its falseness, the lie obliges us to look for the truth. We were never really lovers again, Cleaver recalled. From that point on, it was all a charade.

All at once Cleaver was quite certain he was catching a chill. This'll be the death of you. The back of his neck is icy. Why don't I have my hat on? He turned and walked down the track to Rosenkranzhof. He couldn't remember where he'd left his hat, my nice grey, broad-brimmed hat. The boulders, the outcrops, the nettles and the coloured mosses, the roots fastened to the rocks, the funguses on the tree trunks, they are growing familiar already. Don't turn the phone off, he decided. Let the battery run out. Let it die. His nerves are calming. You must put yourself beyond temptation. Apparently pleased with the decision to turn back, the dog trotted beside him.

It was pitch dark by the time Cleaver reached the house. At some point, I must have been distracted, he realised. He hadn't noticed how rapidly the twilight was deepening. Without a series of appointments, the rigid scheduling of studios and news programmes, one tends to stop looking at one's watch. He breathed deeply. There was still a little way to go and he could barely see to put one foot in front of the other. The track was rutted here. It was a mistake to look up at the sky between the trees; the ground grew blacker. Fortunately, the dog was waddling along in front of him. He makes the darkness visible, just. His coat glistens. In any event, the need to concentrate and watch his step cheered Cleaver up. How dark the woods are! Already it seemed impossible that he had been meaning to phone his son. It was the locked room started it off, he remembered. Was it? Alex, he called the dog. Again he had that vague feeling that he was trespassing. He would be caught. The creature turned, eyes faintly visible, mouth hanging open. Of course I could simply break the lock, Cleaver told himself. Though there was hardly any point if the room was filled with old junk. Why should I care? I have space enough without that. It's not my junk.

He walked extremely slowly, pushing one shin after another into the uneven darkness. Such fresh air can only be good for you, he thought, after London, after a lifetime of studios and offices, taxis and trains and planes. He breathed rather theatrically in self-congratulation. Not a single pollutant, quite probably. The dog padded on a few paces and turned back, padded on and turned back. He wants to protect me. And it was strange the way the creature appeared to understand the man's need to give him a name, even if it wasn't the name he had always been called by. Coming out into the clearing in front of the house, Cleaver stepped in the shit the Haflinger had left. He laughed. Holy Mary Mother of God, he said, touching the beads on the door, remembering the old woman's skeletal fingers up at Trennerhof. He took off his shoes on the threshold. Brought up a Protestant, I lagged behind into atheism. He smiled. Perhaps the only way to get back to God, it occurred to him, rather bizarrely, would be to eliminate consciousness altogether.

But where had he left the matches? In the dark kitchen, Cleaver padded about carefully in damp socks, running his hand over the various surfaces. I will have to be much more organised. The wooden table top was dangerously rough. The torch is still packed away in a box somewhere. From now on I will have to know when it's getting dark, I must be sure where everything is. They weren't on the stove, nor the chairs. He felt the surfaces again. One of the things no film can ever really show, he said out loud, is how it is to be in the dark. They weren't by the sink. Cleaver had come up against that problem on a number of occasions. You can only hint at the mind's confusion in darkness. Again he was puzzled by the thought of all those old valve radios and no electric current to run them. I'm finally beyond the grid, he reflected. For better or worse. Once, he had tried to conduct a few minutes of *Crossfire* in the dark, complete darkness, just to show everyone how essential seeing was to talking, how much the viewer of a talk show was interested in the show rather than the talk. Why didn't my son stick that in his book? There had been three or four guests arranged on two sofas. When the lights went out, nobody had wanted to speak. There were nervous giggles, whispers. Cleaver stood up straight. Where are the matches? The dog whined. He wants to be fed. He stinks. Even inside the house it was cold. I must light a fire and prepare something to eat. I often asked myself, his elder son had written, why my father never did anything to moderate his eating. Cleaver sat on a chair in the darkness. Because Amanda insisted on feeding me like a pig of course. Because we always had guests. Because it would have been antisocial not to eat, not to drink. Because I like eating and drinking. Where in Christ's name did I put those matches! It's so silent here, he thought. Without any warning, there came a knock at the door.

Cleaver stiffened, he stared. The larger shapes of the room were just visible: the cupboard, the table. There is a hint of light from the window, a trickling of water from the tank above the sink. It couldn't be a knock. The dog would have barked. Alex! he whispered. What is a dog for? The creature didn't move. He is half deaf perhaps. The knock was repeated, quite clearly. Two sharp taps. This time the dog got to his feet and went to sit expectantly by the door. When he let out a little yap, a husky female voice said, Uli! With a grating of wood and stone, the door began to open.

Hello, Cleaver said. An ample silhouette filled the pale rectangle of the door. The fat girl, he realised. Uli! she called. Then a stream of words. But now she was taken aback to see Cleaver's big bald head floating there in the pitch dark. Ich kann nicht Feuer finden, Cleaver tried. Hast du Feuer?

There was a rustling noise and a powerful light shone out and swung into the room. Uli, she said again, pointing the torch. Der Hund. At once Cleaver saw the matches on the floor by the other chair. You stepped on a single dollop of shit crossing a clearing, then couldn't stumble on a giant box of matches in ten minutes faltering back and forth around a couple of square yards.

The lamp was on the table. He lit the wick. It smoked. The girl switched off the torch. She stood gormlessly just inside the door, shoulders hunched, one hand raised to squeeze an ear between chubby fingers. In the yellow light he can see a dark green sweater, tight trousers on heavy thighs. She crouched down and took the dog's head in her hands. Uli! That sounds like a girl's name. Uli, komm. She turned to go.

Willst du . . . Cleaver began. The big girl hesitated. She is about seventeen, Cleaver thought. She was wearing a loose smock top, a blue work-jacket. On the table, the lamp was smoking badly. He couldn't decide whether she was retarded in some way. The nose was hooked, the lips very fleshy. No woman, his elder son had written, was too young for my father, no age gap too incongruous. Willst du trinken? They didn't even have to be pretty. Who would have told such a monstrous lie, if not Amanda? And to what end, if not to provoke a battle?

The girl took two paces across the room, picked up the oil lamp and, standing on tiptoe, hung it on a chain that Cleaver now saw for the first time dangling from the central beam. It was a heavy, vigorous body, hidden from the thighs up in loose clothes. Again she pointed at the dog. She was explaining that she had been looking for the dog. Ich habe . . . Wasser, he smiled, Milch, Wein, Whisky. He had lined up his supermarket bottles on a shelf. Und Bier.

The girl was casting her eyes rather furtively round the room, as if surprised to have been allowed the chance to look. Again she raised her left hand to tug at her ear. The dog whined and tried to bite at the root of his tail. She is comparing the place with how it was before, Cleaver thought. There was a look of perplexity in her eyes. The cheeks were chubby, but not ugly. The eyes are small, troubled. Sit down, Cleaver suggested gently. Sitzen Sie, bitte. He wondered if what he said made any sense. It must be full of mistakes.

The girl sat quite suddenly. She said something by way of explanation. She bent to stroke the dog. It must be Frau Stolberg cut her hair so brutally short. Cleaver remembered when Angela had come home with her head shaved. It was as if, his elder son had written, she were deliberately destroying her femininity in protest against her father's philandering. She looked more beautiful than ever, Cleaver recalled. A strange, luminous, vulnerable beauty. He went to pick up a beer. Ist das deine Hund? he asked. The girl didn't seem to understand. Uli? Jo, Uli.

Cleaver had found the bottle opener now. He filled two glasses. The girl got up, scraping her chair back, and moved, tentatively, shoulders hunched, to the threshold of the sitting room. You want to go in there? Cleaver asked. He saw quite clearly now that she had no neck. The chin was weak. And she carried a smell about her, an animal mustiness. It blended with the general damp.

Kalt, she announced. She folded her arms across ample breasts and pretended to shiver. Feuer. She added something that appeared to be a question. Cleaver shrugged, pulled a face of incomprehension. She wouldn't meet his eyes: she returned to the table, picked up the box of matches, stretched to unhook the lamp and walked through into the sitting room. He followed. She had hung the lamp from another chain and was already kneeling by the fireplace. There were split logs in a box, but no kindling wood, no paper, no firelighters. She worked rapidly and precisely, arranging the logs so that three splintered corners were almost touching, then two more above.

The dog arrived and stretched out as if there were already a fire. Cleaver put her glass on the mantlepiece. The smoky light made everything interesting and rather attractive. He sat in the armchair opposite Olga while the girl kneeled and worked. She struck a match. Moving his head he saw she was letting it burn right to her fingertips. At the third match, the flame caught. The three splintered corners began to burn together. The girl stood and turned. Again there was a concern in her eyes. Danke schön, he said. And then: Ich habe eine Tochter . . . he didn't know how to say, the same age as yourself, which wouldn't even have been true. She had noticed the doll now. Pretty, Cleaver said at once, nicht wahr? Sie heisse, Olga. The girl picked up her beer, looked at it and drained it in a gulp. She was ready to go.

Wie heisst du? Cleaver asked. He was aware of the challenge of convincing her to stay. Bier? Another glass? He motioned to Olga's seat. Ich heisse, Harry, he said. Harry is easier than Harold, he thought. The girl hesitated, puzzled. She is not used to invitations, Cleaver decided. She crouched by the dog again. Behind her the fire had begun to disturb the room with its flickering light. Cleaver stood up, took her glass and went back into the kitchen to refill it. It was almost dark here. How strange all this is, your first night at six-thousand feet and you are pouring drinks for a young woman.

Back in the sitting room everything was changed now in the fluid glow of the fire. Wie heisst du? he insisted. Seffa, she said. For one second she looked him in the eye. She was afraid.

Seffa?

Jo.

She looked away. She is not stupid, he decided. He couldn't think now what to say. The fire spat out an ember and the dog grumbled. The girl brushed a hand across the animal's coat. For the first time, a vague smile crossed her face.

Ist Uli dein Hund? he asked again.

Nein, she said. Nein.

She took the dog's snout between her hands and ruffled his fur and began speaking what sounded like baby-talk, her face close to the creature's foul breath. Then very slowly and clearly she said: Aber er schläft in meinem Zimmer.

Cleaver watched. He recognised that over-generous physicality, the rough, exaggerated affection people give to animals. Frau Stolberg was too old to be the girl's mother, he realised. Was it the town-dressed woman? Seffa! she had shouted running into the cemetery.

Ist Jürgen dein Vater? he asked.

The girl looked up from the dog, narrowing her eyes and biting a lip in almost pantomime fashion. She stood up. Then she remembered the beer, crouched down, picked it up off the floor and again drained it in one. From the rush of words she was speaking he picked up Nach Hause . . . zurück gehen. Uli!

Cleaver followed her through the dark kitchen. Where's my hat, I wonder? he thought. It had somehow become an important part of his image of himself living alone in the mountains, a broad-brimmed, grey hat. Where have I put it?

The girl picked up her torch from the table but didn't turn it on as she walked out into the raw air. Her arse is monumental Cleaver thought, but already familiarity had removed that earlier sense of the grotesque. Seffa, he called. She turned. Es gibt, he struggled for words, ein Zimmer, erm . . . Hoch, he pointed up to the little window in the timber above the kitchen. Ein Zimmer geschlossen. Ich kann nicht . . . He made the gesture of turning a key. She was looking at him. Warum? he finished.

Verstehe nicht, she said. She seemed alarmed, turned away.

Achtung, Cleaver pointed, Scheisse! But the girl hadn't heard. She hurried off up the track without turning on her torch.

It was curious, Cleaver thought later, how completely this encounter with the girl had calmed him down. She had returned him to his ordinary, recognisable self: a hospitable, middle-aged man. It was a relief really that she was fat. On the hard narrow bed opposite the locked door he listened to the noise the wind was making in the trees. Perhaps I will have to sleep with my earplugs: that would be ironic, above the noise line. Nice young lady, he had told Olga, returning to the sitting room with a second bottle of beer. He had sat by the fire, toasting his cold feet while the logs burned through. Not that she could remotely be compared with you, my dear, physically. If there was a rule Cleaver had learned it was never to praise one girl to another. Olga's glassy eyes glinted in the firelight. Fortunately, she had no problems with self-esteem. She was unwavering, Cleaver saw, in her Tyrolese pride.

He sipped his beer, staring at the coals. You are curious about that family, he realised later, trying the locked door again before retiring to bed. It was something, he thought, that my son simply refused to acknowledge when he criticised the way I analysed his friends: I am curious. For anyone who read that stupid book, it would seem I had fucked all those women, or appeared on television, out of sheer vanity. Sometimes, his elder son had written, my father would have three or even four women on the go at the same time. But you had no idea of the nature of those relationships, Cleaver protested out loud, the hours of conversation. Did I go to bed with them, perhaps, he wondered, because it was the best way of finding out about their lives? Of possessing their secrets? No, Cleaver shook his big head on the pillow, I went to bed with them to fuck them. He chuckled. But not only. The truth was, his elder son had written, that my father seemed to fear he would cease to exist if he didn't see himself reflected in a young woman's eyes, preferably at the moment of orgasm, just as he feared he might melt into thin air if his image wasn't constantly present on the country's television screens. He always had at least three or four shows and documentaries on the go. It wasn't the truth at all, Cleaver protested. I was genuinely curious. That was all.

Then an alien thought crossed his mind. An idea is breaking in. He recognised that special alertness, that peculiar mix of excitement and anxiety: After Angela died, they were all daughters to you. The fat man lay rigidly still on the old Nazi's bed. Somewhere a branch was fretting against the timbers of the house. I will need my earplugs, he decided. That's why it had never been serious again, after Angela. Or not in the same way. They were daughters. I could write a book, Cleaver had often reflected, *100 Biographies*, or almost, detailing all these women's problems. I talked to them for hours about their futures, their boyfriends, their jobs. I still have it all in my head. Certainly, his elder son had written, my father had far more time for his string of sluts than he ever did for us.

Rummaging in the dark, Cleaver eventually found the box with his earplugs in a side pocket of the suitcase. I must keep them within reach of the bed. But no sooner was the world muffled and hushed, his head on the pillow again, than he became intensely conscious of his isolation, six-thousand feet up in the neck of this wild gorge. I'm utterly alone, Cleaver whispered. The thought induced a primitive alertness. Perhaps it's dangerous to wear earplugs here. But what danger could there be? Now he found himself picturing, as if on some topographical relief model, first Luttach in relation to Bruneck, then Bruneck to Bolzano, then Bolzano to Milan, and finally, on a larger map, Milan in relation to London, to Chelsea, to Amanda. A thousand miles. But that was nothing. It was the winding track from Luttach to Trennerhof that did it, the long steep climb through wolfish pines and stone cliffs up and up to that high plateau, this tremendous gorge. The peasant family in the farmhouse cuts off your retreat, he whispered. Frau Stolberg blocks your return. And the old Nazi. It was a stupid idea. You are suspended here, in a bed at the top of a chasm. Gebirgsgeist. Thank God my feet are warm, he smiled. They were daughters, he thought, after Angela's death they were daughters. You could hardly expect your son to have grasped that. It was strange, though, the way the fat girl kept pulling at her ear lobe. For a moment Cleaver had a powerful sense of Seffa's presence as she drained her beer by the fireplace. Then he knew he would soon be asleep.

VII

THE MOST UNEXPECTED things returned to mind with disquieting urgency. The years of celebrity interviews, shooting scripts and political punditry melted away. I have no interest at all, Cleaver woke up to find, in the fate of Tony Blair. The Booker was already won or lost. Very shortly, he realised, I will not even know who is the President of the United States. I must prepare for the winter, he thought. On the second day of his stay at Rosenkranzhof he discovered the memorial to Ulrike Stolberg. That was also the day he recovered his hat.

He had achieved a great deal in his first twenty-four hours. He had risen early, eaten a full bowl of cereal and christened, so to speak, the outdoor lavatory with reassuring promptness. In a tiny wooden shed at the opposite end of the clearing an old loo seat had been fixed on some kind of metal cylinder, with, to judge by the splash, a fairly deep hole beneath. Re-emerging, still clutching the toilet roll, Cleaver surveyed his property. The gables of the house were dwarfed by the high stone cliff behind. The coarse grass is soaked with dew. To his left the landscape plunged into the gorge where, far below, a procession of small white clouds meandered south between wooded slopes towards Luttach. To his right the track climbed round the house and the cliff through the pines to the high plateau and Trennerhof. For perhaps half an hour, when it rose above the mountains on the eastern side of the gorge, the autumn sun cast a slanting ray that grazed the cliff face above the house and gave its grey surface a buttery glow. The white branches beneath the eaves gleamed like bones. Then it circled behind the rock, leaving Rosenkranzhof in deep shadow, and it was only towards mid afternoon that it sent another obliquely angled beam into the clearing for perhaps twenty minutes before disappearing behind the high western mass of the Schwarzstein. Who would have built a house, Cleaver wondered, in a place that received so little sunlight? He discovered a hencoop together with the stacked firewood on the clearing side of the house. The wood is protected under an old tarpaulin. Amanda, he remembered, was always very attentive to the question of sunlight when they were renting and later purchasing houses. I could keep a couple of chickens, he thought, and have an egg a day, for protein.

The dog returned while he was at work cutting away the remaining trees that rattled their branches against the windows on the gorge side. Cleaver set about his task with a more practical eye this morning, calculating angles, measuring distances, choosing his footing with extreme care on the rocky slope. When the trees were down, he began sawing off their branches, hauling them out piece by piece to the flat clearing, chopping up the slim trunks to add to the firewood. It was exhausting work for a fat man in his mid-fifties. He kept dragging his shirtsleeve across his forehead. The old saw-blade was rusty. His soft hands were soon blistered. I should have brought work gloves, he told himself, not mittens for the cold.

Then suddenly the dog was at his heels, yapping and

whining. Alex! Cleaver was pleased. He hadn't thought of his son's book all morning. What is a book in the economy of a long and busy life like mine? Not Alex, Uli, he decided. Uli, here Uli! It was a she. The dog stuck his nose between his knees and wriggled. When he stopped for lunch, Cleaver gave the animal a bite of sausage. He considered tackling the lump of cheese that Jürgen had given him, but didn't feel quite ready for this initiation. The advantage of a house with no sunlight, he decided, is that you really don't need a fridge. He remembered the smell in the little dairy at Trennerhof. Amanda would never have chosen this place, he thought.

In the afternoon he cleaned the windows, one upstairs, two down. I haven't cleaned a window since I was a boy after extra pocket money. The water was channelled to the house on hollowed-out logs from a tiny stream in the woods above and beyond the cliff. A hosepipe brought it down the rock face, through the roof, to a tank above the sink in the kitchen. Hence the constant trickling and gurgling. It enters at the bottom of the tank, rises to an overflow and disappears down another pipe that empties, Cleaver supposed, some yards below in the gorge. He couldn't find any rags. He used a dishcloth he had brought himself and washing-up liquid. There was an old tin bucket in the cave under the stairs. The water is icy and the glass cheap and thin. Even clean, it seemed opaque. How tiring it is to be constantly raising your arms above your head! He felt a pain in his shoulder, perhaps my chest. He was sweating again. Living this life, you can't not get slim. How my friends will marvel. Cleaver laughed. He even whistled. It was some old signature tune. At least I haven't imagined the camera zooming in, he thought. I haven't spoken into an imaginary microphone.

Towards evening he lit the stove. He tried to light it. It was hard to understand how the girl had got those three logs to burn last night. You should keep the stove alight all the time, he realised. You must always be able to keep warm. Eventually, he used half a toilet roll and a cardboard box and almost choked on the smoke. It billowed into the kitchen. There were levers to pull and push for the chimney and the ventilation. Why didn't Hermann explain all this? For a few moments he could barely see. He was running to open door and window. These people couldn't imagine a life without wood stoves, an adult who wasn't familiar with such things.

At dusk, he sat by the fireplace in the main room with Uli and ate bread and apples. He has brought two boxes of apples. They give the house a good smell. Tomorrow, I will cook, he announced. Perhaps one day I may even bake something. The stove seemed to have a baking oven. Could I manage a pie? But for some reason he was thinking of Amanda's gardening gloves. She kept them in a basket on the windowsill outside the kitchen. You don't look much of a gardener, Cleaver said conversationally to Olga, his mouth full of apple. Though obviously the doll was dressed for high holiday; I'm not seeing her in her ordinary clothes. Amanda was extremely attentive to a house's exposition to sunlight, Cleaver again remembered, and later in life became an avid gardener. *Under His Shadow* mentioned none of this. It is in the way you cut and edit, his elder son had written, or so my father would always maintain when he held forth about his documentaries, that you turn reality into a good story, and a lie. Touché, Cleaver thought. He imagined an obituary note: Over the winter of 2004 Mr Cleaver took time out from his work at the BBC, before returning to head the newsroom at a moment of exciting change and development. He smiled. These days and months will be edited out from the story they make of my life. Assuming anyone bothers. Occasionally, when there was some heavy job to be done, Amanda had bothered her partner to get involved. The patch in the corner behind the horse chestnut needs digging over, Harry. There are some bricks underneath to get out. Cleaver always refused: I don't have time. Hire a gardener, he told her. Amanda never would. There were all kinds of gardening projects she couldn't undertake, she complained, because her non-husband was also a non-gardener. He wouldn't help her. He's completely useless with his hands, so clumsy and impractical. This wasn't actually true. Like my famous impotence. It was the kind of thing she loved to laugh about when they had guests to Saturday-evening barbecues. She would walk them round the lawn, cheerfully pointing and complaining, wry and seductive, while Cleaver sat at the table just inside the French window, pouring out wine for the male company, telling stories, holding court. Here, for example, she would say, we really need a big trellis to hold up these roses, but Harry just won't be bothered. He has no sense of the complete picture. Will you, Harry? She brought her friends back to the table. My elder son missed the pathos of this, Cleaver reflected. And the perversity. Nothing would have been easier for Amanda than to find a gardener. Though of course he did dedicate a whole chapter to my garden shed-cum-office in Wandsworth. Then Cleaver reflected: was it after Angela died that Amanda's gardening became obsessive? He hadn't made this connection before. She dug in. She buried herself.

The dog suddenly pricked up his ears. His rheumy eyes gleamed in the yellow light of the oil lamp. Cleaver listened: Uli! It was a faint cry. Oo-li! The animal whined. Cleaver stood up, went to the kitchen in the half dark and opened the door. It seemed the girl didn't care about the dog during the day, but she wanted him there at night to sleep in her room. The creature trotted off into the gloom. Oo-li! The distant voice was plangent. It can't be much fun for a seven-teen-year-old at Trennerhof. Cleaver was sorry she hadn't come down to talk to him. He wondered if the name Seffa was short for something more recognisable. I can't connect it with anything. Seffa, Jürgen, Frau Stolberg, Hermann, Uli, the town woman, the bead-telling spectre in her black headscarf: they were from another planet. This may be the first day in your whole life, Cleaver realised then, that you haven't talked to a single soul, barring Olga of course, beg your pardon. He made a little bow. And not a great deal even to yourself, he reflected. Soul! Cleaver smiled. He picked up a whisky bottle from the shelf and a grey glass and went back into the sitting room. So what was your son's book all about in the end? he asked out loud, settling into his armchair. What shape did the lad cut out of the whole? Or did he intend to cut? Cleaver filled his glass to the brim and stared into the fire.

There were three sections to *Under His Shadow*, as he recalled. You are now going to think about this with the utmost calm and detachment, Cleaver decided. Part one, part two, part three. That will be a major victory. Get it out of the way. He picked up a log from the box and placed it in the centre of the fire. How fine it was to watch the little flames licking at their new prey! And how compulsive. Once a fire is lit you have to watch it. Perhaps the success of television, Cleaver wondered, had largely depended on the banning of coal and wood fires in built-up areas. The rise of the one form of enchantment, after all, was almost contemporary with the decline of the other. And it was curious, he decided, how much better logs crackled together, in threes and fours, as if collab-orating, or at least twos, whereas the one log alone seemed doomed to do no more than smoke and smoulder. Certainly more interesting than a stock market report.

But don't digress! Cleaver protested out loud. He took a

sip of his whisky. The supermarket in Luttach stocked various brands that appeared to be Scottish, but whose names Cleaver had never heard of before. Flintock's Gold. My father, he remembered his elder son had written – but this was in the last part of the book – was the supreme master of digression. At dinner-table conversation he would routinely prevent any contentious debate from reaching a climax. He hated confrontations, showdowns. One moment you were animatedly discussing nuclear disarmament, and the next, quite suddenly, what mattered were the lyrics of some new Leonard Cohen song, or the increasing number of ladies' underwear shops on Kensington High Street. It was like the three-card trick. No one could ever quite understand where the issue you had been following had disappeared, or how. My father had spirited it away. He had defused whatever clash was brewing. It's filling up time that matters, he liked to say, not deciding how it ought to be filled. He prided himself on a sort of jolly inconsequentiality that in the end was no more than a token of his failure to establish any principle or behave in any way consistent with his responsibilities. When everything is meaningless, what responsibilities can you have? The shape of the whole, Cleaver interrupted himself. He had had that passage on his mind as he went to confront the President of the United States. Concentrate on the shape of the whole, the way the boy cut it, the meaning he meant to give to the whole thing. Part one, part two, part three . . .

Cleaver drained his whisky. The first eighty or so pages had offered, he recalled, as if through a Vaseline-smeared lens, a sort of caricature version of the family's myths and legends. The voice was what critics like to call fresh, ingenuous, the child marvelling innocently at the world he is discovering, while for his or her part the reader understands all kinds of things between the lines: unpleasant things, needless to say, disquieting harbingers of the inevitable disillusion, the unhappy melodrama that every narrative hungers for.

In the first part I come over as a sort of Lord of Misrule, Cleaver told Olga. It occurred to him that perhaps after all he should have brought the book away with him and studied it a little more carefully, though without my glasses of course I can't read anything at all. Not only have I not spoken today, Cleaver now realised, but I haven't read anything either. Not a word. Or heard anyone else speak a word. He and Amanda were presented, in these opening chapters, as the rather comic, larger-than-life protagonists of some upmarket, metropolitan sitcom, glamorous, selfish and endearingly vain, always in need of an admiring audience of celebrity guests, entirely absorbed in the love-hate fizz of a relationship that had them constantly shouting, chucking around the crockery, slamming down the phone and muttering disruptive criticisms to their innocent children of the variety, your father is an absolute pig, that woman will drive me mad, and so on, though without ever arriving at any clarifying showdown. Actually it isn't true I haven't read a word, Cleaver thought. At least a dozen times, he had stared at the black Gothic lettering over the front door: Rosenkranzhof. While he was crapping, for example. The house of the rosary. There seemed no point in closing the loo door. I could hold the beads in my hands, Cleaver thought, and count off my son's lies.

These were the pages that dealt with family holidays, one year in Scotland, where Mother was from, the mythical Galloway, one year in Wales, where my father was from, the mythical Pembrokeshire. Two myths that seemed as incompatible, Cleaver's elder son had written, as Hinduism and Islam, two different worlds that met in a shower of sparks along a line of barbed wire. My father hated Galloway and all the time driving up on the M6 he would take the piss in a fake Scottish accent pretending to be some drunken tartan nationalist. The funnier he was, the more he drove my mother crazy. Were we really such clowns? Cleaver wondered. In the third or fourth chapter his son had described a pact with Angela: the two of them had pricked their thumbs and mixed their blood: Twins Against Strife, they had called themselves: We were all the closer because our parents never stopped arguing.

Cleaver leaned forward, took the bottle from the mantle-piece and refilled his glass. Was that really true? A little left of centre the stone ledge had been broken and a missing chunk replaced with some rough grey plaster. There seemed to be all kinds of these little repairs around the house: wire twisted round the hosepipe where it entered the tank, a leg of the table in a different wood, a patch darned into the upholstery of the armchair, one side of a window frame replaced. Hadn't the twins argued all the time? Cleaver tried to remember. Like any children. Hadn't they also thrown things at each other? He recalled a place where the wallpaper was damaged by a flying shoe. Aged ten or so, his son had been a chubby, taci-turn boy with a big backside and an admirably tidy bedroom, while Angela was a wiry firecracker of irritability and chaos. The book constantly spoke of we twins, but never the fact that they were not of course identical. They were no more genetically alike than any other brother and sister.

Still, Cleaver hadn't minded the first section of *Under His Shadow*. On the contrary. It was good fun. The piss-taking over my famous masterpiece was fair enough. Daddy's in his shed writing his masterpiece! That was how we twins would answer the phone. I can take my fair share of mockery, Cleaver thought. There was even a sort of Falstaffian dash about the father figure, an earthy merriment to his crimes. Amanda was portrayed as a good foil: dour, petulant, lovably unreasonable.

There was the story of how she had emptied a washing-up bowl over a pretty young French journalist whom she had imagined was flirting with her non-husband. The dirty water came complete, his elder son had written, with slimy bacon rind and potato peelings that clung to the lady's blonde hair and one or two items of cutlery that clattered in her lap.

Cleaver smiled. Cutlery that clattered in her lap was good. Even the ancient hearthrug, he noticed, unlacing his boots to warm his feet, had been carefully repaired. Tell me about your family, he asked Olga. The doll, as always, was gaping over his shoulder at the stuffed bird. One of the eagle's wings had been broken and was held up with two thin sticks, like a First War aeroplane. Were its eyes real, or beads like Olga's? Veiled with dust, they stared across the room, searching for some unimaginable prey. Perhaps there are mice in the house, Cleaver thought. I mustn't leave food around. The old Nazi had worked hard, he decided, to stop the rot. Why had he come to live here on his own? For fifteen years. Why hadn't the family taken him back, when he was near the end, when he couldn't keep the trees from the windows? When we moved to the house in Wandsworth, his elder son had written, since there wasn't a room for my father to have a study where he could write his masterpiece, he built himself, or rather he had someone build for him, a large and rather superior shed at the bottom of the garden. It was one of those long, narrow South London gardens about five yards wide by forty long. He put a desk in, covered the walls with bookshelves, set up his stereo and dug a little trench down the side of the lawn for phone and electricity cables. The wires were hooked up to plugs in the kitchen. So there would be Mother, standing over the sink, looking directly down the garden, and my father, behind his desk in the shed, looking directly up it, forty yards apart, and us twins playing in the middle, trying to defuse their two hostile gazes. To tell my father dinner was ready, Mum just pulled the plugs on his phone and electricity. I don't know why I can't have my own study, she would complain to whoever the day's guest was. My job is actually rather more remunerative than Harry's. Isn't it, my love? She was editing the cultural pages of the *Guardian* at the time. It's because you don't have to write a masterpiece, Mum, one of us twins would say, gravely, and everybody burst out laughing. Actually, we're thinking of having a section of the Berlin Wall shipped over to ornament the centre of the garden, my father would remark, pouring wine into big tumblers. My father never pissed about with wine glasses. I was at Heal's the other day, Mother would say, to see if they had a desk that folded out into a double bed. Then we could send him down his food with a cable and winch. Almost every dinner time, a different set of guests would be given an exhibitionist display of my father's and mother's interminable warfare. Just when everybody was convinced they really were splitting up, Caroline was born. And then Phillip.

Rosenkranzhof is a bit more than a shed at the bottom of the garden, Cleaver reflected. The expression, piss about with wine glasses, was infelicitous to say the least. And this time no one can intimidate me by disconnecting phone and electricity. How cold my feet would get in that shed, he remembered. His son's book had had nothing to say about that, nothing to say about the long evenings and grim weekends working at innumerable articles and scripts and programme proposals in two sweaters, an overcoat and a woolly hat. Where have I left my hat? He had always had problems of poor circulation, even back then in his thirties. Why did the old Nazi come here, Cleaver wondered, instead of moving down to Luttach, or to another town altogether? The truth is, I never risked more than so much time on a masterpiece. And what if Frau Stolberg were the man's sister, not his wife? Has anyone actually said she was his wife? Wasn't it curious that even at the end, they hadn't taken him back to Trennerhof? They left him to die here. You're inventing now, Cleaver warned himself. Quite probably the man was fit as a fiddle until his stroke or heart attack.

No, all things considered, he had no quarrel with the first part of the book. There was a sort of generosity and indulgence to the way his own and Amanda's lives had been caricatured in a string of grotesque anecdotes. The reader knew there must be more to it. It was light comedy. But the births of Caroline and Phillip introduced a change of tone. The second section was characterised by a note of scandal and denunciation, even though, oddly enough, the two younger children hardly ever came in for a mention, were never described physically, given no dialogue at all. The whole book, perhaps, is the older child's proverbial lament at being replaced in his father's affections by the younger, Cleaver announced. Could that be true? Olga wasn't interested. Certainly Phillip was the best looking of the children. But almost at once he was again remembering that observation: My father always understood more from any conversation than you had actually put into it, always discovered dishonourable motives you had never imagined. You set out to discuss some problem you were having, or maybe you were just looking for some intimacy, and invariably you came away feeling you were mentally ill, you were acting perversely, you needed help.

Cleaver frowned at the fire, poured and drank off a third whisky. His damp socks have grown warm and smelly. On the other hand it would be crazy not to try to understand, wouldn't it, not to try to get below the surface? Wasn't there something pathological about an old man abandoning his wife to go and live only a mile or so away in the gloom of an Alpine gorge? You wanted to understand. There is a story there. You asked yourself: was it because the wife insisted on living with her ancient mother? That was banal. Amanda had made sure her own mother went into a home. And Jürgen and Seffa? Wasn't there something pathological about a seventeen-year-old girl who sought out her grandfather's decrepit dog to sleep with? But perhaps she wasn't a member of the family at all. How do I know? Perhaps just a maid. You tried to understand, even when you knew that any explanation would be reductive. Isn't that precisely what my son has done with me? He tried to understand and reduced things to a farce.

Cleaver got to his feet and padded round the room. The anxiety is returning. His toasted toes are at once cold on the stone floor. Stupid doll. He hurried up the stairs, brought down a blanket and dropped it over Olga's head. Looking up, he met the eagle's predatory gaze in the yellow light of the oil lamp. How dim it is in here! The eyes gleamed. Like some candlelit chapel. The eagle was the symbol of the Third Reich of course. Cleaver picked up the doll and the blanket, carried them through to the kitchen and dumped them on the table. I must wipe the crumbs off, or I'll have mice about. An eagle is an eagle, not a symbol. A dead bird. He noticed the photograph again. Bozen, Polizeiregiment. That was another word he had read two or three times today. If the old Nazi had served in the polizeiregiment, then he must have been at least eighteen in 1945, which meant that in September 2004 he was definitely pushing, what, eighty? Was Frau Stolberg old enough to be his sister? Phillip, Cleaver remembered, was a full twelve years younger than the twins. Frau Stolberg looked around seventyish. She could be wife or sister.

Yes, the second section of the book – Cleaver went back into the sitting room – combined an unhappy coming-to-adolescent-consciousness with a denunciation of the cause of that unhappiness: Harold Cleaver, of course. Seduced by the comic clarity of the first section, lured into actually liking this self-regarding master of revels, the reader was now invited to witness the gruesome consequences of his ugly, disordered life and recoil in horror. The section built up through the narrator's increasingly troubled adolescence, his problems with first sex, his many identity crises and profound disillusionment (all ascribable to the disturbingly lax and increasingly contentious atmosphere of the Cleaver-Cunningham household), to climax in the tragedy of his twin sister's death.

It's a lie, Cleaver announced firmly, pouring himself a fourth and very large whisky. The other armchair seemed disturbingly empty now. Granted, any explanation is reductive, but over Angela's death his elder son hadn't even tried to find the truth. It is a deliberate distortion, Cleaver shouted. You can't blame a road accident on your mother's and father's turbulent relationship!

He went back into the kitchen, picked up the blanket and the doll, brought the doll back to her chair, set her down – Look at me, damn you! – then sat himself down and covered his knees with the blanket. The evening was turning colder. Olga was still not really looking at him. A doll is a doll. What if, Cleaver suddenly demanded, Rosenkranzhof were haunted by some survivor of the Bozen Polizeiregiment, some frustrated old Nazi Gebirgsgeist determined to possess the new occupant's mind. How silly. He drained the whisky. The second section of *Under His Shadow* could basically be summarised as follows: My mother and my father, but above all my father, who was a special and rather subtle kind of tyrant, were chiefly responsible for my and my twin's directionlessness and desperation, our inability to look confidently to the future.

Cleaver felt a little dazed by the suddenness with which this unfamiliar whisky was now rising to the brain. However inadequate a story is, he thought, or simply downright mendacious, it always adheres to the mind, even the mind of the person who knows it has been made up. This is the scandal of all scandal-mongering, is it not? Even when you know that something had been made up, all the same a trace is laid down in the mind. Mud sticks. Whereas even the worst hangovers wear off in twenty-four hours. He vaguely recalled a very sad tale about incest and child abuse that he had covered for some paper in the early days. A man accused of an act of paedophilia – that was it – had confessed and committed suicide, even though, as it later emerged, he couldn't possibly have been guilty. He had allowed himself to be persuaded by his daughter's supposed reconstructions under hypnosis. Probably he knew the story wasn't true, but he also knew it was true enough.

Write a rebuttal, Amanda had told her partner. She had watched Cleaver closely in those forty-eight hours he was reading the book, the forty-eight hours before the legendary and extremely confrontational interview with the President of the United States. He had barely slept. Any self-respecting mythology, he reflected, has at least two contradictory versions of events. I didn't realise it at the time, Cleaver thought now, but I was under close observation; Amanda was watching me as I read what my son had written, what she had told him about me, knowing that he would write it down. I was the object of an experiment. I was exhausted. Write a rebuttal, Harry. She was forceful. She wanted a confrontation. Sue the shit, if that's how you feel. Yet only the day before she had been proud of her son and his Booker listing. The truth is, Cleaver told Olga excitedly, that while my son imagined that he was declaring his independence writing this book, assumed that he was cutting himself off from the family and cutting me down to size, in reality he was being manipulated by his mother who hoped to spark off a father-son conflict in the midst of which she would become my ally again. Do you see? How about that for a twist? You always came away, his elder son had written, with the fear that your subconscious motivation had been quite different from what you supposed. Cleaver pushed his feet into his boots, crossed the kitchen, dragged open the front door and walked out of Rosenkranzhof into the night.

Why was it that the places I found to escape from Amanda were always so cold? And me with my poor circulation! He remembered coming out of the shed in Wandsworth, shivering, looking through pelting rain to the windows of the warm house where she would be researching some article or other while shouting at the younger children to go to bed. My feet froze in that shed. He typed with gloves cut off at the fingertips and used a laptop so Amanda wouldn't be able to pull the plug on his work. It was my icy feet forced me back home. For as long as I can remember, his elder son had written, in the second part of his book, my mother and father slept not just in separate beds, but in separate rooms. Tonight, at six-thousand feet, the air was chill and very damp with heavy cloud cover. It was cunning of the boy to have waited until the second part to introduce this sad truth, waited until the adolescent narrator was old enough to be upset by this thought of his parents' separateness. Later, when we had a bigger house, they even made a point of sleeping on separate floors. Though, more often than not, Cleaver remembered, having finished working in the shed I would sneak through the passage round the side of the house, get in the car and drive off to some pub or other. Now, having zipped up his jacket, he touched the red beads on the door of the remote Rosenkranzhof. They were draped in a string over two rusty nails. Who had put them there? He turned and started to walk. He hasn't brought his torch with him. There are no stars, he realised, looking up into the gloom. I need to clear my head.

He crossed the flat space outside the house and picked up the track, but in the other direction, away from Trennerhof. You are mad to do this without a torch. As soon as he was among the trees beyond the lavatory, the night was as dark as it had been the previous evening when he was returning from the aborted phone call. The concentration will force you to calm down, Cleaver decided. Your eye will adjust, he told himself.

Almost at once, the track shrank to a strip of stony path that seemed to follow the flat ledge of the clearing as it narrowed around the mountainside to his left. Suddenly, there was a very unpleasant smell. Cleaver stumbled and propped himself up against a tree. Could it be a dead rat, or bird? He held his breath, stretched his foot out carefully. The third section of *Under His Shadow*, it came to him, was a different cup of tea altogether. The gloves were off. The path was taking a downward turn, Cleaver noticed. The smell was left behind. He took one step at a time, setting his feet down carefully among the roots and stones. By this point his son's book had become a savage satire of the father's ideas, a ferocious denunciation of his squalid philandering, a ruthless mockery of his constant presence in the media and supposedly pathological vanity. Amanda dropped out of the picture. Likewise Caroline and Phillip and the now dead Angela. Cleaver definitely remembered that his elder son had used the word pathological somewhere. My father, he had written, was now incapable of not mentioning to every Tom, Dick and Harry who came to dinner all his successes, all the famous people he had recently met on terms of great familiarity. It was *pathological*.

Where does this lead? Cleaver wondered, standing in the pitch dark. A path always leads somewhere, doesn't it? He couldn't remember any of the routine red-and-white signs, the various finger-markers that the Tyrolese tourist board provided for enterprising ramblers. He would arrive at another Rosenkranzhof, perhaps, another gloomy, isolated Alpine hut complete with its own reclusive, geriatric occupant. Or some improbable Stube, some remote mountain hostel. You see a light through the trees and, peering in through a steamy window, you glimpse Hermann with all his friends playing cards in their blue work shirts and banging their beer mugs on the table. Or a chapel perhaps? People build remote chapels in the mountains.

Cleaver stumbled again. His foot had caught a root. He put his hands down to break the fall. No damage done. No doubt it was for this third section, he thought, that they had put the boy on the Booker list. There were no paragraph breaks, no apparent organisation, but quote after quote of Cleaver's aphorisms mixed with detail after squalid detail, generously italicised, of his disordered life. Where had the boy got this stuff from? All very avant-garde. A fizz of fornication, gluttony and exhibitionism, he had written. Evidently, he liked the word fizz. It's fiction, Dad, he would protest if I phoned him. Amanda was little more than a zombie at this point of the tale, a victim long since drained of blood and energy. Not true at all! It was she who had fed the boy all these apocryphal details. The younger siblings, his elder son had written, to all intents and purposes grew up as orphans, dumb beasts in an ideological slaughterhouse. That is truly horrible prose, Cleaver thought. It's so easy to write like that, in a constant stream of overheated indignation. What the public saw, his son had written, was an eloquent, talented man, as witty as he was charmingly overweight: they could not imagine the darkness that this engaging celebrity cast around himself in his private life, like some all-embracing octopus squirting his black ink into your eyes.

Oh please! Cleaver shouted. Spare us the octopus analogy! What in God's name does the boy have against me? I spent enough time with him, didn't I? He wasn't neglected. But Cleaver had been terribly agitated reading this third section. Your hands are trembling, Amanda had remarked, watching him hold the book at the breakfast table. She was curious. He was under observation. Really, I would need to look at it again, Cleaver thought. It was strange, it occurred to him now, how in reality his son had already left home for university some months before Angela died, and hence well before the period covered so aggressively in this third section. We didn't see very much of each other at all in those years. Whereas in the book it was as if father and son were constantly together, constantly inhabiting each other's minds in a sort of furious and exhausting wrestling match. As if the boy hadn't left home at all. I did my best, Cleaver remembered, to get him a good start in life. What I said about the meaninglessness of the work I did, the work he aspired to do, was no more nor less than what I believed, what I am now at last acting on. The opposite of vanity, in fact. His criticisms of my sex life seem desperately immature for a man who is after all in his thirties now. Some people are born philanderers and that is that. Women understand these things. The boy was jealous no doubt.

All at once, Cleaver sensed a different quality to the darkness. There are no trees he realised. The ground is flatter. There had been a change of smell too. The air is fresh. There's a breeze. Lifting his foot to take a step, Cleaver stopped and stared. His eyes pressed against the darkness.

Then, exactly in the spot where he was about to set down his considerable weight, he saw a light. It was as if he caught the gleam of an eye gazing up from directly beneath him; *an eye is looking up at you from the ground, from beneath the ground.* Cleaver stepped back. *I'm hallucinating.* Then he understood it was a prick of light from far, far below. A thousand feet and more. He was on the edge of a precipice.

Shocked, he went down on his haunches. *Why did nobody warn you of this danger?* He felt dizzy. *Because nobody expects a sane adult to go strolling about the mountains at night without so much as a torch. You are not a sane adult,* Cleaver told himself. He must turn round and get back. *This isn't Kilburn or Wandsworth or Chelsea where you can just go out to a pub if your thoughts become unmanageable.*

Still crouching, he backed a little further from the drop. Inexplicably, the path was hard to find. A faint luminosity possessed the emptiness beyond the ledge, but the wood was impenetrable. Then, to his left, apparently floating in the void, he saw a gallows. *It can't be.* Yet staring hard, Cleaver felt sure that a scaffold of some kind was just perceptible in the empty air, and some distance from the brink. *Not possible,* he decided. *These are symptoms of an advanced neurosis.* My father's death, his elder son had begun the last chapter of the third and last section of his novel, *was peculiarly Dantesque in its aptness. To cut a long story short he was hoist with the petard of his irrepressible desire to occupy that limelight he always pretended to disdain.*

Frightened, Cleaver concentrated on the dark wood. *Don't look into the abyss. Let your eyes get used to the dark.* He dropped to his knees and moved his hands slowly from side to side over twigs and pine needles. Then he heard someone moving. *Hello!* he called softly. *Uli! Seffa!* Turning round, he again saw the scaffold looming. *It's uncanny. Seffa!* He called. Hermann! At last, his arm discovered a space free of twigs and stones, a flat space of bare earth. Good.

He began to advance a few inches at a time, always placing the palm of his hand on the ground before he moved. Again he was convinced he heard footsteps. How can there be? You are the only living soul for a mile and more. Breathe deeply. Now is the moment for the victory of cool common sense over nightmare and panic. Very cautiously, Cleaver crawled forward and at once hurt his knee putting his weight on a pebble. Cool common sense would never find itself beside a precipice in the pitch dark.

My father was dining, abundantly of course, his elder son had begun the story, in the restaurant of one of London's most celebrated and expensive hotels – the occasion was some moment of corporate self-congratulation, a collection of BBC bigwigs celebrating their share in the BAFTA awards – when all at once word spread around the sumptuous tables that on the twenty-second floor of the hotel an elderly American businessman was holding his young musician wife hostage, at gun point, in their luxury suite; it seemed he was threatening to shoot her and then himself if she didn't change her mind about leaving him. Already aware, from a trip to the bathroom, of a camera crew setting up in reception to film the arrival of some top model or other, and seeing, as he apparently remarked to the Chairman of the Board who was sitting beside him, that here was the chance for a most extraordinary publicity coup, my father rounded up the camera troupe, Russians as it turned out, and, hurrying to get to the scene of the drama before the police arrived, took them up in the lift to the twenty-second floor, his intention being, he explained, to talk the elderly man into releasing the young woman at once. I know exactly what to say, my father apparently boasted, to a man in that state of mind.

Been there, he laughed, done that. I have all the T-shirts.

Why on earth, Cleaver wondered, resting his back against a tree in the pitch dark, had his son shifted the register of his book so dramatically in this last chapter? Why did my death have to be a farce? Above all, why did I have to be dispatched so quickly, one moment at dinner with the BBC Board, the next in my coffin more or less, as if the boy just couldn't wait to be rid of me? We are all glad he is dead, Hermann had said of the old Nazi. Words to that effect. Having progressed perhaps fifty yards and quite sure now that he was on the path, Cleaver felt a little safer. He was breathing evenly. The gallows would turn out to be some broken tree perched on an outcrop, he thought. Better dead, Hermann had laughed. The footsteps had been a hallucination, or the movement of some small animal, magnified by fear. My son deliberately shifted the book towards the surreal, he reflected, at the moment that was most evidently fiction: the death of a man whom readers would be seeing on TV, perhaps, the very day after finishing the book. That way, he could underline the supposed authenticity of all that had come before. How convoluted! Or did he just want to stress the symbolic content of this fictional death. My death. But what was the symbolic content?

Cleaver struggled to his feet. A few moments of inaction with his arse on the wet ground had made him stiff. His knees were bruised. I'm getting a chill on my neck again. Again he cast about for some kind of orientation. It is hard even to stand up straight in complete darkness. And then, come to think of it, it wasn't even true that readers would be seeing him on television the night after they had read the book, since I disappeared more or less the day it was officially published. I might perfectly well have been eliminated exactly as described as far as the general public was concerned.

Fortunately, there was thick vegetation here each side of the path. Dropping to his knees again, he could feel his way with his hands, the ground to the left dropping steeply into the gorge, to the right climbing up to the Schwarzstein. Nothing, Cleaver thought, had ever wiped out the effect of four whiskies quite so fast as the realisation that he was about to plunge into an abyss. Perhaps one whisky more and I wouldn't have noticed. I would be dead. My father, his elder son had written, at least if one is to take the word of those who ate with him that evening, had polished off at least a bottle and a half of burgundy, plus three or four large Laphroaigs before racing up to the twenty-second floor to have himself filmed saving the imprisoned musical damsel. Not that I would ever allow a small detail like blind drunkenness, he used to quip, get in the way of my better judgement.

This last part of the book, Cleaver recalled, was quite offensively facetious. Soon he should be smelling that unpleasant smell near the beginning of the path. Just rubbish someone dumped probably. I'll say a rosary, he told himself, rather oddly, as soon as I'm out of this. He had no idea how you said a rosary. He stopped. Why had his son chosen to make the young wife of the jealous elder husband a genius musician, after having entirely eliminated from the book any reference to Angela's music, to her genius at the keyboards? She was returning from a concert the day of the accident. Apparently it had been a triumph. The delirium that invests the older man with the much younger woman, my father told the camera crew in the lift – they spoke little English it seems but had already started filming – is the delirium and pathos of ultimate possession. He spoke as if reading from a script of one of his prize-winning documentaries. All the major channels showed the footage the following morning. This is my last romantic relationship, the older man tells himself, my father told the Russian film crew – despite the drink he seemed extremely professional – but also the only one where, by virtue of my greater power and experience, I most completely possess the object of my desire. It is as if he fuses sexual desire and fatherhood. Understand? The Russians didn't, but their equipment was recording; my father was holding forth. They had realised he was a famous man. Tenderness is overwhelming in these relationships, my father said gravely as the lift slowed down and a bell tinkled, but so likewise is the sense of loss when – and clearly he was timing what he said to coincide with the opening of the doors – when the young woman grows up and decides to strike out on her own.

Why on earth, Cleaver wondered, did my son bother to invent this improbable story: Cleaver in the lift talking to the Russian film crew? Couldn't he just have had Amanda, or some unhappy ex push me onto the rails in the Underground? Or a cancer or something. God knows, I'm overdue for a heart attack. The odd couple were in London, his elder son had written, for a concert that the child bride had performed the evening before to rapturous applause at the Festival Hall. How on earth did he expect me to react to this crap?

Crawling forward, reaching out to feel the ground to the right, Cleaver put his hand in something truly horrible. At the slightest pressure, what had seemed like wet pine needles gave way to putrid flesh. Was there a faint gleam of two eyes in the dark? The stench was overpowering. Why hadn't he smelt it yards away? At once Cleaver was on his feet, blundering through the trees, shaking the slime from his hand. A corpse. It must be some kind of corpse. A branch scratched his face. He banged his shoulder. Then at last he was out in the clearing. Rosenkranzhof appeared before him. He touched the beads on the door. Hail Mary full of grace. You are ridiculous, Cleaver snapped.

The oil lamp had gone out. The wick will be burned, damn it. Was there a spare wick? The embers in the fire are just glowing. Cleaver filled the sink with icy water and squirted washing-up liquid all over his hand. You chose this place too hastily, he told himself later, sitting by the fire again with another glass of whisky. You have always chosen everything too hastily, your lifetime partner, your job, as if nothing else would ever be offered. It's so draughty. You never reflected. Perhaps in the end it really wasn't so surreal to imagine that I would have been distracted from a heavy dinner by the prospect of rushing up to the twenty-second floor to talk a man out of harming his young musician wife. I'm so hasty. I don't think. On the other hand, it was one of the greatest achievements of your life, Cleaver told himself, when you finally crushed the desire for romantic love. Had his son sensed this?

The Russians' video, his elder son had written in the last chapter of *Under His Shadow*, shows my father talking softly and persuasively to a closed door with a luxury, black satin finish. From inside the room the microphone is picking up a woman sobbing. There is life after such loss, my father is saying quietly, presumably to the elderly husband behind. See it as a challenge, he is telling him. You have to change, even now, when life had seemed set in its ways. You have to break out of a spell, to find some other impetus. Behind the door the man is grunting. Let her go and she will learn to laugh with you in years to come, my father is saying. He has a very seductive voice. He beckons to the Russians for the camera to come closer. She'll love you in a different way. Beyond the door something scratches and clicks. Come closer, my father mouths to the camera crew. Perhaps a key is turning in the lock, the door is about to open. The lighting in the corridor is harsh neon over ochre carpeting. The crew haven't had time to set up auxiliary lights. You will have other relationships, my father is telling the jealous husband. That's life. However old we are, there is always the new meeting, you know, the new face. And she will be grateful to you, for letting go. You know? You will laugh together. At this point my father takes a step nearer to the door. Come on, why not open up now and chill out, before the police get here and you have to face unpleasant consequences. A woman screams, my father grabs the handle of the door. The camera zooms in, rather clumsily. And a shot rings out, and another and another, splintering through the door. The camera spins. You can just see blood splattering against the wall and ceiling.

What cheap cheap melodrama, Cleaver reflected, snuggling under his quilt to sleep. No harm done in the end, he decided. Bit of a wake-up call actually, nearly stepping into the void. You live and learn. At least my feet are warm. But what on earth was the boy thinking of? Killing me off like that. If it was a provocation, how was I supposed to react? By congratulating him on finishing the book with a bang? By complaining that I would have done a much better job of talking round the old obsessive?

Cleaver gazed across the deep shadow of the bedroom to the locked door where the Stolberg family had stored the old Nazi's stuff. God knows what decomposed beastie he had put his hand in. Amanda wanted me to fight, he decided. Perhaps that is what his son had wanted too. Some kind of determined bust-up about the past. But the boy could have had that any time just by picking up the phone and talking to me. In any event, I outwitted them, Cleaver decided, by disappearing. I beat them there, he smiled to himself, drifting surprisingly pleasantly towards sleep. It will be them having to come and find me, he congratulated himself. Not me them. The wonder was that it was taking them so long.

VIII

THERE IS NO mirror in Rosenkranzhof. Cleaver woke to find himself afflicted with the stiff neck he had expected the day before. He can barely turn his head to left or right. He lay in bed in the grey light, listening to the wind gusting against the panes. One of my father's great gifts in life, his elder son had written, was his ability to sleep whenever and wherever he chose. Because I always have a clear conscience, he inevitably quipped when Mother complained about her insomnia. And this in a way, Cleaver thought, was true. What could I ever be guilty of? Though it surprised him sometimes that he had never been punished. There was cold air shifting about the room, he noticed. It passed across his scalp. The house is full of draughts. I will have to go around blocking them out with strips of felt or plastic, the way old people do.

Massaging his neck, he realised he hadn't shaved for some days. What do I look like? He didn't want to go to Trennerhof for milk and give the impression he was already becoming some kind of wild man. But there's no mirror, he realised. His mind hunted round the house. There's no bathroom in the proper sense of the word. For years and years, evening after evening, Cleaver had sat in front of a bright mirror at the Wood Lane studios while one of the make-up girls carefully dabbed the veins and blush out of his nose and cheeks, turned a glistening home-baked treacle pudding, as his elder son had put it, into a sort of smooth, mass-produced sponge cake. So much for the wit of the shortlisted writer. This for the consumption of an ever more homogenised public, the book observed, with its characteristic note of righteous superiority. The boy missed the potential humour, Cleaver remembered, of their plucking the hairs from my nostrils, trimming my eyebrows, creaming my baldness so it wouldn't sweat.

He got out of bed, went over to the window, but found only a ghost of a reflection against the advancing day behind. He can't see himself. But why care about your appearance once you've chosen to live alone? The Trennerhof peasants are hardly a prime-time audience. Cleaver looked out over the gorge. The complex shift of colours, from the bright greys and greens of the upper slopes to the dark pine and shadow deep below, is growing familiar. Will I ever explore it? he wondered. And he wondered if there was a mirror in the room that was locked. Had the old Nazi looked after his appearance, out of an ancient vanity, perhaps, dreaming of some improbable return to society, to the days of the parade ground and the Bozen Polizeiregiment? Had he too suffered from a stiff neck?

Very carefully, Cleaver tried to move his head from side to side. Don't! To anyone who knew him only in his TV persona, his elder son had written, my father must have seemed entirely natural in his unflagging photogenic suavity; how could the viewers have imagined the effort this heavy eater, drinker and smoker had to make to project that single, reassuring image of himself?

Cleaver couldn't wear the same clothes he had worn yesterday. The trousers were filthy from crawling back up the path. Not to mention the sweat he had produced chopping up those trees. He opened the dusty cupboard. You have one London suit, plus three changes of the sort of shirts and trousers to be found in shops in Bruneck: chequered flannel and coarse brown denim. I shall have to heat saucepans of water to shave, and to wash my crotch and armpits, and to do the laundry. Unless I just put the same clothes back on and the hell with it. Was that a solution? This journey was supposed to be an exit from all effort, Cleaver reflected, the discovery of oceans of meditative space beyond the stress of family conflict and brilliant career. Now it seems all my creativity will have to go into the merest survival: what to heat the water in, where to string up a washing line. Or could I get used to stinking? He made a heap of his dirty clothes. Did the old Nazi take his laundry to Trennerhof? he wondered. Did he have his meals brought down for him? Still gazing out of the window, Cleaver imagined Seffa plodding down the track with a basket in her arms and Uli at her heels. The girl was fat, but not irretrievably ugly. MIT ESSEN, Frau Schleiermacher had written, 450 euros a month. Why didn't I accept? Cleaver was sure she had found him attractive. Husband or no husband. Damn, he shouted. Damn and damn. The only reason for your being here is that you live entirely and utterly alone. There must be no backsliding.

Holding his neck rigidly straight, Cleaver put on his last set of clean clothes. That a jacket is filthy hardly matters, he decided. Of course the milk hasn't been pasteurised, he reflected, tasting his cereal. It was faintly sour. He ate it anyway, contemplating the few objects that lay within his field of vision: the sooty stove, a witch's broom, his backpack and, moving his eyes but not his neck, the old photograph of the young soldiers in three long uniformed lines: a community, a fighting machine. Then the big man raised one ham. The invention of the atomic clock, his elder son had written, quoting Amanda of course, was superfluous, given the regularity of my father's bowel movements. Cleaver got to his feet. Big Ben, Mother claimed, could have been set by the flush of the downstairs loo. For my parents not only had to have separate bedrooms, but separate loos too. Their smells must not mix. Do excuse me, Cleaver apologised to Olga, picking up the toilet roll. More separate than this, he thought, you cannot get.

Outside the wind was sweeping across a clear sky. The treetops bowed under the pressure. Perhaps in the end, he reflected, the boy just wanted to bring me down to earth. Why not? It upsets him that people have such a high opinion of me. He is fed up of being son-of. Yet I never claimed to be anything other than a lump of solid flesh, Cleaver remarked, hard on the splash. Did I?

The problem, he decided, if I were to write my own account of it all, which I never will – though he was feeling bullish this morning – the problem would be to explain to the reader this central contradiction: the appetite for a celebrity that you knew was monstrously empty, the untiring vanity, despite the awareness that it was indeed in vain. On the other hand, what is one supposed to do with life? There's the crux.

Actually, I'd be proud, Cleaver thought, still loitering on the can, gazing across the clearing at Rosenkranzhof, if I'd rushed up to the twenty-second floor to stop a man killing a woman, a young woman at that, and a talented musician in particular. He had to keep one foot propped against the door to stop it banging in the wind. Wasn't that rather admirable? The place stank. Nor would I have done it just for the publicity. Though it was hard to imagine what self-respecting journalist would not make use of a film crew when there was one right there on the spot.

They just can't believe I've disappeared, Cleaver told Olga a few minutes later, replacing the loo roll. That's the truth of the matter. To feel quite sure that he existed, his elder son had written, my father had to see his face on the small screen more or less daily. Not to be on TV would be like not finding himself in the mirror. Well, now I have no mirror, Cleaver announced. He didn't bother shaving. A good session on the john is quite sufficient to remind me I exist, he laughed. They will have to come and get us, he told Olga. They'll have to catch us in flagrante delicto, my charming little poppet! Unless, it suddenly occurred to him – again there was the disturbing sense of a truth simply forcing itself into his mind – unless my unconscious calculation has always been that nothing, in the long run, is more likely to turn a man into a myth, celebrity into legend, than his sudden, complete and permanent disappearance.

Stiff neck or no, Cleaver was determined to see, in daylight, the path that had all but been the death of him the night before. He walked briskly across the clearing. Is it possible that these trousers already feel a little looser than when I tried them on in Bruneck? No. He brushed aside a cobweb strung across the path and almost at once came across the source of the smell that had so disgusted him. An animal had been trapped in a snare. A serpent of wire dangled in the bottom of a narrow gully. What animal? It wasn't a hare or a fox. A marmot, perhaps. He had seen photos at the Tourist Info Centre. The furry creature was half eaten and Cleaver could see where his hand, last night, must have squashed into its intestines.

He hurried on. The old Nazi set traps, he realised. Here and there other animals would be rotting uneaten. He snared animals and skinned them and ate them, presumably. Should I study the traps? If you live in a certain place, does that mean you're obliged to live in a certain way? The woods were full of sound today with the wind pressuring everything to the limit. It was bracing. Scrambling quickly downhill, Cleaver was surprised to notice that the path he had struggled to stay on in the dark had once been a serious track, a continuation, no doubt, of the one that led up to Trennerhof. Just that it wasn't used; the steps and occasional paving were overgrown. At the steepest point there was even the remains of an iron railing on the rock wall. People invested time here, Cleaver thought.

Then he stepped out onto the ledge. The unimpeded wind almost blew him over. The drop was awesome. The gorge opened out and fell away, far, far below to the thread of the Ahrn as it passed, glinting, through some tiny village. Cleaver noticed that the ground beneath his feet had been carefully laid out with stone flags. There was nothing casual here. The gallows was a tall triangular scaffolding with a large, rusty winch wheel. This place must be some kind of loading platform.

Then Cleaver saw a girl's face. To his left, where the ledge narrowed to just a couple of feet, an oval wooden plaque had been riveted onto the rock wall. Sealed under a square of transparent plastic was a photograph. A plastic rose, fastened to the plaque with a piece of wire, was vibrating in the wind.

Edging closer, nervously aware of the terrific drop below, Cleaver couldn't understand if it was his eyes that wouldn't focus or the small photo that was blurred. It's an ID snap. Ulrike Stolberg. The girl was blonde, straight-nosed. He could just make out two dates. 20.4.1965 – 21.6.1990. Then all at once he felt extremely anxious; there was a powerful gust of emotion. I am going to fall. She must have died here, he muttered. The first rock you would hit was at least two-hundred feet below. Cleaver was weeping as he stumbled away up the path. Only when he was almost back at Rosenkranzhof did it feel safe to stop and take a breath. 1990. He stood with his back to a tree. How often he had cursed that year.

Crossing the clearing again, Cleaver decided he would pick up the milk can and go straight to Trennerhof to get it filled. Who was Ulrike Stolberg? But in that case he should take the plate they had given him as well, with the cheese. He had left it on the table. A sharp pain reminded him of his stiff neck. And first I must get rid of the cheese. You can hardly take back what was given to you. Cleaver stared at the gritty grey lump under the plastic wrap. It looked like something dead. He felt disorientated, rushed, though nobody is expecting me. His chest was beating. He knows he will have to go back to that ledge and that photo. Oh the stupid cheese! But he needed to eat. He grabbed the Schwarzbrot from the cupboard.

The moment he released the wrap, the room was filled with the same pungent smell that had afflicted him up at Trennerhof. It was like some self-inflating device, rushing all over the house. Acrid cheese. All the same, Cleaver spread a knife-full of the stuff onto his black bread. He was standing by the table. It crumbled into clots of grey and green. The door was rattling in the wind. Why am I eating? You're not hungry. He pushed the food into his mouth. He was in such a hurry now to get up to Trennerhof. His neck ached as he chewed. Who was Ulrike Stolberg? Then taste and smell fused sharply together and shot up inside his nose. It was so odd to recognise something you knew – yes, it is cheese

– yet utterly different and more powerful than any cheese he had eaten before. He clamped his teeth. It smells like bad sex! Know what I mean Olga? Cleaver burst out laughing. What an incorrigible old roué you are! Simultaneously, he was aware that the sight of that memorial plaque, the reminder of that awful year, had cut him to the quick. I am helpless, he muttered. I never got over it.

He stood by the table munching his bread, jaws aching from this rapid eating. It's as if someone were rattling the door to get in, he thought, to get in to Rosenkranzhof. Cleaver's hand is shaking. He can feel the draught on his neck. My poor neck. My father always insisted, his elder son had written – in the last section of the book this was – that hand-held microphones were ugly, they gave an impression of improvisation and incompetence. He wanted to be miked up, he said, always, at all costs. But the truth was that his hand shook like a leaf in the wind. Christ, what a crap analogy! Cleaver shouted. My father didn't want people to see how unsteady he was. What's the point of being Mr Suave if your hand shakes? It's not hip. So that I often wondered, his son had written, what guilty tension lay behind this tremor. To the quick, Cleaver repeated. Could the boy really not see what had happened? The shaking had nothing to do with it. My hand shook as a teenager, it shook in the cradle most likely. He bit into the cheese again. A sort of vapour rose to his eyes. Did it never occur to him that all that disillusionment, that acid deconstruction of my own achievements, began in the autumn of 1990? Instead, *Under His Shadow* pushed it back across my whole life. As if I'd been born a nihilist. As if the twins' adolescence was poisoned by something that actually only began when Angela's life ended so abruptly.

Cleaver forced down the food and went to the door.

Moving away from routine, it seemed, meant constantly reliving the most intense crises of your life. Mr Cleaver, the doctor took him to one side after the autopsy, there is something you should know about your daughter. Please, no, Cleaver protested. He took hold of the rattling handle. Perhaps one listened to the stock market report every day, he thought, precisely not to hear such voices. The Hang Seng instead of hanging yourself. No, you should wash the plate before going, he decided, or wipe it off at least. The young woman must have died falling from the ledge, he thought. Three months before Angela almost to the day. She was fooling with the winch perhaps. There must have been some kind of system for bringing things up or sending them down to and from the mountain, from Rosenkranzhof. It was strange. Cleaver walked fast up the track. And it was strange too this feeling at once of decision and compulsion: go to Trennerhof. Why? But words are so arrogant the way they divide the world up, and above all the mind. She jumped, Cleaver told himself, she jumped.

Wer war Ulrike Stolberg? he asked. There was no one in the dairy room. The wind slammed the door when he let it go. Under the eaves all those ridiculous trophies that the Tyrolese insist on hanging on their walls were banging and clattering: an ancient scythe, a wooden plough-yoke, a cartwheel, crude little carvings of goblins and clowns. He went to the front of the house, to the room where he had signed the contract. Harry Cleaver. I signed with the name my wife gave me. Paps was always Angela's way. Can I go to the concert, Paps? Come on! I'll go anyway, you know. Oh, let me!

Cleaver's eyes were smarting in the wind. It ballooned in his jacket. Crossing the plateau, where the track came out of the gorge, he had had to bend his back into it. The cheese was still sharp in his mouth. It had stung his palate. This is the flavour of the place, he thought. The peaks all around were tremendously sharp and motionless beneath the fierce pull of the sky, the scudding clouds. Cleaver opened the main door and walked through the porch to the big kitchen parlour. Hello! It smelt of fire and soup again. He had to fight to shut out the elements. Hello, he called. The dusty old radios, the great stove and big stone table seemed to be from a different time, even more remote than the crucifix. Ist jemand da? He has the milk can and plate in his hand. Frau Stolberg?

Jo, a voice said softly. It is a cracked voice. Cleaver walked round the table to where the ancient lady was hunched by the hearth, her back to the door. The same red beads were wrapped round her knuckles. This face is as near to a corpse as you can get, Cleaver thought. She looked vacantly beyond him, a dribble of saliva at the corner of her mouth. The woman was muttering something. Only one side of the mouth moves. She is asking me who I am, Cleaver decided. The words were indistinguishable. He had never seen a skin so papery, so grey. If you fell against her, your hand would plunge straight to the decaying innards. Ich bin Cleaver, he said. He didn't know how to say, your tenant. Ich will die Milch nehmen. Von Rosenkranzhof, he said.

The old woman started. Adelheid! she called. It was a croak. She has no strength in her. Adelheid! The old woman is scared, Cleaver thought. Can she see me or not? She seemed to be staring at him, but blindly. On her lap the beads and knuckles were trembling. How could my son not see the obvious, the complete change in me, after Angela's death? I was more brilliant, more myself, more restless, as if spinning in emptiness. Wer war Ulrike Stolberg? he asked bluntly. It was always a virtuoso performance, after Angela died. The old woman's head tilted. She is focussing all her faculties on me. Wos welln Sie? She started to speak. She was asking something. But he knew by her state of alertness that she had understood his question well enough. Wer war Ulrike Stolberg? I saw her photo. The woman's right hand gripped the arm of her chair. She tried to get to her feet.

Herr Cleaver, said a voice.

Cleaver turned. Frau Stolberg appeared behind him. She was angular and strong-boned in a plain brown dress and apron, the same clothes Frau Schleiermacher wore, more or less. What will she think of my evident state of agitation? he wondered. His eyes were brimming. The tall woman reached out a hand for the milk can and plate. Her mouth was set in an expression of determined indifference. Kommen Sie bitte, she said.

As she led him to the dairy to fill his milk can and place another lump of cheese on his plate, Frau Stolberg started speaking to Cleaver in a slow, stern, reproving voice, though what she might actually be saying, he had no idea. She's perfectly aware I can't understand, Cleaver thought. But strangely this incomprehension allowed him to understand her better. She is lecturing me, he realised, even if the words may be referring to the weather, or the milk. She is putting me in my place.

He took the brimming can and the plate. Wo ist Jürgen? he asked. Was it a kind of joke to give him such a full jug, knowing very well he would never get it down to Rosenkranzhof without a spill? Even if I did have a steady hand. Bei den Kühen, Frau Stolberg was saying. Auf wiedersehen, Herr Cleaver. There was something of Amanda, he thought, in the woman's determined coldness. Amanda too had glittering eyes.

Having already turned to go, Cleaver said, Heute morgen,

ich habe die Fotografie . . . he didn't know how to complete the sentence. Gorge and ledge and drop were not words he had studied for German O level forty years ago. Die Fotografie . . . Ulrike Stolberg ge . . . gesehen. He hoped that in some way his voice might convey condolence, even shared grief. Frau Stolberg had already turned to the sink at the far end of the room. Das ist eine alte und traurige Geschichte, she said.

Was Ulrike Frau Stolberg's daughter? Not a hundred yards from Trennerhof, Cleaver put his milk beside a low stone wall that offered shelter from the wind. There is the clanging of a bell somewhere. It must be the cows. He raised his head. She was born in 1965. And Frau Stolberg is seventy-ish. So she would have been . . . Why can't I do this sum? Why do I always find it so difficult to push people's lives into the past? Thirtysomething. She could well be the mother, then. Ulrike was the daughter. And the town-dressed woman another. You have no right to disturb people's memories like this, Cleaver told himself. Just because your own have been disturbed. And Seffa? He heard the bell again. Seffa is another generation. The cows were on the far side of the plateau, perhaps a dozen of them, grazing on the lower slopes of the Speikboden. I've nothing to do, Cleaver thought. He covered the can with the plate, made sure they were well sheltered from the wind and began to walk.

This panorama is spectacularly outspread, he muttered, looking around him; far more than any screen, however wide, could ever suggest. These are banal reflections. Life is not a framed thing, Cleaver told himself. Like a book or a TV documentary. The natural world is vast. And yet when the two dates are put together – 1965-1990 – people begin to explain a life away. It looks small. It withers. Eine alte und traurige

Geschichte, Frau Stolberg had said. An old, sad story. Your daughter was pregnant, the doctor told him. Cleaver marched across the plateau into the wind. It blows and blows. Perhaps if you know who the father is you might wish to inform him. His eyes searched the slopes. Jürgen is working at a fence, bent down beside a post. It seems strange that there should be fences so high up on the mountainside. Presumably when the snow comes, the cows will have to stay in their barn. Or when people decide to tell your story, to frame you, as his elder son had done to him, then it's as if the two dates were already there. It's over. He was obliged to invent my death, Cleaver reflected. He looked around at the huge landscape, the patches of colour and stone, the grey peaks ranged one above the other beyond the plateau. Closer to hand there was a pool of water for the cows, darkly ruffled in the wind. When all was said and done, who cared how it ended?

Jürgen had seen him approaching, but now kept his head down. Only when Cleaver was within a couple of yards did he realise that there was a sheer drop of some fifty feet immediately beyond the fence. The cows must be protected. Guten Tag, he said. He stood watching. The man grunted a reply. He was using a wrench to tense a wire around a freshly cut pole. Wo ist der Hund? Cleaver asked. The man scratched at the hair above his ear with thick dirty fingers. He was sitting on his haunches, wearing the inevitable blue shirt of the farm worker. Uli ist mit Seffa rausgegangen. He took three nails from his pocket and, holding two between his lips, began to bang the other in with a hammer. All over the world, while I was holding forth on television, men were doing these simple practical jobs. Jürgen was intent, rapid. Amanda's rose trellis had remained in the realm of fancy. When the nail was almost home, two quick blows bent the head to trap the wire.

Wollen Sie was trinken? Jürgen asked. He walked over to a bag hanging from the previous fence pole and produced a bottle. A transparent liquid could be seen through smeared glass. Setzen Sie sich. Jürgen stretched out on his back on the coarse grass in a pantomime of hard-earned rest. It's not his first drink of the day, Cleaver thought.

Wind, Jürgen shouted, viel Wind. Verstehen Sie? He shook a heavy fist at the sky, laughing. Und wo ist Seffa? Cleaver asked. Luttach, Jürgen replied. He began to explain. Cleaver didn't understand. The man sat up and started a little mime, as if they were playing charades. He held the reigns of an imaginary horse. Hermann? Jo-jo. His hand moved downwards, as though descending a hill. Mit dem Käse? Verstehen Sie? Den Käse verkaufen. He pushed out an elbow and brought in finger and thumb to hold his nose over pursed lips, as if disgusted. Zweimal in der Woche. The guy's funny, Cleaver thought. Seffa had gone down to Luttach. Jürgen offered the bottle and he took a swig. It was fierce. Wiping his mouth, he repeated: Okay. Pferd. Käse. Luttach. Geht Seffa für die . . . Shopping? Mit dem Hund. Jürgen roared with laughter. Auf Deutsch! Sehr gut! He seemed to be imitating Hermann.

The man took another very long slug from the bottle. He held it high, waving the drink toward a pale cow that was tearing at the ground a few yards away. Willst du trinken, Isabella. Willst du? Sie heißt Isabella. Isabella! Suddenly, Jürgen was yelling: Willst du was trinken, mein Liebchen? Willst du tanzen? With surprising agility the man leapt to his feet and ran towards the beast, legs wide apart like a clown, waving the bottle. Isabella, willst du trinken? When the cow lifted its head, he put the open bottle under the animal's nose. Trink, trink!

The cow snorted and backed off. Jürgen returned, grinning, stopping to take another slug. Cleaver wondered why he was so amused by the man's antics. Perhaps because I haven't seen anybody for a couple of days. The drink was schnapps, he thought. Jürgen was pressing the bottle into his hands again. The alcohol went straight to his head.

Seine Käse ist sehr gut, Cleaver announced. Only now did he realise he had forgotten his stiff neck. Jo-jo. Jürgen lay down again. Unser Käse ist wunderbar. He put three fingertips together and kissed them in mock ecstasy, then suddenly sat up and yelled at the cows: Isabella, danke schön, Gabriella, danke schön, Lucia, danke schön. He started to tear up tufts of grass and to throw them at the animals. Unser Käse ist wunderbar! What does a man do for entertainment in a place like this? Cleaver wondered. Apart from thinking of Italian names for his cows. Und Seffa? he asked. Wie kommt Seffa . . . zurück?

Zu Fuß! Jürgen cried. Again he jumped up and waddled a few steps, exaggerating the fat girl's walk, stamping his feet down flat. Drei Stunden, mit der Einkaufstasche. He added a heavy bag to his mime, spluttered and sighed and burst out laughing.

Heute morgen . . . Cleaver tried. He had to make a big mental effort. Heute Morgen, ich habe die Fotografie Ulrike Stolberg gesehen. Jürgen's smile faded. He stood still in the wind, his jowls suddenly heavy. Wer war sie? Cleaver asked. Who? Jürgen looked away. Ulrike ist vor vielen Jahren gestorben, he said. He tugged at the skin under his neck. Meine Frau, he added. Cleaver shook his head. The man's wife. Why on earth didn't I make that connection?

Ihr Hut, Jürgen announced. Cleaver didn't understand. The man took off his own small cap and held it out. Hut. He put it on again, pretending it was a cowboy hat, smoothing out an imaginary brim. Ihren Hut haben Sie am Trennerhof gelassen.

Cleaver understood. He wanted to say he was sorry, but didn't know how. Seffa ist Ihre Tochter? he asked. Jürgen turned and stared. His eyes were red with wind and alcohol. Natürlich, he said with unexpected emphasis.

Why do I want to ask these questions? Cleaver wondered, stumbling back down the mountainside. There must be any number of young women who died in 1990. It was after the fall of the Berlin Wall. He stopped a moment. That was November '89. Walking downhill is hard on the knees. Perhaps because of the schnapps, the light seemed blinding now. One longed to be back in the woods. It would be curious, Cleaver thought, to know exactly why it was that the wind moaned like this on these stony heights. A relaxing sound in comparison to the revving of a chainsaw. Some lugubrious friction between gas and solid, spirit and material. There is no noise line, Cleaver told himself. You will never get beyond it. Glancing up, he noticed a black speck circling slowly over the gorge beyond Trennerhof. He watched: some kind of hawk. Like the eagle on the old Nazi's wall. It sails on the elements, gracefully waiting for its prey. When the bird makes its kill, there is the pathos of the victim torn apart and consumed; when it fails to kill, there is the pathos of the predator denied, of patient hunger. Film-makers give their lives to capture such things. But what is the point of these morbid thoughts? Cleaver demanded. Was it really worth being alone if one was merely to think these gloomy thoughts? And how is it possible to be so calm, so free of any plan or purpose, and at the same time so terribly agitated, so vulnerable? Angela, he said softly. The hawk was still circling.

Ich habe mein Hut gelassen, he told Frau Stolberg. He met her in the porch. Her glittering eyes told him he was not welcome. What do I care, Cleaver thought. He was glad he hadn't shaved. I don't have to impress anyone. The woman went out of the room and reappeared with the broad-brimmed grey hat. Why didn't she give it to me earlier?

Wo ist Seffa? he asked. Und der Hund?

Frau Stolberg seemed in no hurry to answer. As when he had first seen her at the funeral, he was arrested by a strange fixity in the eyes. My father would never accept, his elder son had written, the idea that a woman might resist his charms, even a woman he had no intention of seducing. What bullshit, Cleaver told himself. There were hundreds of women he had paid no attention to at all, nor expected anything from. He put the crown of the hat in his right hand and bent his bald head to put it on. Seffa ist nicht hier, Frau Stolberg said. Cleaver waited. He was sure she had something else to say. Speaking very slowly and clearly, the woman eventually declared: Seffa darf nicht zum Rosenkranzhof gehen. Cleaver stared. Es ist verboten, Frau Stolberg said.

Carrying his milk can and the cheese, Cleaver found it impossible to keep the hat on his head. The wind snatched it away. He put down the can and plate to chase it, losing a big splash of milk in the process. Sehr schön, aber unpraktisch, Frau Schleiermacher had said. I bought this hat to cut a figure for myself in the mountains, Cleaver realised. He crumpled it up and stuck it in his jacket pocket. The hat would give me the look of someone who has made a success of his remote Alpine existence. I imagined the cameras arriving to find the TV personality turned hermit, but with panache.

All at once Cleaver was beside himself with rage. Violet ties were his favourite, his elder son had written. Worn over a bright lemon shirt. Or vice versa. The bullets that killed him had to pass first through a white dinner jacket. Could it be, Cleaver demanded feverishly, that the girl had misunderstood when he pointed upstairs and said Zimmer? Surely not. I'm old enough to be her grandfather. Just the thought brought Cleaver up sharp. When did that ever bother me? Should I go back to Trennerhof and have it out with Frau Stolberg? Seffa must not come to Rosenkranzhof, she had said. Verboten. It was verboten. He hadn't told anyone Angela was pregnant. Not even Amanda. He didn't want to. Yet he had always felt the burden of that secret, the same way, at least in the early days, that he used to feel the burden of an affair. Who was the father? Jürgen seemed friendly enough, Cleaver remembered. Except when I asked that question. Is Seffa your daughter? Natürlich, he had said. Why had he seemed so aggressive, angry almost? They can't honestly imagine I'm a threat. But since you didn't want to have contact with anyone, least of all a fat, gormless country girl, what does it matter? Did they have any idea of the kind of women Cleaver had moved among in London?

Back at Rosenkranzhof, Cleaver placed the milk and cheese in a cool corner away from the stove and immediately set out again. He walked swiftly down to the ledge, picking up an unpleasant cut on the old iron handrail. What was it they used to load and unload here? Without even glancing at the photograph of the dead woman, he sat on the very edge of the stone platform, his legs dangling in the void. 1990. June not October. Was it in 1990 that the old Nazi went to live in Trennerhof? Fifteen years would be just before. Two other pylons were visible far below. Then, quite abruptly, he demanded: Why did Angela's death affect me so deeply, so permanently? That is the question you have come to the South Tyrol to answer. Perhaps. Sitting on the ledge, the magnitude of empty space beneath made him feel faintly sick. I would not have reacted like that if one of the others had died, he thought. It seemed strange to admit this only now. He had never had the thought before. You do have another daughter, Amanda told him gently. We have another daughter, Harry. Two other sons. Nor would I have felt the same way about Angela if she hadn't died then, at that moment. That was true too. On the very threshold of womanhood. Your daughter was pregnant, Mr Cleaver. Es ist verboten!

Oh God! Taking no care for his safety, Cleaver got to his feet and scrambled back up the path. Back and forth, back and forth along these paths. I will go straight to Trennerhof now and demand to know why. What have I done? Why shouldn't the girl come down to see me? I don't want to see her anyway. But on reaching the clearing, he stamped straight into Rosenkranzhof, climbed the stairs, crossed the bedroom, lifted his leg and gave a huge kick to the locked door. If they rent me a house, it's mine, damn it! I can see everything in it. The effort sent a pain shooting up his neck. The wood splintered, but didn't give. He must not have closed the downstairs door behind him, because the wind suddenly stormed into the house. There were sounds of flapping, clattering, slamming. A herd of animals seemed to be pushing into the kitchen. Cleaver raised his leg and kicked again, so that all his weight crashed against the door right by the handle. It flew open. Cleaver lost his balance and fell forward. At once something was tugging at his heels. Unable to turn his stiff neck, he heard barking. Uli, he called. The dog was at his face, licking his cheek. Ulrike, Cleaver whispered. Feeling stupid, he climbed to his feet to explore the room.

PART TWO

IX

LET ME PUT it to you, Mr President, that you understand freedom only in the negative sense of freedom from chains. Cleaver was woken by the sound of footsteps. Perhaps there had been the proverbial crack of the twig. At once he was alert. There was no point in going to the bedroom window. Across the gorge, the sun was on the further slopes now. It must be after three. I fell asleep debating with the President of the United States. If there was one thing in our house that was strictly forbidden, his elder son had written, it was to wake my father during his afternoon nap. Who can it be? Cleaver felt muddled. Had he actually said that to the President? Someone was definitely walking around outside the house. Genius must repose, Mother would say. I could peek out of the window in the old Nazi's room, he told himself. That looked out over the clearing. But if Jürgen or Seffa see, they'll know I broke in there. Someone will have to repair the damage.

Nevertheless, he crossed the bedroom boards on bare feet and went through the splintered door. I actually want it to be Seffa, he realised, or Hermann, or even Frau Schleiermacher.

That was unlikely. It didn't occur to him to hurry down the stairs and confront whoever it was. He had to pick his way through the boxes and junk. He hadn't cleaned the place up. There was a crate of empty bottles. How silly, Cleaver remembered of that evening a month before, to have imagined you might uncover some kind of mystery in here. But the accordion had proved a plus.

Even before he got to the window, he saw there was a man with a small backpack on his shoulders examining the door to his john across the clearing. A man in his late thirties perhaps. There was something rather solemn and pensive to his manner. He had a sharp nose, spectacles, thin blond hair. Cleaver watched. A hiker by the looks. A man with a lanky frame. What was he doing so far off the beaten track? There are no signposts or red-and-white flashes around Rosenkranzhof. It is not marked on any map.

The man lifted the latch, opened the door a crack, then closed it sharply, shaking his head. Cleaver grinned. But he ducked aside when the hiker turned round to face the house. As the silence builds up, over two days, three, then a week, then another, you find you don't want to break it. You don't want your mental energy dispersed. I was getting close to something important there when I fell asleep, Cleaver remembered. Now he has forgotten. About the nature of freedom. This whole adventure has to do with the possibility of freedom.

He stood a while with his back against a tall cupboard, trapped by the enquiring eyes of this intruder prowling around his house. I would have been happy to go downstairs and speak to Seffa, if only to reassure myself that they weren't imagining awful things about me. Why did that matter? He poked his head forward again toward the dusty windowpane. Beschütze, O Maria, dieses Haus, announced a faded flowery embroidery hanging on the wall beside, und alle die da gehen ein und aus.

The man was aiming a camera. Again Cleaver stepped smartly back. He caught his heel on a large wooden troll and half sat, half fell on the bare planks. The troll cracked against the cupboard. It was crudely carved out of an upturned tree stump, with a pipe between twisted lips and a cap and feather. The eyes were glass. Like Olga's.

Cleaver sat quite silent, straining for the sound of the intruder. It was disquieting, the tension developed by this unexpected presence of another human being. Whenever freedom is expressed positively by a group of people – for example, in evangelical Christianity, Mr President – it inevitably becomes coercive. Was that the line he had been trying to develop? You won't let a woman abort, perhaps. You don't want gays to have certain rights. The problem was, his elder son had written, that though my father could always fall asleep, any time, any place, the slightest of noises was enough to wake him. You only needed to run down the stairs or to bounce a ball against the garage door and you were being accused of high treason. You had interrupted the repose on which my father's elusive masterpiece depended. You were guilty!

He must be photographing my clothes on the line, Cleaver thought, the chequered shirts and cord trousers. It was a tourist collecting images of the typically Tyrolese: the stoicism of living without utilities at six-thousand feet. He will adjust the frame to make sure he gets in the stones that hold down the wooden roof tiles, and the thread of smoke escaping from the chimney. It had taken Cleaver all morning to wash his few clothes, rubbing the dirty fabrics against each other in tepid water. Amazing how tiring that was. He doubted if they were clean even now. Beschütze must mean Bless, he decided, staring at the dusty embroidery, waiting to hear the man go. Bless this house. Perhaps the town-dressed woman had embroidered this for her father years ago when he moved out of Trennerhof. She loved him despite his battle with her mother. Was Ulrike the daughter, or the daughter-in-law? Cleaver wondered. Perhaps Ulrike had embroidered it. How farcically over the top, though, Cleaver reflected, that section on the afternoon nap had been: the loosened braces on the great paunch, Caroline and Phillip as toddlers taking fright at his snores. A writer sees a chance for caricature and he can't resist it: the pages write themselves, Disney-fashion. After all, I did the same with my documentaries. The public loves it. Everything slots in. Is that freedom of expression? When I'm sure the man's gone, Cleaver decided, I'll go down and walk after him, perhaps, meet him on the path, as if by accident.

He looked at the troll's crooked face. There was dust in all his wrinkles. It was a fat troll with a knotty upturned nose. One wooden hand raised an axe. You imagined you were going to find something significant when you broke down the door, Cleaver remembered. What a strange mood he'd been in that day. Something about Ulrike Stolberg, a family tragedy that bound these people together in uneasy silence, a ghost of the mountains. He definitely heard footsteps again now, but they didn't seem to be moving away. There is something thoughtful and exploratory about this intruder. He is looking for something. Pressed on the floor, Cleaver's hands were black with dust. When you opened the tall cupboard, he remembered, you were convinced that there would be an SS uniform in there. If a man is a Nazi, he must be reduced to his Nazism. Er war ein Krimineller, Frau Schleiermacher had said. Instead there was only this gloomy troll, his face turned to the wall, and the accordion with its red-and-white strap. Everything is traditional in the Tyrol. Everything is in tune: the crucifixes and rosaries and rough pine furniture, the red-and-white Tyrolese banners. The troll was cutting wood no doubt.

With some effort Cleaver got to his feet. Of course, if you do go after the man, you will disappoint him. Despite the grey beard he's grown and his increasingly bushy, unplucked eyebrows, Harold Cleaver is manifestly not your echt Tyrolese; he is an anomaly, an impostor, an escapee. You always speak of freedom, Mr President, as an escape from coercion, the throwing off of shackles – Islam, Communism – the right to choose, as if that were the end of the problem. You never mention the life chosen after the escape, or the kind of unconscious collective ethos where people are so in tune with their conventions that freedom is simply not an issue. Yes, he had definitely launched that provocation. He remembered now. If not exactly in those words. Well, I sure know a man's not free when I see chains on his back, the President had replied easily. Had he understood? Hitching up his backpack, putting the camera away in a pocket, the visitor was striding off down the track that led to the ledge, the old cableway, the photo of Ulrike Stolberg. What would he make of that? Cleaver wondered. Unless, of course, he has come here to look for me.

This thought galvanised Cleaver. Perhaps they have found me! He hurried downstairs, though taking care with that fourth step. He is organised now. He lives in a rigid routine. The stove is never allowed to go out. With every passing day, the late autumn sun is losing its warmth. Keep your clothes dry at all costs. He has hung a clothes horse over the stove. He stacks firewood in the kitchen three or four days before he will need it. He mustn't let his feet get cold. Each morning he walks for two or three hours. He has climbed upward towards the Speikboden, north to the clouded slopes of the Schwarzstein, south along the high plateau beyond Trennerhof. That was where he came across the abandoned mounting frame. It would have been fun to have brought that up in the debate with the President. The cow would be led into the iron frame, Mr President – a sort of small cage really – and immobilised with shackles so as to make it easier for the bull to penetrate her. Cleaver had heard of such things but never actually seen one. The bars were tubular and painted pale yellow. He had run his hand across the rusting structure, surprised at its rather rough, home-made look. There were rubber wheels so that it could be towed from farm to farm, wherever a beast was in heat. There were bars at a convenient height so that the bull could rest its front hoofs while it fucked. All this in aid of meat and milk production. But was the cow unhappy, Mr President, as it was led into the mounting frame? Do cows have much choice anyway? Or any of us? Certainly there were days when Cleaver had experienced sex as an imperative. I felt compelled.

Every fourth day or so he took a shower. He had discovered the old Nazi's system of showering. Cleaver still calls the previous occupant the old Nazi, even if there wasn't a single wartime trophy in the locked room, just boxes of clothes and bric-a-brac, the accordion most usefully, and a cowbell with a bright embroidered ribbon that he has hung from a nail in the kitchen and likes to ring from time to time. Olga! Lunch is served! As he walked each day, the high valleys clanged and tinkled with cowbells. More than once it has occurred to Cleaver that the peasants are perhaps afraid of the silence. Or that the bells are a sort of prayer. Did the farmers remove the cow's bell from her neck for the ritual coupling in the mounting frame? Or did it clang and clang as the bull thrust? The mounting frame was abandoned,

Cleaver thought, because, of course, they use artificial insemination now – it costs less – in much the same way that lunatics these days are constrained with injections rather than straitjackets. There were weeds growing round the flaking yellow bars and stains of rust at the joints. But that only takes the trauma and the pleasure out of the event, don't you think, Mr President, the sense of having really lived, however unpleasantly? Or am I talking to Amanda now? It was so strange how Amanda had always excited him, yet he had got used to not having sex with her. Mother liked to tell dinner guests, his elder son had written, that as soon as it was cheap and reliable, artificial insemination would be much the more civilised method of starting a family.

With some ingenuity, the old Nazi had diverted a small hose from the larger pipe that carried the stream-water into the kitchen. The hose came down the rock face beside the house at the back and, at head height, was made to protrude perhaps two feet, tied to an iron rod jammed deep into a tight fissure. A primitive screw tap was attached. Cleaver had learned to strip naked, stand under the hose – there was a rough slab of stone directly beneath – and unscrew the tap. It was a strong, solid jet. The icy cold burned on his scalp and down his back. He could bear it just long enough to soap armpits and crotch and rinse. If ever anyone felt guilty of anything, he thought, here was a way of imagining you had done penance. The water splashed on his hairy paunch. The flesh was mortified. And I am losing weight, Cleaver noticed. I'm tightening up.

Now, opening the front door, checking the clothes on the line to see if they were dry, it occurred to Cleaver that if he were to take a shower in, say, ten minutes' time, then the intruder, on returning from the ledge – for there was nothing a hiker could do once he had reached the end of that path but turn back – would discover the tenant of Rosenkranzhof naked under the freezing water. His stereo-typed impression of the primitive Tyrolese picturesque would be confirmed. He could set off home content. Unless, of course, the man were to recognise in this shivering hulk the TV celebrity he had been paid to hunt down and promptly snap the photo that would appear the following weekend in one of the Sunday tabloids.

What day is it? Cleaver wondered. And weren't such exhi-bitionist fantasies just another indication of his pathetic vanity? You don't want to confront anyone or speak to anyone, so as not to lose the thread of your precious rumi-nations, yet at the same time you yearn to be photographed naked for the *Sunday Mirror* so that the very few people (women) who are in a position to judge will see that you are standing up a little straighter than of yore and have lost a good stone and more into the bargain. Cleaver laughed. It must be Monday or Thursday, he decided, the days Seffa went down to Luttach. Otherwise Uli would have been here. The dog spends most afternoons lying by the Rosenkranzhof fire before pricking up his ears and whin-ing to be let out on hearing the distant call of the girl from Trennerhof shortly after dusk.

Am I going to confront this intruder or not? Cleaver asked himself. Moving about the kitchen, he put away a pan and checked through the packets of groceries on the shelf beside the window to see what he could eat this evening. Pasta e basta. This incorrigible gourmet, as his elder son interminably referred to him, actually needs neither sauce nor Parmesan. Nor sex for that matter. There was a little butter to help it slither down. Unusually, closing a cupboard door, Cleaver felt the silence of the empty house all around him. I thought I had got over that.

He went back into the sitting room. Olga, poppet, we need to restock the larder. One of us is going to have to break cover and head down to Luttach. Two or three days ago Cleaver had taken his doll out of the house to shake the dust off her dress and kerchief. That old troll is never going to pull his weight, he laughed. She didn't reply. The axe is pure theatre. So, should I bother speaking to this intruder or not, Cleaver demanded? Trolls, he recalled, were supposed to turn to stone in sunlight. Olga sat with her permanent smile on the armchair beside the accordion. What do you think? One plan might be, he thought, simply to sit down and squeeze out a couple of chords on the old instrument. The stranger could hardly help but hear them and would then be in a position to decide for himself whether to knock and meet the occupant of Rosenkranzhof. Perhaps he needs to ask for directions. Where could he be staying, so far from anywhere? Though as soon as he hears a few notes, Cleaver realised, the man will know that this accordion player is not Tyrolese.

Cleaver heaved the thing onto his lap. It was heavy. He slipped his hands under the straps and spread his fingers across the keyboard. At once, he was aware of a slight tension, as though about to go out under the studio lights. You don't relax when you play, Paps, Angela used to complain. She soon gave up asking her father to accompany her singing on the piano. Why can't you relax, Paps? she shook her head. But I do, Cleaver laughed. I do relax. God knows he performed on TV more or less every day. It's just my hand shakes.

Searching his memory, concentrating, he played a few notes. Should auld acquaintance be forgot . . . It was hard to combine the arm action with the fingers on the keys. The sound was more wheezy than plaintive. One of the chord buttons stuck. The day the Stolbergs hear that, Cleaver thought, they'll know I broke into their room. Then there'll be drama. He wondered, in the evenings, when Seffa was calling down for the dog, how far the sound of the instrument carried up the gorge. But perhaps Seffa wouldn't tell the others even if she heard it. It's crazy, Cleaver was suddenly angry with himself, the way you keep assuming that Frau Stolberg is preventing the girl from coming down to visit you. When he went up for milk, though, Seffa was somehow never around, whatever time of day he chose to go, as if she were being hidden, or avoiding him. It was odd too how Jürgen and Frau Stolberg kept pressing the grey cheese on him. He hadn't asked for it. With a raw onion as well, last time, rolling around on the cracked plate. Sehr gut, man muss beides zusammen essen, Jürgen had insisted, pointing at the onion. His rough hand made a gesture to indicate that the onion must be chopped up fine. If this was a fairy story, Cleaver told Olga, I would find out too late that I was being poisoned, or transformed in some way by this mysterious food. That I had grown horns and hoofs. Or that I could no longer leave the Kingdom of the Dead. It would take some miraculous intervention to reverse the process. A kiss of course. What could be more miraculous than for a beautiful woman to kiss a fat old guy who's gorged on grey cheese and raw onions? Jürgen was right, though. The two foods went well together. The palate tingled. Cleaver squeezed out a few notes. A-a-nd ne-ver come to mind! Should auld acquaintance . . . Damn and damn. He put the instrument down, found his jacket and hat and hurried out of the house. He would confront the man.

Cleaver crossed the space at the front of Rosenkranzhof and walked purposefully down the path towards the ledge. He hadn't been this way for a good two weeks. There was no point. I've been very calm these last few days, Cleaver reflected, almost serene. The air was soft and misty. Haven't I? No, the irritating thing about Burns's song, he decided, was that it actually set out to savour the pathos of lost acquaintance, of oblivion, while pretending to be scandalised by it. The words wallowed in imagining the extinction of emotion – friendship forgotten – the better to fall back into it, no doubt with the help of a few pints of wee heavy.

A man who has really left the world, Cleaver told himself, striding along very determinedly after the intruder, in the sense of withdrawn, truly gone out of society, should not have to catch himself humming Auld Lang Syne, of all miserable songs. At the side of the path, the marmot's bones, he noticed, had been picked clean, the smell was gone, though the skull was still caught in the loop of the snare. Old acquaintance could go hang itself.

Is there anyone, Cleaver pulled up short to demand out loud, absolutely anyone, whom I, Harold Cleaver, would really like to see or speak to right now, after a month in the South Tyrol, a whole solid month entirely on my own? No one. I have completely overcome my attachment to the mobile phone. On the other hand, of course, and mainly thanks to the fact that his lifelong partner had been Scottish, Auld Lang Syne was one of the very few tunes that Cleaver really knew how to play on the piano. The only thing that can possibly be said in favour of a Scottish New Year's Eve, my father liked to declare – and Cleaver had actually been rather pleased to find this remark in his son's book – is that it serves as the ultimate benchmark for maudlin sentimentality. My father was brilliant, his elder son had written, at mimicking the drunken, sentimental Scot. Gie us a cup o' kindness, laddie, he would say. The model was my grandfather. Yet whenever Mother's relatives came down to London, he always got drunk with them and he always banged out Auld Lang Syne on the piano and sang at the top of his voice.

That was true, Cleaver thought. He really didn't mind that first section of the book at all. My fingers move to the tune automatically, he noticed, whenever I touch a keyboard. And it was curious, he thought for the hundredth time, how his son's book had simply sidestepped the whole question of music. One of the few pleasures with Amanda had been discussing the different characters of their children. Very early they had noticed their son's stubbornness at the piano. He was determined to impress, but he was trapped inside the score. If he made a mistake, he stopped at once and played the piece right through again from the beginning. It must be done right or not at all. The boy was frustrated. He would slam down the lid of the piano. Or, when once he got it right, he wouldn't play it again. He had done it. He didn't want to risk screwing up.

But Angela plays while she plays, Amanda observed. Mistakes didn't worry the girl. Angela absorbed mistakes into the piece. Or she laughed and played on. Mr President, Cleaver muttered, the problem is not freedom, then, in the negative sense of release from shackles, but the ability to choose the right yoke, to give yourself to a score that you really want to play. This was where his son was in difficulty. And myself too for that matter. Do you ever think, Mr President, about the overall purpose of the society you are leading, American society? It's surely not enough to be negative. Cleaver had definitely asked the man something along those lines. It was the last question of the interview. I believe America has a great mission, the President replied. He had been on automatic pilot at this point. He began to talk about the inexorable spread of democracy.

Angela seemed to inhabit the score, Cleaver remembered. It constrained her, of course, but she transformed it. The score became Angela. Perhaps that is what it means to have a gift. Half the time I'm on keyboards, Dad, I'm playing Bach, she giggled. The guys in the band have no idea! Aged fourteen Cleaver's elder son had refused to go on with his piano lessons. If he can't make up the tune, he won't play, Amanda observed. Rather like someone else we know, she added.

Grüß Gott, a voice announced. Cleaver looked up in surprise. The intruder was only a couple of yards away, walking quickly up the path toward him. Grüß Gott, Cleaver replied. It was the customary Tyrolese greeting. The man was smiling, at ease. The circumspect air he had had outside the house was gone. He was vigorous, swinging his arms energetically, apparently not at all annoyed to have explored a dead end, nor worried to find himself in the back of beyond above six-thousand feet only an hour or so before dusk. Was it an English face? Cleaver wondered. He stopped and stared after the man, who wore jeans and a sleeveless quilt jacket, modern mountain boots. The fact that he said Grüß Gott doesn't mean anything. How did he sneak up on me so suddenly?

Cleaver was in two minds now whether to go on down to the ledge or to turn and follow the man. He hesitated, standing in the overgrown track between slim pines and nettles and boulders. The weather was definitely colder today. Colder and sharper. Perhaps he is a brother of the Stolbergs, of Jürgen and the town-dressed woman. It was a shame she had left so soon. There's a smell of winter, of snow even. Or Ulrike and the town-dressed woman. Though in the end Cleaver felt that the surname Stolberg on the memorial plaque meant that Jürgen would be Frau Stolberg's son and

Ulrike the daughter-in-law. This man was her brother, then, and comes here from time to time from some nearby village to look at the place where his sister died. A sort of pilgrimage. It is mad, Cleaver told himself, to cut yourself off from the world and then spend your time fantasising Gothic romances around a few primitive peasants you know nothing about.

He walked down to the end of the path. The sun was already behind the dark bulk of Schwarzstein to his left. The valley was in shadow. The folds of the land far below merged softly into each other and likewise the greys and greens of leaf and rock. There was a touch of mist. It was almost as if, should you throw yourself out into the void, now, the world would be soft and supporting as water. They must have strung up the cableway, Cleaver had recently decided, to bring down charcoal from the high forests. And Rosenkranzhof had been built by charcoal burners in the nearest place possible to the ledge. They sent down the charcoal they produced and in return received provisions from the village below. Far from being isolated, Rosenkranzhof had been part of the local economy. There's no way of knowing if I'm right, Cleaver reflected.

Every time he looked at Ulrike Stolberg's photo, she was different. The features are quieter and dreamier today. Perhaps the hiker had been her childhood lover and came here every now and then for auld lang syne. Now who's being mawkish? Cleaver smiled. Though it was hard to shake off the thought that the young woman had killed herself because someone had been trying to force her into a mounting frame against her will. Trolls carried off young maidens. Angela had been pregnant when she died. I didn't try to find out by whom. I was too busy trying to deal with the madness of Amanda's having invited Priya to the funeral. Cleaver's elder son was at university at the time. They had barely spoken about it all. I encouraged him in his studies, Cleaver remembered, though it was foolish of the boy to choose Political Science. As he recalled, what the charcoal burners did was to build big fires and then cover them almost entirely with earth so that the wood inside wasn't consumed, but turned slowly to charcoal. He remembered reading something of the kind out loud to the twins as small children, in *Swallows and Amazons* perhaps. Then they broke it up and sent it down with the cableway.

Cleaver took a last look at the gaunt scaffolding with the rusty wheel. There was a very faint sound rising from the valley. Of running water perhaps, or perhaps, very distantly, of traffic. Why did the hiker open the door to my john? Just as he was turning to go, Cleaver caught the smell. Perhaps there had been a shift in the breeze. Yes, it was definitely *that* smell. He went to the opposite end of the ledge. Just inside the trees, before the ground plummeted, he spied the telltale tissues. He shook his head. No wonder the man had had a smile on his face as he hurried past. He had freed himself of a load.

But how could I imagine, Cleaver objected, walking back up the path, that I of all people had anything to tell the President of the United States about freedom, when I daily accepted all the coercive mechanisms of television? He felt angry that the ledge had been violated like this. You don't go crapping by memorials, he thought. How can you even say that you really met or confronted the President when our whole conversation was conditioned by the constraints of the time slot, the sound levels, the concerns with lighting and make-up? After receiving my A level results, his elder son had written – now Cleaver had to lean against a tree for a moment to catch his breath – I went to see my father at the Wood Lane studios to have a last discussion with him about what I was going to study at university. I was in a good mood and ready to rethink things. In any event, I wanted to have it out with him. But in reception they wouldn't let me through. There were interminable phone calls to various studio managers. They were on security alert. Finally, I was marched along a mile of corridors and admitted to a small bright room where my father was being made up beside a tiny young Indian woman, an actress apparently, who was going to be talking to him about Bollywood. She had written a book called *This Spurious Splendour*. I wanted to talk to him alone, but the Indian woman was concerned about the timing of the intervals during which another woman was going to sing. Dad, I got three As, I told him. Angela hadn't even taken her exams. The make-up girl was powdering out the red spots below his eyes. The boy's a genius, my father told the Indian woman, and he's going to waste it all on Political Science! Time, someone yelled, time! Hurrying into the corridor, the Indian woman tripped on a step and my father caught her arm. A year later she was present at my sister's funeral.

X

BACK AT ROSENKRANZHOF there was no sign of the hiker. Cleaver showered, though he had showered only the day before. I'm losing ground, he thought. The gorge was in deep shadow now. The shock of the cold electrified his stout body. What on earth had made his son invent such a ridiculous title for Priya's book? He towelled himself hard and gathered his clothes from the line. *This Spurious Splendour* indeed! The trousers would have to be hung from the clothes horse. He fed the stove. What would they have used the charcoal for, he wondered, down in the Ahrntal? They smelted iron perhaps. Phillip always spoke of his desire to be a craftsman, to work with his hands.

Apropos of nothing, Cleaver had a vaguely prurient idea. He would take the rosary beads hanging on the front door and use them to count off the names of all the women he had had. Instead, he went to the armchair and picked up the accordion again. For some reason he couldn't be bothered to eat. He felt shaken. That troll's a hopeless conversationalist, he told Olga. Treats the place as a hotel. He sat down and put his arm round the girl. If a guest, his elder son had written, or one of us children for that matter, didn't want to sit through one of my father's performances at dinner, we were always accused of treating the place as a hotel. But since it seemed there was no way of communicating with the general manager, I for one couldn't wait to check out.

What tunes did Cleaver know, aside from Auld Lang Syne that is? Actually his son was quite wrong there, he remembered. It was Amanda who accused *me* of treating the house as a hotel when I was so frequently out. But when it's your house, you can treat it how you like, n'est-ce pas? And his son, as far as Cleaver could recall, far from raring to go, had been extremely reluctant to leave home when it came time to depart for university. Amanda had wanted to redecorate his room and Angela had been eager to use it for her keyboards and amplifier, but le petit prince, as they called him, left it to the last possible moment. He wouldn't leave. Cleaver had forgotten how they used to call his elder son le petit prince. It infuriated the boy.

He could play: Rock Of Ages, Abide With Me, Oh My Darling, Guantanamera and Don't Cry For Me Argentina. The mournful tunes were definitely easier. And Amazing Grace. Cleaver listened sceptically to the sounds the squeeze box made as he worked his arms back and forth. It's as if you never quite believe in what you're playing, Angela would complain. Then when his elder son had actually gone, to Durham (the boy had refused even to apply to Oxbridge), he would call home almost daily. He spoke to Amanda. What about, Cleaver had no idea. Is Mother there? he asked, if his father answered. In the end, his room was neither redecorated nor given to Angela.

Irritated, Cleaver thrust the accordion aside. The Buddha did not spend his time dwelling on auld acquaintance. Or amazing grace. How could you believe in such songs? That saved a wretch like me! He hated these emotions. Perhaps an eighteen-year-old girl, he thought, could throw herself heart and soul behind such a song, could put her weight into the yoke without embarrassment, but not a man who knew what Cleaver knew, not a man who had buried that girl. Songs are vehicles for entering into emotions, he thought, for the most part unwanted. It was curious, though, how close that accusation of Angela's was to Priya's: You never let me close to your real life, to what you really believe in. Auld Lang Syne is a sort of mounting frame, Cleaver laughed, which holds the mind still while it is violated by a certain rapacious emotion. Perhaps a bell clangs. And through that emotion the song brings you close to other people, as when everyone sang so movingly at the funeral: Abide with me, fast falls the eventide. Including his partner's lover, and her Scottish parents. It was horrible.

Then Cleaver remembered that other women too had accused him of being detached and cold. For all your kindness, Sandra said quietly, you are frighteningly cold. Women had a way, Cleaver had noticed, of filling oceans of time with airy chatter, before suddenly coming out with something absolutely leaden, lapidary. When I'm with you, Giada had told him in the hotel by the ski lift not ten kilometres from here – Sonnenblick, Cleaver now remembered it was called – it's as if I saw everything quite differently. I feel cool and objective, she said, emancipated even, as if I saw everything from outside. And it's really nice. But I feel it's wrong too.

Cleaver remembered this conversation very clearly, if only because, as his young girlfriend spoke that afternoon, he had been acutely aware that she was telling him that their affair was over. This mountain holiday was to be the end. My last affair, he now realised. I see why my dad's always on at me, Giada told him. You explain my family to me so well. I see what my relationship with journalism is, why I get so obsessed and everything. She paused. He watched her. Cold, I may have been, Cleaver thought, but I always knew at once when a girl was leaving me. It's as if my life was a story, Giada said, that you were reading to me, a story that finally made sense. After the morning's skiing they had spent the afternoon in bed, drinking wine and talking. Somehow it doesn't help, she said. You know? It doesn't help me to live.

There had been no catch in her voice. She was firm. It doesn't go anywhere, she said. You're so perceptive, and kind, but you don't go anywhere, you won't take me anywhere. I'm always back at square one. We're in the South Tyrol! Cleaver had objected wryly. He would never fight a woman who wished to leave him. Perhaps he relished these moments. Exactly, she replied. We're stuck up some frigging cold mountain in the middle of nowhere.

Do you think I'm cold? Cleaver suddenly demanded of Olga. Detached? He struggled to his feet. The house was in darkness and growing chill. He would get the rosary. He hadn't lit the fire and he couldn't be bothered to, but he did shove a splinter of pine into the stove to light the oil lamp. Otherwise it would be hard to negotiate the stairs. He trimmed the wick, lowered the flame. Who had put that rosary on the door? I am parasitic on an environment I know nothing about, Cleaver reflected, fiddling with the vents on the stove. But everyone feeds on the corpse of a world that came before.

Cleaver climbed the stairs and set the oil lamp down on his bedside table. You haven't eaten this evening, he remembered. You haven't cleaned your teeth. You haven't brought in more firewood. You haven't put away the cheese. Let the slide begin. Otherwise what will life be up here but one day after the next on and on, marking time, muttering to yourself? Let's go downhill, Cleaver suddenly decided. Perhaps that's the achievement we're after. I should start drinking heavily. In which case a trip to a supermarket was required.

He lay down on the bed and spread his fingers in the string of the rosary. How many beads were there? Five sections of ten each. Not enough, he smiled. Susan one, Elaine two, Hilary three, Avril four. Beginning was always easy. Or should I say, Hail Avril? No doubt this is the height of blasphemy. Then Katie, Louise, Janice. There had been a couple of pornographic magazines in the old Nazi's locked room. Fairly innocuous things. Nothing sado-maso. Cleaver had them by the bed. He hadn't masturbated, he felt no urge, but he couldn't quite decide to throw them away either. He flicked through a few pages now in the light of the lamp. Hail dear Connie and Ruth and a certain charming girl in Nottingham. These images too follow their metalled ways, he thought. The girl-on-girl shots. The two girls one man, two men one girl. Cleaver of course has a number of his own private snapshots – hail Denise in particular – images that have served him well over the years. Hail Patricia. But that isn't what he is after now.

This question of being detached, Cleaver suddenly thought, wasn't that also to do with freedom in the end? Hadn't the Buddha given his son a name that meant fetter or shackle? He fingered the beads. Whenever he tried to count his women, he always had the impression that he had missed one out. The most important. Hail Susan-two and Marilyn and the Romanian woman who cleaned his office in Farringdon Street. She was middle-aged even then. I was in my twenties. Probably dead by now. But he could well be missing as many as ten. On no two consecutive counts, after all, has Cleaver ever got the tally to come out the same. Sometimes it went as low as eighty, sometimes right up into the upper nineties. Perhaps I've been counting some girls twice. That was why it was such a good way of getting to sleep. The mind began to hunt down dark corridors for missing women. Sometimes you stopped to listen for the sounds of their voices. Sometimes you failed to connect attribute, circumstance and name and counted all three: the ambassador's daughter, the redhead with the small breasts, the moment by the swimming pool after the garden party. I'll never make my century now.

But it wasn't really the number that was bothering Cleaver tonight. And he isn't eager to fall asleep. It's very early. No, the real achievement now, he decided, would be to put these women into chronological order; to understand if there had been some kind of progression to it all. If I could get them in order, Cleaver told himself, and it was rather an odd reflection, perhaps I'd understand what it all meant. Perhaps it was the women who led me here. Perhaps it will be a woman who comes to take me back.

He slept with the windows closed these nights. The dark glass gave back the low flame of the lamp. It was the kind of light women liked to make love by, liquid, soft and mobile: the light most like the mind, as Cleaver had once scored points by observing. For some reason he thought of that ugly troll and his frozen axe. They dragged off their damsels by the hair. And of Amanda. Dear Amanda. Would it ever be possible to see her again? Or would it be like the return of someone who has already taken last rites and said his farewells. No one wants you back when they've already divided the spoils. The liquid mind, Cleaver thought, finds relief when it settles in a well-shaped vessel, a project, an analogy, a home; then relief again when it is poured out. It is free. Free to find another vessel. Another woman. Hail Tracy and Jane. Who came first? He had no idea. Certainly these early affairs, and he ticked off Monica and Sarah and Isabel, had been little more than a declaration of freedom from Amanda. You never really contemplated living with me, Isabel had said, did you? That was the time Amanda had thrown his record collection into the street. The girl was quizzical rather than bitter. She couldn't understand why he had stirred up so much trouble for himself if he had never really intended to leave home. Olga and the troll are brother and sister, Cleaver suddenly said to himself. How do these thoughts come into my head?

In any event, he could remember almost nothing about these women. Chronology seemed irrelevant. The only thing that came to mind were colourful incidents, odd places they had made love: on a train, in a bathroom in Broadcasting House, on the Heath at night. There had been the business, for example, of arriving at Martha's parents' holiday home, near Hove, and having to escape through the upstairs toilet window when her father and *his* mistress arrived in the early hours. Cleaver laughed quietly in the half-light. Martha had been most upset. She had the highest possible opinion of her father and then she had twisted her ankle quite badly slithering down from the roof of the porch. Annalisa, Cleaver counted, and Susan-three. He slid the beads along the chaplet. Every ten there was a larger one to separate the sections, to help keep tally. It was subtly satisfying this tactile business of fingering and counting, the murmuring of the mind and the rubbing of the skin. It was reassuring. He could see how people might get into this, muttering away their time with prayers or women.

Priya is the larger bead, he realised. At once he was on the alert. He gripped the rosary tight. Priya is the watershed. Cleaver bit the inside of his mouth. But to jump straight to Priya would mean to miss at least a dozen others. It doesn't matter. Priya is the different shape that marks the passage between one era and the next. But I won't. Cleaver doesn't want to recall Priya. Count her and pass by. This is a body count, buddy. I can remember everything about Priya, he was aware, unlike the others, but I don't want to. I won't. Something was tugging at his mind. Amanda's grip weakened. He came home half drunk and she drew him into an embrace on the stairs. The kids' bedroom doors were open. We hadn't made love in years. Fuck me, fuck me, fuck me, Amanda murmured. She knew that turned him on. At some point I will have to remember Priya, Cleaver thought. Auld acquaintance should be forgot, another voice told him. There had been other girls of course during the Priya phase. It should never be brought to mind. Amanda's embrace was ferocious. He saw the liquid lights of Priya's apartment, the gold and green hangings trembling on the wall. They would drape a red nightdress over the lampshade. He can see her golden body turned to him from the couch. Priya was a real alternative. That was when the phone started ringing. It is because Angela died while you were with Priya.

Cleaver sat up. For a moment he imagined he had caught the sound of footsteps again. The oil lamp was steady in the bare room. There was the constant murmur of water passing over the roof and down through the kitchen. Some nights it was noisier than others. Angela died while you were with Priya. His hands still gripped the beads, but he knows he has no use for them now. At the funeral you lost Angela *and* Priya together. There will be no more counting. Cleaver sank back on the bed. Why do I feel so exhausted? Who would have thought it could be so hard to be alone? So noisy.

He lay still, waiting, as though expecting to be attacked, or to see a ghost. After Priya you remember everything about your women. He realised that now. Your girls rather. Between one talk show and another. Or do I mean after Angela? I remember them for their problems, their families, their hang-ups. It was quite different from the women before. Why? They were banal hang-ups for the most part. Allison's father had wanted her to work in the family company, waterproof fabrics, but she wanted to go away to Paris to use her French. Why can't I decide? she wailed. Avuncular lover Cleaver had tried to help her. The girl washed her hands and crotch obsessively.

He would have any number of girls at a time now. That too was different from before. He tried to help them all. He tried to explain their lives to them. My father always understood more from any conversation than you had put into it, his son had complained. Though I stopped seeing them, of course, if they didn't want sex. Anna's father needed a kidney transplant. She wanted to donate an organ herself. It had become an obsession. Cleaver dissuaded her. I wouldn't want it if you were my daughter. There was the compli-cated situation in which Jeannie had found herself with her boss on one side and her uncle on the other. Sometimes Cleaver got their problems mixed up. Mary's father had committed suicide. It's crazy to imagine you are guilty, he told her.

But why had he listened to so many sad stories? As if you had no story of your own. Were the lovers before Priya all carefree? Surely not. In the past, he used to enjoy shar-ing erotic details with friends. With Simon and Clive. He didn't listen to sad stories. But not now. He still made love with relish, but that wasn't quite what it was about. The Horny Samaritan, Sandra called him. Maeve called him Uncle, Uncle Hal. And the e-mails Cleaver remembered. And later the text messages. How time-consuming it had been, showing all that thoughtfulness. My father had any number of affairs, his elder son had written, with his various studio groupies. The boy had no idea. He could think only in terms of the dirty old man, an easy stereotype for a best-selling book. One of the reasons I stopped reading pornography, Cleaver had explained to Giada, was that none of the standard descriptions of sex made much sense any more. He remembered the girl who was constantly taking calls from her retarded sister, even while they were making love. Cathy. Why didn't I mind? She was straddled over him talking to her sister on the phone. And meantime his own phone vibrated on the bedside table.

My mind was so deeply embedded in all that electronic back and forth, Cleaver remembered. The text message certainly makes an affair easier, but that doesn't mean it's an instrument of freedom. How thick the web had become. And Amanda texting him too. Constantly. BOOTS, her name appeared on the display. Having a coffee at Georgie's. Kisskiss. Have u seen hoo won Cannes? Kisskiss. Whatever the picture painted in *Under His Shadow*, Cleaver had definitely been kinder to his partner after Angela's death. And she to him. Bereavement brought us together. It was a brilliant move, Cleaver realised now, on Amanda's part, to let our respective lovers witness our togetherness in suffering, to invite both of them to the funeral. What affair could survive such a revelation? Larry too had become a kind of ghost, Cleaver had sensed it. Unlike Priya, though, he had lacked the courage to let the dead bury their dead. Goodbye Harold, Priya said. A simple goodbye. She was gone. But Larry continued to haunt. Perhaps these later girls understood that I wanted to hear their troubles. They sensed I wanted more than sex. And that's probably why they gave themselves to me: I was hardly an attractive physique after all. I wanted sadness, Cleaver thought. Jolly sex and sadness. Certainly I never solved anyone's problems. Rather, I became part of their stalemates. They understood at once that no relationship with Cleaver would ever go anywhere. You wanted them to be real relationships – this was the truth – precisely in order that they go nowhere. We have so much potential, Sarah sighed.

Potential! Cleaver lay still. The words are on his lips now: The death of a talented young woman, he whispered into the shadowy air of the dusty room, a talented and pregnant young woman, your daughter to boot, is more or less equivalent to the death of meaning, tout court, is it not? The music Angela would never play, the love Angela would never know. That was when your mind detached itself from the world, when you began your journey to Rosenkranzhof. You could not take a talk show seriously after Angela had died. Not really. You would not fight to keep Priya. Truth was understanding the illusion of potential. There is no point, he told Giada. And Sandra, and the others. Each time, with each girl, you savoured the death of that potential, of the thing that cannot be, the death of the young woman. He definitely chose them younger after Priya. Love was most present to me, Cleaver decided, when both near and impossible, when savoured but already lost, in the unreal space of the hotel bedroom. A future that wasn't to be.

Cleaver remembered a girl whose nervousness getting past the reception desk of the Kensington Palace Hotel always brought on an attack of runs. She was so grateful that he didn't mind. And yet you didn't give up the talk shows. He chewed a lip. Or the sex. You didn't stop behaving, or appearing to behave, like a jolly roué. My father jealously defended a celebrity he claimed to despise, his elder son had written, no doubt because it guaranteed him a constant supply of ingenuous young women. He had given Melanie five-thousand pounds to pay her way through drama school. What would the critics think if the boy had stuck that in his book? Her father was a rich man, but insisted the girl pay her own way. I want you to realise your potential, Cleaver had told her. She was barely adult, on the brink. How many years had gone by like this? You must find another boyfriend if you want a family, he had told Sandra. He had certain formulas now. You should have a family, he told her. There was a solemnity to it, a ceremony of loss. Of all of them it was Sandra who had understood him most and most refused to accept what she understood. Run away with me, she insisted. Astride his thighs, she daubed MY MAN on his stomach with menstrual blood. He remembered her reaching a hand between her legs then smearing the blood on his stomach.

Angela died while I was with Priya.

Cleaver shook his head. The room brooded. A whole month has gone by and you have got nowhere, he announced. Crossing the roof, the piped water murmured its prayers. You have made no progress. A month of silent living and you are still buzzing with interviews, with protests, with accusations. You see an abandoned piece of agricultural junk in the midst of the most breathtaking landscape and at once you are thinking about the conundrum of freedom, coercion, sexuality. You are thinking about yourself. Same when he had seen two large and ugly beetles toiling over each other among the pine needles. Endless reflections.

Cleaver tried to lie still and concentrate on the small sounds of the house. Something creaked somewhere. If I could see the landscape as a whole, he decided, when I was out walking, or even just standing at the window; if I could apprehend the wholeness of it, perhaps then this voice and the past would dissolve outward into that whole and the mind would be still. Or if you could just concentrate concentrate concentrate on the simplest of physical truths – a rock, a tree – and really get the damn thing into your skull. Hadn't that been the plan, the first or second day: to contemplate simple silent shapes and forms, cutting out all the noise, the television and traffic and text messages, really to be there where you actually were with the objects around you, eliminating all false consciousness, eliminating false interest in things you had no connection with, developments in Sudan, gay-couple adoptions? Yet a month later, in a silent room lit by a smoky oil lamp, the mind was even louder than everything it had rejected. The mind was deafening. Did the old Nazi talk to the troll? he wondered. It was the waterfall in the deep wood. Is that a solution or a symptom? I must stop talking to Olga, Cleaver decided. I should get rid of her. After all, it wasn't my plan to bring her here. She was foisted on me. He remembered Frau Schleiermacher's laughter. Ihr Mann ist ein Jäger, Hermann chuckled. A hunter. Pam, pam. I will lock her up in the cupboard with the troll, Cleaver suddenly thought. Or chuck them both off the ledge into the void. Please Harry. It was Amanda's voice. He heard it quite distinctly.

Cleaver is sweating now. Did you remember your tranquillizers, Harry? How well she knows me. Having T with Larry. Wish it was U. How many messages she must have sent these last weeks, not even knowing whether he was reading them. How many interviews my son will have given. Maybe he did win the prize. He's famous. They're making the movie. If I phone him he will insist it was fiction. It's just a novel, Dad. He is expecting me to phone. If you can't concentrate on a single visual image, Cleaver decided – which after all was hard in this flickering lamplight – perhaps you could just repeat a single word. One word, muttered over and over, would break the flow. He assumed that was what mantras were about. A sort of crowbar to smash one's way out of the trap of reflection. Even you, Mr President, once had a serious alcohol problem. Isn't that so? You needed help. Troll. Cleaver began. The word had a nice round dull sound. Troll, troll, troll, troll, troll, troll.

Cleaver fingered the rosary beads. Mantras and beads couldn't be far apart. Didn't they have prayer wheels, blown by the wind, or turned by mountain streams? Not unlike the cowbells. The world was turned into a praying machine. Prayers that kill thought, Cleaver told himself. Perhaps that was what religion did. Troll, troll, troll, troll, troll, troll. It was close to doll too. Troll doll troll doll. But a monk doesn't comment on the mantra he repeats. Then his fingertips touched one of the larger beads. Angela, Cleaver whispered. Angela, Angela . . .

There came a fierce knocking on the door downstairs.

Engländer! Someone was shouting. Engländer!

XI

CLEAVER HURRIED DOWN the stairs. He was so relieved to be called out of himself; this voice was so urgent. He trod heavily on the fourth step from the top. Engländer! The stair splintered. It gave. Cleaver's foot crashed through and he fell forward. The oil lamp flew out of his hand, bounced on the stone floor and sent a sheet of flame up the wall. Tumbling onto his wrists, Cleaver had a vivid impression of the stuffed eagle garishly illuminated above the ever-complacent Olga. By the time he had recovered his wits, the flame had sunk to a small fierce fire against the nearest armchair. Water, he thought. He was shaken. Engländer! Wo ist Seffa? Someone was pounding on the door. I must have bolted it.

Cleaver dragged himself to his feet. A pain shot up from his ankle. By the light of the flames, he hobbled breathless round the armchairs, through the kitchen and pulled the bolt. Jürgen thrust his way in. Wo ist Seffa? The man began to speak urgently. Feuer, Cleaver protested. Hopping to the sink, he turned on the tap. Jürgen's clothes smelt of the cowshed. His eyes were bloodshot. Realising what was happening, he ran through to the sitting room. Then Cleaver picked up the sound of heavy boots on the stairs. Achtung! he shouted. He heard the man stumble but apparently survive. Seffa, he was calling, Seffa! Then Cleaver was just hobbling toward the armchair with a bowl of water, when Jürgen came racing down with the open sleeping bag that had been spread on the bed.

The fire had caught a corner of the upholstery. Olga continued to smile into the flames. Cleaver slopped his water on the chair and Jürgen threw on the sleeping bag. The light died. Jürgen was holding the quilted bag around the fire, pressing his body against it. Disorientated, Cleaver smelt smoke. The room is filling with smoke. He started awkwardly toward the window. He can barely put down his right foot. Wo ist Seffa? Jürgen demanded. He was scrambling to his feet. Somehow the two men banged into each other. There was a stink of cow shit and spirits and chemical fumes. Then a torchlight snapped on in the kitchen. The beam swirled with smoke. Jürgen, Herr Cleaver? It was Frau Stolberg. Wo ist Seffa? She seemed stern, but anxious. The voice was measured. Wo ist sie? Jürgen pushed open the window. Das weiss ich nicht, Cleaver said. I don't know.

There was no spare oil lamp. Why hadn't Cleaver prepared for such an emergency? Jürgen took the torch and went to examine the fire. Mehr Wasser, he said. Frau Stolberg had started to climb the stairs in the reflected light from the torch. Seffa! she shouted. Her voice raised, she produced a torrent of words. Achtung, Cleaver told her. The stairs! Jürgen was speaking too. Seffa! Frau Stolberg cried.

Cleaver turned on the tap again. While the bowl was filling, he pushed open the window. The air was cold, the water icy. There was time now to locate his own torch on the shelf. The beam trembled in his hand. I'm shaking. He hobbled back, clutching the torch against the bowl.

The room was lit by a flame again now, but it was only Jürgen's lighter playing over the wood in the fireplace. The smoke was thinning. Kommen Sie doch, he told Cleaver. It was strange to hear the sounds of footsteps clattering over his head. Frau Stolberg must have found the splintered door, perhaps the pornography by his bed.

Seffa ist nicht hier, he told Jürgen. Ich habe nicht Seffa gesehen. The flame on the logs finally caught. Jürgen stood up and shouted something to Frau Stolberg. The woman came carefully down, speaking all the while. She was angry. Jürgen poured the bowl of water into the burnt upholstery of the armchair. My sleeping bag is ruined, Cleaver thought. He sat down heavily on the chair opposite Olga.

Herr Cleaver. Frau Stolberg reached the bottom stair and came to speak to him. The room was flickering with the flames catching in the fireplace now. She turned off her torch. Her eyes were as steady as they had been at the funeral, her back rigid in a heavy coat. She wore a black headscarf. Wo ist Seffa? she insisted.

Sitzen Sie, Cleaver said. He gestured to the armchair. The doll could be moved to the floor. Entschuldigung, he tried to explain. Die . . . stair ist brochen . . . gebrochen. Jetzt. Ich bin ge . . . He had no idea how to continue. Drink? he asked and turned to Jürgen. He felt sure the man would understand. Trinken? But Frau Stolberg had started speaking very rapidly. Jürgen went to the window, tugged it open, pushed his head out and in a tremendous voice yelled: Seffa! SEFFA!

Cleaver was aware of the cold air flowing in. The door was open too. They think I might have staged the accident to give the girl time to get out of a window, he realised. He protested: Es ist vier wochen ich sehe nicht Seffe. He held up his fingers. Four weeks. I haven't seen her. Seffa ist nicht hier. Willst du Whisky trinken? Es gibt eine Flasche in der Kuche.

The two began to talk again in the firelight. Jürgen wore a heavy leather jacket and the small cap he used for milking. The girl has disappeared, Cleaver thought. Perhaps she hasn't come back from shopping in Luttach. He felt overwhelmed. It must be the effect of these days without speaking to anyone. How could they have imagined she might be with him? Wo ist der Hund? he asked. It was grotesque. He had to repeat before they would pay any attention. Der Hund? The girl couldn't be involved in a traffic accident, he thought, surely. They didn't reply. Frau Stolberg hadn't said anything about the upstairs door being broken.

Watching mother and son discuss the matter in the light of the fireplace, Cleaver had the distinct impression that it was Frau Stolberg who was the more anxious of the two; Jürgen was actually smiling now, protesting, as if, having found that the girl wasn't with Cleaver, all danger was over. It was something silly Frau Stolberg had imagined. Has the girl been dropping hints about me in order to cover up something else that's going on? Cleaver wondered.

Es gibt, he announced, nein, es gab . . . how to say it . . . ein anderer Mann hier, heute. Another man, he repeated in English. Why he had decided to say this, he didn't know. Now they were paying attention.

Wer war das? Frau Stolberg wanted to know.

A hiker, Cleaver said. He didn't know the word. Ein Junge, am Fuß, mit Rucksack. Er ist am . . . He had no idea how to say gone to the ledge. Unter gegangen. Unter? Cleaver struggled to his feet, hopped to the window and pointed down past the lavatory toward the track. There.

Suddenly the two Tyrolese were arguing. Frau Stolberg

seemed extremely determined. She was giving orders. What could the handsome hiker have to do with the unattractive Seffa? Cleaver wondered. He limped back to his armchair.

Sie isch mei Tochto! Jürgen was yelling. All at once a personality came into focus in his face, as if he were truly present for the first time. His unhealthy eyes gleamed. Sie isch *mei* Tochto!

Frau Stolberg stared. Daughter? Cleaver wondered. Jürgen shouted another sentence which definitely included the word Engländer. It appeared to be spoken with scorn. Cleaver had to twist his neck to follow now since they were moving through to the kitchen. He got to his feet and again had to put all his weight on the left.

Sem gea i alluon, Frau Stolberg said. It sounded like alone. Jürgen was beside himself. As Cleaver rounded the back of the armchair it was in time to see the man plant himself in front of the Bozen Polizeiregiment and spit on the glass. Without a word, Frau Stolberg picked up her torch and walked out into the night.

Cleaver made to lift his ski jacket from the hook and follow her. A heavy arm barred his way. Das macht nichts, Engländer. The peasant laughed rather sourly. He had a good forty-eight hours of stubble on his chin. As on the day he had found him mending the fence above Trennerhof, Cleaver wondered if Jürgen wasn't a little drunk, or mad.

Wo ist sie gegangen? he gestured to the door, though he knew perfectly well where the woman had gone.

Das macht nichts, Jürgen said, shaking his head.

Apparently having no trouble finding his way in the dark, he walked round the table to the shelf where Cleaver kept his bottles. Uncorking the whisky, he noticed the cowbell. Wie schön! He clanged it vigorously. Mariangela! Bruna! Puttane! He rang the bell, laughing raucously, took a deep swig and offered the bottle to Cleaver. Though he didn't actually want any, Cleaver also took a swig. There was something wonderfully stormy about the man. Since in the end, Cleaver's elder son had written, my father never had the courage to break entirely with convention and reputation – why else would he have worked so long for the BBC, why else have stayed so long in a relationship without love? – he was always attracted to crazies, to people who went to extremes, which probably explains why his talk shows were so successful.

Entschuldigung, Tatte, Jürgen was saying. Once again the farmer was standing in front of the photo of the Bozen Polizeiregiment. When he lifted the bottle, Cleaver was convinced he was about to smash it through the glass. Instead, in the reflected light from the fire in the other room, Jürgen touched the neck of the bottle against the glass and raised the bottom so that a trickle of whisky dribbled down the severe young men of sixty years before. Ha! Das is gut, Tatte, nicht wahr?

He is speaking so I can understand, Cleaver realised. Tatte must mean father. He is enunciating carefully. It can only be for my benefit. Jürgen laughed again and lifted his elbow to rub away both whisky and spit. He rubbed hard, grunting and laughing. This is pantomime, Cleaver thought. From the distance, Frau Stolberg's voice came faintly through the cold air, Sef-fa! What did she hope to accomplish, going to the ledge; and what if she smelt the hiker's fresh shit and imagined it had been Cleaver? Verrückt! Jürgen was pointing a forefinger at his temple and twisting it comically from side to side. Sie ist verrückt!

Still drinking from the bottle, Jürgen now went back into the sitting room. It seemed they must wait for Frau Stolberg. It was almost midnight. Vielleicht ist Seffa in Luttach, Cleaver said slowly. She stayed in Luttach. Jürgen was not paying attention. He picked up Olga, sat down in the still-smouldering armchair and placed the doll beside him. Ein hübsches Mädchen! Mmmmbw! He kissed the doll on the forehead, then bent down, picked up the accordion and immediately, vigorously, began to play.

Hopping after him, Cleaver was aware of having every right to feel outraged by a landlord who burst into his house in the night more or less accusing him of philandering with an unconscionably fat daughter. Had they noticed the rosary missing from the door? Especially when he had chosen this house in order to be entirely alone. And now he was being kept awake with accordion music of all things, with sentimental folk tunes. Not to mention the broken stair, the smashed lamp, the ruined sleeping bag. Yet his only consideration was that if Jürgen was so relaxed as to be playing the accordion, there could hardly be any real danger for Seffa. He must know of some friend she has, down in Luttach, Cleaver decided. He was humouring his mother coming here to look for her. Why was the old lady so convinced that the girl had come down to Rosenkranzhof?

Jürgen played with gusto, occasionally stopping to grab a swig from the bottle. It was as if the man had been waiting to have an accordion stuck in his hands. His powerful forearms pulled and pushed. They were tunes you could dance to at village fairs. Jürgen tapped his foot and smiled at Cleaver, at Olga. Raucous, sentimental things. The musician wasn't embarrassed by them. Yet even this man, Cleaver decided, is hamming it up. He found himself watching Jürgen carefully. The hair was unshaven on his rough neck. The ears were large and wide. You ham a tune up, Cleaver thought, so as not to find yourself overtaken by a storm of emotion, to keep control. The girl's safe and sound down in Luttach, he decided.

Mein hübsches Mädchen! Jürgen rubbed his stubble against Olga's face. He pushed the whisky bottle at Cleaver. Trink! Cleaver took a swig. Jürgen launched into another tune, nodding his head extravagantly to the beat. He wants his mother out there to hear it, Cleaver suddenly realised. That's it. He wants her to know that he is not worried, that it was futile for her to walk down there in the night. Yet it was *his* wife had died at the ledge.

Warum . . . Cleaver began. He had to concentrate to find the words now. Jürgen raised a comically bushy eyebrow. This really would make excellent TV. My father, his elder son had written, always invited the wildest people to his talk shows, so he could make fun of the crazy energy that he himself lacked. His charisma was the charisma of someone who always steps back from the brink, while ironically applauding those who take the plunge. Warum ist . . . Ihre Vater . . . hier gekommen . . . in dieses Haus?

Jürgen stopped playing, and placed a rough hand theatrically round one red ear. Cleaver repeated. Why? Why had the old Nazi come here? Jürgen grimaced. Again he made the gesture of rotating a forefinger against a temple and at the same time shaking his head in mock sorrow. Verrückt! Mad.

Hoch, Cleaver pointed upstairs, es gibt ein . . . he didn't know the word . . . Troll, he said. Jürgen was drinking again. Troll, ein kleiner Mann. Mit Pfeife. Cleaver made the gesture of smoking a pipe, of wielding an axe. Jürgen wiped his mouth on his sleeve. The same sleeve that had wiped the photo. He was laughing. Jo, jo. Der Troll! He dropped the accordion heavily and jumped to his feet. In the low light from two glowing logs he hurried upstairs again, leaping across the gap. Cleaver recognised an alcohol-fed energy. Upstairs, he must have tripped over something. It would be darker up there. Der Troll! It must be the same word. There was a heavy bumping and banging. Jürgen reappeared on the stairs holding the thing by its wooden hat. Er ist sehr schön, nicht wahr? Ein schöner Zwerg. Mit Axt!

Jürgen set the creature down by the fire. Können Sie spielen, Engländer? Spielen Sie. He pointed at the accordion. All at once, he seemed very excited. Spielen Sie! The troll too had a bright face in the firelight. A red glow played over the dust and varnish, the painted blade of the axe. The eyes gleamed. Cleaver reached forward and picked up the accordion. He rested it on his knees. His right foot was throbbing. Wie geht's dir? Jürgen was enquiring of the troll. Mußt du noch viele Bäume zerhacken?

Cleaver began to play. Should auld acquaintance be forgot, he began, a-and never brought to mind. Jo, jo, Jürgen laughed. Das ist gut! He arranged the troll so it was facing into the room, set the bottle down on the mantlepiece, picked up Olga and began to waltz. Should auld acquaintance be forgot, for the sake of auld lang syne. The words didn't seem as odious to Cleaver now as they had earlier on in the evening. The effect of the whisky, no doubt, and the company. Jürgen had begun to sing. Apparently there were German words. Burns in German! The man did a pirouette with Olga in his arms. The movement was surprisingly graceful. There are tears in my eyes, Cleaver realised. Jürgen! Frau Stolberg snapped. The woman stood in the doorway with her torch pointing at the floor.

Later, rearranging his bedding, Cleaver recalled what seemed to him one of the most perceptive remarks his son had made in his generally unforgivable book: When my parents played together, they played at having arguments, he had written. There had been an element of rehearsal, Cleaver thought, in the way Frau Stolberg and Jürgen had shouted at each other this evening, the son clowning with the troll, the mother making her eyes intense and cold. In any event, neither had addressed another word to Cleaver.

We played at arguing, he remembered, climbing into bed, because it was the thing we knew how to do best. We knew all the steps. Sometimes, his elder son had written – and this was towards the end of the first section of the book – they would shout such horrible things at each other that we would cry, then Mother would burst out laughing and explain that they were only playing, they didn't really hate each other, while my father picked us up and hugged and kissed us. Clearly at some point Jürgen had said something terrible about Frau Stolberg and the old Nazi. He said it facetiously to the troll, as if expecting a reply. Cleaver had listened, like a child who can't really understand what the adults are talking about. Scheiße! Jürgen said. Frau Stolberg refused to shed her fiery coldness. Cleaver had been listening for the name Ulrike. Or Tochter. Instead, Frau Stolberg kept saying, Seffa. Perhaps she was insisting they leave at once. They had to find the girl. And Jürgen was resisting. But it was a fake resistance. He would give way just as soon as he had thoroughly annoyed her with his clowning. My parents made each other who they were – like the classic theatrical double act, you couldn't im-agine one without the other – then whenever there was an audience they played those parts quite consciously, hamming and rehearsing their arguments for fun. That was a perceptive remark, Cleaver decided. Though it hadn't always been clear to him when he and Amanda had been playing and when they were in earnest. You grew so used to irony, to an illu-sion of control. Then events overwhelmed you.

After his visitors had gone Cleaver poked his nose out of the door before bolting it for the night. The temperature has plunged, he thought. The sky was intensely clear, pulsing with starlight. There was the sharp cracking sound of something contracting, freezing. This business with my foot is serious, he thought, limping up the stairs. To get over the gap, he had to make a big effort heaving himself up on the handrails. Do I miss those fake arguments? Cleaver wondered, stretching the sleeping bag over the bed again. Burnt patch or no, he needed it. When we played like that, it was as if we accepted destiny, ourselves, and laughed at it too. There were no real arguments after Angela died, Cleaver remembered. But nor did they play at quarrelling any more. Climbing into bed with his socks on, he fervently hoped that the Stolbergs would find Seffa at home when they got back to Trennerhof.

XII

Waking early, Cleaver found his ankle had swelled enormously. When he tried to put weight on the foot, the pain almost made him pass out. He had to sit on the bed again. The nausea was slow to clear. It might be unwise, he heard a voice say, to find yourself too far from essential services? Who had said that? It was hard to dress, hard to pass his ankle through his trouser leg, almost impossible to get a boot on. He found the rosary between the sheets and slipped it into a pocket. And this was the very day he had meant to walk down to Luttach to see Hermann about bringing up supplies. As it was, it took an age just to negotiate the stairs.

Cleaver steadied himself against the mantelpiece. How much do we have to eat? he asked Olga. That old eagle hasn't caught anything I suppose? A rat perhaps? A marmot? My breathing seems rather louder than usual, he thought. He coughed. The troll was still watching the place where Jürgen had danced. Hangover? Cleaver enquired. There was something odd about this morning. Hopping round the kitchen, he found two packets of spaghetti, biscuits, some apples, a couple of tins. Good for a day or three. But almost at once he changed his mind. You have your famous Norwegian walking poles, don't you? He spoke out loud. Get moving. Go to Trennerhof. This foot needs seeing to. Otherwise you'll be a cripple for the rest of your life. No sooner, his elder son had written, did my father have the ghost of an ailment than he was convinced he was on his way to being a ghost.

Cleaver pulled on his ski jacket, jammed the felt hat onto the now straggly hair surrounding his bald spot, and hopped to the door. He took his walking sticks. Outside the wind was bitter cold. It was incredible though, now he thought about it, that the Stolbergs hadn't enquired about his foot. They must have realised he had fallen on the stairs. They are so wrapped up in their own problems, he told himself, it didn't occur to them to worry about me. But now he turned back. He hadn't even crossed the clearing before it became obvious he would need scarf and gloves. My fingers are red. What a strange silence, he noticed again. The morning light was intense and steady, but somehow grey too. There's no water running, he realised. He went to the tap. It was down to a trickle. Why should the Stolbergs worry about you? Didn't you ask to be alone?

Crossing the clearing again, he saw the air had magically thickened. It's snowing. His heart started with pleasure. They were big thick flakes, falling soft and steady. The wind had dropped in an instant. He turned to look back at the house. With enchanting swiftness the black roof had frosted. The smoke from the stovepipe curled up among the flakes. Rosenkranzhof. How pretty! The larger landscape has disappeared, Cleaver realised. The peaks have gone. There was just his tiny house, the woods, the gorge and the thickly falling snow.

He turned and climbed, digging his sticks into the uneven ground. He would never have believed snow could settle so fast. He stopped to rest. He had skied in a snowstorm with Giada one day. He remembered the snowflakes melting on her lips. Beneath the trees the ground was still dark in patches, but where the track was exposed it was already a smooth white. Fleetingly, he remembered Caroline a few years back complaining how the snow never settled in the borough of Westminster. I hardly think of the younger kids at all, he muttered. Did I ever throw a snowball with Phillip? He honestly couldn't recall.

Cleaver hobbled on. There was ice forming on his beard now. He put a glove over his mouth and breathed warm air into it. Keep walking. He bent into the slope. Everywhere the snow fell with wonderful steadiness. He had filmed a gypsy camp in the snow once – that he did remember – with Amanda and Larry. In County Clare. Very picturesque. Amanda and Larry had been obsessed by gypsies. Cleaver stopped. It was a while since he had thought about this. Life gets to be so long. There had been a green caravan with a red chimney. Always on the brink of insolvency, Larry's little publishing house churned out books about gypsies and by gypsies and Amanda reviewed them glowingly and with passionate indignation. He remembered in particular a memoir by a Hungarian gypsy who had been in Belsen. Cleaver had read a few pages himself. There had been grants from the Arts Council. *Under His Shadow* had said nothing about the way the author's mother found justification for her long relationship with Larry in their shared commitment to minority causes. At least I only used to say I had some party or editorial meeting when I stayed out. I never expected anyone to believe me.

Resting on his sticks, Cleaver shook his head. What a

figure I must cut, a bearded, limping, long-haired hulk on sticks with a broad-brimmed grey felt hat. He felt good, though, photogenic even. When you're on the move, he thought, out in the landscape, especially in these extreme conditions, then it's a pleasure to remember things, however painful; whereas alone in the house the head gets so pressurised, the thoughts implode. At a certain point, he recalled, Larry and Amanda had asked Ken Loach if he would make a documentary about some Irish gypsies. Larry was publishing a book about them. Amanda was very excited. Cleaver had had Loach on a talk show where the director spoke of the plight of a mentally-ill adolescent, the main character in some early film of his, as being emblematic of the individual's struggle against society. The family in this early film, Loach said – it was part documentary, part fiction – had crushed the girl, refused to recognise her special needs, to the point that she withdrew into mutism, since, even if she spoke, no one listened to her. The family was a dangerous and repressive institution, Loach said. This was the sense of his film: the unequal struggle of vulnerable individual against cruel society. God that was a long time ago, Cleaver reflected.

Was it because of his aversion to repressive families that Loach had turned down Amanda and Larry's proposal for a documentary on gypsies? The controversial director had come across well on the talk show. You do it, Harry, Amanda had asked him. Arms hanging at her sides, she had leaned heavily into his paunch, face upturned to his. Larry has it all set up, she said, script and everything. Amanda was a beautifully slight woman beside Cleaver's bulk. Unseemly bulk, his elder son had written. Do what, begging your lady's pardon? Cleaver had asked. She looked up sweetly into his eyes. It was a parody of pleading. Her mouth was small and twisted with irony. Then they both laughed. Our fun and our arguments were always parodies of fun and parodies of arguments. This show has been running as long as *The Mousetrap*, Mother used to joke; so Cleaver's son had written. Alas, the original rodent decomposed long ago, my father invariably added. Not even a whiff of the blighter. Did I really say blighter? It didn't sound very Cleaver. *No-Mad* proved a milestone in the history of aware-ness-raising, *Under His Shadow* had rather generously pronounced of the humdrum gypsy documentary. Awareness-raising is horrible, Cleaver thought. But the boy said nothing of the strangeness of his father's agreeing to work together with his partner's lover.

Cleaver leaned on his sticks and swung his good leg forward. Actually, we were quite a happy threesome on that trip, he remembered now. The film conveyed nothing of course of the stench inside the caravans, only their pictur-esque and poverty-stricken exteriors. Two or three had defi-nitely been repainted for the film. Even the snow seemed to be laid on to make the camp prettier. Cleaver recalled a close-up of tender blades of grass pricking from the ice beside a caravan wheel with a flat tyre. What made me do that for them? he wondered. When it came to the final cut, Larry wouldn't accept anything that showed how the gypsies treated their children. He felt it would be inappropriate to complicate the public's response. Cleaver had agreed. He remembered a little girl forced to stand barefoot in the snow. They didn't show it.

Already there was more than an inch of snow. It was making that nice squeaky sound under his boots. The air was still and icy. The flakes came down so thickly that even a broad-brimmed hat couldn't keep them out of your collar. Cleaver shivered. He had done the film, perhaps, because he guessed how much it would disturb Larry to witness the well-oiled mechanisms of his and Amanda's arguments. And of course Amanda would be obliged to compare my efficiency with his dithering. Even the decision to go back to London for a couple of days in the middle of the shoot was done to show them I was in control. Though officially I went for Angela, he remembered.

Suddenly the snow in front of Cleaver exploded. He had been contemplating the steep hairpin where the rockfall had blocked Hermann's cart that first day. About a third of the way, he told himself. There were icicles hanging from the weathered fractures. Then the snow flew up in his face as Uli came bounding and slithering down the track. Banging into him, the dog barked and tugged at his trouser leg. He's happy to see me. He wants to go down and sit by my fire. No, we're going up not down, he told the animal. We have to go to Trennerhof. Uncle Harry's hurt his leg.

He thrust his sticks in the snow and swung his good leg forward. The dog barked and snapped. Cleaver bent, picked up a handful of snow and threw it at the creature. Uli yelped. Larry had seemed rather left out when he and Amanda had thrown snowballs at each other. Larry wasn't a playful guy at all. He had an irritatingly slow, earnest voice. You're spoiling the girl, breaking the trip just for her, Amanda had complained. You should say no. But she was grateful he was going, of course. She was torn. We were always torn.

The dog tugged at Cleaver's trousers again and this time he slipped and fell. Back on his feet, brushing himself clean, he hesitated. If anything, the snow appeared to be coming down more heavily. It was getting treacherous. His foot wasn't hurting so much now. Perhaps it's an ordinary sprain, Cleaver thought. All at once it seemed stupid to sacrifice his solitude for an ordinary sprain. The first snow always thaws as soon as it's fallen. In a day or two you'll be able to walk up to Trennerhof with no problem. You still have food. Whereas if you go now you'll be taken down to the hospital in Bruneck. You'll be tempted to turn your phone on, check your e-mail. Amanda will have written. Before you know it you'll be back in London to see a specialist.

The dog came and thrust her snout in his lap. Ugly thing. He stroked the animal. What a strange moment that had been when he had flown back to London so that his daughter wouldn't be spending the night alone in the house with a man she hardly knew. But really, perhaps, so as to show Amanda and Larry that he had no problem at all with their spending the night together. Okay, he told Uli, we'll go down. Once I have the dog in the house, Cleaver reasoned, if I don't let him out, someone's bound to come and get him. Quite probably Seffa. If the dog was back, no doubt she was too. Then he could explain about his foot. They would bring him some supplies. He had cash.

The walk back was very beautiful. It seemed the mountain landscape had been waiting for this. The snow suffocated all sound but the snuffling here and there of the dog, the quiet squeak of Cleaver's tread. What I should have suggested to Loach, Cleaver thought, was that actually there is nothing society enjoys more than to savour the struggle of the individual against society. Cleaver propped his poles against a rock and tried to adjust his collar. Angela had met the guy at some provincial concert where everyone was drunk or high and any conversation impossible thanks to the deafening volume of the music. Nothing new about that. Nevertheless she was in love. Please Paps, she had begged on the phone to Limerick. Cleaver's daughter was far from mute. Logorrhoeic rather. She took after her dad. Please! Craig lived in Glasgow, he couldn't afford to come to London without somewhere to stay and since he worked during the week he could only come at the weekend, this weekend, she said. Please, Paps, I'm in love.

The younger children, as Cleaver recalled, had been spending half-term with their Scottish grandparents. Cleaver's elder son could not promise, as he had put it, to be in that night, because he had a party on. First he had promised he would be around, to see that all was okay, to offer a reassuring presence for his sister, but then he had said actually he couldn't promise. Just tell her she can't invite the bloke, Amanda insisted. She wanted Cleaver to leave her and Larry alone for a couple of days, but not in order to indulge Angela. Nobody ever lets me do what I want, just because I'm a girl, Angela wailed. Why can't I have a friend over? You should be glad I bothered to tell you.

They had reached that point in the documentary where they needed to go through the footage they had and see where they were up to. I'll go back to London for the weekend, Cleaver said, while Larry takes stock. It's his film. That way Angela can have her friend over and there'll be no danger. I'll be around.

Amanda was furious. You spoil her, she raged. You always let her have her way. Imagine we say no, Cleaver was adamant, and she invites him anyway, since she knows we're not there to check. Then when they're alone in the house he won't take no for an answer and rapes her. As far as they knew their daughter still hadn't had sex. So what do we do then: say we told you you shouldn't have invited him?

It had been marvellous, Cleaver remembered, watching Larry's growing embarrassment during that long argument. How the man was diminished by not having children of his own to argue about and be responsible for! But why did Amanda and I take such pleasure in tormenting, in playing those games? Catching himself by surprise, Cleaver suddenly sat down on the path.

How silent it was. He turned his face to the sky and let the icy flakes fall on his closed eyes. Why did we do that? Such light, soft touches. Then, surprising himself again, he actually lay back and stretched out in the snow. Perhaps the cold ground would be an antidote to all this feverish thinking. Unexpectedly, he felt quite comfortable. Perhaps the snow is my element, he thought. For a moment he imagined himself buried in whiteness. The steady flakes would sift down filling the wrinkles of jacket and trousers, slowly smoothing over the great mound of flesh that was Harold Cleaver. The idea seemed oddly luxurious.

Cleaver must have lain there for four or five minutes. The dog came snuffling round him. Shoo! Leave me in peace! The creature wanted to lick the snow from his beard. Tickled, Cleaver sat up. But for some reason he was reminded now of his son's last comment on *No-Mad*: My father made astonishingly sensitive documentaries, his elder son had pontificated, on behalf of those like the Romanies who were getting a raw deal in life. In this case, his use of the snow as a metaphor of human coldness was extraordinary. But in private he despised the rhetoric of charity, perhaps because he was such an uncharitable old miser himself. Certainly I never saw him give a copper to a beggar, whereas his credit card was always available for champagne and nouvelle cuisine.

On his haunches in the snow, Cleaver burst into laughter. He grabbed icy handfuls and tossed them in the air. What had the boy been reading! If ever I go back, he resolved, I'll write directly to the *TLS* to protest about the Booker people shortlisting scribblers who write clichés like a copper to a beggar. He struggled to his feet. It had been an excellent idea, he told himself, to buy these Norwegian walking sticks.

Perhaps five minutes later he rounded the bend and Rosenkranzhof came into view. A deer stood motionless right by the door. Its proud antlers seemed the perfect ornament to what was now a fairy-tale cottage. How beautiful, Cleaver thought. He looked across the clearing. Snow lined every window ledge. How lucky I am to have this refuge. The proud animal held its nose raised, eyes alert. Then Uli arrived and dashed at the beast. The ugly dog slithered and slipped. Spirit-like, the deer was gone.

XIII

It had always fascinated Cleaver that a cleaver was something that chopped things in two, meat usually, while to cleave might also mean to cling to someone, to become part of them. A man shall cleave unto his wife and they shall be one flesh. One meat. He had never bothered looking into the etymology of this. But then he had never married either. Can you really become part of someone else? On the other hand, could I ever properly separate myself from Amanda? You have separated yourself, for Christ's sake, Cleaver protested.

He was sitting on the armchair before the fire. The dog was on the hearthrug. Outside the snow fell steadily into the gorge. More separate than this you cannot get. Perhaps Rock Of Ages, it occurred to him as he warmed his hands, combined both meanings. Rock of ages, cleft for me, Let me hide myself in thee. Cleaver picked up the accordion and began to play. How gloomy. His fingers were stiff and swollen. He had often crooned the hymn to the twins as a lullaby. When I soar through tracts unknown, See Thee on Thy judgement throne. It had a soporific effect. Closing his eyes, Cleaver imagined expanses of gleaming snow stretching up into the peaks. *Cleaver Cleft* might have been the better title for his son's book. Footprints would lead upwards across the ice to a dark cave, a narrow fissure in the rock. Let me hide myself. He understood that emotion. Abruptly, Cleaver stopped playing.

Tired as he was, he had worked hard on returning to Rosenkranzhof. My ankle is just a sprain, he decided, and this first snow will thaw at once. It's not December. He felt he had an insurance policy now the dog was here. The Stolbergs wouldn't abandon their dog. Still, he brought in as much wood as possible, stacking it carefully against every bare section of wall. You must keep warm. Despite the protection of the eaves, the snow was already lying heavily on the tarpaulin that covered the stack outside. Cleaver hopped back and forth with a basket, carrying four or five logs at a time. Then he wasted half an hour trying to get a splinter out from under a nail. He hoped he had got it all out. Perhaps there was something still in there. The light was so grey and his eyes are so poor. The finger hurt if you pressed. It was sore. He sucked it. I'll have no lamp when night falls, he realised. Just the fire. And my torch. He felt excited.

Going out again to check the weather, Cleaver discovered that he could put the heel of his foot down now, but still not the flat. There was a sharp pain. Should I try to clear a path to the loo? He looked in the cubbyhole under the stairs. Unlatching the door, the air was damp and chill. He had to hobble back to the kitchen for the torch. The beam found a pair of snowshoes hanging on the rough wall. You didn't see those before. He shivered. There were bundles of wire for snares and a pair of clippers. Nothing useful. Carrying out the shovel, he tried to get going on a path to the loo. Otherwise I'll be shitting by my own front door. But already there was a twilight feel to the day. He was sweating. This is back-breaking work. The snow sifted down effortlessly, as if the very act of falling were voluptuous. What he'd cleared was instantly covered. Suddenly, Cleaver was exhausted. How on earth had the old Nazi managed? he wondered. Der Winter ist sehr schwer da oben, Frau Schleiermacher had said. No doubt Seffa brought down his food from Trennerhof. And he set traps of course. Cleaver still hadn't eaten today. Eat one solid meal, he decided.

The tap wasn't even dribbling. The stream has frozen. Cleaver filled a pan with snow from the area to the left of the front door. Worst comes to worst you can shit and piss on the other side. There was still a tin of ragout. Towards three he was at last sitting in front of a blazing fire with a plate on his knees. Uli whined. Don't you ask for any, he told the troll. Olga's too nice to you by half. You expected Angela's man to be a troll, Cleaver remembered of that occasion when he had flown back from Dublin. Perhaps because she had insisted on referring to him as a man rather than a boy. At seventeen, Angela had a track record of finding men ten or twelve years older than herself, invariably of the lowest social extraction, school dropouts playing in second-rate rock bands. Cleaver's elder son had refused point blank to miss his party and play babysitter when the man arrived. Just tell her no, he insisted on the phone to Ireland. I don't ask people I've barely seen before to stay over while you're away. Why can't you be hard on her, Dad?

The calls to London had been made on the gypsy documentary's expense account. They hadn't had mobiles in those days. Larry began to complain of the tightness of their budget. Was there some alliance, Cleaver had wondered, between Amanda and their son against his twin sister's impatient sexuality? Angela didn't disguise the fact that losing her virginity was now an absolute priority. Paps, I do know how to say no if I want to, she protested. Don't you think I've been asked a million times? All I do is say no. Still, she seemed to appreciate her father's decision to be around at the weekend. I won't interfere, Cleaver had promised. I mean, in the end, I can't stop you doing whatever you want to do. In the end, he repeated. I'll just be around the house, in case . . . In case what? she teased. Remember, Cleaver had told Larry, that if you invite me to be away from home for a month you can hardly deny me ordinary contact with my family.

Putting down his plate for Uli to lick, Cleaver picked up the accordion and played Rock Of Ages. These maudlin tunes were drummed into me when I was a kid in church, he thought, and the older I get the more I regress. Nothing in my hands I bring, Simply to Thy cross I cling. I know you don't give a damn, he broke off to tell the troll, but it does seem to me that this hymn betrays a desire for oblivion, a desire for the merciful earth to open up and swallow the singer whole, once and for all.

Cleaver sat awhile gazing into his fire. He sucked his sore finger. The flames in the grate had the same voluptuous constancy of movement as the steadily falling snow, the same power to mesmerise, to annul the mind. Fire and snow. The body burned, the body frozen. You didn't really plan to change your life when you came here, Cleaver realised now. There were dozens of noble, charitable and even sensible ways of doing that. You planned to end it.

Uli still licked obsessively at the plate. Cleaver smiled. The dog was eating her own saliva now. She was hungry. Getting to his feet he pulled a log from the pile against the wall and thrust it in the fire. Spark and fizz, you bastard. He laughed. I'll have to get the finger looked at, he thought. The splinter was deep. What was the point, he wondered, of having an accordion if you couldn't play anything you would ever want to listen to, just melancholy hymns that confused paradise and oblivion, desire for auld acquaintance and desire to have done with all acquaintance? Thatcher had told people like Ken Loach, Cleaver suddenly remembered, that there was no such thing as society. Did she really say that in so many words? It was curious how you thought you had finished a discussion to your absolute satisfaction only for it to rear its ugly head again an hour, or even five hours, or fifteen years later. For all her unpopularity in media circles, Cleaver had tended to agree with the Iron Lady. He knew what she meant. Society is an imagined thing. But were there such things as individuals either? Could you call a man an individual when he couldn't stop humming all the maudlin tunes drummed into his head before age ten, when the thing he appeared to desire most was to lose his voice forever and dissolve into the landscape? *That's why I came here. To catch an everlasting cold.* It was extraordinary how his son hadn't appreciated that this was the shadow yearning behind every exhibitionism. Only an exhibitionist, Cleaver decided, can really yearn for oblivion, can perhaps actually want to be shot by the jealous husband behind the bedroom door. Only a name-dropper of the magnitude that you were. That was the truth behind the stupid story that closed *Under His Shadow*. *I wanted the man to shoot me.*

Would you like to eat with us, Dad? Angela had asked. I behaved atrociously that evening, Cleaver remembered. *I name-dropped unforgivably.* He had been planning to eat with Priya. He had imagined the kids would stay out till late. *I didn't come back from Ireland for Priya,* Cleaver had told himself, *but now that I am back I might as well see her.* Angela had mentioned a concert, a pub somewhere. She always went out Saturday evenings. She knew every small concert venue in London. Instead they stayed in. To Cleaver's considerable surprise, Craig was black. He was tall, but stooped. The face was handsome, but lopsided. One ear stuck out. He was Negro.

We *want* you to eat with us, Angela insisted. They were already cooking. It was something rather elaborate. Nah, Craig explained, it's that the group Angie wanted to see are crap. He reached out and took Angela's hand across the table. She was wearing one of her satanic bracelets, spikes and skulls. In Cleaver's regard, the young man seemed respectful, but independent. Better to stay in and play ourselves, he said matter-of-factly. He had brought his guitar with him, from Glasgow. His fingers, Cleaver noticed, were the fingers of a smoker and a guitarist. Priya took it badly when he cancelled. It's as if I had two wives now, Cleaver told himself as the voice complained that he never found space in his life for her. Without marrying once. But Priya complained in a soft, elegiac way, quite unlike Amanda.

At the dinner table Cleaver had been extravagantly jovial, opening an expensive bottle, telling anecdote after anecdote about famous names he'd worked with. Craig smiled quietly and said, Right, yeah. He exchanged glances with Angela. Dad, we do know you work in TV, she interrupted. But Cleaver pressed on regardless. His mind was buzzing. The conversation with Priya had unsettled him. I sleep with an Indian woman and am disturbed about my daughter having a relationship with a black. My father, his elder son had written, only asked people about their lives because whatever story they might tell him he was sure to top it with a better story of his own. Cleaver hadn't asked Craig anything about his life that evening. Only later did he discover that the boy had grown up in an orphanage, worked as a welder and played in a rock band.

Towards four, Cleaver went out to relieve himself in the snow. Memory equals mortification, he said out loud. Already there was more than a foot of it. He cleared a path of about three yards so as to establish a little distance should he need to shit. Uli came floundering out and wanted to piss by the wood stack under the eaves. Cleaver chased him off. The flakes still fell thickly. The landscape was unimaginable now behind the opaque air. Since we've done the cooking, Angela had wound up the meal, can you take Ivan out, Paps? The big dog was waiting at the door. It was always me taking the dog out, Cleaver remembered. Ivan was far more hand-some than you, he told Uli. Angela looked wonderful with cropped hair, he remembered. Perhaps the real masterpiece, he suddenly told himself, would be to cut oneself off entirely, inside the head as well as out. To go mute *inside* the head, that was the real challenge. Was the girl mute *inside* her head as well? he should have asked Loach. Had she stopped talk-ing even to herself? Perhaps she wasn't unhappy at all.

Cleaver went back into the house, picked up the troll by the brim of his wooden hat and, using the thing as a walk-ing frame, carried it out of the house. Time to get a little fresh air, old chap. He planted the wooden statue in the snow. The troll has his axe raised. No. Cleaver pushed him over. Lie down, face down in the snow. It seemed impossible to abandon the thing without thinking in these terms. Uli barked at the prone figure. The axe was buried now. You too, Cleaver told Olga. Your time's up, love. He carried the doll in his arms and stood her with her face to the wall under the eaves beyond the wood stack. Good. The Stolbergs would come for Uli around dusk, he thought, or shortly before. Not long to wait now.

Cleaver hopped uneasily about the house. He checked and rechecked his store of food: one full bottle of whisky and one a quarter full, one decent bottle of Chianti, one spare set of batteries for the torch. For perhaps half an hour he stared out of the upstairs bedroom window down into the gorge. There was nothing to see but the white tops of trees and the flakes swirling slowly in the void. They didn't even seem to be falling now. They hung there. It's so soothing, Cleaver thought. He had an image of icy dampness cooling open sores. Uli followed him up the stairs and began to fret. Her claws scratched on the floorboards. Cleaver ignored the animal. Once, he thought he glimpsed the tall crags on the further side of the valley. For a moment the landscape had depth and shape. Then it was gone again.

Lying on the bed with the quarter bottle of whisky, Cleaver waited to hear the Stolbergs' call, though they would surely realise that the snow was too deep now for the dog to climb back alone. They would come with a sled perhaps. He had definitely seen a sled at Trennerhof, propped against the wall beside the chicken coops. What if they see I've put the troll and Olga out in the snow? They'll think I'm mad. Cleaver didn't care. Verrückt, Jürgen had said standing in front of the photograph of his father, wiping the spit from the glass. Mad. Cleaver presumed the old Nazi was his father. Tatte was the word he used. Verrückt, Jürgen had said of his mother when she walked down to the ledge, shouting after Seffa. He pronounced the word very carefully so that I could understand. Mad. Sie isch mei Tochto. Jürgen had said. My daughter. Madness was obviously an unremarkable condition in these parts, Cleaver thought. Jürgen himself was hardly a paragon of sanity, dancing with Olga and accusing the troll of jealousy. Cleaver definitely felt better now that he had dumped the two of them outside. We'll get on better when you've left home, he had told his son. There'll be less friction. Not to mention offering schnapps to his cows. Had Ulrike been mad that night she fell from the ledge? But how do you know that it happened at night?

Cleaver was in the dark now. He listened. Surely this is the quietest it has ever been in Rosenkranzhof. No running water. No branches rattling. Very occasionally the flakes make a soft tapping on the windowpane, as if Olga were asking to be let back in. The mountains are full of ghosts. Really to be rid of them, you would have had to burn them, Cleaver thought. But they weren't mine to burn. Then you'd have caught yourself scattering their ashes.

He could hear Uli's faint breathing as he slept. It was quite dark now and they still hadn't called for him. Cleaver was sure he would have heard. Perhaps the clocks have been moved back, he thought. He listened hard. Something sparked in the fire. They'll come tomorrow, he decided. They won't want to come down in the snow tonight. He remembered listening hard that night in the house with Angela and Craig. The truth of the matter was that you didn't want your daughter to lose her virginity to a Negro. Somehow it seemed important to use that harsh word. To watch my father's documentaries, his elder son had written, and then to hear the views he fielded at the dinner table, was to live in the crossed wires of chronic hypocrisy, to breathe the acrid smell of the moral short circuit, of repelling poles forced into contact. What guff. Yet at the same time you were having an affair with an Indian woman, Cleaver reflected, a small dark southern Indian woman, perhaps the only affair you ever had that could honestly be described as passionate, the only real alternative to the life you have lived. Priya means beloved, she once told him. He had loved her. With Priya everything was simple and easy. Their conversations had been quiet. No torment. There wasn't even the need to avoid confrontation.

The times they spent together were always a pleasure. Those dolls lining the stairs of Frau Schleiermacher's house were my old girlfriends, Cleaver suddenly told himself, the roll-call of my women. He remembered the bright smiling faces and Tyrolese headscarves on the first-floor landing. Every one the same. Why do I have thoughts like this? You should have counted them, he chuckled. Only Priya wasn't among them. They were all rosy-cheeked. I liked Craig, though, Cleaver told himself now. The boy had seemed articulate enough, if only I had left him a little more space to talk. It was funny that he had Amanda's Scottish accent. Certainly he could play the guitar.

Cleaver had lain on his bed in the house in Chelsea, listening while his daughter and her new boyfriend jammed together in the basement. Angela put down a few simple rhythms on the keyboards and Craig played guitar. This young man is a very serious guitarist, Cleaver realised. He woke up. Priya phoned to say she was sorry if she had sounded sulky. Guy's a hell of a guitarist, he told her. Seems Angela's dying to sing in his band. It's just I'm jealous of your children, Priya said, you know, the way they have your unconditional affection, the way they will always be part of your life.

Towards midnight the music had stopped. They've moved to the TV, Cleaver thought, the sofa. He waited. The dog was padding about in the hall. Priya had said she thought it was sweet he was black. Amanda phoned. She's checking that I'm really here, Cleaver decided. An improvement on the last troglodyte, he told her. He said nothing about the colour, or the accent. Apparently Larry felt they needed more of a sense of movement in the film. A lot of the footage was rather static, not nomadic enough. He wanted a shot of caravans on the move, some traditional dancing, by firelight, in the snow hopefully. He was trying to arrange something with the head man. Cleaver lay awake thinking what a prick Larry was. The gypsies had been parked in that field in County Clare far longer than Cleaver had ever lived in any house.

Then they were coming up the stairs. Lying in his bed in Rosenkranzhof, Cleaver could hear the sound of his daughter's giggles. They passed his room on the first floor and headed for the second. Ivan's tail was slapping against the banister poles. Angela had promised that Craig would sleep in the guest room. Cleaver had promised he wouldn't check up on them. She had never slept with a man. Her father was only there for her safety. Is she a girl or a woman? Cleaver wondered. How on earth could Loach say the family was such a repressive institution? Are there institutions that are not repressive? He heard whispering and doors opening and closing. They were pushing out the dog. They're whispering because they think I'm asleep, Cleaver realised. It's a sign of respect. He climbed out of bed, dressed, crept silently down the stairs and drove to Priya's.

Cleaver felt for the torch on the floor by the bed. I must have left it in the kitchen. That was stupid. He hadn't expected to stay up in the bedroom till dark. He had imagined himself hobbling down to meet the Stolbergs come for their dog. But it didn't matter. He has the whisky bottle to pee into. He could empty it out of the window. Downstairs, the stove was well fuelled. The house is as warm as I can make it, he decided. All the same, even wrapped in the three blankets and the sleeping bag he couldn't get properly warm. He shivered. Have I got a fever? The hole in the bag didn't help, but it surely wasn't just that. Olga and the troll will be blocks of ice, Cleaver thought. Uli had curled up among the dirty clothes in the bottom of the wardrobe.

During the night, Cleaver dreamed that a chair in the kitchen was provoking some strange psychic activity. You sat on it and things moved around. The drawers flew out of the sink unit and cupboard doors opened and closed. It was the kitchen in Wandsworth. It was the chair Angela had sat on at dinner with Craig in Chelsea. She sat down and Craig took her hand for a moment across the table. It was a charming gesture. How could his son have written that she was rejecting her sexuality when she cropped her hair? They had made some kind of casserole. Cleaver was telling a story about when he had interviewed Pete Townshend. Suddenly, the chair sprang back across the room and hit the wall. There's a poltergeist in this house! Cleaver cried. He had always known there was a poltergeist. That's why I worked in the shed at the bottom of the garden. He went round the table and moved the chair back to its old place. It sprang backward and flew into the wall again. The fridge door swung open. The room filled with cold. Only then did they realise that Angela was gone. Angela! they started calling. Craig too was alarmed. Angela! It was a poltergeist. The air was chill. Cleaver sat in the chair himself. It will take me to where she is, he said. I'll go and get her. I'm not afraid. It didn't. It behaved like a perfectly ordinary chair. It allowed itself to be pulled up to the table. There was Angela's plate full of casserole, a glass full of wine. Cleaver stood up and the chair shot back and slammed against the wall. Food began to fly out of the fridge. Milk cartons. Graukäse. The room was freezing. A cold wind was blowing. In a torment of anxiety, Cleaver shouted, Her bedroom! He ran up the stairs. The carpet was loose. He tripped and fell. He had hurt his ankle. But she was there. Angela is alive. She is sleeping peacefully in her bed. Her young face is soft and absorbed in sleep. Cleaver bent down to kiss her and woke up.

It was an old dream. Tonight's variations didn't alter the substance. Cleaver climbed out from under a pile of bedclothes. His heart is beating fast. The poltergeist dream. Ow! He had forgotten the bad ankle. He felt in the dark for the bottle to pee into. Now he has forgotten the sore finger. Christ! There was definitely something under the nail.

He limped across to the old Nazi's room and tugged open the window above the clearing. The snow was still falling. There was a strange luminosity. Perhaps it isn't that late, he thought. They have put back the clocks. Seffa, Cleaver called softly. Seffa! The silence swallowed up the sound. For miles everything is deep in snow. Ulrike, he shouted. Angela!

He put his elbows on the sill. Angela! The cruel thing about the poltergeist dream was the extraordinary relief he felt on finding his daughter safe and well in her bed, followed at once by waking, by reality. He had broken his promise coming home at dawn that night from Priya's. Very softly, he had opened the door of her room and peeked in. Amid the usual chaos, Angela was sound asleep, her face turned to the black youth's naked back, the dog on the rug beside. Cleaver looked at his daughter. There was a small tattoo on her shoulder that he had never seen before. A butterfly. A year later Craig was driving her back from a gig when they hit a truck. The child was Craig's, Cleaver knew. I would love to have been your daughter, Priya whispered. She was in tears at the funeral. I wish it had been me, she said. It was the end of their relationship. Staring out in the dark through the drifting flakes, Cleaver whispered: Imagine a female figure coming out from the trees, she is walking to you across the snow. He stared and stared.

Cleaver's lips are icy now. I want to die, he said softly. He closed the window and limped back across the bedroom and sat at the top of the stairs. Lowering himself carefully, he bumped down on his backside. Achtung at the fourth! He gripped the banister. In the sitting room there was a red glow. Cleaver caught a glimmer in the eagle's eyes. That too would have to go. It's you or me, he told the bird. We're the last. Why do you ham this eternal jocularity? he wondered. It must be the result of those years of TV patter, all that automatic familiarity. My father liked to boast that he could chair a TV debate in his sleep, his elder son had written. Which is pretty much what it sounds like to me, Mother replied. You couldn't say they didn't keep their dinner guests entertained.

Eventually he found the torch on the windowsill in the kitchen and the first thing he saw when he switched it on were mouse droppings. There are mouse droppings on the draining board, and between the burners on the oven. Cleaver swung the beam rapidly across the table, the shelves. No sign of the beast. But they were definitely droppings. This show has been running longer than *The Mousetrap*, Mother used to say.

Cleaver went back into the sitting room and stoked up the fire. An interminable double act, his son had written. No wonder my sister turned to loud music and pills. Uli appeared on the stairs, whining. It was dead of night. Six weeks ago, Cleaver thought, two months, three, you were mainly interested in Iraq, the presidential election, global warming, the fate of Blair. Then as soon as you were alone, your family invaded your mind. They possess me.

Could it be, Cleaver wondered, staring into the fire for minutes at a time, that people's political passions, their ideo-logical take on events, their commitments and hobby horses, were in fact nothing more than the displacement of some family embroilment, a different manifestation of the same ghosts? Mr President, may I put it to you that all your political adventures have been an obsessive emulation of the father figure whom you both admire and feel the need to outdo. How reductive!

Cleaver brought the chair as close to the fire as it would go. On the other hand, wouldn't it be more surprising if things were otherwise, if people actually held their opinions, as it were, purely, out of mere rational and intellectual conviction – what could that mean? – and then, having arrived at those opinions purely, they set about working out the consequences in public life, engaging in politics and charities and pressure groups on the basis of the most scrupulous ratiocination. Amanda's thing with the gypsies was definitely a provocation in my regard, Cleaver decided. I always sensed that. No doubt Ken Loach had been through some shit with repressive parents. When asked to explain what was meant by political correctness, his elder son had written, my father would say: Political correctness means not being able to say what one really thinks of gypsies. Yet his film *No-Mad* was surely one of the most sensitive portrayals of gypsy life we are ever likely to see. Such was the conundrum I grew up with, his son had written: There was simply no space that my father didn't occupy, no opinion he didn't simultaneously hold and reject. If you don't catch that mouse soon, Cleaver told the eagle, you're out on your arse with the others. He had always hated, he decided, the kind of journalism that had the presumption to deploy the first person plural.

XIV

WRAPPED IN HIS ski jacket, hat crushed on his bald spot, Cleaver had eventually fallen asleep with his feet on the grate. Now he woke to the smell of scorched socks. Ow! Jumping up, he quenched his burning soles on the cold stone floor. Oh Christ! His ankle hurt. But at least I didn't dream anything. He hobbled across to the window and found it beautifully patterned with frost. How long is it since you saw that? He ran a finger round the crystal shapes, then pulled the window open.

Dawn was breaking and the air was empty now. Just a few flakes were blowing about. Across the clearing, everything was softly curved, blue and grey. Cleaver boiled a pan of snow for tea. I've nothing to give you, he told the dog. Uli followed him about snuffling. The Stolbergs will be here soon. He found four biscuits he had forgotten in one of the cardboard boxes he had brought that day with Hermann. The mouse had got there first. The wrappers were shredded. We've got to get this mouse, he told Uli. The dog padded about whining and sniffing.

Cleaver spent the early morning examining every inch

of the walls, the floors, the backs of cupboards, looking for a small hole. The Stolbergs didn't come. Only now did he realise that the moss between the planks on the first-floor walls must have been laid there on purpose as a form of insulation. The soft green cushion grew into the gaps, feeding on the damp and blocking the drafts. Eventually he found a knothole in the bottom of the kitchen cupboard. There was a suspicious smell. Trying to think what to block it with, he remembered the cat in *The Tailor of Gloucester* who traps mice under china teacups. There was a snowstorm in that story too. He put a Tyrolese beer mug over the hole. Gnash your teeth in outer darkness! It had been Phillip who loved *The Tailor of Gloucester*. Finally a memory of Phillip. Their youngest child liked to copy the drawings in all his storybooks. He was hopeless at school. Unlike the others, Phillip never competed. He was quiet, but not mute, a great copier of pretty drawings, a happy boy. Caroline too had always seemed happy and composed in her studies. To the point that I hardly noticed her. Would the mouse be able to move the mug? Cleaver wondered. An interesting experiment, he promised Uli.

For lunch Cleaver gave Uli half the remaining ragout and drank the Chianti. It's folly to drink all of this, he thought. There were still a few flakes sifting down. Soon it will start to thaw. He floundered as far as he could along the track he had shovelled the day before and shat in the snow. It was sad to soil such gleaming whiteness with a great turd. Acting on a strange impulse, he hobbled back inside the house and collected together every single item that he had brought with him from London. Everything left over from your old life, he muttered.

On the bed he laid out his dark suit, the bright pink shirt, lemon tie, green socks, blue underwear, his watch, a leather coat, the two mobile phones, gold cufflinks, a signet ring, patent leather shoes. He stared at them. Something inside him is hungering for a symbolic act. Burn them. Don't be ridiculous.

In the jacket pocket he found his passport. Look at yourself! Cleaver saw the intense, clean-shaven, pork-pie face that had been so effective on TV. He shook his head. In his wallet were credit cards, driving licence, a wad of cash, receipts, two theatre tickets, his Wood Lane security pass. Cleaver liked to carry cash. And Angela's photograph. His elder son hadn't mentioned the fact that he kept Angela's photo in his wallet. Perhaps he resented it.

Cleaver studied the picture. She looks quite different from Ulrike Stolberg. He knew the face too well. It was just an old piece of cardboard. My lips, Cleaver muttered. Angela had her father's round full cheeks. All the more so with her hair cropped. He tugged at his beard. What on earth do I look like? Uli? All this crazy growth. Now he had got out all his old things he couldn't decide what to do with them.

Outside the afternoon was uncannily still. It had stopped snowing but there was no sign of a thaw. Going out to fetch more wood, Cleaver noticed tracks on the snow. You're not alone, he thought. If you sat quietly enough at the window you would see deer and marmots. Perhaps a fox. You could set snares. He remembered the hiker looking for a place to shit. Only a man of monumental vanity could have assumed that the first casual intruder was an investigative journalist. Put them in the Nazi's wardrobe, Cleaver announced out loud. He opened the fresh whisky bottle and hobbled upstairs again. Life alone isn't a meditation but a constant back and forth, up and down stairs, clothes on and off, piling logs on the fire, cleaning out the ash.

Clambering over the broken stair, Cleaver couldn't decide

whether his ankle was worse or better. The pain was sharp, but I'm used to it. I will not trap animals, he decided. He picked up jacket and trousers and hobbled across to the little room. I don't want a new life. There were no hangers in the wardrobe, but pegs driven into splintery pine. It was strange seeing his clothes hanging next to the old Nazi's. There were half a dozen rough blue shirts, brown overalls. He felt in the pockets. He knew there was nothing there. He had felt in them before, three or four times. The first time he had found a bird whistle. Where did I put it? By the window. Perhaps I should try the overalls on, then I would get a sense of how big the man was.

Cleaver shivered and shut the wardrobe door. I could put planks across and nail it shut, he thought. I need never see those clothes again. Drinking directly and deeply from the whisky bottle, he thought how strange it was he had never got some kind of cancer, or a heart condition. Both his parents had died of cancer. Actually, that was quite an attractive death your son invented for you, Cleaver decided: the gunshot through the lacquered door. He sat down in the room's one chair, rickety and straight-backed. I should be grateful to my son for having dispatched me so elegantly. Though I would have made a more persuasive appeal to the idiot with the gun. What would you say, Cleaver asked himself now, to an older man who was about to shoot the young mistress who wants to leave him? Think of her as your daughter, I would say.

For some time Cleaver sat very still, staring at the small bare room. What had it been used for? There were two wooden boxes full of junk, some books. Why had they locked the door, he wondered, if there was nothing to hide in here? Why was there a lock on the door in the first place?

He decided once again to think about Ulrike and the

Stolberg family. What motive could she have had for committing suicide? If she did. It must have been a year or two after Seffa's birth. It was unlikely she did pills, as Craig and Angela no doubt had. Cleaver had invited various experts on post-natal depression to his talk show once. No one had dared field the idea that a woman with a newborn child might fear she was no longer attractive to her lover. She was stuck with her husband again. Cleaver was sure this had been the cause of Amanda's depression after Caroline was born. She had lost her figure. Larry had slipped off the radar for a while. Or what if Jürgen had discovered the child might not be his? Was that why he insisted, Sie isch mei Tochto. Ulrike's father-in-law, Jürgen's father, had abandoned the family house around that time, to come and live in Rosenkranzhof. Cleaver chewed his lips. How old would the man have been? Sixtyish.

There were cobwebs in the corners. Cleaver took a swig of whisky. When the thaw begins, I'll hear dripping. He listened. Silence. This is the silence you always longed for, he told himself. Jürgen will have brought the cows into the stall. Perhaps Ulrike and the old Nazi used to meet here. In Rosenkranzhof. In this room with the lock on the door. The young woman and the father-in-law. Perhaps she was pregnant again. Or she met another lover here and was discovered by her father-in-law. He used the place for hunting, perhaps. He sat at this window with his gun, waiting for deer to come. Or he blew his whistle to attract some bird or other. Ulrike begged him not to tell. Then there was a secret in Trennerhof. And Frau Stolberg would have sensed that secret. She is that kind of woman, Cleaver thought. Did Ulrike confide with the town-dressed woman, her husband's sister, the rebel of the family, the one who left? Did she tell her that baby Seffa wasn't her brother's daughter? Or the baby that was on the way? I was often sorely tempted by my elder son's girlfriends, Cleaver remembered. He remembered in particular the neurotic girl who always fell ill when the two of them were supposed to move in together. I tried to warn him. What an extraordinary physical presence that girl had had, a knowing smile beyond her age. He couldn't remember her name. But I never did touch them.

Cleaver shook his head and drank again. I could mull over this stuff for eternity, he decided. On the other hand, there was the time when his elder son had tried to date one of his, Cleaver's, girlfriends. Unknowingly, of course. Melanie had told Cleaver every detail, giggling her head off. Or perhaps she didn't tell you everything, Cleaver thought. He wouldn't have put it past her. He had never imagined his girlfriends were faithful to him.

Cleaver moved his chair to the window and forced it open. The cold air flowed in. He leaned on the sill and looked across the clearing. His loo was half buried. The snow was deep. To the left the trees climbing the gorge were silent, their branches sagging with whiteness. Cleaver picked up the whistle he'd left there and blew on it. The shrill sound seemed to connect his thoughts with the world outside. The hunter mimics his victim, offering company, then, blam!

Cleaver whistled again. My father was a wonderful mimic, his elder son had written in those spirited opening chapters, so much so that you sometimes wondered whether he really had a voice of his own. That famous voice, for example, that was to become the news voice of the eighties and early nineties was actually a studied amalgam of a thousand mimicked mannerisms.

Cleaver blew again. He stared across the clearing. He blew once more, long and hard and stared. Sure enough, a young man has appeared, climbing the path that leads up from the ledge, from the charcoal burners' cableway. He is a hand-some, sombre young man, in jeans and denim jacket. For some reason his feet don't sink in the snow. Suddenly, he raises his eyes to the window, the window of Rosenkranzhof. Cleaver stares. Is it Ulrike's lover? The young man has a shotgun slung over his shoulder. Alex, Cleaver breathed.

Uli howled interminably all afternoon. There really is noth-ing left to eat now. You brought no emergency rations, Cleaver reflected. In films people always have emergency rations. No chocolate. No muesli bars. He gave the last strands of pasta to the dog. The whisky will do for me. Towards dark he was afflicted by a desire to go out and check on Olga, but he resisted. Suicide was a form of communication. He had read that somewhere. The very fact of the suicide, the timing, the method used, they were all forms of communication far more powerful than any letter of farewell. Aimed at one's nearest and dearest, of course. The young mother who throws herself into the void is declaring her independence, Cleaver thought. One could hardly say, nearest and coldest, nearest and harshest, nearest and grimmest. She is cutting loose from a thick web, from a society that has decided that words like nearest and dear-est must cleave together. It's an independence that can come only at the cost of your life. That's another thing I might have said to Loach, Cleaver told the dog. Uli was whining, scratching the floor. Whereas murder, dear doggie – he took the creature's head in his hands and shook it – murder is an even more direct form of communication. Savvy? Uli? But all at once Cleaver was shocked by an extraordinary light of recognition in the dog's deep eyes, as if you looked over the brink and found eyes in the void staring back. She understands. Cleaver pushed the creature away.

During the night he dreamed again. This time it was a new dream. He was fucking a rat. A large furry rat with a great wet red vagina. But what appalled him was that he was doing it without a condom. Am I mad? He would contract some filthy disease. Cleaver woke. He was upset. It was the unnecessary ugliness of the dream that galled him. It was unpleasant. Life is waste, he thought, a waste of vivid and unhappy mental images, a waste of young lives, a waste of effort. I've wasted enough time, were Priya's last sad words. Beloved. Goodbye Harold. What had become of all those years of televised debates, the screen filling and emptying? Even in your dreams you avoid your son, a voice said.

Lying stock-still in the dark Cleaver was alert, electrified. It was the same feeling he had had that afternoon when he woke to find someone stalking round the house. Have the Stolbergs come, he wondered, in the middle of the night? Have I been tracked down? There's a wind blowing now, he realised. There was noise. He limped to the window. A strong breeze had swept the snow from the tops of the trees. Even in your dreams you avoid your son.

He hurried to get back under the blankets. It was true. But when had it begun? When did I begin to avoid him? From the day he smelt a rat. Cleaver felt about for the whisky bottle. My son became a sort of fundamentalist, he thought. Not religious. But he always knew what was right and wrong. He was always sure of himself. Selfish and priggish. *Under His Shadow* is the work of a fundamentalist, yet fundamentally self-serving. Cleaver waited. He heard the sound of snow sliding off the roof, but it wasn't a thaw. The wind was rising. Perhaps you identified your son with a part of yourself that you wanted nothing to do with. Con-science, my father would quip to his dinner guests, equals the science of conning people into behaving.

Drinking from the bottle, Cleaver tried to remember those scenes around the dinner table. His son would lean forward in dogmatic stance. He would repeat my ideas to whatever guests we had, but in crass form. Phillip and Caroline whispered and giggled together. They were too young to take part. When your son presented your ideas, Cleaver remembered, you suddenly realised how crass they were. You had to retreat from them, contradict them. He repeated them of course because he wanted your approval. You hated that. Angela never asked for approval. She did just what the hell she wanted. You hated the way your son always took Amanda's part. It wasn't necessary. She had no need of him. First he wouldn't leave home, then he was constantly on the phone to his mother. God knows what about. And after fifteen years avoiding him, he writes this book. It was an ambush, an assassination. I had found a strategy that made it possible, despite everything, for me to live, to survive, and he blew it away. You must confront your son, Cleaver told himself.

This is a trick. Cleaver lay very still, like some animal who still hopes to avoid the hunter's eye. He is alone in an expanse of snow but still hopes not to be caught. This thought is a trick to drag you back to the world, to have you lose all the ground you have gained here. You avoided your son from the moment the boy smelt a rat. He repeated your opinions in your presence, and at the same time he was accusing you of not really holding those opinions, certainly not living by them. The more he repeated them, the less you held them. The wind tugged at the house now. The cold trees creaked. For a long time, Cleaver lay silent. But he knew he was caught now. Alex, he said at last. Damn you.

He waited till dawn. All at once his mind is made up. He was excited. He went back into the old Nazi's room and retrieved the red mobile from the pocket of his jacket. We're going, Uli, he told the dog. Move your arse. He dressed in the heaviest clothes he had, buckled the snowshoes to his boots and opened the door.

The wind was whipping up the snow. The sky was a frozen pewter. The peaks were huge all around. Uli howled. The ice in the breeze stung the eyes. The dog plunged out into the snow and at once turned back. Come on, Uli! The creature plunged again, and again turned back. Cleaver lifted the big snowshoes and thrust them forward. He tried to lean on his walking sticks but they sank deep. You would need ski poles. He left them sticking in the snow. I'm going anyway. He slid the snowshoes across the white surface and tried not to lower his weight too suddenly. All the same his ankle sent jabs of pain up his spine.

He walked, crossed the clearing, entered the wood. His mind swung wildly. This is a terrible mistake, a trick. This is absolutely necessary. His body pressed on, regardless. The pain didn't touch him. It was happening to someone else. On the track beneath the trees, snow was tumbling all around as the branches bent in the wind. Cleaver's moustache and beard were brittle. The snowshoes were heavy. He pushed forward with the right foot and pulled the other up along-side. The hell with the dog, he thought. She can go back and hide under the eaves. She won't die.

Amazingly, the wind was growing stronger. It was being funnelled up the gorge behind him. The snow rose like smoke. It swept past his feet. But I'm making decent time, Cleaver thought. Now there was cloud again. He smelt it coming. He smelt the weather turning again. Far from feel-ing cold, he felt extremely hot, feverish. Before leaving London, you should have confronted your son. Then you could have bowed out in peace. Then you could have spent your time here more profitably. You could have meditated quietly, in Rosenkranzhof.

Alex! Cleaver shouted. He felt excited. You have decided now. You will rise to his bait and confront him. Under his shadow indeed! The pain made him grit his teeth. I'm glad the weather is so harsh, he thought. This is what you came to the mountains for, after all. For harsh weather. Did Frau Schleiermacher really imagine I didn't realise the winters were hard at six-thousand feet?

Half an hour later, as Cleaver reached the top of the gorge and came out of the trees, the gale almost swept him away. The ice flew in his face. He glimpsed the plateau. Great puffs and spirals of snow were racing across the horizon. He had to turn his back. He was absorbed in whiteness. He tried to face the path again. Where was it? Where are the poles? he wondered. Hadn't there been tall poles that should mark the track when it snowed? Why can't I see them? He couldn't see Trennerhof. Cleaver advanced a few paces. They had been yellow, he thought, yellow and black. The snow was deep and constantly moving. It tugged at the big shoes. He pressed on, an arm over his eyes. I can see nothing. Then the left snowshoe came off his boot. That was his strong foot. The straps were old and rotten. His leg sank in thigh-deep. Jesus! Cleaver sat and tried to put the shoe on again. The strap had broken. His gloves were too thick to work with. He took them off. His fingers were stiff. They were blue. He was sitting deep in the snow. Keep calm. You must confront your son.

He got the strap fixed, but couldn't get to his feet. He was half sitting, half on his back deep in the snow. Hilfe! he shouted. Help. Eventually he got to his feet. He stumbled on for perhaps five minutes. Trennerhof should be visible now. Where is it? He could barely open his eyes into the wind. The lids burned with cold. There seemed no end to the whiteness. Now the shoe was lost again and he sank down. Hilfe, he called. Hilfe! You never sound like you believe it, Paps, when you sing. Hilfe! Cleaver didn't believe anyone would hear him. He had the sense to dig himself deep, to keep out of the wind at least. Doing so he realised his feet were numb. His hands are numb. My lips are numb. Some minutes passed. I can't get up. For Christ's sake. This is it, Cleaver decided then. It's happening. He didn't feel angry or desperate. Only yesterday you dreamed of it. Now it had come much sooner than he imagined. There will be no confrontations, he muttered. Hilfe! Cleaver called. Weakly. The world all around was astonishingly white and shapeless.

XV

CLEAVER IS IN a state of beatitude. Everything is empty, painless, thoughtless. Yet there is a faint muttering in the background. He's noticed it now. Fortunately, it is in a language he cannot understand. Everything is white, muffled, quiet, yet from time to time a baby's nagging cry ruffles the blank surface of his mind. This is not my baby, Cleaver thinks at once.

The muttering is louder now, it is German. It is conversation. No, it's a quarrel. There's a smell too. Then Cleaver is aware that he is lying on his back. He is aware of warmth. Don't open your eyes. Don't move. He fears if he opens his eyes he will be seen. It's a smell of cooking. I don't want to eat. I don't want them to know I'm here. Some kind of stew, it smells like. Then he distinguishes a voice. Frau Stolberg.

Cleaver won't open his eyes. Frau Stolberg is angry. His whole body, he appreciates now, is thrilling with heat. The skin wants to be scratched. Yet his arms don't move from his sides. A man's voice is answering. It's not Jürgen. The bustle seems to be coming from below him. I'm onstage, Cleaver thinks, about to begin my show. There is a silence, his skin is smarting and tingling, then another angry exchange, another woman's voice. Or am I a ghost hovering in the air? Frau Stolberg speaks again. She is sharp and grim. Crossfire. There is a clatter of plates and chairs.

Cleaver listens. He realises now that he has been listening for some time and that he has no choice but to go on listening to the sound of chairs scraping, the banging of doors, furious voices, the nagging cry of a baby. This is not my baby. I have no responsibility. Then he hears cattle. His legs are itching to be scratched but his arms are still by his sides. The cattle are moaning to be milked. I will not show I'm awake, he decides. I will melt in the thaw and trickle away down the mountain. Skandal, he hears Frau Stolberg shout.

Herr Cleaver! A voice is speaking close to his ear. Cleaver is lying quite still. It is dark now. He senses that. I must have fallen asleep. Herr Cleaver? It's a woman's voice. A hand is holding his wrist. Herr Cleaver, are you awake? The doctor is here.

Warily, Cleaver opens an eye. This is strange. A ceiling of square wood panels is just three or four feet away. It is lit from below him. He tries to pull himself up. The light seems orange. At eye level, to his left, is a shelf with half a dozen dusty valve radios. Trennerhof. Beneath the shelf is a door. I'm on the stove, he realises. He is lying on a thin mattress on the pine planks over the stove. In the far corner he glimpses the crucifix with the corncobs. The old woman in her armchair is below. He can hear her snoring.

Herr Cleaver! To get near him, the town-dressed woman has to stand on the pine bench that runs round the bottom of the stove. A short ladder is built against the side. Cleaver recognises her now. I don't know your name, he says. Speaking, he realises his lips are cracked. They're sore. The woman exchanges a few words with a man who is on the floor below her. The doctor wants to look at you.

Cleaver was aware of his legs being uncovered and handled. They felt at once numb and fiery. Are you okay? the woman asked. Her face was lit obliquely by torchlight. You are warm, ja? It is very warm here. She patted the mattress. The doctor was inspecting his legs with a powerful torch. It was all strangely pleasurable. What's your name? Cleaver asked again. She smiled. She has apple cheeks that have aged and weathered, soft eyes, bright blonde hair tied back tight. My name is Rosl. You have luck, Mr Cleaver, my mother has found you in the snow.

I have to speak to my son, Cleaver said. He struggled to his elbows. Then the doctor spoke again. His face was hidden behind the torchlight, but Cleaver caught the gesture of a young man pushing back his fringe. He wants to know if you can feel when he puts his hand on you. Cleaver nodded. It's itching, he said. The woman didn't understand. It makes me want to scratch. She spoke in German. The doctor wants you to drink something now, she said. At once the two of them disappeared.

Cleaver managed to sit up and look about the smoky room. Did the old woman always sleep in front of the fire, or have I taken her bed? There was just one oil lamp over the table in the centre of the room. Now there are voices raised in the corridor. A man shouted. It was very loud and fierce. Perhaps somebody kicked something, the wall or a cupboard. Cleaver needed to pee. A woman protested and began to cry. Then there was barking. It's Uli, Cleaver realised. They have recovered Uli. How long have I been here? While the man shouted in another part of the house and other voices were trying to calm him, Cleaver tried to look at his watch, only to discover that his hands were wrapped in woollen scarves. His watch was gone.

He had just lain down again when heavy footsteps came

hurrying into the room. All at once another face was beside him, blond and moustached. Englishman! The mad Englishman! Bright eyes were laughing in the frame of a woollen balaclava. There is someone who is asking for you, Englishman, in Luttach. He wants to speak to you.

Hermann!

You are warm now, ja, you feel good? You are lucky. Hermann was zipping up his jacket. He was in a hurry.

Someone for me? Cleaver asked. I don't want to see him.

You rest. Hermann laughed. I must go. No more walks in the snow, eh, Mr Englishman!

Du Kriminello! Hermann had just gone out through the porch when Jürgen rushed across the room after him. Raising himself on an elbow, Cleaver glimpsed his small leather cap beside Hermann in the open doorway. The oil lamp began to sway slightly. Jürgen was yelling. Du bisch narrisch, Hermann said coldly. Verrückt. Wie dein Vater.

Doktor! Hermann called back into the house now, Los! The doctor was already crossing the kitchen with his bag, but now there was a cry. Jürgen must have thrown a punch. There was a scuffle just outside the front door. Cleaver could hear shouts and grunts. The doctor rushed out. Cold air flowed into the room. The lamp was swinging. The town-dressed woman reappeared. Cleaver has forgotten her name already. He must tell her he needs to pee, but she too hurried outside to shout at the men in the snow. There was a jingle of harness. Rosl, he remembered. The shouting went back and forth. A horse neighed and stamped. Now Jürgen and Rosl came in pushing and pulling each other as they headed across the room to the corridor again. Dumm, she was saying angrily. Jürgen thrust his way past her. Betrunken! Cleaver heard Hermann calling to his horse. Juli, ha! Across the room, skeletal face lit by the fire, her shadow stretching and contracting with the swinging lamp, the old woman snored. Cleaver sank back on the bed.

Cool hands are on his legs now. Cleaver opened his eyes. The doctor told me to make this. It was Rosl. She was standing on the ladder at the foot of the bed. It is antibiotic, she said. She held up a tube of cream or ointment. For a moment Cleaver panicked. I need to pee. She didn't understand. Bathroom, Badezimmer. You can wait? she asked. I am fast finished. Her hands were strong and sure, rubbing a cool cream into his ankles. Perhaps he could wait. It was strange to see a woman's face over his legs in the half-light. Now she had taken a foot in both hands and began to bandage it. What was all the shouting about? he asked. Rosl smiled at the foot, fastening a safety pin. She looked up at him from shrewd eyes. She is pretty, Cleaver thought. A pretty blonde forty-year-old.

She helped him roll over and put his knees over the platform by the ladder. She took a bandaged foot and placed it on a rung. His legs were leaden. There was a sharp pain from the ankle. On top he still had his shirt and pullover, but below they had stripped him to his underpants. As soon as he had steadied himself on the floor he saw the flesh over his knees was pink and blistered. He moved stiffly. Here, she said. She offered a shoulder. In the toilet, Cleaver unwrapped the woollen scarf from his right hand. The fingertips were covered in bright red blisters.

Later he woke again to a shriek. Someone was shrieking hysterically. Now the only light was the glow from the fire. What time is it? Cleaver wondered. What is going on here? When the scream came again, he swung his legs over the edge of the bed and climbed slowly down the ladder.

Someone's in pain. He stood for a moment, leaning both tingling hands against the stove. It was insulated with a white padding. Holding onto a chair, pressing a hand on the wall, he hopped to the door. The sobbing came from upstairs. There was a broad corridor in deep shadow. Everything is panelled with wood. A door slammed and a woman was shouting.

Cleaver couldn't see. Feeling left and right for support, he limped into the darkness, found the stairs. An oil lamp crossing the landing up above showed him antlers and perhaps a stuffed fox, a framed embroidery. There was mayhem in a room whose door kept opening and closing. Cleaver pulled himself up as quickly as he could. Only a few hours ago, I was dead, he thought. I was buried in the snow. Then he collided with Rosl. Herr Cleaver, kommen Sie! She was wearing a nightdress. Kommen Sie! She pulled him after her. The girl was shrieking again.

Stumbling through the door, Cleaver was aware of a large bed with tall thick wooden posts, a ponderous dresser, the smoky light and smell of the oil lamp. Seffa was crouched on the pillows, breathing hard, one side of her body pressed against a monumental headboard. She wore a white nightdress and was hiding her face in her hands. Jürgen was leaning over her shouting. He grabbed a wrist. What's going on here? Cleaver asked. It didn't occur to him to speak in German.

Herr Cleaver, said a voice. Cleaver turned and saw Frau Stolberg standing by the drawn curtains. Still dressed, she wore black. Then he realised that her arms were cradling a baby. Please, she said in English, go.

Cleaver looked back to Seffa. She had dropped her hands and he could see her face was bruised. Jürgen was speaking sharply to her. His massive hand grasped her wrist. Rosl whispered: They want that Seffa says the man that is the father.

Stop, Cleaver said. He had to steady himself against the

door frame. Stop! Downstairs the dog was barking. Jürgen ignored him. Na, des isch et woar! Seffa whined. She seemed distraught but adamant. Jürgen slapped the girl.

Jürgen! Rosl shouted.

Leave her alone! Cleaver lurched across the room. His right leg buckled. Falling, he had to grab at Jürgen from behind. The peasant shoved an elbow into his chest. Everyone was shouting. Climbing to his feet, Cleaver stumbled sideways, and, as Jürgen turned to yell at Rosl – Walsche! Scheiße! – he managed to sit himself on the bed between father and daughter. He spread out his arms. The blistered fingertips were throbbing. Leave her alone. You can talk about it some other time. What's the hurry?

Jürgen stared at him. The man had been drinking. His rough, broad cheeks were flushed. Downstairs the dog was yapping constantly. Das war Hermann! Jürgen yelled. Na Tatte, des isch et woar! She was denying it. Cleaver kept his arms spread out in defence of the girl. What's the hurry? he demanded. Leave her be. He felt sure they must understand.

Rosl said: He wants to kill the man who it is.

Frau Stolberg said something to her son. Jürgen hesitated, grimaced, then spat. Cleaver felt the spit land in his beard. Jürgen turned on his heels and strode out of the room. Tatte! Seffa called. Na Tatte, des isch et woar! She burst into tears. They could hear him pounding down the stairs, the dog barking furiously. Rosl ran out of the room.

Cleaver rubbed at his beard with the wrist of his pullover and found his lip was bleeding. Looking up, he saw Frau Stolberg watching him from her steady eyes. The baby in her arms was snuffling, her great-grandchild, Cleaver realised. I have to thank you, he said, for pulling me out of the snow. The woman gave no signs of either understanding or acknowledging. So Seffa had disappeared to give birth, Cleaver realised.

The doctor came for mother and baby, not for me. Danke schön, Frau Stolberg. Sie hat mich . . . The words wouldn't come to mind. Hilfen, he said limply. Gehilfen? Geholfen?

Frau Stolberg ignored him. She said something to Seffa that seemed to involve the words waschen and essen. Perhaps. All at once both women were leaving the room. Only now did Cleaver notice Jesus holding a bleeding but luminous heart in a heavily carved frame over the headboard. He felt confused. You died and woke in another world. Struggling to his feet, he saw there was a mirror over the dresser.

It was a tall mirror. Cleaver crossed the room. In the dim light a thickly bearded face was looking at him. I've changed. He hadn't seen himself for a month and more. The nose was starker, the skin chapped and wrinkled. Looking down, he saw that if his legs were hardly thin, still the flabbiness was gone. Then he caught his eyes. They are the same, the same bright mixture of assertion and vulnerability. Feeling strangely pleased with himself, he limped to the door.

You were very . . . Rosl didn't know how to finish the sentence.

Back in the kitchen, Cleaver had been sitting for half an hour or so at the big stone table. He didn't feel ready to tackle the ladder over the stove. Then Rosl appeared. Very . . . mutig, she said. Thank you.

Mutig?

Ja. She pulled a stern face and held up a tense clenched fist. Strong, she said.

Cleaver smiled. You're welcome. Where's Jürgen now? Is he going to start again?

He is gone, Rosl said. Will you drink?

Gone? Cleaver didn't understand. Where, how? What time is it? It was halb zehn, she said. Half-past nine. Cleaver had assumed it was the middle of the night. He shook his head in amazement. Only half-past nine? Rosl brought him a glass and a bottle of schnapps, a jug of water, then a wooden plate with bread and speck. He has taken the . . .

Again she was lost for words. She came to sit opposite Cleaver at the table, then got up, climbed on the bench by the stove, pulled a blanket off the bed and brought it to him. She bent down and put it over his bare knees. He has taken the Schlitten, she said. She looked around, couldn't find what she was after, then, smiling, lifted her arm and slid the palm of her hand down an imaginary slope. Whee! Schlitten fahren!

Sled, Cleaver said. Her face across the stone table was a refined version of Jürgen's, he thought. She had a trim, unused air about her, as if of a younger woman whose life has been suspended, preserved, while her troll-like brother was wizened almost.

Uli came to sit at Cleaver's feet.

So, is it a boy or a girl? he asked.

A girl.

I didn't realise she was pregnant. I thought she was fat. Then I haven't seen her for weeks now.

Rosl didn't reply. When he sipped the schnapps his lips smarted.

Your hand, she said. She held up one of her hands and made it tremble. You are cold?

My hand always shakes. I'm okay. Then he asked: You don't have a mobile here?

She had her chin propped on her forearms now.

A telephone? Cleaver repeated.

Ja ja. She pulled an expensive-looking silver gadget from her pocket.

Does it get a signal?

Here, she said. Call.

Cleaver was taken aback. Maybe tomorrow, he said. I'll pay obviously.

The two of them were silent for a while. Only now did Cleaver realise that the ancient woman had disappeared. She has gone to bed. He chewed a slice of speck. Uli moved to settle down on the hearthrug. There were still embers in the fire. Upstairs footsteps moved along the corridor. Cleaver was aware of resisting all kinds of questions, all the Gothic scenarios he had imagined in that month at Rosenkranzhof. The Stolberg family is not your business, he thought. Finally he said: You are not worried about Jürgen?

Rosl sighed. I worry and I don't worry.

After a few moments, Cleaver said: This is the first conversation I have had for more than a month. With a person that is, he added.

Rosl smiled. She got up to tend to the fire.

I won't ask the next question, Cleaver thought. The silence grew longer. He broke a piece of bread and ate it piece by piece. Finally Rosl came back to her seat and said, My mother, you know, has found you only ten metres from the door here. She is bringing in wood and she sees your hat.

That's incredible, Cleaver said. I thought I was in the middle of nowhere.

Jürgen carried you.

Carried me!

Rosl stood up, pulled a comically grim face and threw an imaginary sack of potatoes over her shoulders. Staggering under the weight, she trudged a few steps, legs splayed in snowshoes, as if through deep drifts across the parlour. Cleaver laughed. At the same time he felt he might weep. In her blue nightdress and thick woollen socks, the blonde hair tied back from a glowing face, the woman was so beautifully present to him. I had got used to the dolls, he thought.

Mutter is angry that it is not a boy. She wanted a boy for Trennerhof.

Ah, Cleaver said.

Trennerhof is from Mutter's family, not from my father. Trennerhof, Trennerhof. She is thinking only of that.

You don't care for Trennerhof, Cleaver said.

No, I am a Walsche. I am not existing. Ppph! She made a gesture of contempt.

A Walsche?

An Italiana. I married an Italian.

Right. Cleaver remembered that Hermann had used the word.

I live in Bozen. Bolzano.

Where your father was in the Polizeiregiment.

Ja. Many years ago.

There is a photo in Rosenkranzhof. Of the regiment.

Oh? Rosl didn't seem to be interested. My father was the radio man. He had the radios. She pointed up at the shelves.

Cleaver was perplexed. But it made more sense than Hermann's version. Funny the radios without the electricity, he said.

Rosl laughed. Mutter wants no news in Trennerhof. Only a man, for the . . . Kühe.

She has Jürgen.

Jürgen drinks. He drinks all the time.

At least he shaves, Cleaver said. He mimed a man using a razor. Rosl smiled. When there was a silence, Cleaver drained his schnapps. It was good. He studied the blisters on his fingertips. They were painful, but seemed harmless enough. He was aware of a great sense of mental well-being. Rosl seemed in no hurry to go to bed.

You have left Rosenkranzhof now, she smiled.

Cleaver shrugged. I hurt my ankle. That's why I tried to

come up here. Ankle, he repeated. He pushed back his chair and tapped the injured part. I can't walk properly. Then he told her how it had happened, the late-night visit from Jürgen and Frau Stolberg, the broken stair. At once he sensed a new tension in the woman. She was alert. She hadn't known about this. Frau Stolberg, Cleaver said, your mother, went down the track, to that ledge at the bottom, that place where there is the cable down to Steinhaus. With his hands, Cleaver traced the sag of the cable draped down the mountainside. Rosl jumped to her feet. She turned to the fire, crouched down to stroke the dog. Rosenkranzhof is a horrible place, she said.

Cleaver watched her. Have a drink, he said. She shook her head. Then they heard the sharp wail of the baby. Because it's a girl, Rosl said quietly, I will ask to bring her to live with me in Bozen.

You don't have children? Cleaver asked.

No.

Perhaps you should take Seffa, too.

I wanted to bring Seffa, many years ago. But she is not leaving without her father. She loves her father.

Or the father of her baby.

Rosl was still stroking the dog. Now she stood up and seemed ready to go. She shook her head. Then Cleaver had the distinct impression that Rosl knew who the father of the child was. Both women knew. He wondered now if he had understood right when Jürgen had said: Das war Hermann. Does the baby have a name? he asked.

Sie heißt Ulrike, Rosl said.

XVI

Alex? Cleaver asked.

It was as if he were calling through smoke.

Alex!

Dad!

Cleaver woke in a sweat to the sound of footsteps crossing the room. Wer ist da? He asked. Schlafen Sie, said Frau Stolberg. He heard her pulling on boots, pushing open the door. Then he was aware of the cows complaining and almost at once someone else was by the table. He turned on his side and saw Rosl buttoning a coat.

What's happening?

Jürgen isn't home. Die Kühe . . .

Can I help? Cleaver asked.

You sleep, Rosl said.

Cleaver climbed down from the bed and went out into passageway to the toilet. Where did they put my watch? The house was quiet, but the cows were bellowing loudly outside. Over the door going back into the kitchen there was a bunch of dried heather and to the right, built into the wall, a small iron door for stoking up the stove on the other side. No dolls in Trennerhof, he noticed.

Limping about in the dark, Cleaver found a basket of logs by the hearth and laid two side by side in the embers of the fire. His fingers were stiff and extremely sore. He blew on the coals. Where were the matches for the lamp? He stripped a long splinter from a log, lit it from the first flame that sprung in the grate and carried it carefully to the table. The wick took at once and the room steadied in a shadowy yellow light. Only then did he remember the splinter under his nail. The pain of the frostbite had masked it, but it's still there. The fingertip is inflamed. He could see a black smudge beneath the nail. Ow! Don't touch.

Cleaver looked around for his clothes. Uli was on the old lady's chair. She wagged her tail but didn't get up. Trousers, shirt and sweater were folded on the bench under the stove. Dry. Why doesn't this pain bother me more? Cleaver wondered. Fingers and feet were craving to be scratched, but his mind was calm. Something about the big room with its clutter of boots by the door, its silent old radios, its stove and bric-a-brac and smoky smell, made him feel rested.

In the porch, the only thing that would fit on his swollen feet was a dilapidated pair of wellingtons, Jürgen's presumably. What if Jürgen had set off last night to have it out with Hermann?

Outside the air was raw. Dawn was hardening a skyline of peaks and cloud beyond Luttach. To his left the huge mass of Schwarzstein was weirdly blue and white. It's so vast, Cleaver muttered. A grey field of frozen snow stretched away to the cut of the gorge.

Cleaver replenished the firewood basket from the log pile under the eaves. He could hear chickens clucking in the shed beyond. Long icicles had formed from the guttering near the chimney. He breathed deeply, the air is good, then walked round the house to the cowshed.

There was a heavy wooden door, and after that a curtain of thick black plastic. The smell of straw and shit and warm animal breath was overpowering. He waited for his eyes to grow accustomed to the dark. The cows were standing side by side, their backs toward him, their heads trapped between the vertical wooden bars between stall and feeding trough in the main part of the barn.

There was the dull sound of a dozen pairs of jaws champing on hay. Cleaver walked along the line and found Rosl with her head pressed into a cow's belly, a three-legged stool strapped round her thighs. Milk squirted into the pail in sharp spurts. The woman was sighing with the effort. Her wrists tensed as she pulled down, relaxed coming up. The hands clenched and unclenched on the teats. She doesn't wear a ring, Cleaver noticed.

Can I help?

She didn't move her head to look at him. She must already have been aware he was there. Ein moment, she said. The cow shivered and kicked out a leg in irritation. Rosl said a harsh word, and slapped the creature on the flank. Then she lowered her head again.

Frau Stolberg, Cleaver saw, was working at the other end of the line. The cows seemed oblivious to anything but their eating. There was fresh shit in the gutter behind their hoofs. Go round, Rosl said. Da hinten, sehen Sie? She pointed. And give more Heu. Heu, you understand?

He had to go back outside, along the wall of the building where a path had been shovelled clear of snow and then in again through another larger door. Now the cows were on his right. A lever could draw apart the vertical wooden bars corresponding to each cow's head. They thrust their necks through the gaps to eat, then the bars closed again. They are trapped when they eat and trapped when they fuck, Cleaver thought. The cows didn't seem to mind. Only where a couple of animals had finished the hay in front of them did they twist their necks and stretch out long pink tongues to lick at their neighbour's fodder. The trough was grey stone and their tongues when they licked made a low rasping noise.

Opposite the animals, there was a wall of tightly packed hay. A loose pile was ready in the centre of an otherwise meticulously swept floor. Cleaver was surprised by the pleasure of its sweet smell, as if, on this icy morning, he were breathing in summer. The stalks pricked his sore fingers. Limping along the trough, he shared the hay out. His body ached. The cows stretched their necks impatiently. The soft pink noses snorted. Without thinking, Cleaver found himself talking to them. Here you go, sweetheart. Easy now. Hey, give me time, give me time! The cows resumed their eating. Through grimy windows the light was coming up.

Later, Cleaver watched Rosl set up the filter in the dairy room where the Graukäse was made. It was a sort of child's construction game of differently perforated cylinders, discs and blotting papers that assembled in the form of a conical tower, perhaps four feet high. With tense hands, Cleaver lifted a full pail and poured. The milk streamed across the silvery steel shedding flecks of grit. Where's Jürgen? he asked.

Rosl seemed exhausted. He drinks, she said. He is betrunken. Then he sleeps in the bar. On the . . . the Boden. She indicated the floor. Maybe two or three nights.

You don't think he went to hurt Hermann?

Rosl shrugged. Her mood has changed, Cleaver thought. She was cooler.

If you want me to leave, he offered, I can go down to

Luttach today. The path should be easy from here.

You must rest, she said. It is . . . soon for you to walk in the snow. Your feet . . . But if you want, go.

Then she showed him how to wash the filters. It is years I don't do this, she said. She gave him rubber gloves and a plastic apron. There was a gas boiler fed by a cylinder and an impressive armoury of nylon scrapers. Everything must be one hundred per cent clean, she said. Sauber? Cleaver said. Sauber sauber.

The hot water on rubber gloves was torture. Cleaver enjoyed it. He spent twenty minutes and more removing every trace of milk and dirt from the various utensils. It was a simple, demanding job. I am calm, he kept telling himself. How did that happen?

The day was bright when he walked out again. The sun had topped the peaks to the east. The white landscape gleamed. Cleaver stood still, listening intently. He put an experimental foot in the snow. It had lost its crust. Over the door, water had begun to drip from the round green sign that advertised Forst beer.

Guten Morgen, Cleaver said, going back into the parlour. Frau Stolberg's ancient mother was dunking bread in milk. She lowered her shawled head to push soggy chunks between her gums. Cleaver had realised now that the curtain to the left of the stove behind the bar led through to the kitchen proper. Again he went to offer help. The ceiling here was low and black and the place smelt strongly of smoked ham and frying. Setzen Sie sich! Frau Stolberg shooed him back into the parlour, then followed with a plate of perhaps a dozen eggs. Seffa appeared, carrying a large battered holdall. Morgen, she said. It was only when she set the holdall down on the chair beside her and leaned over it that Cleaver realised the baby was inside. Can I see? he asked.

The girl seemed barely changed from when she had come to Rosenkranzhof that first night for her dog. Her shabby clothes were loose, the limp hair was cut without style. But one cheek was deeply bruised and whereas Cleaver remembered her expression as vacant, now there was a troubled alertness about the eyes. Warming her hands round a bowl of milk, she glanced towards the door at the slightest sound.

Kann ich das Kind sehen? Cleaver repeated.

Rosl and Frau Stolberg were eating in silence. Seffa shrugged her shoulders. Leaning over the holdall, Cleaver saw the baby wrapped in white wool, eyes closed, puffy lips frowning, a small pink cap on her head. Acting on impulse, he plunged his hands into the bag and picked the child up. Herr Cleaver! Frau Stolberg objected. He lifted the sleeping baby to his shoulder, careful to keep her soft skin from his beard and patted her gently on the back. How light babies are, he said to Rosl. Sie ist sehr . . . hübsch, he told Seffa. The girl was anxious.

There was a sudden cackle of laughter. Grotesquely gaunt, her toothless mouth gaping, the ancient lady peered up at Cleaver and the child. She said something loud and fast of which Cleaver could distinguish not a word. The gnarled hands made an expansive gesture. He would never have imagined there could be such vitality in the old skeleton. She belched and laughed again and pointed at him. Frau Stolberg was speaking too, in a voice that seemed unusually soft. Listening without even trying to understand, Cleaver felt the slight trembling of the living child, so unlike poor Olga. Ulrike, he said gravely, Guten Morgen.

The old lady laughed and clapped and exclaimed to the others. Seffa was upset. She reached out to have the baby to herself. Cradling the bald head in one hand, Cleaver bent forward to pass the tiny girl to her. My father, he remembered

268

Alex had written, always came across as a very fatherly man, though it was more rhetoric than reality. No doubt he'll make an excellent grandfather, Mother would say wryly. Sitting down again, he asked Rosl, Can I use your phone?

Rosl had left it in her room. Eat first, she said. It is hot now. Cleaver had a plate of eggs and speck and black bread in front of him. As he ate, he listened to the women talking. They spoke in low, business-like tones, but with an edge of tension. They were discussing the question of Jürgen, he guessed. Perhaps Rosl had offered to use her phone to call down to Luttach. How long would her battery last? Frau Stolberg seemed resigned.

All at once, the ancient lady leaned across the table and shook her daughter's wrist. Mutter! Frau Stolberg said. There was a faint smell to her. Oma – that is my grandmother – Rosl eventually translated for Cleaver, says you are . . . She hesitated, A fine man. And very, how do you say, handsome.

Cleaver was chewing speck. Is that so? he smiled. He turned to the ancient creature and bowed his head in acknowledgement. It was obvious she was all but blind. And my mother, Rosl went on, asks, How are your hands and feet this morning?

Cleaver turned to Frau Stolberg. Es geht mir gut, danke. He remembered that formula. Only, I have a bad splinter. He showed his finger to Rosl. She got up and stood behind him so as not to block the light. She laid his blistered hand across hers which was dry and cool. Das ist schlimm, she said. It was infected. Mutter? Kommen Sie. Frau Stolberg stood and bent stiffly over the hand. She shook her head. Na, ich sehe nicht gut. Die Augen. For the first time she spoke in such a way that Cleaver could understand. Ich kann das nicht sehen.

While he was finishing his breakfast, the women prepared

a bowl of scalding water. Rosl indicated that he should put his hand in it. It will be . . . schmerzhaft, she said. Pain. Frau Stolberg moved a chair to the window. Setzen Sie sich hier hin. Hier ist Licht.

Rosl left the room to fetch needles, nail clippers, tweezers, scissors and even a small knife. She pulled up a chair opposite him so that their knees were touching. Ow! Cleaver let out a wail and pulled his hand away. Sorry. Then the baby began to cry. The ancient woman laughed. She hadn't understood what was going on. Seffa got up and began to walk the child back and forth across the room.

Hier, Frau Stolberg said. She poured Cleaver a glass of transparent liquid from a bottle without a label. He sank it in one and immediately recognised the taste. Gebirgsgeist. He had to shake his head. Now the woman was putting a dishcloth in his hands. You can bite, Rosl said. Bite? No? Frau Stolberg indicated he could clench his teeth on it.

Cleaver accepted. He watched Rosl's puckered mouth and squinting eyes as she tried to ease a needle under the nail. The fingertip was swollen. The pain was extraordinarily sharp. He bit on the towel. One moment, she said, withdrawing the needle and standing up. Pulling the cloth out of his mouth, Cleaver took a breath. Rosl brought over another chair, put the bowl of hot water on it and pushed in Cleaver's hand. Hold it there. She had lanced the pus under the nail and the finger began to bleed into the water. Hold it. She grabbed his wrist when he started to pull it away. The water was scalding.

They sat silent together for perhaps a minute, watching the blood cloud the water. Then Cleaver asked: Just to pass the time, you know, can you tell me why there is a bar in the room, a counter, for beer, and that Forst sign outside the door?

Rosl had taken hold of his finger now and was squeezing

out any remaining infection. For a moment, he thought she was refusing to answer, or hadn't understood. Then, still intent on his hand, her face grimacing as if the pain were hers not his, she said, Since many years, my father had a Stube, here in Trennerhof. For the tourists, you know? The walkers.

She took his hand out now and dried it on a towel on her lap. The people could sleep here, she explained. Even ten people. In summer it was always full. She moved his hand under the window and studied it carefully. People liked that there was . . . keine Elektrizität. It was an adventure. Hermann and his father came with their horses. They brought the pony-trekkers. She looked up from the finger into Cleaver's face. This is very bad, you know. We must take away the . . . Nagel. How do you say? You will perhaps wait. You go to hospital.

No, Cleaver said. You do it. But pour me another drink. He smiled. Why did the bar close?

She frowned. Why do you want to know about my family? This is pain now, she said. Using the knife she began to saw horizontally across the base of the nail.

Cleaver closed his eyes. Through his teeth he said: I'm curious. Ever since I went to Rosenkranzhof I wanted to know why your father went there. I kept going to the ledge where there is the photograph of Ulrike.

Rosl was making sure she had cut the edges of the nail where it curved into the skin. Why have you gone to Rosenkranzhof? she asked.

Cleaver was breathing deeply. This is stupid, superficial pain, he told himself. It means nothing. It will end as soon as the splinter is out. I don't know, he said. To prove something maybe. To live in silence.

Rosl picked up the scissors. And you have succeeded?

It was a very noisy silence.

And now you want to telephone someone?

It's just a call I should have made before I left.

And then you go back to Rosenkranzhof?

Cleaver winced. In a sudden movement, she had levered back his nail so that it broke along the line she had scored. Cleaver let out a cry. Mehr heißes Wasser, Rosl called to her mother. Using the scissors she cut the nail free. Frau Stolberg came and took away the bowl. The baby on her shoulder, Seffa leaned over to look. She grimaced, said something. The raw skin was bleeding along the line where the splinter had entered. The broken piece was deep inside. What does she say? Cleaver asked. She says, not so bad as to have a baby, Rosl said. Seffa nodded. She understood the word baby. Already Frau Stolberg was back with fresh hot water. Rosl pushed his hand in. Cleaver tried to concentrate on her face. The small mouth and faintly wrinkled eyes had that soft grimness of a woman who is hurting a man gently, for his own good.

So you will go back? Now she pulled the hand out.

I don't know, he said. She began to study the fingertip, picked up the tweezers, then changed her mind and chose the needle again.

Perhaps the silence will be quieter after this phone call, Cleaver said. Or perhaps I won't want to go back at all. But you still haven't told me why your father lived there.

She went into the flesh. Cleaver winced and shook his head fiercely from side to side. She had reached the splinter now. He was determined not to complain.

Ulrike has worked in the Stube, Rosl said. She was very beliebt, popular. You know? She married Jürgen. One day my father has killed a man. After that, he has gone to live in Rosenkranzhof. The Stube has been closed. Ulrike has wanted to leave Trennerhof, but Mutter has not let Jürgen go. Then they have been intending to open the Stube again, but Ulrike has had an accident at the Seilbahn . . . the telepherique. For to bring up the things.

Rosl was working with the tweezers as she spoke. She didn't look up. Cleaver could see the delicate skin behind the ears where the hair was tied back. It was a good neck. There was a small mole. Frau Stolberg had begun to sweep the floor under the table, but Cleaver sensed she was listening. She knows Rosl is telling me their story, he thought.

Now!

He breathed hard as she made a first attempt to fasten on the splinter. There was a pause.

Why wasn't your father put in prison?

Here no one has said who has done it. The police have not insisted.

Why not?

Because . . . because this man . . . war schuld. He was . . . schuldig . . . it is his fault.

This was about Ulrike? Cleaver asked.

Achtung, she warned. She pulled the splinter out. Cleaver shut his eyes. He felt its length retreat from deep inside his flesh.

Gut. Fertig.

Surprisingly bloodless between the points of her tweezers, the fragment of wood was almost a quarter of an inch long.

She smiled, pleased with herself. Yes, it was about Ulrike.

Cleaver sank his hand into the water. After a few moments, he asked: And Ulrike used to take your father his food at Rosenkranzhof?

Rosl stood up, shaking out the towel, pulling down her cardigan.

Now I go to get you the phone, she said.

Frau Stolberg propped up the broom and came to study his finger. The nail was gone almost to the base and the exposed flesh was cut deeply in two places. To Cleaver's surprise she went to a cupboard and returned with a pack of sterile gauze. Eyes fixed as ever, she patted the skin dry and secured the gauze round his finger with sticking tape. The baby started crying again. Seffa went to sit by the fire near her great-grandmother, pulled up her sweater and pushed the child's mouth against a breast.

Man weiss nicht wo ist Jürgen? Cleaver asked.

Frau Stolberg did not reply, though Cleaver was sure she had understood. She went into the kitchen, returned with a large basin full of potatoes and began to peel them.

The field indicator on Rosl's phone showed one notch. Seffa glanced up with an interest more intense than anything Cleaver had seen on her face so far. She wants her own phone of course. Is it possible she has a lover? Then he realised: I've forgotten the number. I have it in my phone, he explained, but the battery is dead.

Okay, give me yours, she said.

Cleaver's ski jacket was hanging by the door. The phone was still in his inside pocket. The battery is dead, he repeated.

Sitting at the table again, Rosl rapidly took his phone apart, removed the SIM card and inserted it in her own phone. Frau Stolberg watched, uncomprehending. Rosl turned on her phone. The screen glowed. Cleaver took it, but didn't understand how the thing worked. It wasn't his familiar Nokia. Open the Phone Book and call Alex he told her, A-L-E-X. He wondered for a moment if you needed to add the international code. Rosl pressed and tapped, then handed it to him. Apparently not.

All four generations of women were watching Cleaver now. The old lady had her beads in her hands. He could see the fist working as she pushed each bead between finger and thumb. I must ask why it was called Rosenkranzhof, Cleaver thought. But he heard the phone ringing now with faint faulty tones.

Alex? he said. The signal was coming and going. Alex?

Dad! Cleaver's son was already speaking. He must have seen his father's name come up on the screen. Dad! Then Cleaver realised that he had no idea what to say beyond pronouncing his son's name. The frenetic mental activity of the last month had completely evaporated.

How are you, Alex?

Dad, I'm fine. Listen . . .

The line broke up for a moment. Cleaver felt anxious. It was supposed to be a momentous call. The women were watching. Why didn't I go on my own somewhere? Rosl had lit a cigarette.

Alex, I just wanted to say, about the book. It's okay.

Dad . . .

No, it's not okay. I mean, I hate it. I think it gives a completely false picture of me. All the same, I wanted to call – Cleaver knew his voice had gone cold, he was losing it – to say, well, that I don't want the book to be the end of it, of us.

Dad! his son kept trying to speak. The line came and went. Cleaver was still trying to say the thing that had to be said, whatever it was. I mean, a son is more . . . than a book. That sounded hopeless. Alex, I've been thinking . . .

Dad!

But what finally stopped Cleaver talking was the look on Rosl's face. As she breathed out cigarette smoke, a flicker of irony lit her blue eyes, as if, even without understanding the nature of this exchange, she knew she was listening to an old performer.

Dad, for fuck's sake let me get a word in.

What? Cleaver asked.

Guess where I am.

What?

The line went again.

Guess where I am, where I'm speaking from.

Why? Cleaver wondered. Where? Manchester?

No.

Home, Chelsea?

No.

I don't know. You're being interviewed on TV. You're going to Stockholm for the Nobel.

I'm climbing a mountain.

Good for you.

There was a pause.

Where? Cleaver asked.

I'm sitting on a sled.

Cleaver was alarmed.

With a guy called Hermann. Above a place called Luttago.

Luttach, Cleaver corrected. You haven't brought your mother along, have you?

See you soon, his son said.

XVII

PERHAPS JÜRGEN IS dead and I will take his place here at Trennerhof. Cleaver had insisted on mucking out the stall. Where are you going? he asked Rosl. She was pulling on her boots at the door. To make clean the Stalle, she said, die Kühe. Someone had to clean out the shit. I'll do it, Cleaver offered. She shook her head. Your hand . . . I'll be okay with gloves, Cleaver insisted. The moment she heard Hermann was coming, Seffa had been anxious. Und Tatte? she broke in now. Kommt Tatte auch? Rosl and Frau Stolberg spoke together in low voices.

Jürgen has died drunk in the snow, Cleaver thought, and I will take his place here at Trennerhof, I will milk the cows and muck them out and make Graukäse and gather hay and listen to silent radios through winter nights while the old woman mutters her rosary.

They had given him blue dungarees, a blue jacket and he had put on Jürgen's boots again. Rosl showed him where the tools were. Why not wait your son in the Stube? she said. It is warm. I can make clean. She is curious to meet my son, Cleaver realised. She is curious about me. No, I want to help, Cleaver insisted. You saved my life. She shook her head. She knew he knew it wasn't necessary.

Like this, she said. There was a long pole with a heavy rectangular scraper at the end, made of slate it seemed. First you used a pitchfork to lift the dirty straw onto the wheelbarrow, then you dragged the scraper across the cement. It squealed. My mind's starting to mill again, Cleaver realised. The piss gathered in a shallow drain behind the animals' legs. Rosl was watching him. The calm is over, he told himself. He worked despite smarting hands, aching legs. The cows stepped out of the way of the pitchfork with surprising agility.

That's it, she said approvingly. The air stank as the smell of the shit was released. You don't need to stay, he told her. First I must show you . . . She was at a loss for words. She pointed at the wheelbarrow, Kommen Sie, and began to walk behind the cows across the stall.

The wheelbarrow had no sides. The handles were very low. Cleaver was amazed how heavy the shit was. Trying to get it moving he almost toppled the load back on the floor. He limped after her. The ankle was fine till you put weight on it.

There was another door at the other end of the stall and outside, across a small yard, rose a great flat mound of straw and shit, perhaps six feet high. A broad plank had been laid against the side to form a ramp. Rosl indicated how it was done. Cleaver could see that a few loads had been dumped up there since the snow had fallen. But he doubted he could manage. The plank looked slippery. The wheelbarrow steamed in the cool morning air. He set it down at the bottom of the plank. What if Amanda is with him? he wondered. I'm not going back.

You must run, Rosl laughed. Stooping to grip an im-

278

aginary wheelbarrow, she huffed and puffed and ran at the plank. She is pretty, Cleaver thought. Why no ring? She said she was married. He remembered that Jürgen had been good at miming. What do you do in Bozen? he asked. What's your job? Computer graphics, she said. For the first time her accent was perfect. Cleaver shook his head in wonder. I have no problem, she laughed, with words like, co-ordinates, three-dimensional, rotate clockwise. But this – she gestured to the farmhouse, the old tools, the stacks of wood, the shit pile – this is not . . . international.

Cleaver pulled the wheelbarrow back and took a limping run. The load surged and wobbled. The wheel bumped onto the plank, climbed a yard or so, then, halfway up, he lost control, the wheel slid off and the load was spilled down the side of the mound into the surrounding ditch. Macht nichts, Rosl shrugged.

As they went back into the stall, he asked, Why was it called Rosenkranzhof, anyway? He picked up the pitchfork to resume his work. Why did they give it that name? Keine Ahnung, she said. Then mimicking an American voice she must have heard: I ain't got the slightest.

Seffa is scared of her father coming back.

Rosl shrugged her shoulders.

You know who the baby's father was, don't you? Why don't you tell?

Mr Cleaver, she said. Please.

Back in the gloom and stench of the stall, Cleaver worked methodically. The skin on his fingertips was itching. It's a pleasure to be around these animals, he thought. He liked the touch of their flanks. I forbid you, he told himself, to fantasise about living with this woman. When will you have had enough of life? On the other hand there was no question of packing up to go back to Amanda.

Keeping the load on the wheelbarrow smaller, he was able to push it up the plank quite easily. Another plank ran along the top of the mound. It sagged as the wheel trundled across. Cleaver tipped the shit onto the snow beside what he judged to be the most recent dumping. They build up the pile of shit, he realised, consolidate it, then move the plank on top of the new level. Shit on shit. C'est la vie.

Still up on the muck heap, he put down the wheelbarrow and gazed at the landscape. The panorama rose and fell in range after range of white peaks. The sun glittered on the melting snow. Everywhere there was the sound of dripping and trickling. My son is climbing the gorge, Cleaver said out loud. Who cares why the place is called Rosenkranzhof? What difference does it make to you if some old charcoal burner died there alone with a rosary in his hands and then his friends nailed the beads to the door and called the place Rosenkranzhof? What can it matter? Or that an old Nazi retired there to pray for forgiveness? I want to make this a place of prayer, he thought, and he nailed a rosary to the door. Seffa went down the track with Uli to take him his food. In the sky over the gorge a hawk was circling. How did my son find me? He will be here any moment. The whole world is a place of prayer, Cleaver muttered. Since when did you have thoughts like that?

He went back into the stall and picked up the pitchfork. Perhaps all my thinking at Rosenkranzhof was conditioned by the name Rosenkranzhof. Hoist by the petard of his own thirst for celebrity. Cleaver heaved a clump of straw and shit onto the wheelbarrow. Can one be so easily led astray, by a name, a name he had only responded to because of his son's book? Had it made any difference, he wondered, changing all the place names around here from German to Italian. Brunico, Luttago? Had it changed people's minds. Was that why Jürgen gave his cows Italian names? And why do you keep expecting to uncover some secret, Cleaver demanded of himself, some revelation that will explain and resolve things, that will open a new way for you? Amanda spoke directly to Priya, perhaps. Could that be the truth? After Angela died, Amanda and Priya sorted out between themselves who should have you. I wouldn't be surprised. Like farmers bargaining over an old bull. Or they tossed a coin even. Seffa is her grandfather's daughter, maybe. Melanie told Alex that she was my lover and that I was paying for her to go through drama school. You preferred Angela to me, that is what he is going to say. You preferred my sister, and after she died you filled your life with Angela substitutes rather than pay any attention to me. You always ignored me. Cleaver can hear his son's rather high-pitched voice. Of what possible interest could it be to me, he thought, to know who is the father of Seffa's baby, to know if it was Jürgen who insisted on his father being banished to Rosenkranz-hof: Either he goes or I go, he told Frau Stolberg perhaps. In German of course. In Tyrolese. Despite the sweat on his face, Cleaver shivered. A cold draught rushed into the stall.

Dad!

Cleaver looked up.

Christ, you need a shave!

Amanda wasn't with him. Relieved, Cleaver, smiled, or half smiled, indicated he couldn't embrace, or even offer his hand in his present state and insisted on finishing his job in the barn. Five minutes, he said. Small and neat in bright red skiing gear, his son sat on a milking stool and stared at his father. Christ, he said again. He looked young for his age. I promised I'd help here, Cleaver explained. These people are in a bit of a crisis. There's a baby just born and now the guy who does all the work has disappeared.

Cleaver took pleasure forking straw and shit very carefully onto the barrow. The pains in his hands seemed quite unimportant. You always did cut a figure, I suppose, Alex laughed. Of one kind or another. It was a nervous, eager laugh. God, it stinks though! Cleaver breathed deeply. It's going to be more like ten minutes, he thought. Alex watched in silence, then said: Actually, I think that must have been the guy who came up with us.

What?

The farmer here. Seems he was out on a binge last night. He walked up beside the sleigh. Had snowshoes. Big stocky man with a funny leather cap, long arms, morose.

That's him, Cleaver said.

Fantastic place you found, Alex chattered on. These mountains. Quite something. I've never been to this neck of the woods before. I had no idea.

But Cleaver was marvelling at his own sense of disappointment on hearing of Jürgen's return, as if this were more important than his son's arrival. You really did think that might be a way out, he realised, taking Jürgen's place. It was hard to get the scraper right into the final corner. Old age on the farm. There was a glob of soft dung. Cleaver trundled the wheelbarrow out of the barn, very conscious of his son getting to his feet to follow. He took a shambling run and forced the barrow up the slippery plank. How ridiculous I'd look if I fell over now. He had to put all his weight behind the thing to heave it over the lip. He was gasping. Done it. The barrow creaked across the top of the mound. The plank sagged. I might as well be on camera, Cleaver thought. I might as well never have left Chelsea at all.

You're limping, Alex said.

I hurt my ankle.

Cleaver took off his gloves and went into the dairy to wash his hands, allowing his son to trail after him like a dog, or a second-string production assistant. Two churns of milk stood in a tank of chill water. The wall was an array of hooks and curious utensils. It's the cheese they make, Cleaver laughed, explaining the smell.

Mind if I take a photo? Alex asked.

Cleaver had his back to him. He washed carefully, keeping the water away from the dressing on his middle finger. Material for another book? he enquired over the sound of the tap. An illustrated version perhaps? Or is there to be a website? Then, pulling the plug and tearing a sheet of towelling paper from a roll on the wall, Cleaver turned and faced his son at last. Alex had a small camera in his hands.

Snap away, Cleaver said.

You look so different, Alex laughed, without the smart suits. And it's quite a beard. Mum will be amazed.

Cleaver couldn't contain himself. You were a little runt writing that book, he said.

His son held his gaze with troubled eyes. It was a handsome but always troubled face. They had seen each other so rarely these last few years.

A runt, Cleaver repeated.

There was a long silence. Water trickled into the cooling tank and out through a drain under the floor.

You understood nothing of the relationship between myself and your mother. Nothing. And what you did understand you distorted. You distorted everything. You presented me as a fake, a hypocrite and a buffoon.

Cleaver was aware that he hadn't meant to speak so soon or so forcefully. But the words came. His elder son listened to him. The muscles round his small mouth had stiffened.

You talked to people who were jealous of me. But never

to me. You had no time for my version. It was disgraceful. An assassination. Cleaver was trembling. And you were jealous yourself. Of me. Of Angela. What crap that stupid last scene in the hotel. What utter bullshit!

Alex Cleaver ran his tongue over his lip. He had put a hand on the stone counter.

So when you phoned me, he asked – his voice was low and tense – was it to tell me this?

More or less.

Go on then, if there's more.

Cleaver took a rapid step across the room and slapped his son hard across the face. He has never slapped a face in his life. Then he crossed the dairy and pushed through the thick curtain and out of the door. His hand was ringing with pain. He banged his elbow on the stone lintel. Just an hour ago you were so calm! He threw himself down on the wet snow beyond the track and pushed his hand into the ice. For a moment he almost passed out; the big landscape reeled. He shook his head and breathed hard. The cold filled his lungs. Then, as his dizziness settled, he became aware that Alex was standing watching him from the door to the dairy.

Why did you come? Cleaver asked. How did you find me?

Get up, Dad, Alex said. Come on. Get up. He hesitated. Mum's really upset, you know. The young man lifted a hand to rub his cheek. We always knew where you were. More or less.

Always?

You made a big purchase in Brunico. Mum talked to someone at the credit card company.

That easy?

She really wants you back, Dad.

And so?

So, I came to tell you. In case . . .

Suddenly Cleaver was livid. First you write down all the shit she tells you to write about me – how many hours did you spend on the phone together? – you make it funny, you make it appetizing for the public, you package it, you sell it, you get famous, and then you obey orders and come out here to bring me back.

Dad, can't we . . .

What in God's name are you doing here? You didn't come to see me at all. Just to bring a message about something that has nothing to do with you. My relationship with your mother has nothing to do with you. All right? It's not your business. Invent stories about it by all means, but if she wants to send me messages, she can damn well do it in person.

Dad, get up. Please.

Cleaver struggled. One foot sank into the melting snow. Alex offered his hand and pulled him up. As Cleaver stumbled to his feet, his son opened his arms. Cleaver pushed by. Let's go inside, he said.

In the parlour, Rosl offered warm milk. Mit Schnapps, mit Schnapps! Hermann cried. As always the man has his cowboy hat tipped back from his long red face. Uli barked and snapped at their feet. Engländer, Hermann roared, grabbing Cleaver by the shoulders. Now you are ein Landwirt! He gave Cleaver's beard a little tug and took a handful of the blue peasant's work jacket, shaking his head in fake amazement.

Jürgen was sitting at the table with his chin on his hands. His coarse face seemed dazed. Tausend Dank, he muttered in Cleaver's direction. He scratched the back of his neck, tipped his leather cap forward so it was almost covering his eyes. Frau Stolberg brought a tray with mugs and a bottle.

This is my son, Cleaver said. Mein Sohn.

Alex nodded, Hello everybody. Erect and compact, a white

woollen hat in his hand, he looked younger than his age. How old is he now? Cleaver wondered. His smile was handsome, faintly sardonic. Thirty-one, thirty-two?

Er heisst Alex. Alex, this is Seffa, Rosl, Frau Stolberg.

Frau Stolberg bowed slightly and stiffly, but already Hermann was chattering. Jo, jo, jo hait znacht schun, he slapped Jürgen on the shoulder, du muisch kemm. He spoke insistently, almost bullying. Kimm, kimm, kimm!

Jürgen seemed reluctant, but about to give way. The two men argued back and forth. With her baby in the holdall on her lap, Seffa watched them from the fireside, smiling blandly. How quickly the family has recomposed itself, Cleaver marvelled, after the bust-up yesterday evening. Jürgen picked up the bottle, poured himself a small schnapps and tossed it back in one. Stimmt, he grunted. Genau. He banged the bottle back on the table. Hermann stamped his foot and clapped. Gut gut gut! Cleaver sipped his mug of warm milk. Perhaps a slap round the face clears the air, he thought. Perhaps Alex wanted to be slapped. Then the family gets back together. It's a formula. He felt tired and his hand was aching.

Erklär! Hermann shouted at Rosl now. Or at least this was one of the words. Erklär es dem Engländer! We must make come the Englishmen.

Rosl brushed a strand of hair from her forehead. She smiled. Tonight is the first night of the Klöckler . . . How do you say klocken? she asked Hermann.

Klocken? Klocken ist klopfen.

So. Frau Stolberg rapped her knuckles three times very slowly on the breadboard. Klopfen. She is relieved her son is back, Cleaver saw. She has things under control again.

Knock, said Alex.

Richtig! shouted Hermann.

Tonight is the first night of the Klöckler, the men who knock. It is a tradition, Rosl explained. She had changed into a skirt. People go from house to house, you know, in the night to knock on the doors.

Hermann went to the porch, picked up a tall wooden staff leaning beside the coats and banged it on the wooden panels. Loud, he said. We knock loud.

And they . . . dress . . . Rosl shook her head. Das weiss ich nicht, Hermann. They dress . . . funny.

Hermann turned to Jürgen and fired off a question.

Jo, jo, Jürgen reassured him.

They dress up, Alex said.

Right, Rosl smiled at Cleaver's son. Hovering in his bright red ski suit, gloves hanging from a clip, white woolly hat in his hand, the young man looked more dressed up than the others would ever be. He wore his hair brushed back stylishly from a centre parting. That was new, Cleaver noticed. The first adult wrinkles were gathering around his eyes.

Right, they dress up and they knock, in the night. It is a tradition. It is to chase away the silence and . . . Again she looked to Hermann. Hilfe, she laughed, she said a few words.

Hermann took off his hat, pulled a long face, dropped his shoulders, bent his knees and slouched slowly to a chair. He sank down, buried his face in his hands and appeared to be on the edge of tears. Seffa giggled. She likes him, Cleaver thought.

To chase the silence and the . . .

Traurigkeit, Seffa offered.

The sadness, Rosl translated. Yes, the sadness of the winter nights that in the mountains are very long.

Then we drink and sing, Hermann added. It is a party. And with some Damen – he winked at Cleaver – we dance.

Jürgen filled another glass, raised it and drank it off. He

didn't seem convinced. Frau Stolberg made a dour comment. There was a brief back and forth between herself and Rosl. Asleep by the fire, the ancient mother let out a long soft snore. Hermann produced a torrent of words that had everybody laughing. He rushed round the table, still with the staff in his hands, and pretended to knock on the old woman's skull. Only Frau Stolberg had her lips set.

Every Thursday, Rosl finished, for three weeks before Christmas, we have the nights of the Klöckler.

Sounds fascinating, Alex said amiably. Then he asked: I was saying to Dad, I want to see the place where he has been living, is that possible?

Rosl and Hermann conferred. Schneeschuhe, Jürgen said.

Irritated, Cleaver asked what had become of his watch. Did he really want to take his son to Rosenkranzhof? It galled him to think Amanda had known all along. I need to change, he told them. His trousers were filthy from cleaning out the cows.

The watch was found at once on the mantlepiece. Und Ihr Hut! Hermann cried. He ran to the pile of things on the shelf by the door. The broad brim was battered now. Hermann crushed it down on Cleaver's head. Was für ein Landwirt! he laughed. You look great, Dad, Alex said. My son is determined, Cleaver thought. After years of indifference, years when we barely spoke, and then everything that he wrote in that obscene book, he is determined to be reconciled. I'm exhausted, he complained, and it's not even lunchtime. Müde, he repeated. Ach, die Kühe. Hermann shook his head. Very hard work, Englishman, die Kühe. Like women! Nicht wahr, Jürgen? Jürgen, hoi, woch au!

I will make you a picnic, Rosl offered. Her skirt was dark green and she had a high-necked, rust-red sweater. For the first time her blonde hair was loose. It is streaked with grey. You have hurt you-self . . . here, she said to Alex. She touched her cheek and nodded to him. It is red. What has happened? I banged my head, Alex laughed. No, I *knocked* it. He made a great play of using the word they had just learned. Knocked. On a door post. He went to the door and mimed a man turning and walking into something he hadn't seen. Without words we all become clowns, Cleaver thought. Perhaps it was preferable. Faking dizziness, his son grabbed a chair. That slap seems to have cheered him immensely. Cleaver smiled. Rosl was at least six or seven years older than his son, he guessed. Hermann said that if the two Englishmen walked down to Rosenkranzhof, he would come later and pick them up with the sled before returning to Luttach for the night of the Klöckler. Frau Schleiermacher salutes you, he told Cleaver, and he winked again.

Nice people, Alex remarked a little while later as they set off. Rosl had given him a knapsack with black bread, speck and Graukäse.

The trick with the snowshoes, Cleaver told his son, is to lift your feet high before pushing them forward, and always plant them flat and well apart. One foot at a time. Otherwise, you trip over yourself.

A steady breeze was blowing across the snow now, chilling the sunlight on the high plateau. They wore hats and gloves. Alex put on sunglasses, but as they descended into the gorge the air became icy and grey and the snow hardened. They walked in silence.

So, who won the presidential election? Cleaver finally asked.

Your man, the President, of course.

Despite my interview.

That was a brilliant interview, Alex said. I wanted to tell you.

He kept slowing his step to let his father catch up. Cleaver could hardly put any weight on his ankle.

I was in a rage because I'd just finished reading your book. I took it out on him.

After a few moments silence, Alex said: Perhaps that interview was your masterpiece, after all.

My famous masterpiece, Cleaver smiled. Actually, he conceded, I quite liked the first section of your book. If you'd left it at that . . . the rest just seemed infantile and vindictive.

Funny thing is, your reputation skyrocketed, Alex said. I couldn't believe it. You'd have cleaned up if you'd stuck around.

I cleaned up long ago, Cleaver remarked sourly. A few yards on he relented. He stopped for a breather, leaning on a rock. So, did they give you the big prize?

You bet! Alex bent down, scraped some snow together and threw it at his father.

No! Cleaver stood still and let the snowball fly just inches over his head.

Alex laughed. Are you joking? They gave it to some pc thing about five generations of a gypsy family. Discrimination, romance, incest. Dark wisdom of antique civilisation. Bit of magic realism. Quite a cocktail.

Huh, Cleaver said. He found it hard to hide his relief. Well, Larry will be happy, he said.

Right. I hadn't thought of that. Alex threw another snowball that hit his father on the knee. Author was pretty too. Anita something. You would have liked her. Younger than me. Tits. Latin skin.

No comment, Cleaver said.

Speaking of which . . . Alex put his arm in his father's now. Cleaver let him, but wouldn't respond. Walking close together, the snowshoes clashed. Cleaver stumbled. His son held him. Yes, you would have laughed. When you left, like, when you disappeared, everybody thought you must have run off with a woman. You know? The tabloids ran a sort of roll-call to see if anyone remotely associated with you had gone missing. It was quite a list.

Cleaver grimaced. Gratifying I'm sure.

That Melanie Clarke phoned me to ask if I knew who it was, the woman you'd run off with, that is. Remember Melanie? She wasn't one of your girlfriends, was she?

Cleaver felt uncomfortable. It seemed inappropriate for father and son to talk women. Where was the angry voice of *Under His Shadow*? he wondered. Where was the outrage, the accusation, Cleaver the source of all evil?

If she was, I wouldn't say, he said stiffly.

Anyway, everyone was most disappointed when all the suspects turned out to be present and correct.

People only want the obvious stories, Cleaver said, because they already know how to tell them and how to respond. As he spoke, he remembered that the presence of younger people always made him pontificate. Don't.

A few minutes later they turned the last twist in the track and there it was. Long icicles hung from the rock face over the roof where the sun must have struck earlier on. Wow. The young man took off his sunglasses and read the name: Ros-en-kranz-hof. Very pretty, he said. Remind you of anything? Cleaver asked. Alex frowned. Rosenkranz and Guildenstern are dead, I suppose. He didn't seem to recall what he had written in his book.

As always, the door scraped on the uneven stone floor. The hinges squealed. Then, while Cleaver lit the fire, his son explored. Tell me if you see a mouse, Cleaver called. What's with the broken stair? Alex shouted from above. Cleaver explained. He listened to the footsteps moving back and forth. The flames caught in the grate.

And the bloodstain?

The what? Where?

In this little storeroom.

Cleaver pulled himself up the stairs. Even after only a day's abandonment Rosenkranzhof had taken on its old musty smell. Their breath hung in the air. I must have mistaken it for a shadow, Cleaver said. Are you sure it's blood? He opened the window to get a little more light. My eyes are crap. In fact it was quite a sizeable stain on the wooden floor beneath the chair in the old Nazi's little room. This room was locked when I arrived, Cleaver said. Perhaps the guy had an accident, Alex suggested.

Downstairs again, Cleaver boiled snow for tea. There were still some tea bags. I thought it was going to thaw, he said, but it was just a bit of warm sunshine. Sitting in front of the fire, his son asked: So what are you writing, Dad? Where's the desk, the old laptop, the notebooks?

I'm not. There isn't one.

The younger man seemed perplexed. He leaned forward to warm his hands. Looking at the sharp nose, the narrow, eager mouth, Cleaver was strongly reminded of the young Amanda of years ago. They both had the same irksome resilience.

Really?

Really.

Oh . . . Sorry, I just assumed that's what you must be doing out here. Like, you'd finally retired to produce the great work. Or the great rebuttal even.

You were worried? Cleaver asked.

Alex reflected. Not really. He paused. He seemed newly alert. So what *are* you doing?

Nothing.

The young man's eyes narrowed. Nothing, like . . . ?

Like eating, shitting, walking, thinking, Cleaver said.

Oh. But in your head . . . you're planning something.

Cleaver began to laugh. No, absolutely nothing. No project, no grandiose ambitions.

It doesn't sound like you.

Well, there you are, Cleaver said.

Alex drank his tea, warming his fingers on the cup. It's a shame though, he said after a few moments. I know Mum was hoping that's what you were up to. She kept saying, let's leave him a month at least and he'll be back in fine form and with the definitive object, the great work.

I was left alone to write my masterpiece.

Alex smiled. I guess so.

Something that would rival *Under His Shadow*.

I think that's what Mum thought. She said it was good you'd been spurred into action.

Cleaver shook his head. He had to breathe deeply. That's not going to happen.

There was a long pause. The logs crackled and settled. Then Cleaver put down his cup: Alex, there are millions of masterpieces. They change nothing.

His son frowned. Who needs to change things? There's always the work itself, isn't there? The pleasure of something well made and the feeling . . .

Cleaver was exasperated. How could his son not see there was a stumbling block the size of a cathedral between them? You do it then, he said sharply. You write a masterpiece.

Dad . . .

Alex, I bequeath you this task. Okay? You can write my

masterpiece. Cleaver produced a frighteningly harsh laugh. He stood up and limped quickly to the window. What is happening to me? he wondered. The whole encounter was unreal. I was only left alone so I could write my master-piece. I hadn't hidden myself at all. Put your boots back on, he announced sharply. There's something I want to show you.

What is it?

Put your boots on. Let's go.

Outside the house, Cleaver fussed back and forth to find where he had tossed away his walking poles. The wind had dropped and the air was freezing again. In the shade, the snow was frozen hard. The cold bit into their cheeks and fingertips.

They crossed the clearing and started down the track towards the ledge. Alex was silent for a while, but quite suddenly Cleaver exploded again. He could not contain himself. Just tell me one thing. What on earth put it into your head to write that stupid last scene?

Take it easy, Dad.

Inadvertently, Cleaver had lifted one of his poles. Tell me why you wrote it!

Alex hesitated. Okay. To be honest, you know, I didn't know how to finish the book. I needed an end of some kind, but in reality the more I thought about you, Dad, the more I couldn't imagine you ever doing anything but more of the same. If you see what I mean. So I went and invented something weird. Like, a bit of a joke, to finish with a bang, I never really asked myself whether it was offensive or not.

Bullshit.

Alex sighed.

Bullshit, Cleaver repeated.

They had reached the place where an iron railing was

fixed to the rock. The track had crumbled and what was left was deep in snow.

Take off your snowshoes for this bit, Cleaver said. You'll need to dig your toes in.

Where are we going?

You'll see, Cleaver told his son. He felt a bitter determination to open his eyes somehow, to place him before his crime.

Tricky . . . Alex said. Damn! A shred of his smart ski suit had torn on the rusty railing. The woods above and below lay in deep silence.

As if to lull his son into a false sense of security, Cleaver resumed: So at the end of the day you just couldn't imagine me doing anything but fighting with Amanda Cunningham in a house in Chelsea while playing celebrity journalist in interminable talk shows.

Pretty much, Alex admitted. He was beyond the railing now. After all, Dad, most people would kill for a life like that, wouldn't they, the kind of celebrity you have? He buckled his snowshoes back on and began to walk swiftly down the last part of the track to the ledge. It was steep here, curving sharply to the left and downwards. The snow was icy and Alex slithered. He laughed and tried to skate on one snowshoe. All the rocks and contours were gone in a sheet of ice. I should have brought skis, he called. Way hey! He slipped again and slithered down a yard or so.

All at once, limping behind, Cleaver guessed the danger. Stop, he yelled. Stop, stop, stop!

Dad? Alex grabbed a small tree and tried to stay on his feet. What's up?

Stop. Alex, please, just stay where you are. Right there. Don't move. Cleaver approached slowly, placing his feet sideways to the descent, digging in his walking poles. He halted a few paces above his son. Where the ledge should have been, some ten yards below, the snow stretched smooth and sheer in a steep slope right to the edge. It was a chute. All the footholds were gone. You wouldn't see the drop until it was too late.

Alex, don't move! Cleaver suddenly felt nauseous. He sat down on the ice. His breath steamed about his face. Just stay where you are. Okay? Stay there. He was shaking. His son would go over the ledge. Cleaver could hear his cry. He saw the body falling.

Dad, Alex scrambled toward him, but slipped.

Stop, I said stop! Stay there. Hold onto something. Don't slip, for God's sake.

But what's up?

I've made a mistake. We have to go back, Cleaver shouted. Take this. He threw one of the poles to his son. The younger man missed it and it slithered down the ice.

Don't go after it. Don't!

Can't I just take a look? Alex turned and peered. He made to go down again, treading carefully.

No! Cleaver yelled. It's a sheer drop. There, where it looks like the path turns. We shouldn't have come. Take this one. Carefully now. He slid the second pole down towards his son and this time Alex got it. Staying at the edge of the track, grabbing the trees that clutched the side of the gorge, he climbed back up to his father.

Alex.

You're crying, Dad.

Let's get out of here, Cleaver said.

They negotiated the section with the railing and began to climb. Then Cleaver explained: he told his son about the ledge, the photograph of Jürgen's wife. He was still trembling. I wanted you to see. Just that I hadn't thought of the snow drifting and then being frozen like that.

It's okay, Dad.

Cleaver's thighs and calves felt unsteady. His ankle ached. Actually, I nearly stepped over myself the first evening I went, he admitted. I should have thought. He shook his head to clear the dizziness. His son took his arm. It's the date, Alex, I wanted you to see the date. Cleaver stopped and looked into his son's eyes. She died in 1990, remember? 1990. His son held his gaze. Your book would have been fine, Cleaver said quietly, without the stuff about Angela.

Alex turned away. Let's get back, he said.

Rosenkranzhof had its usual sly, picturesque look. The smoke drifted almost vertically from the chimney. The rosary beads looked like berries against the black wood of the door. Inside, they pulled out the food Rosl had prepared. The place was warmer now. Chop up the onion and eat it with the cheese, Cleaver said. There were four bottles of beer. This is cheese? Alex asked. It's disgusting.

They sat at the table, eating. The black bread was hard work. Bloody mouse is still around, Cleaver complained. There were droppings by the stove. You wonder what he finds to eat. His son was intrigued now by the system that brought the water across the roof. How long are you planning to stay? Cleaver asked at last. Where are you going to sleep?

I just came to find you, really, Alex said. I mean, Mum thought it was time someone came and talked to you.

Sweet of her.

And that's all. Are *you* staying?

Cleaver looked at his son. The younger man had unzipped the front of his ski suit over a bright white pullover. He looked so neat.

I'm in a dilemma, Cleaver said.

Alex raised an eyebrow.

In the sense that it will be hard to stay here now with the snow. I'm limping. Walking is hard going. I need someone to restock the larder.

Rosl had packed some sort of fried doughnuts in a white paper bag. If you ask me, it's crazy, Alex said. He licked his fingers. Exciting for a while, I can imagine, but, hey, enough is enough. Why not come back with me? You've tried it now. You've done it. What is there to prove? You said yourself that books and films mean nothing. People forget. They won't bother you about what I wrote. I noticed . . .

Alex, Cleaver interrupted, Alex, sorry to disappoint, but I didn't come here *just* because of your book, you know. Perhaps you haven't grasped that.

Dad, I was only . . .

Cleaver lifted a ham and farted. Both men laughed.

Tell me why then, Alex said.

There's nothing to tell. It's just that I can't go back. I mustn't. I can't stay here and I mustn't go back. If I go and immerse myself in it all again, if I'm just *around* televisions and newspapers, all that endless churning of information and opinion, and your mother of course, your mother most of all, I'll die.

Rubbish, Alex said crisply. It's more likely you'll come back to life.

No doubt, but not the kind of life I want. Then Cleaver added: Remember the newspaper-reading scene in your book? The Sunday mornings? Or your description of me arguing with the TV? Well, now I'm like one of those ex-alkies who knows that they must never touch the stuff again. Never. A single drop would be the end. Same thing with Amanda.

You're far more likely to die here, Alex pointed out.

I'm not worried about that, Cleaver said.

Alex pursed his lips. It's like, you're denying who you really are.

I wish I could.

But Mum . . .

If your mother wants to see me, she can make the trip herself, can't she? Since she always knew where I was . . .

So you're staying? Alex said.

Cleaver shook his head. I don't know.

His son looked at him: You're voice has changed, he said. There's something different about it.

How.

It's like . . . Alex looked puzzled and smiled. Then his face cleared: Just different.

I'll take it as a compliment, Cleaver said.

They opened the remaining beers and moved to the armchairs and the fire. Alex noticed the eagle above the fire-place. Someone's broken his wing, he said. He stood and examined it. The bird had been frozen as if in action, its neck outstretched, claws extended to kill, but the feathers were dusty and the stick propping the broken wing very obvious.

I did think there might have been a fight here once, Cleaver said. He pointed to the chair-leg that had been repaired, the conspicuous stuccoing on the mantelpiece. Like someone had heaved some furniture around. There's a dent in the wall too, Alex noticed.

For perhaps half an hour, then, they discussed the Stolberg family. Alex was sitting in the chair where Olga had sat for a whole month. Perhaps Jürgen killed the old man? he suggested. Someone's got patricide on the brain, Cleaver smiled. He shook his head: You don't know how much time I've spent thinking about it. It's a sort of mental trap. At the end of the day I came to the conclusion it must have something to do with the triangle: old Nazi, Frau Stolberg, Jürgen; father, mother, son. There's some negative dynamic there. Or there was. Rosl is an escapee, the one that got away, the one who became Italian. Ulrike was a victim, and maybe Seffa's going to be another. There's something up with the old struldbrug too, the old lady, but I can't work it out. Then Alex remarked that he had read about an old man in the Scottish Highlands who had confessed to having had sex with five generations of his own womenfolk: grandmother, mother, sister, daughter, granddaughter. You see how well behaved I was in the end! Cleaver laughed. Alex grinned: Can you play? he asked, pointing to the accordion.

You try, Cleaver said.

His son put the thing on his lap and moved his fingers over the keyboard. He could remember the right hand to Alla Turca but was put off by the problem of squeezing the air in and out of the bellows. After a couple of tries, he gave up. Can't do it. Show me.

Cleaver pulled the instrument onto his knees. He played Auld Lang Syne, hamming the thing. Alex laughed. Granddad's Hogmanays, he said. Then Cleaver played Rock Of Ages. The mournfulness of the tune began to take over. He crooned a few words. Not the labours of my hands . . . You used to sing it as a lullaby, Alex said. Angela hated it. Cleaver stopped, put the instrument down. Enough, he said abruptly.

There was silence. Cleaver looked at his watch. Wonder when Hermann will be coming? I'd better get my things together. Whatever I'm going to do, I won't be sleeping here tonight.

Alex hesitated. Dad, actually, there was another reason for my coming.

Cleaver looked at his son.

Alex sighed. There's something I wanted to tell. Maybe. I didn't know . . . There's something I'd like you to understand.

Cleaver felt anxious. What?

Don't worry! Alex laughed. I've already destroyed your reputation, remember?

Tell me.

Give me a moment to think. I wasn't sure that I was going to tell you this.

Cleaver stood and went to feed the fire. He placed two logs crosswise. Maybe the biggest pleasure, here, he told his son, has been watching logs burn. I mean, really concentrating and watching. He blew to get the flames going. I love it when the pressure builds up inside the wood and the heat forces a jet of gas out of one end, following the grain I suppose to where the log was cut, and the jet catches light, like a Bunsen burner. But not steadily. In sudden little spurts. You never know when it's going to start or stop. Blue flames sometimes and even green. They really rip, then suddenly the flame goes out and there's just smoke coiling and writhing. I suppose the mixture changes. Then the flame again. There's a little roar when it catches. You know what I mean?

Sure.

I've spent whole afternoons here, watching that. It must be the closest I got to not thinking.

Fires are mesmerising, Alex said. But he was ready now. Okay, he said, listen. So, four years ago, I went to live in Manchester, you remember?

I remember I told you not to.

Right. You told me not to, his son smiled. When did you ever tell me I was doing the right thing?

Alex, I . . .

301

Just listen. The main reason I went to Manchester was to get married.

You what? You're married?

Yes.

But why didn't you tell me? When? Does Amanda know? Are we going to be grandparents?

Listen! No she doesn't. I'm going to tell you now.

Alex paused. He looked at his father as if weighing him up. When I was doing my postgrad at the LSE I met this girl studying at art school. The Royal College actually. She was a big talent, lively, bright, good-looking. We started living together. That was when I had that place on Balls Pond Road.

Again Alex paused, as if daring his father to interrupt. Cleaver restricted himself to shaking his head.

And she was rich too. Her parents were rich. She had already had a show and made a couple of sales.

I'm surprised someone like that wouldn't have wanted to stay in London, Cleaver said. What's in Manchester?

Wait, wait Dad.

Does the lady have a name? I always think girls should have names.

Alex swallowed. Letizia.

Quite a name.

Her mother was from Sicily. Dad, let me tell you, it isn't what you're expecting.

I'm not expecting anything, Cleaver said.

We started living together, but it wasn't going that well. She was very extrovert, very moody, always flirting with other guys, self-confident. Ambitious, even arrogant.

You mean bossy? Cleaver asked.

No, not bossy, but arrogant, like, brushing other people aside. I'd just got my first job with *Business Week*, remember?

She did nothing but take the piss. Only art mattered, everything else was dull. Etc, etc.

So, Cleaver said, you were going to split up when she tells you she's pregnant.

Dad, I said wait. It's not your story. About six months into it, we were having this crisis, trying to break up and not quite managing sort of thing, when she fell ill. She sort of ran out of energy, couldn't do anything. It was unusual for her. She was a whirlwind normally. I thought it was psychosomatic, because of us arguing and everything. Anyway, she went back to her parents in Manchester and I assumed it was over. I was upset, but not that upset.

You did have something of a track record with psychosick girlfriends.

Then her mother phones me to say she's got leukaemia.

I'm sorry, Cleaver muttered.

Quite. Alex hesitated. So, I went up to see her. I mean, she didn't know her mother had called me. She didn't know I knew she was so ill. She was very subdued, changed and tender, and we sort of fell in love again.

You mean you felt sorry for her, Cleaver said.

Please don't tell me what I mean.

Okay, Cleaver said, sorry.

Then about a month later, her mother asked me if I would marry her.

I beg your pardon?

Letty was only going to live six months or so, if that. That's what the doctors said. She hadn't been told. Maybe she guessed. I was the only guy who had stayed with her more than a month or two, lived with her. The mother begged me. To make the last part of her life happy.

But that's completely mad! Cleaver burst in. That's crazy. And you agreed?

Alex put both hands in his thick hair. I asked her and she said yes.

But why didn't you talk to me? Or your mother. Jesus! I thought you talked to Amanda more or less every day. Weren't you always on the phone?

I didn't talk to you or Mum because I knew you'd come down on me like a ton of bricks and I'd have to hear what an idiot I was and how stupidly I was behaving and why didn't I come and work in London in a decent newspaper and so on and so forth.

Go on, Cleaver said. Let's not get sidetracked.

Anyway, like I said, when I went to stay up in Manchester we were sort of in love again. It was easier at her house than in London. There was a strong sense of family. There was the mother and father – he was much older, he'd never wanted Letty to go to art school and seemed almost happy she'd had to come back – then two younger sisters. It was as if I was the son they hadn't had, the only boy, the young man of the family.

Again Alex hesitated. Cleaver grimaced but waited.

In the end, though, Dad. Alex bit his lip. In the end, though, I think it had to do with Angela.

Their eyes met.

I mean, that I married her. It was like being close to Angela. Letty was that sort of girl, artistic, charismatic. And she was dying. I don't know why, but I was glad of the chance to be close to death. It was as if I'd missed Angela's dying, it happened so quickly and I was too young, I felt guilty, she was the talented one, and now it would really happen and I would play my part. I thought, it's only for six months, a year at most. It was as though, I was giving time to a part of me that had been buried too quickly. Afterwards I'd be able to put it behind me.

Cleaver was shaking his head slowly from side to side.

We got married. The parents are rich. Or he is. There are all kinds of business interests. He found me a job in a computing magazine, I was doing the promotions, and they set us up in a sort of separate flat on the top floor of their house, a mansion really.

Alex, Cleaver breathed, Alex! I can't believe you didn't say anything. Leave aside the question of advice. You could have just told us.

What did you ever tell me about your real life?

But Alex, it's not . . .

Let's leave that argument to another time. Let me finish. And by the way, I did tell Phil and Caroline. They came and visited. They came to the wedding and we all agreed there was no point in upsetting you and Mum with it all. You always had your own shit to deal with. Alex paused. Anyway, the fact is that she didn't die.

Cleaver watched his son. He was hunched forward, slim hands clasped together, lips frowning, as he had once hunched and frowned over his homework. There is something extremely resilient about my son, Cleaver thought. Always has been. Something hard and prosaic. Like Amanda.

It *seemed* she was going to die. They put her in hospital. I went every day. It was a ward where people went to die, really. I must have seen seven or eight people die, usually children. But Letty hung on. The doctors couldn't understand. Her mother kept saying it was my love. Alex sighed: Anyhow, after about three months of this, they found a perfect bone-marrow match, you know they have this international tissue-typing register now, in Holland. It was one in a hundred thousand. They did the operation, and slowly, but very slowly, she started to get better.

Cleaver sighed. Looking around the room as his son took

305

a breather, the stone floor, the rugs, the window, he had the impression that Rosenkranzhof was changed. To sit here in the future would not be the same as it had been in the past.

But really slowly, Alex resumed. It must have been four or five months before she got to her feet. Meantime, the mother says to me, if I need a woman, she'll find me one.

I beg your pardon!

Alex smiled. She's canny the mother, she's Italian, quite young still, she married a guy twenty years older than herself when she was eighteen and pregnant; so she's thinking, here's a young man and he needs sex and Letty can't give it to him, and she wants to keep control of it all so that it doesn't break up the family.

For a moment the figure of Frau Stolberg crossed Cleaver's mind. And so?

So I told her to mind her own business. I mean, I was really angry, especially when she had these friends over from Sicily and there's this woman in her early forties all over me, clearly acting on orders.

Cleaver shook his head.

Finally Letty was back on her feet. She came home. But she wasn't herself at all, she was sleeping fourteen or sixteen hours a day, completely listless. The whole core of her was gone. She didn't draw or paint or even want to look at art. The only thing she could think about was dragging herself through the day.

No creature comfort, Cleaver said.

It was unthinkable, Alex said. Anyway, at this point I was already having an affair.

Ah.

That's cheered you up, Alex smiled. His eyes shone in the flames from the fire.

I'm just glad something was going for you.

Wait. Alex paused. It started, or, no, it sort of half started way back, more or less when Letty first went to hospital. I met this girl in the gym.

Not the gym.

Alex smiled wanly. She was much younger, still at university. But no, there was no sex. We just spent time together and it was sort of tacitly understood that after it was over, after a decent interval . . .

Like a fortnight, Cleaver said.

Please, Dad, whatever. After an interval, we'd become lovers.

Cleaver was about to remark that his son had always found women who wanted to put things off, but he stopped himself. Go on, he said.

Actually, I still haven't come to the reason why I'm telling you all this. You can't imagine.

So go on. I'm listening.

Okay, when Letty is getting better, but not really better, and I realise she'll never be the same, I start going to bed with this other girl.

Name please, Cleaver asked.

Marilyn. Alex pronounced the name quickly but with the utmost caution, as if it were broken glass in his mouth. Then Cleaver understood. For a moment he was overwhelmed with pity. He had seen to the end of the story.

Alex began to speak more rapidly and with less expression.

Okay, we started making love. It was all so intense and poignant and happy. She begged me to leave Letty, and I said, how could I, in the situation I was in? We made love in her student dorm, or in the car, or sometimes in hotels. I would tell Letty I was coming down to London to see you and Mum, and instead I took Marilyn to the Lake District, or even Blackpool, wherever. So, it had been going on a year and more when she was due to graduate. She was going back home to Portsmouth. Then I kind of had a breakdown. I said I'd leave Letty and come and live with her. Only Marilyn said no. Maybe at the beginning it would have worked, she said, but not now. She broke it off.

I went crazy, Alex said. I lost it completely. I was banging on her door in the middle of the night. Stuff like that. Letty must have guessed what was going on. Certainly her mother did. But nobody said anything. Then one day she just disappeared. Marilyn. She left the dorm, must have changed her e-mail and mobile number. All of a sudden this woman I've been seeing every day just disappears from my life, completely. Not a trace.

Priya, Cleaver thought. I'm truly sorry, Alex, he said. Really, really, really sorry.

And that's when I started writing *Under His Shadow*.

Alex looked up into his father's eyes. It was a look of challenge.

At first, it was a kind of therapy. I thought it would take my mind off things. I'd even been thinking of killing myself. Banal. I'd never have had the courage. Then the more I got into it, the book, the more mixed up everything got in my mind. The real energy of the thing was how angry I was, with Letty's mother, with Letty, with Marilyn, with myself. But at the same time, it was your fault too. You'd always given me the impression I wasn't the talented one. That was Angela. Genius died with Angela and so on. It was as if I'd become the nobody you always took me for. I started feeling angry about it. The cynicism. All those bad jokes about infidelity, and the famous dinner guests. It was awful. And I realised I'd partly married Letty in reaction to how cynical you were. To be different somehow, better. I'd fallen into a trap you set for me.

Alex stopped. His voice was defiant. Cleaver had his head in his hands. He wouldn't reply.

Actually, I think the book's pretty accurate, if you want to know. And I don't feel sorry for having written it at all. You made our lives so unpleasant sometimes and, most of all, confusing. Do you have any idea? A minute ago, you asked, why didn't I talk to you? Because whenever I did, in the past, you were always more interested in showing how clever you were at analysing psycho situations than in me. Every situation you come across is a sort of gymnasium for your talents, a possible documentary. It's the same with these people here. You don't give a damn about this Frau Stolberg and Rosl and whatever they're called. You just like wondering if you can sniff out an incest.

Cleaver sat silent. The whole portrayal of Angela was a lie, he thought. A deliberate lie. But now is not the time to tackle it.

Anyhow, I just thought you should know – Alex suddenly smiled rather too brightly – now I'm here, that at the end of the day the anger in that book wasn't only to do with you. I mean, what mattered to me at the time was the mess I was in over Marilyn.

Again the two men caught each other's eyes. Cleaver was shaking his head quickly and rhythmically, in a kind of trance.

Alex waited, as if making sure that he had given his father enough rope to hang himself. Cleaver wouldn't speak.

Then the younger man relaxed. He sat back. Anyway, as you see, your Alex understands now that life can get complicated, and the book was just a book, Dad, just one possible take, when I was trapped in a kind of gloomy state of mind. Perhaps I overdid it here and there.

Alex, Cleaver finally said. I feel completely drained. And I need a pee.

Cleaver hobbled outside and stood in the snow in the cold afternoon. Without a jacket, he shivered. Count yourself lucky I didn't pee on you, he shouted at the troll. My son is in a serious state, he thought. Or maybe not. Maybe he just needed to tell his story. It was because of Angela, he had said.

Going back into the house, Cleaver climbed the stairs to gather some clothes. Alex was staring into the fire. So what's the situation now? Cleaver called from upstairs. He pushed trousers and socks and shirts into his suitcase.

Sorry?

What are you planning to do now? He wouldn't go to the old Nazi's wardrobe for his shirt and tie. Just your mountain clothes, Cleaver decided.

Oh, I'll go back down to Luttach. With the Klöckler.

No, I mean, with your life.

I don't know. There was a pause. After the book came out, I was offered a job with some radio show on one of the London stations. A sort of avant-garde arts magazine.

Take it, Cleaver called. Normally I'd say to stay a million miles from arts magazines and broadcasting in general, but take it. Move away, then maybe divorce. He sorted out his underwear, then added: You see now the wisdom of not marrying.

Alex didn't reply. After a few moments he shouted: If you had married, you'd be able to get divorced now. Think of the relief.

Good point! Cleaver came downstairs. Or you could stay here with me, he said.

Here?

In Rosenkranzhof, for a while.

Alex smiled. Dad, nobody can live outside of everything, which is what you're trying to do. I have to deal with this stuff.

Cleaver sighed. There are places on the margins, he said, outposts. You can take a break.

And you're really inviting me to stay?

Why not? For a while. Live on the edge. Get some perspective.

We'd kill each other.

Quite probably. Cleaver laughed. Bet your mother would be out here in less than a week, though, if you decided to stay. We'd be the holy family all over again.

Alex looked puzzled.

You and I were supposed to argue, Cleaver explained. She wanted me to take you to court over the book, you know. That's what she wanted to happen when she asked you to come out here. For us to fight. She'd be jealous if she thought we were getting on, and her all on her own. She'd be on a plane in twenty-four hours.

No, that's unfair, Alex said. And please, don't tell her this stuff I've told you. It would only upset her.

Suddenly, Cleaver was moved. He went over to where his son was sitting and opened his arms. Alex stood up and they embraced, faces in each other's shoulders.

Friends, Cleaver said.

Friends.

Alex – Cleaver spoke in a low voice – Alex, find your-self a nice girl and make me a grandfather. Then I'll come back. Promise.

Dad . . .

Sorry, only joking.

Dad, no, there's one crazy thing I didn't tell you. The boy laughed nervously.

Fire away. Cleaver squeezed his son's shoulders. He was looking into the fire.

One day, like, when . . . I don't know why, I was really

mad, I started going to bed with her mother.

Cleaver disengaged. You did what?

Alex lifted his hand to his mouth. With Letty's mother. She's staying in Bruneck.

She's in Bruneck, now? Your wife's mother?

Alex nodded. She's called Clara. We're going to do some skiing. There was a facile grin on his face, but his eyes were troubled. She's a fan of yours, actually. She says she'd like to meet you.

No, Cleaver said. He shook his head. No, no and no.

Dad . . .

And you should get out of it, Alex. Run.

But, Dad, she's . . .

I'm not criticising you, I'm just saying, cut loose. Don't even go back to Bruneck.

I knew you wouldn't understand, Alex said. He tried to smile. Clara's a wonderful person.

Without waiting for Hermann, they shut the house and had crossed the clearing and started dragging the suitcase up the track when a jingle of harness announced the arrival of the horse. Hermann was braking the sleigh on the steep slope and Rosl, in a red woollen hat and gloves, was striding behind in snowshoes. Uli barked excitedly and launched herself from the sleigh into the snow. You must come with us to do the Klöckler, Hermann began at once. Yes, Englishman? Cleaver wanted to hit the man. No, wait, Hermann said, die Ziehharmonika. He hurried across to the house to retrieve the accordion.

Cleaver put his suitcase on the sleigh and sat down with Uli's big paws on his lap. His mind was quite empty. Hermann walked ahead, talking and clucking all the way to the fat Haflinger, while Rosl and Alex trudged behind in the snow.

Cleaver didn't listen to their conversation. He stroked the dog. The creature seemed grateful. When the others spoke to him, Cleaver didn't respond.

Later, he said he was too tired to go down to Luttach and knock on people's doors. I'm too tired to have fun. My foot is aching. My fingers hurt. He pulled a face. The silent sadness of the long winter nights is fine by me. I wouldn't want anyone to knock.

Rosl laughed. Hermann and Jürgen had dressed up in smart black baggy trousers, blue aprons and black trilby hats with red ribbons round the crowns. Now the masks! Hermann announced. He had a grotesquely large, white, dog-like mask covered with sheep's wool but with a red nose. The thing had obviously been made years ago and smelled. Jürgen's mask was dark blue. He put it on and roared and knocked his cowman's staff on the panelling on the wall.

You go, Cleaver told his son. The cows had been milked. The men were in a hurry to set off before dark. There were various farms to go knocking at on the way down. You go, Cleaver insisted. And can you ask your mother, he turned to Rosl, if I could sleep here and help with the milking in the morning? That way Jürgen can stay in Luttach. I'm happy to help. You said she wanted a man. Rosl spoke to Frau Stolberg for rather longer than seemed necessary. The older woman hesitated, then nodded stiffly.

Just outside the front door, Alex said goodbye.

Remember what I said, Cleaver told him. Run.

I'll think about it.

Oh, and tell Amanda I'd be happy if she came to see me. Really. We could live together in Rosenkranzhof. Tell her I've become a handyman at last. She can have her trellis.

Alex laughed: You're clutching at straws, Dad. Anyway, I thought I wasn't supposed to carry messages. He seems cheerful, Cleaver thought. Perhaps I'm the first person he's told. He feels relieved. It wouldn't last.

Tell her, if she comes to live with me in Rosenkranzhof, I'll marry her. I promise. Upon my word, he added, grinning.

Alex laughed even louder. He was almost in giggles. Rosl watched him with an indulgent smile.

He's been drinking already, Cleaver told her. Don't let him have too much this evening. He's a delicate creature.

Oh, I look after him, Rosl said.

The party set off as the light was failing. Hermann was on the sleigh to brake and steer down the slope. He held the reins in one hand and a flask of schnapps in the other. Or perhaps it was Gebirgsgeist. He was whistling. Rosl and Alex sat behind, a blanket on their laps. Jürgen walked beside with the accordion strapped to his shoulders. He squeezed out a few notes. Only at the last moment, when he noticed Rosl's pale blue suitcase on the sleigh, did Cleaver realise that she wouldn't be coming back. She was escaping to Bozen. He hopped out of the house and hurried over the frozen track in his socks. Rosl! She turned. I have to work tomorrow, she said. I have my car in the village. Cleaver gave her his hand. Auf wiedersehen, he said.

In the parlour, Frau Stolberg served soup. The ancient mother dunked her bread. The baby was nagging. Seffa walked her back and forth. The girl looked calm and thoughtful. She is intelligent after all, Cleaver decided. While he ate, the conversation was desultory and completely incomprehensible. There was goat's meat now, in a stew. It tasted good. The old radios need dusting, Cleaver noticed. They've been silent so long. Then it occurred to him that he hadn't asked Alex about Iraq, about Blair or British politics. The fire crackled.

Occasionally his eyes met Frau Stolberg's. They glitter with reticence, he thought. I like that. Ich bin sehr müde, Cleaver told her. Ich will schlafen.

Carrying a torch, she showed him to a panelled room two doors down from where there had been the drama the previous night. They must have fobbed Jürgen off with some story about the father, Cleaver thought. They'll have invented some tourist just passing through. Frau Stolberg lit the lamp and left at once. Gute Nacht, she said.

Cleaver sat on a high bed. There was a fireplace that hadn't been used for years and he guessed at once that the sheets would be damp. He studied an arrangement of dry flowers on the dresser. He was tired. These people love dry flowers. A Madonna looked down over the bed. Perhaps it was better to die in a road accident, in the fullness of life, after being wildly applauded on stage, he decided, than to be gutted forever by a lingering disease. Small mercies. He opened a cupboard and found extra blankets. Or perhaps all lives are the same life: the ancient lady sleeping away her senility by the fire and the bellicose President beginning his second term. Faintly, from downstairs, he heard Seffa crooning to her baby. In which case it was futile to dwell on old sores or conjure up Gothic tales.

Undressed, Cleaver went to the window. There was no moon, just a very faint luminosity from the snow. I shall stay here and reopen the old Nazi's Stube, he said out loud. Yes. He shivered. It wasn't thawing at all. We could get some English guests perhaps. An ad in the *Spectator* would do it. Some posh young women. Then I could teach Seffa a few words so she could serve beer and Knödel and schnapps. You're clutching at straws, Alex had laughed. It was because of Angela, he said. How was I supposed to take that? How was my son supposed to take the suggestion that I would marry Amanda if she came to live with me in Rosenkranzhof? The window had misted now. She'll never come, and I don't want her to. Our games are over, Cleaver muttered. He rubbed the glass with the sleeve of his pyjama and peered out into the night. What if I saw a sign? For a moment he remembered the pleasure of holding the tiny child in his arms. A shooting star, for example. But was he facing north, south, east or west? Cleaver frowned and went to find the bathroom.